S0-AWY-249

MADAME ZEE

MADAME ZEE

PEARL LUKE

HarperCollins*PublishersLtd*

Madame Zee
© 2006 by Pearl Luke. All rights reserved.

Published by HarperCollins Publishers Ltd.

HarperCollins books may be purchased for educational, business,
or sales promotional use through our Special Markets Department.

HarperCollins Publishers Ltd
2 Bloor Street East, 20th Floor
Toronto, Ontario, Canada
M4W 1A8

www.harpercollins.ca

Library and Archives Canada Cataloguing in Publication

Luke, Pearl, 1958–
Madame Zee : a novel / Pearl Luke. – 1st ed.

ISBN-13: 978-0-00-200513-5
ISBN-10: 0-00-200513-1

1. Madame Zee – Fiction. 2. Brother XII, 1878–1934? –
Fiction. 3. Vancouver Island (B.C.) – Fiction. I. Title.

PS8573.U5354M33 2006 C813'.6 C2005-907405-1

HC 9 8 7 6 5 4 3 2 1

Printed and bound in the United States
Set in Stempel Garamond

In memory of

Amanda Rae Richard (née Hilles) 1981–2002
David Bruce Chapman 1951–2004
William James Eckenswiller 1955–2005

PROLOGUE

In the large meeting room she sits impatiently off to one side. She ignores the questioning stares of the others and instead tries to reduce her anxiety by sketching Bo, who stands at the front of the room. She has taken up sketching again as a sort of therapy, drawing from memory the images she has seen. Over the past week, she has had several, all frightening, each one of the same catastrophe. Underneath one, she has written: *it is worse than you think.*

Externally, she has healed nicely, and is no longer bruised and disfigured by the abuse, though two thin scars may never fade, and stretch like pale pink worm lines across her upper lip and jaw.

Worse than the scars are the internal changes. She fights almost constant anxiety, as if she needs to relearn certain realities of consciousness—the brightness of daylight, the grittiness of dust, everywhere. Too many sounds leave her feeling jittery and impatient—dishes clattering over the sound of talking, an automobile clanking up the road. Even the sound of chewing—her own or others'—is sometimes an almost unbearable annoyance. She is quick to startle, and intensely restless. The term *thin-skinned* means more to her than it used to, and she imagines that she has lost something, as if a protective glaze over her nerve endings has been peeled off.

Her clothes rub her in a most uncomfortable way, and if others misunderstand her intentions, or don't answer quickly enough, or disappear just as she needs them, she can barely contain her frustration. Even when she is alone she feels explosive, and when she cannot contain the feelings, she expresses anger differently than she used to. Where before she may have responded with silence, now she lashes out both physically and verbally before she has time to consider her response. When Sarah bumped her plate off the table and claimed it was an accident, she shocked and embarrassed everyone, including herself, by kicking the plate halves and bits of food across the dining room. When Alfred ignored her request to tighten the spring on the screen door, a message Bo had asked her to relay, she slammed the door three times in quick succession, creating a sound like gunfire, and then she slunk away.

Now Bo nods at her from his position at the front of the room, and then he motions for everyone to quiet. They do so immediately, and he looks out at them for at least ten seconds without saying anything. Finally, he speaks.

"I find myself in need of a foreman, someone who speaks for

me and reports only to me, and the person I have appointed to this position is Madame Zee. As of now, you should regard her as my eyes, my ears, and my tongue."

PART I

CONSCIOUSNESS
1897–1926

CHAPTER 1

1897

Edith Mabel Rowbotham lies contentedly in a lowland meadow in Lancashire County. Partially hidden atop a soft bed of flattened fescue and sedge, sweet vernal grass and cocksfoot, saxifrage and marigold, she and her older sister Honora stare up at the hard blue sky suspended overhead. A small, copper-toned butterfly lands delicately atop a spike of crested dogstail, and a brown hare races close, stops still and grinds its teeth in startled warning, then makes a quick zigzag around their legs to disappear as quickly as it arrived.

She giggles and nudges Honora as the hare bounds away, and then she settles back on the grass. A moment later, not knowing how it is possible with her eyes wide open, Mabel sees herself, perched atop a large boulder, facing water. Sharp, wartlike barnacles encrust the sides of the rock, but its smooth bald top holds the sun's heat and warms her from below. Salt air mingles with the odours of seaweed and fish, and gulls circle with their anguished child's cry. Waves—greenish, greyish—roil toward her, and when she turns her back on them the incoming surf roars up behind her as if it means to crush everything in its path. Bits of kelp and floating debris catch in the shoulder of each wave before it crests, and then they smash against an outcropping of rock with such force she wonders why the earth's surface doesn't shatter like glass beneath her feet.

She hears each explosion like a cannon shot and sees the resultant spray discharge in all directions. A splash hits her leg, as cold as a bucket of ice water, one tiny portion of one vast arc that might have drenched her from head to foot and sucked her out to sea.

The ocean is powerful in its attack. Rock is equally powerful in its resistance. But for all their fierceness, the waves, momentarily expended, lap the innermost shore like a gentle, healing tongue, so that as each one withdraws, she hears the pleasant rattle of shallow water draining off pebbles.

And then all the tin-plate colours of rock and sea—all the sensory information she can't possibly know—recede, so that once again she lies motionless in the meadow with Honora. Her sister's hot, familiar arm encircles and supports her neck and, rising from it, Honora's faint ocean scent joins forever in her memory with the smell of crushed grass.

"I had another daydream," she says, breaking the silence. Honora has explained that daydreams are like night dreams but easier to recollect.

"Just now? Was it good?" Honora rises on one arm so her face hovers over Mabel's.

"There were birds and the sea. It was warm, but the water was cold."

"Well, you're the lucky one. I never see anything, even when I want to."

The yeasty scent of fresh baking lures the two girls inside, into their grandmother's kitchen, a haphazard space with a low, wood-beamed ceiling, where pastries and pots share workspace with any number of more improbable items—buttons, string, pins. Supplies lie where their grandmother last laid them, rather than where a more orderly person might put the same items. Squat, reflective jars of canned goods sit like colourful lanterns on the floor along one wall. A green towel dries over a chair, and a papery gold onion glints on the windowsill, atop a copy of *The Adventures of Sherlock Holmes.* It is mid-afternoon, but here the sun filters through windows surrounded by ivy, giving the room a cool aquatic quality despite the heat and welcoming aromas.

Mabel emerges, blinking, into the kitchen and drops Honora's hand to begin a separate exploration of floured countertops and painted, freestanding tables. The two girls exchange a glance. *Is it here? Or here?*

Grandmother Castle's cottony head lifts as they enter, and her smile contains just enough hint of impatience that they keep their distance—until she beckons both girls over to where she has sugar cookies cooling on a rack. As hot as it is, three loaves of fresh-baked bread also rest on the counter, and alongside them, a pan of cinnamon rolls.

She has shaped the largest cookies into numbers. Last year she baked threes, sixes, and eights; today she passes a seven to Mabel. "Careful of that pan now. It's still warm." She slides the hot tray farther back on the countertop and selects the number nine from the rack for Honora. She calls her by her pet name. "Your last single digit, Honey. And when William wakes, I have a *four* for him." She scoots both children aside. "Now, out from under me so I don't step all over you."

She no longer cuts and bakes the ages of Mabel's four elder brothers into cookies. They are past all that, but hidden amongst more mundane shapes on a plate of circles, diamonds, or crosses, they'll still discover a boot, a hat, a moustache—any of the rich possibilities their grandmother sees as she slices through the dough.

"You're almost *ten*." Mabel latches on to her sister's freckled arm, a look of awe on her narrow face. "And there are ten of us."

"Imagine that," Grandmother says. "Ten already."

Honora has crammed her mouth full. She pops the last bit of cookie between her lips just as their mother opens the kitchen door and pushes through, her face damp, her expression hazy.

The two girls rush over.

"You're a welcoming sight." Margaret Rowbotham drops her shopping sack on the floor and stumbles as her daughters throw their arms around her waist. "Let me put this down before it tears open." She carries another package, brown-wrapped and tied with hempen yarn, which she sets securely on a wooden chair, and then she stoops to give her daughters a joint hug. As they pull away, she glances around. "Where's little William? Still asleep?"

The girls nod, and Honora accepts her mother's hat and hangs it on a peg next to the back door.

"I'd better check on him."

Honora's face has flushed petal-pink, and their mother hardly leaves the room before she nudges Mabel. "Do you think that's it?" Her eyes go to the parcel on the chair.

"Let's feel it," says Mabel.

All summer they have admired the new child-doll propped in the shop window two doors down from their father's pawnshop. It has younger features than most dolls, with blue sleep eyes that open and close, curled fingers, and two tiny, rounded teeth between parted lips. They each have a rag doll already, simple stuffed figures their grandmother sewed for them in their infancy. Maggie belongs to Mabel and Holly to Honora, but they're nothing compared to the beautiful, bisque-headed child in the window. They pleaded for her, just the one doll to share.

"Look at her." Their mother gazed through the window with open admiration when they showed her. "Skin finer than an eggshell. Even if we could afford her, she'd be in pieces in a minute."

No amount of begging or cajoling has changed her mind since, but Honora wants nothing else for her birthday. Not a new dress, or shoes, or a satin ribbon. Only the girl with the two darling white front teeth, the pouty pink mouth, the fine painted brows.

"Oh no you don't." Grandmother heads them off as they move toward the chair. She shoos them away with a mock frown. "I heard that. Both of you, out of my kitchen now."

"But, Gram. *Is* it? Is it the doll?" Honora looks covetously at the package.

Grandmother Castle rubs her nose with the back of her hand and then secures a few loose tufts of grey hair into the distracted knot on the back of her head. "I honestly don't know. You'll have to wait until tomorrow. Now out with you both. Play with William, or I'll set you to washing up."

She softens the brusque words with a quick peck to the tops of their heads, and sets them free. As an afterthought, she touches her hand to Honora's forehead. "If Billy's awake, play with him in the shade, why don't you. It's too hot in the sun."

The three children sit in a semicircle around a tin bowl of water and a large heap of dandelions collected from the patchy meadow across the lane. They remain in sight of the family gate so they can watch for the return of their father and brothers. Mabel squeezes sticky white milk from a stem and touches it to Honora's arm.

"Don't." Honora pushes her away.

Mabel feels the sudden surprise of rejection, and then a little cramp of anger that demands retaliation. She turns to William. "Smell this." She holds a dandelion beneath his nose and pushes the golden crown into his nostrils so that a hundred fine petals tickle him. "Smell the pee-a-bed."

"Don't." William copies his sister's warning and bats at her hand with his chubby, sun-browned fist.

"Leave him," Honora says.

"Mother makes him smell the pee-a-bed so he won't wet the mattress any more."

"I don't pee the bed!"

William's wide blue eyes begin to fill, and Honora immediately changes the subject. "Did it work when Mother put dandelion milk on your wart?"

She examines her fingers. "I don't have a wart."

"Then it must have worked. Gram says they bring good luck, too."

She nods. She has helped her grandmother wash young, tender dandelion leaves for salads, brew spring roots for a medicinal tea, and dry larger ones in the sun to be ground for coffee. She tosses a handful of dandelions into the air. "If the pee-a-beds bring luck, then you'll get your baby doll."

"It won't matter." Honora's words belie her expression, which says it matters very much. "Gram must know something. They must have bought me shoes like last year."

Big thick brown ones, Mabel remembers. She watches as the neighbours' black-and-white cat sidles near a dignified covey of feeding quail. Their soft *pit, pit, pit* sounds escalate, and the cat's rippling, well-groomed coat shimmers as it moves—a black silk jacket over immaculate white trousers. The cat approaches stealthily, nose twitching.

"Or a new winter coat so I can give you my old one."

"No. They can't have!" Her exclamation is so sudden that the cat darts away; two leaps and a bound and it is gone. The quail scatter—a gentle drum roll from those that take flight for a few feet, the others propelled in all directions by comical stick legs racing.

"Why should this year be any different? They mightn't have the money for a doll. And I can't hurt their feelings, can I? Whatever they've got me, I'll be happy for it." Honora glances at Mabel. "I *will.*"

She turns away from Honora and holds a dandelion under William's chin. *She* won't be happy with a stupid old coat. She checks for the amount of yellow reflected against her brother's skin. Bright means he is very sweet, pale means he is not. The bottom of his chin is bright gold.

She pulls the flower off the dandelion. "You're not very sweet," she lies.

"Of course he is," Honora says. When Honora turns her gentle smile on him, William's face loses its threat of tears, and he rolls over in the grass and laughs.

Mabel ignores him and slides closer to Honora, so close that their arms press together. Honora's is hot and dry. Hers is damp and sticky. Together, they pull all the heads off the hollow dandelion stems.

"We'll make a chain." Honora demonstrates to William how to poke the thin end of the long stem into its larger, opposite end to create one link after another. "And then we'll go inside. My eyes hurt."

Later that evening, Margaret Rowbotham boils huge pots of cabbage and potatoes, saving the fattened chicken for tomorrow's birthday dinner. The family eats the meal with a little bacon fat and thick slices of brown bread as they sit around the table—Grandmother Castle; Mabel's parents; her brothers Angus, Julian, Paul, Albert, and William; Honora; and she—all of them grinning wide moon-slice grins at one another.

After dinner, Julian swings William up onto his shoulders. Second oldest of the boys, Julian is underweight, his shoulders square, broad, and bony. But his face is angular and cheerful because he resists all things unpleasant, and at nineteen, he is not too old to play. With William clutching his head, he chases Paul and Albert outside, where the three brothers engage in a game of catch, an hysterical William tossed between them.

Mabel watches for a while, until William wets himself and the fun stops.

"He stinks," Paul says.

Julian swats him when William's shrieks of laughter turn to wails. "Don't say that."

"Why not? It's true."

"Doesn't matter if it's true. He has feelings, too."

Angus, the eldest, the quiet one, reads by the window. It is his copy of *Sherlock Holmes* on the windowsill. He looks up when he hears his brothers arguing, but he's never drawn in easily, and *Frankenstein* holds him fast.

Mabel joins Honora, who is already washing and dressing for bed. She combs Honora's hair. In exchange, Honora hums "Brother John" over and over.

"That's all," Honora finally says. "My throat's sore."

So the two girls curl together under their flannel blanket. She rubs the smooth surface of Honora's thumbnail with the pad of her own smaller thumb, the circular movement slowing until she falls asleep, still holding Honora's hand in their narrow iron bed.

Near morning, when light at the window is no longer black but is not yet bright either, she wakes to find Honora breathing in rapid gasps, shivering so violently that Mabel can hear her sister's teeth tapping together.

"I'm cold," Honora whimpers, when Mabel pushes her face close. "So cold."

She wraps her arms around Honora. "Is that better?"

Honora pushes weakly against her and cries, "You're cold. You're too cold."

She's not cold at all, and Honora is as hot as the sun. "Wait," she says, thinking fast. "I'll get the lamp."

The coal-oil lamp is on the bureau, pushed to the back, close to the mirror. She can just see its tin bottom in the dim light, but she'll need a chair to reach it. Her parents have said she's not to touch the lamp ever, not even to turn it down and certainly not to light it, but this must be an exception. Honora is shaking, and the lamp will be hot enough to warm her.

She slides a chair in front of the bureau drawers and stretches forward. Oil spills onto her hand as she drags the lamp closer, but she is careful and it stays upright. She wipes her fingers on her nightdress and checks the top drawer of the bureau for the box of kitchen matches kept there. Finding them, she lifts the glass globe with the wire and strikes a match against the brick set on the bureau for this purpose. She has seen her parents do this a hundred times, and Honora as well.

Proud of herself, she lights the wick, lowers the globe, and blows out the match. Now she has only to take the lamp closer to Honora.

But something is not right. She pushes the lamp back and bats at a ring of fire still burning on the bureau. As she does, a flame ignites on her wrist. She screams out in real pain and terror, and rubs her hand against her nightgown. When the flames ignite there as well, she panics and tumbles off the chair, rolling onto the floorboards.

As the chair knocks against the bureau, the lantern tips and shatters on the floor. Quicker than the hare in the meadow, fire jumps forward and the bedclothes near Honora ignite.

CHAPTER 2

She is staying the weekend with Henry and Eve Stanton, friends of her parents, and parents of Julian's fiancé, tiny Beth Stanton, who has auburn hair exactly the colour of Mabel's. Not even a year has passed since Honora's death, the only other time she stayed overnight with the Stantons. This morning, Mrs. Stanton put extra sugar on her porridge, and Beth spent most of the afternoon teaching her to cut paper dolls and fold birds. Even Henry has been fussing over her, trying to teach her how to play a willow flute he whittled just for her. But fuss as they may, she isn't fooled.

William is ill; her parents told her that. That's bad enough, but it's not the real reason she's here. He has been ill before and she remained at home. The last time she stayed with the Stantons, Honora went to heaven.

"Because I started a fire?" she asked at the time.

No, of course not. She was called home by Jesus, her mother and Gram said, both of them so closed and hurt-looking she didn't dare ask anything more.

She tried her brothers, but they didn't have many answers either.

"You lit the room on fire," Paul said. "What did you expect?"

"Shut up," Angus said. "Leave her alone." Then he turned to Mabel. "It wasn't like that at all. But do you have to keep talking about it?"

You did it, Paul mouthed, behind his brother's back.

She flopped in a chair and stared wide-eyed at Paul, then turned to Angus. "But how did she get to heaven?" And how could she be in heaven if she was under a cross in the graveyard as well? Could she breathe there?

"She doesn't need to breathe," he said. "She'll sleep forever in the graveyard. But the part that made her breathe, and laugh, and think, *that* part's in heaven."

"But what about worms and beetles?" She could hardly stand to think about how many of them there might be. She had watched worms. They can crawl in one hole and quickly curl out another. "Won't they be there, same as in the meadow?"

"They won't be. They know where they can go and where they can't."

"But how?" Her own insides ached with not knowing.

"They just *know,* Mabel, that's how. Same way you know you can't walk certain places or you'll fall through."

The way he spoke, she could tell he'd finished answering questions. Angus's patience had limits, and when his voice got gruff, he was best left alone. None of the answers helped make anything clearer anyway, or helped to make her miss her sister less. Only Honora would have answered as long as Mabel had questions, until everything fit, and no one had properly explained to her why her sister was not there to do just that. Why would she go to heaven when she could have stayed right here? It made no sense.

At first she made mental lists of things that happened during the day, things she wanted to tell Honora as soon as she saw her, forgetting that she would not see her at all, and sometimes she even went behind the house or over into the meadow in search of Honora, only to remember after a few steps that she wouldn't be found. Then she'd sink down and squish the stink out of pepper saxifrage with the heel of her hand until her eyes watered, or would throw stones at the hares that still bounded there. She'd make her list anyway, and would tell it to Honora at night, pretending her sister lay beside her in the narrow iron bed, just as she used to.

Sometimes Gram would peek in to see whom she spoke to, so she learned to whisper quietly so no one else would hear. And, finally, she stopped talking to her sister aloud at all, and only did so in her head, because she could do that day or night, preferring talk with Honora over any sort of interaction with her older brothers.

And now, faced with the Stantons and all their kindness, she is certain that when she is allowed home, William will be gone to heaven, too.

On Sunday, just after lunch, she packs her small bag of clothes and stands with it by the door. She waits until Eve Stanton notices her, and then she says, in her politest voice, "I'd like to go home now, please."

Mr. Stanton sits at the head of the table. He lowers his newspaper. "What's the matter? You don't like playing the flute?"

Mrs. Stanton stops wiping the counter and shakes her head at her husband, so Mabel instantly sees to which of them she should address her plea. It will not be enough merely to beg that they allow her to return home, so she tries logic. "I don't mean to be rude, but Gram says visitors are a lot like fish. More than two days and they both stink. It's time for me to go home now."

"Mabel." Mrs. Stanton comes to where she stands and stoops to her height. "We're happy to have you, child. And your parents said they'd come for you themselves as soon as they can."

Mabel stares her down. "Will William be there when I get back?"

"Well . . . William . . ."

She stamps her foot. "I want to *be* there."

"Yes, yes. I'm sure you do." Mrs. Stanton's homey bosom heaves forward as her arms encircle Mabel.

She looks stubbornly from one to the other of them, and then Mr. Stanton takes his hat up off a chair.

Grandmother Castle pulls Mabel into her soft, warm lap and holds her tight. "You can take comfort knowing he's with Honora in heaven. They're happy there together."

At that, she struggles to free herself, twists and wrestles in Grandmother's arms as she tries to crack her hold. She struggles so forcefully she breaks into a sweat, but still Grandmother holds her tight. Finally, when her fury exhausts her, she turns and pushes her face into Grandmother's shoulder.

"*I* should have got to go. *I'm* the next oldest."

"Hush, Mabel. You don't know what you're saying. We go when God calls us, not before, and we don't get to choose. Life is not fair—"

Grandmother's voice breaks when she says that, and Mabel puts her thumb in her mouth, frightened into acquiescent silence. She has seen her mother cry, and her father once, after Honora died, but she has never seen her grandmother shed a tear.

For months after, the house is quieter than it has ever been. Her older brothers all work. Angus sells goods from her father's pawnshop in a rough wood stall near the docks. Julian cleans the stables at Clark and Sons, a long low building with numerous squared-off doorways beneath small transom windows, and greasy black straw rarely glinting yellow. Paul and Albert both peddle newspapers at the train station, and come home with hands and faces blackened by soot and ink. Along with her father, they are all gone until evening, and for the first time, she feels like an only child.

When she closes her eyes, she sees Honora as clearly as she used to when her sister was alive. She doesn't know how this is possible if Honora is in heaven, which she understands to be somewhere up above the sky, but she doesn't question her presence. What bothers her is that however close Honora appears, she remains separate and distant, as if she communicates through a closed window. Nevertheless, Mabel continues to silently share secrets with her, and while occasionally Honora smiles or reaches out, an invisible barrier remains between them, so that Mabel can never quite feel her sister's touch, though her whole body strains toward it.

With William gone, too, the days are agonizingly long. What is there to do with neither brother nor sister? Often, now, she curls alone in a chair, not even her doll for comfort, and bites her nails, her eyes squeezed closed, straining to bring the image of Honora closer. If she can see her sister so clearly, why does she stand there, silent and unattainable, hour after hour?

"I hate you! You're mean and dumb and I hate you!"

Gram comes running. "Good God, child, who on earth are you yelling at?"

She allows her grandmother to hold her briefly before she breaks away and flounces down in the chair again. "It's Honora. Why won't she talk to me? I can see her but she only stares and won't say anything at all."

"Oh, Mabel."

She hangs her head and pulls at a thread in the upholstery until a naked line grows noticeably long behind her fingers, and though her grandmother must see it, she says nothing to reprimand her.

Grandmother Castle strokes her hair for a few seconds more, and then she says, "I think about Honora often, too. I don't know why she can't be here to talk to us, but I wish she were."

"No, but I *see* her! Do you see her, too?"

"Every day, child. I remember her when she was just a little tiny baby, and I remember her when she was the same age you are now."

"But she's *here,* and she won't talk to me." She looks up at her grandmother, her eyes blurry and hot with unshed tears.

"Where is she? Where do you see her?"

She can't decide where to point. Where is her sister exactly? She can't point to that corner, or that chair. She can't even point to the space immediately in front of her, though when she closes her eyes, Honora stands in front of her, not above or below or off to one side.

"I don't know. In here, I guess." Sulkily, she points to her forehead.

Her grandmother hugs her with such ferocity that she squirms to escape. It is a hug the opposite of her mother's embraces, which are loose and infrequent now, not hugs at all, really, just arms draped reluctantly around her from time to time when Mabel pushes in close.

"I'm sorry, Mabel. I really am. I know how much you miss her." Her grandmother considers her with a sad, worried expression, and then she leaves the room.

As she does, Mabel closes her eyes again. There is Honora, bearing the same patient smile, as if she merely waits, one hour the same as many.

She sleeps with the German doll her parents bought for her immediately after Honora died, when she wet the bed several nights in a row like William used to and spent the better part of many nights wide awake and tearful. She named the doll Trea, short for treacle. She would have called her Honey, but she saw what happened to her mother's expression when her father said, "Pass the honey." Mabel's mother no longer cries openly, but her eyes continue to look as if someone has poked them, and questions asked of her often go unanswered.

Because Mabel is tall for her age, she has almost grown into the new navy skirt and matching wool sweater Honora would have opened on her tenth birthday, had she lived. The clothes are brighter and much crisper than her own good set, and while they have remained neatly folded in her bottom drawer, she sometimes opens the drawer and eyes them with dread. She has been hoping that they will somehow disappear before she is required to wear them, but now she understands that they are going nowhere. When her mother finally notices her enough to comment on the shortness of Mabel's skirt, she pulls the clothes from the drawer, rolls them in a tight ball and hides them behind a box under her bed.

One day, not long after her grandmother overheard her yelling at Honora, her father invites her to come with him to his pawnshop. She's been there before, but now he takes her with him two or three days a week.

She sits on a wooden stool behind the counter and watches customers, or sometimes squats alongside the glass cabinet, through which all things become wavery and distorted.

"What's this?" Her father reaches behind her ear and pulls a tuppence from nowhere. He shows it to her and then makes it disappear again. A second later he opens his palms and wiggles empty fingers at her.

She laughs aloud, a delighted sound she hasn't made in months.

"What? What's it doing in your hair?" This time he pulls a coin from her curls.

"How're you doing that?"

"I don't know. There's money everywhere. Grab me some, why don't you?" He reaches up and pulls another coin out of the air. "Like this, you see?"

Another time he takes his handkerchief from his trousers pocket and casually pulls a crumpled wad of paper from it. He takes on a baffled expression and tosses the ball in a bowl on the counter. He shakes the handkerchief out so that she knows it is empty, and a second later, he pulls from it another wad of paper. Each time he moves to return the handkerchief to his pocket, he finds another ball to toss into the bowl. After a few minutes of this, he takes the bowl from the counter and holds it out to her.

"Toss those out for me, would you?"

But when she jumps off her stool to do as he asks, there is no paper in the bowl.

"What did you do with them?" her father asks. "They were there a minute ago."

At first she is puzzled, and a bit afraid she has done something wrong, but when she sees the glitter in his eyes, she narrows her own.

"Never mind." Her father shakes his handkerchief out a final time. "There's no shortage of them." Once again, he moves to return the cloth to his pocket, only to find another mysterious wad of paper stopping him. He pulls it out, looks at it curiously, and this time, he tosses it over to Mabel and pockets his handkerchief.

She pulls it apart. It is nothing more than an old receipt wadded up. "Tell me," she pleads. "Tell me how you did that."

"Tell you what?" he says. "I don't know where they all came from."

After that, he has a new trick each time she accompanies him, until he has shown her a dozen or more. He ties knots in his hand-kerchief with the flick of his wrist, or blows on others to make them disappear. He cuts a string in half, and makes it intact a minute later.

Always, she is reduced to giggles and pleads with him to reveal the secrets. How does he *do* that?

"A magician never tells," he says.

But she decides she will learn. Gram informs her that people sometimes learn tricks from books, and the same shop that sells dolls also sells books.

So she asks old Mr. Barton. "Is there a book with tricks in it?"

"Tricks?"

"Yes. Handkerchiefs and coins. Things like that."

"Not here, there's not."

"Oh." Her shoulders drop. "My Gram says that if you don't have it, and Father doesn't have it, it probably doesn't exist."

"Your Gram might be right about that." He removes his glasses and polishes them on a cloth while he thinks. "I'll tell you what. I don't have the book you want, but I know a few tricks myself. You straighten shelves for an hour, and I'll teach you one, how's that?"

They shake on it.

When business is brisk, she stays out of her father's way. Sometimes she goes down the street to visit Mr. Barton, and some-times she amuses herself with items in the shop—belts, bottles, boots, various pieces of furniture, luggage and cases. Her father has a scale with heavy iron weights, and she balances disks of iron against pawned items, adding and subtracting either weights or goods until the two scooped trays hang evenly. Sometimes she stands silently at the window, peering out, holding Trea tightly under one arm. Unknowingly, she rubs her thumb over Trea's tiny fist.

"So many *things*," she says. "They make me wonder about the people who owned them." She discovers that when she holds a woman's hatpin, her chest aches the way it aches when she thinks of Honora, and a thick, leather-bound notebook causes her to imagine a man with a large curled moustache. Some items cause her head to feel noisy and full. A little glass dish makes her want to laugh.

"When people are down on their luck they pawn their belongings in a certain order," her father says. "First the watch." He points to an entire row of big round pocket watches. "Then the rings. After that, it's the knife, their false teeth, and finally their pistols. Most of them will give up their knife before their teeth, but the revolver is always the last to go."

The next year her father sells the shop and moves the family to London, where he has purchased a coal warehouse along Regent's Canal. And with horse trams and workmen's railway fares allowing so many others to move to the suburbs, he is able to purchase a small home for them in the city as well, down a narrow cobbled lane, only a five-minute walk from the crowded tenement building where Julian and Angus will live. Her mother is tired after the move, but radiant also, and her eyes show signs of enthusiasm in a way they have not for months.

"The warehouse is a big, ugly, rundown thing, but it's ours," she says.

In fact, it is large and dark and requires many repairs, but the bank has sold it to her father for back taxes and the assumption of delinquent loans. It takes everything he has saved in the past fifteen years, but now he and his sons can work together.

"This is good for you, too," her father says. "We can send you to a proper school."

So far, Mabel's education has been at home with her mother or grandmother supervising generic lessons provided by the county. She has learned to read and write a basic sentence, and she is proficient in simple mathematics.

"A school with other children?"

"Of course there will be other children!"

"When can I start?" she asks. Maybe in London she will find a girlfriend her own age to talk to the way she used to talk with Honora.

"Soon," her father says. "As long as it's practical. I don't want you educated for the drawing room."

Rather than send her to an expensive boarding school with a non-academic program, her parents enrol her in North London Collegiate School. It is the first girls' day school to offer an academic curriculum as broad as any boys' school, her mother says.

She stops still when she sees the school on Sandall Road for the first time. Built from brick, it sprawls behind spacious lawns, rising three storeys high with two square towers soaring higher still. The roof is all angles and peaks, with various chimneys and outcroppings framed against the sky. She counts dozens of tall, vaulted windows, multipaned and impressive. Inside the entry, both her parents

and she seem smaller, dwarfed by wide hallways and graceful archways that shimmer with colour reflected off stained bevelled glass.
Imagine. She will go to school here!

When she begins attending in 1900, the first thing she notices
is that the days seem much shorter. The school day whizzes past,
and in addition to her academics, she learns not to slur her *r*'s and
how to sit straight and how to dip a pen and blot ink properly. Her
teachers encourage her to read for pleasure as well as for information, and she soon devours *A Clever Daughter, The Four Miss
Whittingtons,* and *A Queen Among Girls,* all books that encourage her to gain an education and become a responsible and self-
supporting woman.

"Maybe I can own a coal warehouse someday," she tells Gram.

"Is that what you want? To supervise big, gruff men all covered
in coal dust?"

"I never thought about it." It is the first time she has reason to
think about what she *does* want, and suddenly she looks at everyone with new eyes, observing how others earn a livelihood—who
look pleased with their occupation, who do not. Who looks prosperous, who does not. It occurs to her that the rag-and-bones man,
who clomps past their house with a big old Clydesdale and a cart
that creaks and groans, a man who does not appear prosperous at
all, nevertheless looks as contented as anyone.

When she is only twelve, after she reads about Elizabeth
Blackwell, the first American woman to become a physician, she
thinks that perhaps she would like to be a physician, so she can
help people, children in particular, and prevent their early deaths.

"That's so disgusting I can't even entertain the idea for a
moment," says Paul, the most conservative of her brothers. Once,

when he chided her about reading too much, he also warned her that no man wants a wife smarter than he is.

"Why should being a physician be any more disgusting than being a nurse?" she snaps. "Women have been nursing for ages."

"At any rate, you won't be allowed—will she, Father? Women physicians aren't allowed in England."

"Is that true?" asks Mabel.

"It used to be true," her father says, "though I don't think it is any more. I do remember something about Queen Victoria not allowing physicians from America—female physicians—to attend an international medical congress."

"Held here, in London?" She gapes at the injustice.

"Yes."

"How's that fair if there are women physicians in other countries? Why shouldn't they practise here as well?"

"No one's saying it was fair, Mabel." Her father seems far less concerned than her brother that she might consider such a career.

"They should never be allowed," Paul says. "Women are meant to be feminine, not mucking about with blood and nakedness. I can't imagine anything more repulsive."

A couple of weeks later he purposefully brings home a mangled dog. "Here you go, Mabel. How'd you like to practise some medicine?"

The animal is near death already, and one look at the maggots writhing in its wounded side causes her to gag and turn away, from the animal and from her brother's knowing smirk.

She cringes again when she hears the sound behind their house that tells her Paul has shot the creature, and wonders if he may not be right. She does not like the sight of blood, and if she is honest with herself, illness makes her fearful and unreasonably anxious.

Later, when her mother discovers what he has done and lays into him, Mabel stops her. "It's all right," she says. "He's right about me, but he's not right about other women. Plenty of women have a stronger constitution than mine."

"That's very fair of you, Mabel, considering your brother acted like a brute." She glowers pointedly at him until he gives in.

"I'm *sorry,* Mabel. I was a brute." He smiles charmingly at them both.

"Better," her mother says. "Much better."

If at first she thought school would be all about sitting at a desk, it is not.

"Our sports clothing is the best," she reports to her mother, who has sewn her gymnastics costume according to the school's standards—a dark blue serge dress, belted at the waist and worn with a light blue tie. She wears her normal skirt and cape over the dress as she walks the streets, and discards them once inside. "Not having stays in our undergarments allows me to move freely and breathe, and no tight collar, either. Everything is loose and comfortable. Almost like boys' wear!"

"Now don't go telling your father that, though between the two of us, I'm a bit envious." Her mother lifts her own long brown skirt and then drops it to brush a stray hair from Mabel's cheek.

Mabel is legally old enough now to leave her classes and never return, but she becomes sullen when some of the other girls do just that. That her friend Catherine has left, in particular, causes her to complain to her grandmother.

"She's my best friend! And we've been tennis partners for two years. Why would she go work in a boring millinery shop when she could have stayed in school?"

"Sometimes people don't have a choice."

"I'm always left behind."

She says this with such self-pity that her mother joins the conversation to snap at her, "Would you rather quit school and work in a shop as well?"

"No, of course not! I want to continue."

"Certainly she should continue," the Headmistress assures her parents. Sophie Bryant is petite and elegant with greying, upswept hair. She sits at her huge mahogany desk with the erect posture of a woman taught deportment at an early age, all relaxed and solid gracefulness—a woman of many "firsts," her father told Mabel.

Dr. Bryant is a member of the London Mathematical Society, the author of the first paper the society published by a woman. She was the first woman in England to become a Doctor of Science and, of only slightly less importance, he said, she was one of the first women in England to own a bicycle. Her husband, once a respected surgeon, died of cirrhosis at thirty, only one year after they married. In the thirty-two years since, Dr. Bryant has devoted herself to an academic life.

She has several texts open on her desk as she speaks to them, but she has pushed them aside. Mabel is a favourite of hers, she tells Mr. and Mrs. Rowbotham, addressing them over still, folded hands.

"Your daughter thinks for herself, and at a very young age. She doesn't cause trouble. Rather, she avoids it, and yet she isn't afraid of her own ideas. That's a valuable quality."

Dr. Bryant says she wishes some of the other girls would show a little spirit, stop sitting like colourful sponges, all aligned in their seats, ready to absorb and obey rather than to learn and think. "Any girl fortunate enough to have access to an advanced education needs both discipline *and* courage, not one without the other."

She observes them all seriously—mother, father, daughter. "She is first in her class, and particularly strong in mathematics and science. I can count on one hand the number of students who apply themselves as she does. It would be a great cruelty to take her out of school when she has just begun to blossom. She should continue here with us until she's older, and then go on to Cambridge, possibly Newnham or Girton college, as others of my students have."

She opens a folder and passes it to Mabel's father. "Have you seen these? She has an interest in botany and sketches the plants skilfully. It would be a crime not to encourage her."

Mabel breathes shallowly and reads her father's movements peripherally as he examines the sketches. If it were up to her, she would do nothing but sketch and read and play sports. She showed him an early sketch once, when she had just begun drawing, but he brushed it aside, more interested in her answers to the mathematics and science questions she had also brought home. Ever since, she has been careful to offer the academics for his approval and keep the drawings to herself. What is practical about drawing,

34

after all? Especially when she puts images on the page so easily. All she needs to do is examine an item once, and later she can visualize it repeatedly, the image retaining all the detail of the original, so that she merely copies its dimensions to the page, one part at a time until the whole is complete. Sometimes she forgoes tetherball, a sport she loves, to sit with her back to the brick wall, drawing something from memory, even when the other girls chide her.

"You're drawing in your sleep," Alison said only yesterday, teasing her when Mabel closed her eyes to look closer. Alison is the most effervescent of the girls, always giggling with someone about something. Then she rushed off with the others while Mabel sat apart. It seems to her that all of the other girls laugh so much more readily than she does, though she is never sure why that is. Sometimes she feels such frustration at her own inability to get the intricacies of behaviour right that she must dip her head to hide her face from them.

Yet always she takes some solace in the constancy of Honora's comforting presence. Do her friends have someone always with them, like Honora? She thinks not. She tried to ask Olive once, because she is quieter than the other girls and seems the most likely to, but she quickly changed the subject when Olive looked puzzled and confused.

But her father appears pleased with the sketches. He passes the folder to his wife and reaches around behind her back to squeeze Mabel's shoulder.

"Then she'll continue as long as she likes."

CHAPTER 3

On March 20th, 1905, she turns fifteen. Her mother, not her ailing grandmother, bakes her cake, and the family gathers to celebrate. Julian and Beth have twin daughters now—Elisabeth and Eloise—and they chew on Mabel's fingers and clamber at her legs for her to hold them. She lifts them one at a time, and then settles in an easy chair with them both on her lap. She nuzzles their cheeks with her nose and takes turns resting her forehead against each of theirs to stare into wide brown eyes. Their warm, chubby hands and snuffling exertions send feelings of pure joy straight through her, and she watches them endlessly, thrilled by the expressiveness of their tiny faces, their small mouths ever moving, even in sleep.

Angus has also married, to Hetty, who is as talkative as Angus is quiet. They have no children, but they will, Hetty says, six or seven at least, if she has her say. Paul and Albert tease her, tell her she is as fat as a dumpling and probably has one or two hiding under her skirts already.

Mabel, who has never completely forgiven Paul for the incident with the dog, pokes him in the ribs and says, "You'd better be content with nephews and nieces, because who else would have you?"

"Or you," he counters, but he loops an arm around her shoulder when he says it so that she knows he is teasing, and is aware that he knows she was, too.

Everyone laughs together and jokes easily before dinner, and then they all sit down for roast beef with Yorkshire pudding. For dessert they have birthday cake, a lemon layer cake, with raspberry preserves and whipped cream. She blows out the candles, all in one breath.

Later, they present her with pencils and drawing paper and a flat board folder with ties to keep her drawings safe. Her *portfolio,* they call it, as if the plants and flowers she draws are of real importance and should be protected.

No one says, *Honora would have loved . . .* or *Remember when William . . .* Everyone misses them still, but they belong to private memories now, beloved and seldom mentioned.

At school, the Headmistress stops her in the hallway. "I had the pleasure of reviewing your file over the weekend. You're doing exceptionally well. Keep up the good work."

She feels herself blush, and is as mortified as she is proud, but she stands tall and returns Dr. Bryant's smile as if she is accustomed to such singling out. "Thank you. I will. I'm so glad you're pleased."

"Very pleased, Mabel. Well done."

When she continues down the hall, Alison takes her arm and imitates the Headmistress. "Well done, Mrs. Pet! What did you do to deserve that?"

"I don't know," she says honestly.

She continues to draw plants skilfully, everything from a blade of grass or a dandelion to a hydrangea in full bloom, but every so often now, she sketches an image of Honora as well. Her sister has not stayed the same in appearance, but has grown older along with Mabel, and while she cannot understand how it is possible to see her sister always older, always in contemporary dress, she draws what she sees, and occasionally holds drawings side by side to compare them. In the privacy of her bedroom, she transfers all of the drawings to her portfolio, studying them in the process.

Her sister's face is no longer childlike but has the tender delicacy of a young woman on the cusp of adulthood. Her hair, once worn either curly or plaited, is now parted on one side and swept back off her face in a modern style that shows only the lobes of her ears. And although Mabel cannot see her sister in colour, envisions her only in shades of black and white, she sees that where once her sister's locks were blonde, they have gradually grown darker to become light to medium brown. This, too, is reflected in the drawings.

Honora's eyes have matured, and the last two drawings now show them gazing out from shadowed sockets below dark arched brows. Her nose is straight, her lips full on the bottom, thinner on top, and most often gently curved in a slight smile. Most memorable is the way her chin angles in to a point and forms a perfectly round swelling, almost as if someone has tucked a portion of a tiny ball under the skin. Her neck is long, her shoulders narrow and slightly sloped beneath a plain white blouse, buttoned, with a sash at the waist.

She closes her eyes and sees Honora from her own interior perspective, and then she opens her eyes and looks at the last drawing. The faces are similar, but very different as well, the way any living person is different from a photograph or sketch.

Mabel stands before the dressing-table mirror and props the sketch up so that she can compare it to her own reflection. Her hair is dark auburn, not red exactly but hinting at red, and worn down—not up—and to her shoulders in an unruly tangle of spiral curls. Her eyes are not yet set so deep as Honora's, though they are beginning to look as if they may end up that way, and her brows are thinner and straighter than Honora's. Perhaps the strongest resemblance between them is in the overall shape of their faces, both long with high, strong cheekbones, both with jaws that angle in to end in a pointed chin.

She turns her face slightly to the side, and then juts her jaw in toward the mirror and up. Though she would not mind if it did, her chin does not have the same swelling as Honora's. Nevertheless, she sees enough of a resemblance to feel satisfied, and she slips the last drawing back in her portfolio.

Mabel often completes her homework in the kitchen while her grandmother bustles around her, but for those occasions when she needs quiet, her father built a small desk for her that fits neatly into a corner of her bedroom.

She is sitting at the desk, chewing on a pencil, when she experiences a strange tightness in her chest, a mere tug at first, and then a painful fist squeezing like nothing she has felt before. A face she cannot recognize, pale and bloated, surfaces from the pages of her algebra text, a male, eyes bulged to twice any normal size. She brings her palms to her chest, and the face at first fades and then surfaces again, gashed and horrible in a pool of dark water.

She sits very still and watches as an old man and a younger figure trudge along a snow-packed path—an animal trail or a route of their own making. The older man pulls a toboggan, and spruce boughs bend low with the weight of snow. Their boots take noisy bites from the icy, trampled path—she doesn't hear this so much as she knows, without ever having heard the sound leather soles make on ice.

She sees the figures, close enough to discern how they shift their heavy packs, and then the older one tumbles forward so that in half a second he is gone, dropped through the ice in grainy black-and-white images.

And then, just as the pain in her chest subsides, Honora appears to Mabel, her expression unsmiling but serene. Seeing her sister has a calming effect, and Mabel focuses on her face as the final clenching in her chest subsides. Is there some connection between Honora and the old man and the boy, and if so, what is Honora trying to tell her? If only Honora would speak, wouldn't everything be so much simpler?

She goes in search of her mother, her pulse still racing. This is important.

Her mother glances up and then rushes to her side. "Are you ill?"

"I don't know. I had a daydream and I'm not sure what it means." She tells about the tightness in her chest and about what she saw in the middle of her textbook, everything except that she also saw Honora, and has always seen her. She omits this detail not because she thinks her mother won't believe her, but to protect her, because what if her mother was once again to become the diaphanous, moulted shell she was when Mabel was younger?

She tries but fails to describe the vision accurately. "I've had daydreams since I was small, but I never saw anything like this. And they never hurt before." She presses her hands to her chest, can almost feel the pain again.

"Daydreams?" Furrows in her mother's brow deepen, but she reacts as she often does when Mabel's behaviour puzzles or displeases her: she lays a comforting hand on her daughter's forehead and observes her with a bewildered expression. "I think you're tired," she says. "You need more rest."

That weekend she finds it impossible to study. What do the images mean? Why did Honora appear after them? And how will she ever know? She lies perfectly still in bed, trying to summon an image of Honora, but as hard as she tries, she cannot summon her sister or feel her presence. Has she somehow disappointed her? The thought that her sister might never appear to her again keeps her awake, adrenalin coursing through her body as she tosses from her back to her side through most of the night. An annoying tic starts under her eye, and when the birds begin their morning twittering, a sound she normally loves, she only wishes them silent.

On Monday, school is an escape from home, and she forgoes both sports and drawing, choosing instead, when her classmates go outside, to visit the school library. After some minutes randomly inspecting shelves, frustrated, not sure how to find what she searches for, she reluctantly approaches the librarian.

"I'm wondering about people who sometimes see things in their heads."

Mrs. Walsh puts her own head on a tilt and considers her for several seconds before speaking. "People who are mad?"

"No," she says, startled. "Not that."

"You mean someone who has a vision, like the Apostle Paul?"

"Yes. More like that. How do I find information on people who've seen things in this century? I want to know why they see what they see."

Mrs. Walsh laughs. "I'm sure they'd all like to know that." She sorts through a box of cards. "The newspapers are filled with that sort of thing, of course. There's that Edgar Cayce in America. He claims to give healing advice to sick people while he lies in a trance—"

"Does he see things?"

"I'm not certain, but we can retrieve a few of the articles. And there is Madame Blavatsky, the founder of Theosophy—"

"Excuse me?"

"A religion of sorts. They claim to have some sort of mystical insight into the nature of God and the soul."

"Oh." Religion. That's not what she wants.

"They're Spiritualists, some of them. They believe the dead can communicate with the living. There seems to be a lot of hocus-pocus involved, and Madame Blavatsky certainly claimed to have visions."

"Truly?" She tries to keep her voice calm. Theosophists and Spiritualists. The dead communicating with the living. She asks about the correct spelling and makes notes on a piece of paper.

"For something more scholarly, but along the same lines, there is the London Society for Psychical Research. SPR, they call it."

She waits, assuming correctly that the librarian will explain.

"They're relatively new—since the early 1880s—but they've published some papers on clairvoyance."

"Clair . . . ?"

"Clairvoyance. The ability to perceive outside the usual senses. Seeing things not there, if you will."

"Honestly?" How fortunate that Mrs. Walsh has taken her request so seriously. She thought she would be lucky to find anything.

"Of course, and there is telepathy as well—a sort of silent communication between minds. Sir William F. Barrett, of Cambridge, is involved with all that at the society, and Dr. Henry Sidgwick, too, before he died. He was from Cambridge as well. Dr. Bryant admired him because he supported higher education for women. She sniffed at his interest in the supernormal, of course, but she still visits his widow."

Mabel receives that as a reminder that she shouldn't make assumptions. However much information is available, she imagines most people would be skeptical if she were to tell them what she sees.

Nevertheless, by the time she leaves the library, she can't believe her results. She has an armful of books and a further list of materials and reports she can peruse within the confines of the library. In addition, Mrs. Walsh has provided her with the address of the London office for the Society for Psychical Research at 20 Hanover Square.

Alone in her bedroom, she sits hunched over on her bed, her back touching the pale plaster wall, and reads about Theosophy. She learns that its doctrines aim to bridge the gaps between science, religion, and philosophy—three facets of one whole field of knowledge that no one should attempt to separate—and that the society has three chief objectives: 1. *To form a Universal Brotherhood of Humanity without distinction of race, creed, sex, caste, or colour;* 2. *To study ancient religions, philosophies and science;* and 3. *To investigate the unexplained laws of nature and the psychic powers latent in man.*

She thinks of her brother Paul and wonders if a universal brotherhood so devoid of prejudice can ever exist, but even the idea that others want such a thing excites her. Theosophists believe in the unity of all life, that all living things derive from the same source and energy, and are hierarchical in nature; as the body is composed of organs, which are composed of tissue, which is composed of cells, so too are plants and animals arranged according to the same hierarchy. Not only that, Theosophists believe in the immortality of the soul, which may reincarnate and take another form to further its divine purpose. They believe in karma and spiritual evolution. Good karma and bad karma accumulate according to one's actions in this life, and affect every phase of one's continuing existence. Kick a dog today and that bad karma will have to be lived, in some form, somewhere else. Act kindly and kindliness will prevail, in this life or the next, or in some distant embodiment on the way to enlightenment.

And what of their investigation into psychic powers? She reads ever more avidly, taking the information in as if it were a large complicated puzzle, spurred on by the smallest piece that fits with what she already understands. The more she reads, the more interested she becomes. Madame Blavatsky heard voices, and she saw images, just as Mabel does. She received notes from unexplained sources, and could move items without touching them. But she attributed these gifts to the Masters of Wisdom, and strived always to be receptive and learn more from them.

The Masters—known fully as Masters of Wisdom, Compassion, and Peace—are highly evolved beings, and make up a spiritual brotherhood of the highest order. Known as Brothers of the Great White Lodge, together they guide the destiny of the entire human race as its individuals reincarnate over and over in their attempts to reach enlightenment.

The doctrine of reincarnation, Helena Blavatsky wrote, states that everyone derives from a much higher, blissful state of spirit. The higher, spiritual part, when incarnated, lives as a mortal endowed with a profound sense of individualism and separateness from others.

For as long as Mabel can remember, she has felt intensely separate. *But,* she reads, for most people, glimmers of the higher consciousness will break through this diminished life. The frequency of these experiences depends on the individual's spiritual advancement, but each flash of higher consciousness is a reminder of that knowing, blissful state to which everyone returns, and of the enlightenment toward which one might strive.

Immediately she thinks of her daydreams. Are these the glimmers of knowledge and higher consciousness of which Madame Blavatsky wrote? And if they are, what is she meant to do about them?

However often she starts down this path, asking herself these questions, the answers always remain just outside her grasp. Thinking about them is akin to running after soap bubbles—just as she stretches far enough to think she is near an answer, the bubble pops and she is left staring helplessly into vacant air. Whatever the answer was, now even the question evades her.

Mabel's brother Albert is next oldest to her. He is seventeen, tall and thin, taller than any of the other boys, though he is now the youngest. He is almost as serious as Angus, but he is the most adventuresome, unable to sit still. When he is not working, he often goes off by himself, returning for dinner with stories of the London streets he has seen, lanes so narrow that people pass items from one balcony to another across them. One that is wide at one end and narrows to a closed point. Another where the women stand outside and approach men as they walk past. He didn't mean for her to hear that, but Albert and Julian didn't know Mabel had wrapped the draperies around herself to keep warm, and stood behind them, gazing out the window.

She believes there is much Albert does not tell about his experiences, and for this reason, he is the brother she approaches when she wants to visit the offices of the SPR. She has caught him alone on the back step, where he sits chewing on a piece of grass.

"Let me get this straight. You want me to take you to an address, but you don't want me to ask you any questions?"

She nods.

"Does this have something to do with some boy?" He looks at her in an appraising way, as if he wonders what another might see in her.

"Don't be stupid. I wouldn't need you then, would I? I'd have the fellow to help."

"Is it a doctor?"

Perhaps he has imagined something too horrible to speak of, because his expression changes, and he looks at first shocked, then angry.

She holds up her hands. "It's nothing terrible, Albert. I only asked you because I thought you could keep a secret."

"It's not a secret if I don't know."

"It's my secret."

He turns away from her and spits, then he shakes his head. "I won't do it."

She glares at him. "If it were Julian who had asked you, or Paul, you would take them in a second!"

"Tell me what you're hiding."

"I'm hiding nothing. I have a private interest I wish to keep private, nothing more, and I thought my older brother might help me. It's obvious I was wrong."

"Tell me the address."

"20 Hanover Square."

"I'll think about it."

Too late, she realizes he has tricked her. He will go there himself and he will know anyway. "*Fine.* If I tell you, will you take me?"

"I have to know first."

So she tells him about the society, about how they investigate ghostly phenomena and other paranormal activity. Mind reading. Second sight.

"You must be joking," he says, grinning, and then, when she assures him she's not, he laughs so hard he almost chokes on his blade of grass. "Are you off your knob? Why would you want to go there?"

"If you think I'm going to tell you anything more when you act like that, you're the one who's off your knob!" How dare he laugh at her? She trusted him! She lifts her skirts and turns her back on him.

"Wait a minute, Mabel. Hold on. I'm sorry."

"You're not."

"I am. I won't laugh any more. I promise."

She eyes him mistrustfully.

"I might like to visit there, in fact. I'm only surprised, that's all. How do you know about them, anyway? And what do you hope to learn if we go?"

What does she hope to learn? She only wants to know what is there, what the members of the society *do* at the office. And most important, is there anyone there she might talk to about her own visions? But she doesn't tell Albert any of that, and says instead, "I suppose I want to know if they have classes or books that would teach me how to be like that."

"To read minds and all?"

"No, not that. I don't know. More to understand why. *Why* do they see what they do?"

"Tomorrow, then. We'll go, the pair of us."

In May, she has a second experience. She is at school when she "sees" her mother flip a pot of scalding water onto her arm. She is sitting at her desk when it happens, and she can do no more than grip the sides of her desk and close her lips tight, hoping not to make a sound. Perspiration breaks out on her forehead, and just as before, her chest hurts terribly. The image rises into her vision with no effort on her part, obscuring everything else in her sight, and she sees her own kitchen at home.

Her mother catches the handle of the pot on her apron top as she bends over the stove. Mabel watches helplessly as the water cascades over her mother's arm, and just as she begins to feel the burn herself, the image and the burning sensation fade. And once again, as the pain subsides, Honora appears.

Mabel hasn't been able to conjure a clear image of her sister since the first vision, so although she felt nothing but horror only a moment before, now she has to stop herself from laughing aloud. Even as Honora's image fades, she feels certain her sister will return. Mabel will endure these images and the resulting discomfort every day if they will bring Honora back!

Since her visit to the library, she has been reading almost

constantly, and what she has all along called "daydreams" are, in fact, clairvoyant episodes. She still does not understand what she is meant to learn from them or even why she has them, but she will not stop trying to find out.

She thought she might learn something at the office of the SPR, but when Albert took her there in March, the office could not have been more disappointing—little more than a small cube containing a large desk and numerous filing cabinets. The man inside was sweet-faced, slightly built, and balding, with round spectacles on a nose made longer by its thinness. Not someone who inspired confidence, as she had hoped. He was neither friendly nor helpful, and said only that the office was not open to the public. He didn't even provide his name when they provided theirs, and when Albert asked where he might learn more about the society, the man shook his head.

There was nothing for anyone to learn about them, he said, until the society made their findings public, which they had not yet done. Their meetings were private, their findings were private, and there was nothing more he could do to help them.

She could have argued that their findings were not entirely private if she was able to review them in the library, but she would have argued only for argument's sake. She had envisioned something else entirely, a place where people came to discuss their experiences, where she might, as well, and the office was nothing like that.

"Satisfied?" Albert asked, when they had left the office and were once again outside.

She shrugged and nodded. Nothing she reads or does leads anywhere. It interests her to learn about others who believe they see images or help heal people, or who communicate with the dead, but nothing in the books or papers has explained how to control the clairvoyance, why she has the ability, or what to do about it. There must be *some* reason she sees what she does, but if so, what is it?

And now she worries all afternoon that her mother has hurt herself. She rushes home after school expecting the worst. She bursts in and calls out, but her mother greets her as usual, unhurt, not at all concerned about anything except whether or not Mabel would like a cup of tea.

"Are you all right?" She takes her mother's arm and checks it for signs of the scalding.

"What are you doing? Of course I am. Why wouldn't I be?"

"No reason. I'm glad you are, that's all." She gives her mother a quick hug, and decides not to worry her. "I'm going to read," she says.

"That's all you ever do!" But Mrs. Rowbotham smiles to show she is not nearly as concerned as she pretends.

So what is going on? Is she doomed to see frightening images for no good reason?

She has almost forgotten the event by the time she arrives home, a few weeks later, to find her mother's arm covered in gauze.

"I was so foolish." Her mother recounts how she flipped the pot over on herself. "A dozen times I've almost done that, and still I haven't learned."

Mabel is horrified. "I saw that happen to you. In a daydream." She still calls them daydreams for her mother's benefit. "I saw it just as you described it to me." And if she had told her mother immediately after she saw the accident clairvoyantly, would it have happened anyway, or could she have prevented it?

Her mother brushes the admission aside. "Of course you didn't. Don't say that."

"No, Mum, I did. I have clairvoyant episodes. I see things. Sometimes I smell, or hear, or feel them. There's no other explanation for why I would. I felt you burn yourself. I almost yelled out in class. And remember, I looked at your arm when I came home from school?"

She can see by the change in her mother's expression that she remembers.

"What are you saying? That you see the future?"

"Not usually the future. But I don't know. I saw this." Her mother has that pursed-lip look she gets when she plans to turn a decision over to someone else. "Please don't tell Gram or Father."

"Why not?"

Because they won't understand? Because they won't believe her? Or is she afraid they *will* believe her? What would they do then? In the end, she chooses the only reason she thinks her mother will accept. "It will frighten them."

Certainly her mother looks frightened enough.

"Oh, Mabel." Her mother sighs, as if there is no way to under-stand her daughter. "This is not right."

What does she mean, *this is not right?* Will she consult Father after all? Does her mother believe she is ill? Or that something is wrong with her mind? This thought occurs to Mabel often enough, especially now that she has read a few of the reports opposing psychical research. There are plenty of doctors who would diagnose her as mad and lock her away, were she honest with them.

But she's not mad, is she? In her heart she feels she's not, but why are so many doctors certain that all psychic phenomena can be explained away as psychological delusion? As mass delusion, even? She read one report about a group of people all pointing at the sky in a stupor, an entire group who believed they saw an assembly of angels. One man could see nothing, and finally he took the shoulder of another who looked undecided but still entranced. "There's nothing there," he said.

"Thank you." The man appeared visibly relieved. He shook his head and became much more alert. "I knew there wasn't, but I could almost see it for a minute there."

And she has heard about Bedlam, too, an asylum for the insane. People there see what others do not. They hear voices and talk to empty space. Are they looking upon loved ones as she looks upon Honora? Ordinary people used to visit the asylum for amusement, observing the antics of the patients. Gram said that has all been stopped now—but who knows when it will start again? If the essence of sanity relies on distinguishing between what is tangible and what is imagined, might she not one day be confined there herself? She lies on her bed and pulls the pillow over her head. She has spoken to none of her friends, her brothers, her teachers. Who would not laugh at her? Who would not presume she is mad?

Sometimes when she's really anxious, she pulls hairs from her head one at a time to distract herself, and she pulls one now. The tiny twinge is a kind of penance, though her family is Protestant, not Catholic, and even then they only attend services occasionally, for a few weeks after the pastor makes his yearly visit.

At dinner she eats only tiny forkfuls when her parents or brothers turn to speak to her. In between, she moves the fork to her mouth with almost nothing on it. She spreads the food around on her plate, tucks some into her handkerchief, and when she takes the plates away, no one notices that hers has hardly been touched.

The tic below her eye returns. Looking in her hand mirror, she sees cheeks even more scooped away than usual, and when she presses the pads of her fingers below her eye to stop the tic, she is surprised to find the trembling skin there as dry as paper.

Some of the reports she reads offer suggestions on how to develop her abilities. Her *psychic* abilities, though this is a word she hesitates to use in reference to herself just yet. She worries that accepting the term will make her an oddity, a misfit who believes she can see what others can't. Or arrogant, someone who assumes she is somehow capable of knowing more than others possibly can. Either way, she is not quite ready to claim this "gift" she may or may not have.

Still, she is not content to do nothing about it, either, so in the evenings, when she used to do her homework, she sits on her bed with an ordinary pack of playing cards, flipping cards one at a time, guessing whether the card will be black or red. She goes through the entire deck this way, guessing each time, and unremarkably, she is right about half the time. When she makes the task more difficult and tries to guess the actual suit of each card, her success rate increases slightly, and the cards match her guesses about thirty or thirty-five percent of the time.

A five-to-ten percent deviation from normal chance means very little. Memory could be enough to account for the difference—as more black cards turn up, she may consciously or subconsciously guess red more frequently. To challenge herself further, she returns each card to the deck in random order. Her success rate falls, and though it remains slightly above the norm, she never consistently guesses more than thirty percent correctly.

Despite this disappointing lack of success, she uses the cards every evening for several weeks until she tires of the unrewarding tedium. Then she changes her strategy. Instead of speculating about the cards, she lies on her bed and attempts to clear her mind, relaxing and leaving herself open to whatever image might arise.

She does this for an entire week, most nights falling asleep when she relaxes, but on the eighth night, after a period of quiet waiting, she sustains a dreamlike state where she sees Dr. Bryant extend a diploma. The experience is ordinary, fleeting, and even predictable, because the Headmistress surely will pass her a diploma soon at the graduation ceremony. But the image arrives with chest pain, and is layered over her eyes like a negative she peers through, so that her surroundings fade out in that telltale way they have in the past, and reappear only after she has also seen Honora, smiling.

Is this a coincidence, or did she will this image into being? She sits on the edge of her bed, tense with excitement. For the first time, she might have exercised real control! And if she did, if she genuinely did, mightn't it be possible that one day she will see clairvoyantly whenever she wants to? Imagine that! Just imagine if she could turn the knowledge off and on as she wished. What sorts of things could she know and predict? Who could she help? Maybe she will even learn how to communicate with Honora or others. The possibilities are endless, if only she can develop her ability. Forget about botany. Forget about mathematics. How can she learn to be more clairvoyant?

Chapter 4

Toward the end of the school year—her fifth at North London Collegiate School—Dr. Bryant calls Mabel into her office to interview her alone.

"Has something happened at home?"

Mabel knows full well that her grades have suffered. Instead of studying, she has been reading about paranormal abilities and preparing her mind with meditation. She has been expecting this discussion, has even imagined how she might respond to the Headmistress's questions with questions of her own: What does it mean that I can see these things? What should I do about them? Are the images ever likely to be useful? But instead of asking the Headmistress, who may indeed be willing to discuss these questions, she remains silent, in part because she remembers what the librarian said that first day: *She sniffed at his interest in the supernormal, of course. . . .*

"Nothing has happened, ma'am."

Dr. Bryant holds her gaze for several seconds, until Mabel looks away, and then she speaks gently. "I was happy to hear that you would return this year, Mabel. But I can't help you if I don't know where the problem lies."

"There's nothing, I promise."

"For heaven's sake, Mabel!" Her tone is exasperated. "You're pale and distracted. You've lost a stone, at least. I'm told you're a million miles away in class. You missed an exam, and even the assignments you complete are not up to your usual standard. How can you sit here and tell me nothing is wrong?"

She has never admired anyone as much as Dr. Bryant. When the Headmistress visits the classroom, she often scans the tables before she speaks, and when she spots Mabel, she smiles at her specifically. She calls on her by name, too.

No. She will not risk Dr. Bryant's estimation of her by admitting to something the woman is almost certain to scoff at.

The Headmistress shakes her head. "You won't get into Girton or Newnham at this rate. Have you thought of that? The application deadlines are approaching."

"I'm sorry, ma'am. I won't be applying."

"But why not?" her mother says. "I don't understand."

"There's no point wasting Father's money. I'm not interested in botany any more. It just doesn't hold my attention the way it used to."

Dr. Bryant expected her to attend a Cambridge college, and if only she could go on to Trinity College, where the founding members of the Society for Psychical Research once taught, perhaps she wouldn't need to disappoint everyone, but women do not attend Trinity. And despite the SPR's association with Trinity, even that college offers no classes in anything related to psychic research. If they did, perhaps she could speak to someone in person, ask if she might be allowed to do the coursework, whether the professors graded it or not. But what is the point of attending any college if they can teach her nothing about the only subject that interests her? Isn't she better to study on her own?

"Wasn't your goal to become self-supporting?" her mother asks. "This is so unlike you, Mabel."

"I'll think of something."

It has already occurred to her that the study of psychology might provide some opportunities for psychic research, and for honing her own skills, but when she obtained the listing of courses from the librarian, they focused exclusively on child rearing and school counselling. Even then there was no mention of dreams or imagination, or how the mind works. The articles she read about women in psychology, thinking she might learn something that would steer her in the right direction, were primarily written by men, and the tone was disdainful. Several articles stated outright that, as in medicine, the presence of women dabbling in science lowered the status of more serious professionals. She decided right then that she'd rather work in a dress shop than constantly fight against men like her brother Paul, who would waste their own time in obstruction, if only it meant they would prevent her achieving her goals. She is not like Dr. Bryant. She is not a woman of "firsts." She admires women like that, but they are braver than she is.

But she can share none of this. If her mother believes Mabel has lost interest in academics because of a passion for the occult, she will blame herself for not consulting with Father, and she will talk to him immediately. Mabel can easily imagine his reaction. *I've credited you with more intelligence than that,* he'd say. She heard him say something similar to Albert once. And he has several times referred to a group of Spiritualists as idiots, as fools and charlatans, so there's no reason to think he wouldn't doubt her intelligence in the same way. Better to let him think she is interested in nothing at all than have him believe she has been taken in by idiots, when she is not yet prepared to argue their worth.

Her mother lays her stitching aside and studies her daughter without comment. "I think I understand," she says at last. "It must be difficult to watch your friends making marriage plans. You want all that, too—to be courted, to marry. That's perfectly normal. But you will—"

"Mother! I'm only sixteen."

"Yes, that's far too young, I agree. But you feel left out. You've said so, many times."

"Not about marriage!"

"And don't think I haven't heard your brothers. Paul was wrong when he said a fellow won't be happy if he thinks you're smarter than he is. Intelligent men like intelligent women."

Mabel shakes her head. Only one of her friends has marriage plans. Olive works in a good dress shop, and has such a knack for it that she has already built a regular clientele amongst the "fine silk" crowd. Catherine has become a milliner, and now blocks fashionable hats for the same sort of women who frequent the dress shop. It is only silly, giddy Alison, one year younger than Mabel, who is already planning a wedding to Arthur Bailey. Arthur owns the Duke's Head Ale House in North London, and Alison can speak of almost nothing but him, which makes for dreary conversation.

"I'm not interested in a lot of flirtatiousness."

"There's time enough." Her mother smoothes her skirt and broaches a new topic. "In the meantime, if you're no longer interested in botany, that's your choice. There are other options, other fine schools."

"To study what?"

"What interests you most?"

"I don't know. Drawing. Reading." Silently she lists the others. *The occult. The mind. The soul. Death. Spiritualism. Mesmerism.* She wishes she could test even one of these out on her mother for a reaction, but even supposing she did not question her intelligence the way Father would, she would think of such interests as leisure activities, not career-worthy pursuits.

"I've always thought that teaching is a very practical and versatile profession, and Homerton is a very good teaching college."

"Aw, Mum. I don't want to spend my life in some large house tutoring spoiled children. I'd be a glorified children's maid, and not paid much better, either."

"Not these days, you won't. New schools are opening all the time, and people send their daughters to them. That means more positions in the classroom, like at your own school. You'd do well at it."

Her mother has a point. Academically, she is almost prepared now. The training will take only six months or another year at most. She will have access to books, and can read whenever she likes. Her father may be disappointed, because there is no prestige associated with teaching, but she will earn a living. A poor one, perhaps, but more important, the teaching itself need not be demanding. She will have plenty of time to read and cultivate her own interests.

And if she doesn't earn enough, there is always her drawing. She has been sketching faces from memory, has attempted to visualize others aside from Honora as a means of improving and sharpening her visions, so isn't it possible she could earn a little extra by sketching the occasional portrait, by selling a few botanical drawings?

"All right then," she says agreeably. "I will pursue a teaching career."

"You will?"

The surprise on her mother's face makes her smile. Perhaps she should have resisted a little, if only to reassure her. "Yes. Tell Father. You came up with a good idea and I like it. You're worried I'm humouring you, but I'm not."

When she graduates from North London Collegiate School later that year, Dr. Sophie Bryant congratulates her and extends the diploma, just as in Mabel's vision. Later, when everyone is milling around, shaking hands and accepting the good wishes of others, the Headmistress asks about her plans.

"A children's teacher?" Her eyes question Mabel and a slight frown pulls at her mouth.

She could not feel worse if she had told Dr. Bryant she planned to stay home and knit sweaters. "I've given it a lot of thought, and it's what I want."

"Your mother's idea?"

They both look to where Margaret Rowbotham stands talking to another woman. She appears drained today, as if the day has already exhausted her. Mabel understands how Dr. Bryant might see her mother as no more than a sad, jumpy woman, and she feels protective.

"Mine. My sister and brother both died when they were very young, so I'll enjoy being around children."

"And your father?"

"I think I disappointed him. He liked the idea of a botanist in the family."

"Then perhaps you'll change your mind?"

A botanist must be a serious scientist, a biologist who concentrates on distinguishing details and minutiae. As a botanist, she would be expected to investigate and discover what is new, to write papers about her findings. Even supposing she is ever able to focus on such things again, it would take all of her time. And were there any time left over for her own interests, messing in the occult would jeopardize a career like that. But the Headmistress values education for its own sake. Neither the practical nature of her decision nor the impractical nature of her passion would please Dr. Bryant.

So she says only, "My father would like that."

CHAPTER 5

1910

"I've bought farmland in Canada," Mr. Rowbotham announces. His excitement extends to the quivering wiry hairs that poke out from his eyebrows.

"One hundred and sixty acres for ten Canadian dollars. That's hardly more than two sovereigns, for a quarter section." He waits for their understanding. "My farm in Saskatchewan will be as large as an entire English village!"

He has never farmed before, but that won't stop him. He has a history of success, and for that price, he says, he can afford to make a few mistakes. He will leave the warehouse in his sons' capable hands and they will sail for Canada in the summer.

Mabel is twenty years old now, and teaches at Francis A. Bishop girls' boarding school in West London. Last year, she read about the Fox sisters—two American sisters, Kate and Maggie, who had reached old age and died when Mabel was still a toddler. The oldest, Maggie, was four years younger than Mabel is now when she and her sister purportedly received messages from the dead. As hundreds, and then thousands, saw them and believed they really did communicate with their deceased loved ones, the Spiritualist movement began. If more than a million Americans can believe in the possibility of speaking to the dead, perhaps Mabel should visit there.

She might meet someone like Edgar Cayce, who heals with information gained in a trance. Maybe he could teach her how to do more than merely visualize Honora. But America has always seemed so far away, and besides, her interest in the United States has never extended to Canada. Nor has she ever imagined that she would actually *live* in another country.

"I'm not certain I want to move," she tells her mother. Did they mean to go without her? And if not, why had her father presented the move as a *fait accompli*? Couldn't they have forewarned her?

"Your father has been discussing this off and on for months," her mother says. "You can't tell me you haven't heard him talking about Canada—I can't count the number of times he's brought it up. He's only been waiting until you were grown."

"I never imagined he would *move* there! What if Gram dies while you're there?" Lately, her grandmother does little more than sleep in an upstairs bedroom. Lily, the new housekeeper, often returns her food to the kitchen untouched.

"If Gram were to survive the summer," her mother says, "she would stay with Angus and Hetty—but she won't, Mabel. You need to prepare for that."

"How do you prepare for the death of someone you love?" Except perhaps to believe that they will return. She puts her face in her hands. Will Gram appear the way Honora has, or will she disappear the way William did? It is too unpleasant to think about.

Margaret Rowbotham rises and walks to Mabel's chair to stroke her hair. "She's been with us a long time. We have to accept that she can't hold on much longer."

She leans into her mother, and then wraps her arms around her knees. She still can't stand this sort of talk—people she has to let go, others off to some Christian heaven. What of the fact that Gram simply won't *be* here?

"So what am *I* supposed to do?" she asks.

"You can hold her hand and talk—"

"I don't mean Gram. I meant when you go to Canada. Am I to find somewhere else to live?" She takes a swipe at her cheek, impatient that she can't hold back her tears.

Her mother rubs her back. "We never intended to abandon you, but we can't make the decision for you either."

"How do I know I'd even like Canada?"

"You don't, of course. I'm not sure I'll like it either, but it means a great deal to your father, so I'm willing to go."

"What about Paul and Albert?" They are unmarried and have remained at home, though both are grown men. "Where will they live?"

"They want to rent a flat together near Julian and Beth."

"And why Canada of all places? Why couldn't it be an easier choice? Why not America?" She dries her eyes on her handkerchief and tucks the bit of lace into her sleeve. Then she stands, and when her mother takes her own chair once again, Mabel notices that she does not move as easily as she once did. Has her father aged as well? She hasn't thought much about their mortality until now.

"Few choices are easy, Mabel. When they appear to be, they're often not the best choice at all."

"If I stay in London, I suppose I could board at the school."

"There *are* schools in Canada. You may have an advantage there—"

"Of course there are. But—"

"You don't need to decide right away. Why don't you think about it?"

She studies her mother seriously, and then leaves the room. What if her parents go to Canada and she stays here? What if she never sees them again?

She likes to walk the streets of London, if only to look in shop windows or peer at the houses lining both sides of the street. Each street is different, and she notes how ornamental details— scrollwork, pillars, and railings—save some houses from being little more than brick boxes, how some are enclosed by gates and rails, sometimes covered with ivy, while others can't be seen at all and remain hidden behind high brick and stone walls. Low-roofed pubs appear unexpectedly on corners smelling of ale, and church spires often rise behind them. Gardens are mostly private, with locked iron gates, but some beckon invitingly through sculpted green archways. Occasionally she ventures into one and sits for a while, but mostly she walks, hands stuffed in the pockets of her coat, hat pulled down to her ears. Father said that the weather in Saskatchewan is very cold in the winter and very warm in the summer.

She dislikes the cold. And yet she can't let her parents go off by themselves. Who knows how long it will be before she sees them again? Though this is also true of her friends. When will she ever see them if she leaves?

Not that she visits with them often any more. She rarely encounters Alison now that she is married, though she has twice gone to their apartment above the Duke's Head Ale House. The apartment was dark and noisy and not at all what she expected. And Olive and Catherine are always so busy at work. She counts back to when she last saw Catherine, the quietest, her favourite of the three friends. Could it really be four months already?

But think of all the new opportunities the move could provide. Not for work—she will be lucky to find a better position than the one she already has—but in its proximity to the United States, where there is a large Theosophical movement. Are there Theosophists in Canada, as well?

When her decision is made and done, everything happens quickly. Most memorable is the six-day trip from Liverpool to Quebec City across the Atlantic on the *Empress of Ireland,* a floating monument to Edwardian grandeur. Mabel shares a second-class cabin with her parents, a bright white space hardly large enough to turn around in, but that is a novelty in itself. She explores and fills the tiny cubbies and marvels at the crisp sheets turned down each evening. And since she has never dined out in London, the ship's second-class dining room, with formal place settings and four-course meals, awes her into silence.

For part of each day, the sun's reflection shimmers off mercury-tipped waves, and from the deck, she stares endlessly, burning this remarkable sight into memory. She will draw it later, if only she can invent a technique that will do justice to the silver glitter that stretches as far as she can see in any direction. Playful dolphins have frolicked alongside their ship for several days in a row, and on the last day, as they enter Gaspé Bay, a thirty-foot minke whale jumps so near the ship she can almost count the throat grooves beneath its triangular snout. The creature is enormous—six to eight tons, a steward says—and it emits a raspy vocal as loud as any engine. This spectacular sight sets her heart thudding, and for two hours after, she refuses to go below deck on the off chance she might see the whale again.

They reach Quebec City and stay only one night before boarding the train west. Narrow cobbled streets remind her of London, and in the tiniest bookshop she has ever seen—a disappointment only because all the handsome books have French titles—she nevertheless buys a thin silver bookmark, punched with a hole from which a scarlet tassel dangles.

But if Quebec City feels somewhat familiar, she greets the rest of Canada with surprise. Her first daylight impression of rural Saskatchewan is after almost two weeks of gruelling travel in a second-class Canadian Pacific Railway "colonist car." The car is as hot as she imagines the engine room must be, and crowded with other immigrants. Sometimes she thinks she will swoon from the heat, which open windows cannot lessen. For twelve days she has done little more than sit and mop her brow. At night when they fold the sleeper down over their seats, she goes to bed eagerly, for when sleep eventually arrives, those are the only hours that pass quickly. At mealtimes she goes with her mother to the kitchen at the end of the car and prepares simple food with other immigrants from Britain, Poland, and Ukraine, amongst others.

For the first two days, the journey is sociable, and passengers resort to smiling gestures when language is a barrier, but after several days of almost unbearable heat, noise, smoke, and stench, talk is limited, and there is little to do besides stare out the window. What Mabel sees is an empty land.

This impression does not change when they finally arrive at her parents' homestead. Where are all the people? She believes she'd find more occupants in one overcrowded London tenement than inhabit the entire village of Lemsford, near her parents' farm. And yet the surrounding acres are by no means desolate and barren. Wheat tops ripple in the breeze throughout summer and sometimes remind her of the wide open Atlantic. By fall, cut grain lies in long skeletal spines, with jutting golden stooks stretching ten miles or more in every direction. Sunsets turn everything melon orange, and the harvest moon in September looms so large and yolk-coloured that she can only stare at it in amazement, the world so new and unknown.

Her parents photograph heaps of vegetables—carrots, squash, potatoes, cabbage, pumpkin, onions—and send these photos back to her brothers in England, proving the rich fertility of Saskatchewan soil. And of their new home nearly finished: a modern two-storey with attic gables and verandas on all four sides.

Her brothers must wonder why there are no trees, for while there are some between her parents' property and the neighbouring farm, the photographs show only a few small, now leafless poplars—along the driveway, and a small cluster of equally leaf-less willows around a muddy slough in the distance. And won't they laugh at photographs of the town? At rural architecture so unadorned that most of the shops are nothing more than plain wooden boxes with the simplest gabled roofs? At wooden plank sidewalks sitting atop dust or mud, depending on the day, and nothing at all surrounding them, except perhaps a horse or cow in the background, because even the shops—few as they are—are not adjoined, but sit solitary and alone, so far apart that two or three more could be built between them.

Yet, if her brothers chuckle at the sheer expansiveness of such unprecedented space, they would only gape in astonishment if they could see the enamelled blue bowl upturned over the entire province when the sun shines. *Imagine azurite,* she writes. *Or French enamel . . . or blue sapphire . . . and even then, none of them is blue enough. And my disappointment on a cloudy day—when the sky is not blue, here, it is the same woolly grey of London in the winter—and all the unpainted boards of these plain buildings disappear into it.*

She finds a teaching position almost immediately in Macoun, with nine students in the one-room schoolhouse. As in Lemsford, the streets are dusty when the weather is dry and muddy when it is wet, so that the hems of her dresses are always in need of scrubbing.

She lives in a rooming house, and when she first arrives, a few families invite her to join them for Sunday dinner, but none of the visits foster further real friendships. The women have husbands and children to keep them busy, homes to run, and endless chores. None of which leaves much time for Mabel, even when she tries to befriend the women by stopping by with small gifts of coffee or sugar, and although no one is unkind, after the first few months it seems inevitable that most of her relationships will remain superficial.

Occasionally she visits her parents on weekends, curious as to how their farm will have changed each time, outbuildings built, and finally the main house complete, but most of her evenings are spent alone in her room at the boarding house.

She works her way through a box of books she brought with her from England. When she has finished reading them, she learns that there is no place to buy more locally. There are books—romances and westerns, religious adventures—but nothing of the sort she has brought—books on Theosophy, magic, and ancient religion— and so she rereads the ones she has and begins a notebook where she records her thoughts.

If arcane knowledge misapplied is sorcery, and used beneficently it is wisdom, what are ways of knowing only happened on, like mine?

A medium is a passive instrument. An adept actively controls himself and all lesser forces.

Adonis: the Jewish Adonai? Really?

Do I believe that all the world is a Brotherhood? Perhaps, or at least that it was meant to be.

She reads that some people have received spiritual messages through a practice called automatic writing, so she tries it herself. She sits in a wooden chair at the small table in her room with her feet flat on the floor, her back straight. She holds a pen over a piece of paper for several minutes at a time. When nothing happens, she places the nib directly on the paper, but this action only results in a large blotch of ink. After several minutes, she closes her eyes and allows her hand to move lightly over the page, but when she stops and examines the paper, she has written nothing legible. Perhaps she has misunderstood. Maybe she is meant to write whatever comes into her head, and not expect her hand to simply begin moving on its own. So now she scribbles any thought that occurs to her, and she writes steadily, without stopping, until she covers several pages.

When she reads what she has just written, it is no more than a mundane and convoluted transcription of confused thoughts.

The realization of the unknown is only possible alongside a willingness to accept the unexpected. However, the unexpected may not be recognized or recognizable, in which case—is it possible to experience something profoundly meaningful at a level beyond understanding, and unknowingly feel and respond to its effects?

There is nothing in all the pages that brings with it a shiver along her spine, a flash of certainty, an image of Honora, or anything else that would suggest the exercise has been worthwhile.

Three years slip by like mist, quiet, uneventful, vaguely obscuring. Visits to her parents, long walks down mostly untravelled dirt or gravel roads, reading, attempts at psychic practice, teaching, and occasional bits of writing, mostly in her notebook or in the form of letters to England. It occurs to her that many more years could pass in exactly this same manner—but is this what she wants? To be the unmarried schoolteacher living in the boarding house into old age? And if not, what will she do to change her course? Look for a husband? Move to a larger city? The thought of doing either causes her to feel great lassitude.

Sometimes when she sees two girls hanging on each other at school, she feels such a pang she has to force back tears. After all, they are children, and how wonderful for each of them to feel so close to another. She doesn't wonder why the image moves her as it does, or if she does, she recognizes only that she is lonely, that forming friendships is no longer as easy as it once was.

When she misses her friends in London, she practises imagining them, tries to see them clearly, as she still sometimes sees Honora. She does this either by lying in bed with her eyes wide open, or, if she is tired and risks falling asleep in a prone position, by sitting at her desk with pen and paper. When she sees something meaningful she writes it down so she won't forget about it, and because sometimes the importance of an image becomes clear only weeks later, as she reads through her notes. When she is successful, the images of her friends are sometimes accompanied by memories—the sound of their voices, words they once spoke. One night, in meditation, she sees Alison as she has never seen her before, holding a baby in a long white christening dress. Though it should be impossible to know, she is certain the baby is a girl. She sees the child so clearly she can practically smell her, and she knows the image is important because of this strange certainty, and also because of how she feels physically. Just as her visions are almost always preceded by chest pain, these other moments of knowing are accompanied by an intense energy, a rush of adrenalin that sets her heart pounding and leaves her flushed and excited.

The excitement returns when, more than a month later, she receives a letter from Catherine reporting that Alison gave birth to a baby girl, Ethel, born a week before Mabel visualized her. She laughs aloud at the news, and still jittery with adrenalin, she starts a separate notebook to keep track of incidents like these, too uncanny to explain. And where previously she meditated an hour a day, she increases the time to an hour morning and night.

In her fourth year teaching at Macoun, one of the parents, known to her only as Mr. Herbert, father of William, issues a complaint against her because she showed the children a magic trick, the same handkerchief-and-ball trick her father once showed her. Not one to confront anyone on his own, he does not address the issue with her personally, but complains to the school board, which sets a meeting of the parents. Mabel, in her distress, forgets the name of the chairman the moment she hears it.

"'Miss Rowbotham's behaviour is sacrilegious,'" Mr. Herbert begins, reading from a piece of paper. His hands shake and his voice is tentative. "'It goes against the values of the community and it is outside the mandates of the school curriculum.'"

"It was a children's trick!" she says, affronted. "I amused them for a moment with a simple trick anyone here could do."

"But we wouldn't," Mr. Herbert says.

"What about the mail you get from the Theosophical Society?" Miss Audley says. She is the postmistress, a thin grey woman with no husband and no children of her own.

Her tone is so accusatory and angry that Mabel blinks. This meeting is about something more than one magic trick. She wonders what Miss Audley knows about the Theosophical Society and why she is present at this meeting at all. "What right do you have to discuss my private correspondence?"

Miss Audley addresses the chair. "You can tell a lot about a person by their mail. The sort of person who'd teach *magic* to small children." She stresses the word *magic* so that it sounds as if Mabel has done something vile.

The chair nods. "Carry on."

"And she's also written to Edgar Cayce, and got several letters back."

"Who is Edgar Cayce?" the chair asks.

"An American psychic." This comes from another parent. Josephine's father, she thinks. "Anyone who's heard much of him knows he's a Satanist. He hypnotizes himself, and allows Satan to speak through him."

"He would attribute his gift to God, not Satan." She allows herself to use their rhetoric for a moment. Nor does he hypnotize himself, she would like to add, but she does not quibble. He simply lies down and allows himself to relax. In this relaxed state, he has given accurate instructions to heal hundreds, if not thousands, of people with illness. "He correctly diagnosed a spinal injury in a little girl thought to be mentally ill. He recommended herbal medicines, dietary changes, and exercises for one man's chronic liver problem, and the problem cleared in days. He pinpointed the exact location of a tumour thought to be inoperable, and even offered precise directions for a successful surgery."

"I see," says the chair, and somehow his dismissal of these facts suggests her naïveté in believing them, or perhaps that anyone who hypnotizes himself might just as well be a Satanist. The chair is an older man, partly bald, with his remaining fringe nearly grey. Until now he has appeared almost bored with the proceedings, only reluctantly present. Now he leans forward. "Are you a Satanist, Miss Rowbotham?"

"Certainly not! Nor is Mr. Cayce, as far as I know." She assumes he wants to know if she is some devil-worshipping evildoer. Few Satanists are. Aleister Crowley has often been accused of Satanism, and while he is not one, he's quite clear on the subject—most Satanists view Satan as merely a symbol of dissent and individualism, not as a deity to worship. But why are they caught up in this, anyway? Why should she be subjected to this line of questioning? What has it got to do with anything? She lifts her chin and faces the chair. "Really, isn't my personal correspondence my own business—?"

"Not when it means harm to our children," Miss Audley interrupts.

"The children I teach, you mean?" she challenges her. "Not yours, surely?"

"Is it true you are in communication with these people?" The chair sounds very stern.

"I've requested information from Mr. Cayce, yes. I had hoped to visit him, but he discouraged me." She still remembers how she smarted when she read his last letter. *To pursue these visions of yours would be a folly. Having seen the ridicule and shame that too often befalls young women like yourself, and having endured much of the same, I must advise you to let go of the dream that this ability will one day amount to good.*

"And the other?" the chair asks. "The Philosophy Society."

"The Theosophical Society, yes." Cayce had a few words about them, as well. *It is not a Godly organization, and I would not like to count you amongst them.*

"What is your interest in these people?"

She considers for a moment the angle that will least harm her. "Mr. Cayce heals people. I am intrigued by that. And I had a child-hood interest in Theosophy. Theosophists believe in one religion for all—all the people of the world working together for a common purpose." Even as she says it, she realizes how idealistic it sounds. Were such a thing possible, it would require the interven-tion of a most powerful spiritual force.

"They believe in reincarnation!" Miss Audley interjects again. "And they claim to communicate with ghosts."

"And you?" the chair asks. "Do you believe in communicating with the dead, Miss Rowbotham?"

"I'm not sure," she answers truthfully. He uses the word *you* only in its most general sense, and has not asked about her own abilities, about which he could not know. "I lost a brother and a sister when I was quite young, and my grandmother died three years ago. It's comforting to think they might somehow contact me, but there is no substantial evidence that would prove it."

"So you believe in reincarnation."

She waves a hand impatiently. "Let me ask you this: having arrived once, would it be any more miraculous to arrive again?"

"This is what she's teaching our children!" says Miss Audley.

"No, I'm not! But I'd like to think I'm broad-minded enough to consider the possibility!"

Mercifully, after an hour of questioning the meeting ends. The chair leaves her on probation. She is to perform no more magic tricks, and is to curtail contact with anyone connected to the so-called supernatural.

In addition, the chair says, she must follow the curriculum more closely and not allow the students as much time as she has been allowing for individual interests. She need not teach music and drawing at all, as they waste valuable time better spent in other pursuits. The children can sing in church, and drawing is simply unnecessary.

She has been trying to read, but whenever she gets to the end of a page, she realizes she remembers nothing of what came before. She slams the book closed and gets up to prepare herself a cup of tea.

How dare that busybody examine her mail and have her teaching motives questioned? She sets a kettle of water on the electric ring in the corner of her room. She remembers few of the arguments put to her in the meeting, but she retains an imagined image of Miss Audley peering at the return address on each piece of mail that comes to her.

She spoons tea leaves into the teapot and pours hot water over them. She feels more than chastised. This is oppression. She will apply for other teaching jobs, and she will not stay in Macoun any longer than she must.

In June, she is offered a position in a new school in Eagle Hills. The new town is even smaller than the last, but she has no immediate choice—it is the only school to offer. The fall passes routinely, but in December she deviates from a strictly Christian perspective and introduces a story about Hanukkah. Her supervisor, Mr. Andrews, has always struck her as unnaturally jovial, but he isn't smiling the morning she finds him seated behind her desk. He rises to greet her and gets straight to the point.

"There is no mention of Hanukkah in the curriculum," he says, "though I understand our students are learning about it, irregardless."

"That's true," she says, ignoring his error. "But one of our students is Jewish. I wanted him to feel included, so I read one story." She has already argued the validity of her choice successfully with her father, and she feels confident she chose correctly. So what if the majority of the other children celebrate Christmas? What harm can it do to teach them that not everyone does? If the world is ever to approximate the ideal of one Brotherhood for all, cultural variety should be shared, not repressed.

Mr. Andrews brushes her sentiment aside. "Irregardless of that, this is a Christian school, not a synagogue. Send the boy to a Jewish school if he wants to read about Hanukkah."

She forces herself to speak calmly. "But you know there's no other school in Eagle Hills."

"Precisely. But his parents could school him, and they have the option of moving him elsewhere—to Toronto or New York, somewhere they can mix with their own kind."

It takes a moment before she has any response at all. She recalls that in their first meeting he dismissed the theory of evolution as heresy and told her never to discuss it. She imagines all the people and ideas a man like Mr. Andrews has to dismiss as lesser or irrelevant in order to believe in his own superiority. *Irregardless,* he would say.

She shakes her head in dismay. "I can't believe what I'm hearing."

There is a long pause in which both she and Mr. Andrews look away from each other. Her eyes fall on the blackboard and she sees the careful letters she traced along the top of the new chalkboard at the beginning of the school year, *A* to *Z*, each letter boldly shaded. She remembers how diligently she worked to get each one correctly drawn, and how the younger children's eyes lit up when they first saw them. She believes that learning should be fun and meaningful, tailored to each child's understanding of the world.

Above the chalkboard hangs an oval of polished wood with the carefully painted phrase "In God We Trust." She has read the words many times, has even found them comforting on occasion, but sitting here with Mr. Andrews, she sees how easily they can become ominous and self-righteous.

Mr. Andrews is the first to break the silence. He is certain she cares about her position. The parents expect more from her. He expects more. He knows she is up to the task or he would never have hired her.

"We want you to use the curriculum as the Department of Education has defined it. Is that so difficult?"

"No," she says. "In fact, it would be easier than doing what's right."

"We're in agreement then." He is smug, so certain he has brought her behaviour into line.

When he leaves, she sits erect at her desk. In the silence of the empty schoolroom, she slides open her desk drawer and retrieves the scarlet-tasselled silver bookmark she bought in Quebec City. She drops it into her open bag and scrutinizes the rest of the drawer's contents. She has collected nothing of interest.

"I don't understand you, Mabel," her father says. "How many times do you think you can walk away from a position before the school board will no longer accommodate you?"

She wears a serious expression. She gets the seriousness from him, she has often thought. Her pride, too. She would rather keep these incidents from him, not discuss them at all, but she can't return home mid-year with no explanation.

"It's not as if I mean to come up against them." She really doesn't. And yet how is it that she so often does? It is irritating to intend to do something good only to have it so often judged wrong.

"At this rate, you will lose any allies you have."

"But how is it wrong to speak out when their policies are so unfair?"

"That's as it is when one is employed. I didn't always agree with my employers either, nor your brothers necessarily with me, but that's the way of it. The world is divided into two kinds of people, Mabel, those who follow the rules and those who don't. And you can be certain of this: those who follow the rules have a much easier time of it. Without them, we'd have anarchy."

"With too many we have status quo! And how is it fair to ignore Jacob in favour of the others? Why shouldn't I help to *make* the rules?"

"Good Lord." He heaves a small sigh and lowers his head into his hands to massage his temples, impatience flashing across his features. "Why are you always so preoccupied with fairness? Is it fair that you were born into comfort while others are born into abject poverty? I'm pleased that you want to help others—but how will you help anyone when you're in the poorhouse yourself?" He raises his head again and smiles grimly. "Kindness and patience are the two great virtues, Mabel. You have the one. The other needs development."

She wishes her mother would join in these conversations. Her absence is no indication that she disagrees with Mabel's father, but she doesn't take the same interest she once did. In England she was much more vocal about her opinions, but she's changed in Canada.

Mabel supposes they all have. It hasn't been easy to find a foothold, what with the cold and the hard work, so many people all struggling to acquire their dream, yet separated by distance and unspoken disappointment. It must be difficult for her mother. She must miss her friends and Mabel's brothers. She would miss them more than her father would, because he has joined the Orangemen and he meets with a group every week.

But it can't only be loneliness. She has offered to keep her mother company, to help or visit, to go for a walk, but still her mother retreats.

"That's lovely of you," she'll say, "but I have too much work in the kitchen."

She seems disconnected, somehow. Her kitchen is large and ordered, in stark contrast to the small muddled ones Gram presided over in England for so many years. Warmth and spicy scents fill it, but in many ways it is less welcoming than the old ones, for although her mother occasionally stops long enough to sip a cup of tea in front of the large window, perhaps even admires the stretch of lawn she looks out on, she rarely invites Mabel to do the same. This new kitchen is her mother's territory, and she hides in it.

She's aged here, too. Lines and puckers have settled into pouches of tired flesh, and her eyes have lost their flash. In that department, her father has fared no better on the Canadian prairie. While he spoke to her, she observed him silently. He has developed jowls and dark empty sacks under his eyes.

He looks like a man who has worked hard, and it shames her to cause him extra concern.

"I'm sorry, Father. I'll try harder." He wants the best for her, both her parents do, and she can't bear to fail them. She vows to do better.

Alone in her own room, she lies on her bed and practises an exercise she calls "mind tending," whereby she attempts to pay attention to whatever spontaneous message her mind might offer up. Instead of trying only to *see* something, and bring on a vision, she wonders if she might not also hear or feel something. Maybe the reason she has fewer visions than she'd like, and finds them difficult to understand, is not because the information isn't there, but because she has only been tuning in to a small part of the whole message, as if she blocked the sound when someone was speaking and watched only their lips moving. Usually this mind tending only turns up something odd and seemingly meaningless, like "*one hundred tetherballs*," but occasionally the message is more intriguing, as when she paused for a minute or two on the veranda last night and heard "*pathological liars be damned.*" That surprised her in the way an odd dream can surprise, and she was left wondering, Where did that come from? She considered the phrase for several minutes afterward, even meditated on it before she went to sleep, but its meaning never came clear. And now, the voice in her head is certain, but all it says is, "*Go to the bathroom,*" and that because her bladder is full to bursting.

With a deep sigh, she rolls over and heaves herself off the bed. Nothing is happening as she had hoped. Teaching is not the easy job she had thought it would be, and if she has learned a few methods meant to develop her psychic ability, the results have so far been negligible.

CHAPTER 6

1915

One farm over from her parents, Mr. and Mrs. Parsons have a son, Leo, who lives with them and who will one day take over the farm. He has straight, sandy-coloured hair parted down the middle and the same round, cheerful eyes as his mother. When she first met him, she felt a flutter of excitement, the recognition of one looking for another, but over time, the flutter settled and a feeling of easiness rose to take its place. He stands shorter than Mabel and always wears two jackets at once, instead of one heavier one. In the winter, when he removes them to sit at the table, long underwear pokes out of his shirt cuffs, the edges grey and worn. He smells like salt water, except for his breath, which is often minty. Still, more often than not, when she writes ahead to say she will visit her parents, she arrives to find Leo already there.

They take innocent walks along the trails that run between her parents' farm and his, through the narrow wooded windbreak that separates them. In the winter, spruce boughs hang low under the weight of snow, and once, when she hears the sound of their boots on the icy path, the sound triggers something from a long time past.

"I saw a path just like this in a dream when I was a child," she says, not attempting to explain that it was a vision, not a dream. "Before I'd ever seen snow, I heard the sound our boots are making."

Leo rewards her with a curious look. "My grandfather used to say that the mind is a window. He says anyone can see anything that ever existed or ever will, if only they'll sit still long enough to look.

"He's deaf now, and he doesn't talk much, but I used to walk this path with him every winter when I was a boy. He trapped up and down the river right up until a few years ago. Coyotes, beaver, otter. He pulled supplies on a toboggan and sometimes we'd camp overnight in a lean-to."

Now, gulping huge mouthfuls of cold air as she walks, she considers confiding in Leo. Then she stumbles and extends her bare hands to break her fall, but almost before she has hit the snow, Leo has her on her feet again. He holds her hands, already as rough as roots from the unrelenting cold, and rubs them to warm her.

"One year the ice was soft and he fell in. Good thing I was with him."

She takes a sharp breath and hopes Leo will interpret it as surprise or empathy, but in reality she remembers the unknown face in her book, how it took on such a dismantled look, the skin frightening and blue, the eyes not quite focused, everything pulled askew.

"How old was he then?" she asks. It may not be the best question, but her mind is cluttered with ones she can't ask. Did his lips turn dark and his nose a necrotic white? Were his eyes bugged out and frightening?

"Almost seventy. He caught his boot and tripped on a frozen clump of grass. He should have been able to right himself, like you just did, but the ice didn't hold and he broke his wrist as he went through."

Leo doesn't have to tell her how the stumble catapulted his grandfather's body forward, or about the brittle snap of ice breaking, and elderly bone. She has already seen the gaping cave of water that took his grandfather whole, first his head and shoulders, then his back and his woollen rump as he tilted forward in a slow slide under and into the icy pool. She knows how his heavy parka absorbed water and how the cold numbed him, his senses going dark one by one.

She breathes the cold air now in gasps. All her attempts to control her visions over the past few years have gone nowhere. She rarely has premonitions, and when she does, she seldom understands them until after the fact, if then. But if the inexplicable face that appeared in her textbook all those years ago is connected to Leo, isn't it possible that every other image may someday connect to some other aspect of her life? A surge of adrenalin sets her heart beating rapidly. She stops on the path and presses the heel of one hand between her breasts.

Leo stops, too, and tightens her scarf in a gesture of manly tenderness. "Don't worry," he says. "Somehow I got him out without going in myself." He tucks the ends of her scarf inside her lapels. "I piled pelts on him and was able to pull him home on the toboggan before he froze."

"Oh my God." She tries to still the excitement building inside her. Has she finally stumbled upon a clue? Then she imagines the long, painful ride home for Leo's grandfather under stinking animal hides. "I'd like to meet him," she says.

Leo arranges for her to meet his grandfather the next time she is home. The old man sits in a wooden rocking chair facing a small window. He is bent and wrinkled, with small, watery eyes that look empty one minute but peer out bright and quick when Leo introduces her.

"He won't have heard the introduction, but he'll know you're a friend."

She pulls up a small stool and waits for him to speak. She is not sure what she expects from him, but the coincidence—her vision, the circumstances of his fall—are too great to ignore.

Finally, he stretches out his hand, and she holds it.

"Do I know you?" he asks. "Do you want to marry our Leo?"

Leo colours and turns away when she shakes her head *no*. They have carefully avoided that discussion. He works hard, but she sees how he takes for granted the work of his mother and his sisters, who clean, garden, cook, bake, iron, knit, sew—and bear many children. It goes without saying he will want someone similar, someone like her own mother, and his, not someone consumed by some vague longing she doesn't yet understand.

The old man is disappointed. He turns back to the window and stares into the distance so long that she thinks he has decided to say nothing at all.

He still holds her hand, and then gradually his grows so warm she is uncomfortable holding it. And when he finally turns back to her, his eyes are not as bright as they were. They seem to fade even as she watches, and then he speaks in a rough, forced whisper, so she has to lean forward to catch the words.

"You must never live by the sea."

"Why?" she asks, hoping he can read her lips.

"It's too easy to drown," he says.

The next time she feels the familiar chest pain that precedes a vision, she is teaching in Lancer. The one-room school sits on the edge of town, surrounded by bare poplar skeletons and acres of Saskatchewan prairie. The children write quietly, and no one notices when she grasps the arms of her chair and holds on, hoping that whatever happens will be quick and silent. She stares straight ahead until the back wall disappears, and then she sees herself sprawled on the ground, arms splayed out, a book off to the side.

That's all.

Just the one fleeting and disconcerting image before the wall returns and the squeezing in her chest subsides. The image could mean something or nothing, but it leaves her longing for the day to end.

At final recess, she almost has her wish. She patrols the grounds as she always does at this time of day, ostensibly to keep peace and ward off trouble, but mostly to keep warm. The youngest girls skip along beside her. Fallen leaves crumple beneath the soles of her sensible shoes. An earthy, mushroom scent wafts up from the ground, and clear play sounds ring out all around. What pale sunlight exists originates too far south to add any warmth to the autumn air, so she pulls her walking coat closer. She is about to call everyone back inside for the last hour when angry voices rise behind her.

She turns toward them and the hem of her coat sweeps behind her as she hurries to a corner of the school grounds where a cluster of boys have gathered. Even from a distance she can see which two boys are at odds from the confrontational tilt of their chins. Brian Connor is the pale, plump one. Nicholas Slobovian is the darker of the two, and more than once she has heard his name shortened unkindly. As she draws close, she hears Brian's voice, derisive, over those of the others.

"Stupid bohunk!"

She lengthens her stride and leaps between the boys. "You apologize right this instant. That kind of talk is unacceptable."

She is taller than both of them, but they are stronger and heavier. She hopes they will lose their belligerent, cocky sureness before someone is hurt, but Brian, predictably, can't give in easily.

"I'm not apologizing. He's got no business here."

"What's that supposed to mean?"

Nicholas takes a step forward and attempts to get around her. "Your family wasn't born here either, fish belly."

Nicholas's skin is light brown and smooth, like a fine brown egg. Brian's, in contrast, looks lardy and raw. He is the son of the only barrister in town, and in their home "Canadian" means

"British colonial," with few exceptions, and Protestant with no exceptions. She gleaned this from her first interview with the father when he hired her. He grilled her about her family's religious ties, and stressed that any Catholic sympathies were cause for dismissal.

Catholics, Jews, blacks. They are all the same to men like Mr. Connor and Mr. Andrews, and the Connor boy is very much like his father.

Brian imagines himself superior, the only one capable of leading any school group, and he repeatedly bullies the younger children until they run away in sullen tears. Once he tormented one of the smaller boys until the boy wet his pants in terror, and Mabel had to send him home in shame because she could not allow him to sit there, dripping, while the others either pitied or despised him.

Nicholas's parents emigrated from Ukraine. They live on a settlement some miles out of town, and while the other children on the settlement take their lessons in Ukrainian, Nicholas wants to study in English and be like his uncle Yaroslav, a "song plugger" in New York City. According to Nicholas, Yaroslav works for a publisher of popular music in Tin Pan Alley, a street in Manhattan where pianos pound all day long. He earns fifteen dollars a week to sit in a booth and play brand-new songs for vaudeville performers who need fresh tunes for their performances. He told Nicholas that if he hadn't learned English he'd be playing the piano in church for less than a glass of homemade wine. With the help of one of his aunts, Nicholas practised English until native Canadians stopped asking him to repeat himself. Then he approached Mabel. She agreed to let him join the class immediately, and she assumed it was within her power to do so.

"You assumed wrongly," Mr. Connor said. "The purpose of your position is to teach, not to make decisions better handled by myself or the parents. So be warned. One sign of trouble and that kid is back where he belongs."

And this looks very much like trouble. Nicholas is as hot-headed as Brian. He pushes past her to stand face to face with Brian. Accidentally, he knocks the book from her hand, so that it falls and splays open on the bare ground. Brian throws the first punch, missing Nicholas and hitting only empty air.

"Stop it," she screams. Part of her wants to stand back and allow the boys to rip at each other until their blood flows, proving the same brilliant red from each. She bends to save her book, and as she rises Nicholas's fist connects with her shoulder. Her book takes another spin. Her legs give and she lands on the frozen ground. One of the children shrieks, and then Nicholas bends over her and offers his hand.

"Miss. I'm sorry. I didn't mean—"

"I know."

But Brian swats his hand aside. "Look what you did to the teacher." He ignores her completely to take a free shot at Nicholas, and she hears the crack of bone from where she still sits on the ground. The other children gasp, a semicircle of open mouths and confused eyes.

"Brian!" She tries to lift herself off the ground, but her limp arm impedes her efforts. "Go home. Now!"

Nicholas has dropped to the ground a few feet away. He steadies himself on hands and knees. Blood streams from his nose, but he moves toward her, his eyes on Brian as he tries to rise.

"No!" She yells the warning the instant she notices Brian step forward, but he raises his foot defiantly and gives Nicholas a final kick in the stomach. She screams, and immediately regrets her response when some of the children begin to cry.

Brian throws a derisive glance in her direction, and then he takes off across the schoolyard at a run. Over his shoulder, she hears his parting shot: "My dad will take care of you!"

She isn't clear whether he means Nicholas, who has sagged back onto the dirt clutching his stomach, or her.

CHAPTER 7

1917

The Lancer bank closes at three-thirty, and at three-fifteen she taps her foot on the tiles and wills the people ahead of her in line to conduct their business quickly so she will reach the lone clerk before he closes his wicket. As she waits, she counts off the passing seconds on the large clicking, humming clock that hangs above a portrait of King George V. It is the first electric model in town, often either fast or slow, and not everyone agrees that it is an improvement on the old wind-up one it replaced.

She has been earning a salary of forty-four dollars a month, paid weekly. Normally she withdraws ten dollars a week and saves one dollar, but this week she plans to close her account and reclaim her small savings, as well.

She reaches the head of the line at precisely 3:25 and makes her request. The unsmiling clerk stares at her. He is thin and sharp-shouldered and has the peaked look of someone who has recently suffered a bad bout of diarrhea.

"It's too late to close your account."

"And why is that?" She tilts her chin and smiles at him with what she hopes is an expression of goodwill. "The bank is still open, and I have, after all, been queued up for nearly thirty minutes." Normally she would have said *lined up* in the Canadian way, but she reverts to the British idiom when she hopes to charm or intimidate, the latter often as successful as the former.

"The manager needs to approve the request. We have to do the paperwork. And the bank is closing."

"What can there be to approve? If you'll ask your manager to come out, I'd like to speak with him myself."

When she lifts her eyebrows and glances toward the office door, the clerk reluctantly leaves his wicket and raps on it lightly before entering. Printed on the frosted glass in serious black letters are the words, JOHN COULSON SKOTTOWE, JR., MANAGER. She supposes they convey the dignity of the occupant, undoubtedly some portly, cigar-smoking type who doesn't wait in lines himself, but has others do it for him.

Well, then. She has no further need for his bank, his officious clerk, or Manager Skottowe himself.

She keeps her back to the people waiting behind her and tries not to imagine their resentful stares. She hopes they won't be turned away as a result of the delay she has caused, but she can readily imagine the clerk slamming the wicket closed just as the next person steps forward.

After a minute or two of silence, the door to the office swings wide and the manager steps out behind the clerk. She has never seen John Skottowe or had reason to meet him before now, and she quickly clears her expression of an unflattering frown.

Mr. Skottowe's suit hangs very well on him, broad at the shoulders and slim at the hips, and his lean, angular lines do much to soften her annoyance. He looks no more than thirty-five to her twenty-seven. Certainly he's not more than forty. Too bad she hadn't met him sooner.

His progress toward her is slow and appraising, as if he has all evening to squander and is happy to spend the time sizing her up. When he also holds her gaze a fraction too long, and when she chooses not to be the one to break contact, he has the decency to look sheepish.

He lifts a portion of the counter and motions her through. "Miss Rowbotham?"

She stands five foot ten and considers herself tall, too tall for most men, but he smiles down on her. She allows him to take her elbow and propel her along, and when he closes the door and shows her to a chair across from a large desk, she doesn't even bother to look around the room, but meets his gaze directly.

"Is there some problem?"

"Perhaps that's a question I should ask you. I understand you want to leave our bank. Have you been so unhappy with our service?"

The Union Bank is the only one in town, so satisfaction or dissatisfaction is a moot point, but if he intends to act as if he's concerned about her insignificant savings, she supposes she can respond as if she believes him.

"I wasn't unhappy until a few minutes ago, but I'm relocating and I need to close my account." *Relocating* sounds odd and stilted and she wishes she had said *moving* as she normally would have. *I'm moving.*

It's a phrase she has used too often. Her parents' friends will be tactful. No one will ask her outright why she has left Lancer after little more than two years, as well as Eagle Hills and Macoun before that, but the silence says as much as any question. They expect her to be embarrassed, and she is, a little. But she will defend her position, as well. Why shouldn't she make decisions that affect the students? She is the one who sees them together, who knows their personalities and how they interact with each of the others.

Nevertheless, the dismissal has left her vulnerable. She worries that her father is right. With her work history, she may not be offered another job. She may have to leave the province, and even then, won't another school board want references? Won't they be in touch with this one?

Mr. Skottowe has a habit of rolling his pen horizontally between thumb and forefinger, and as her eyes are continually drawn to the motion, she can't help but notice that he wears no rings. His fingers are long and well shaped, and the nails are nicely manicured and buffed.

They peer at each other over the clutter on his desk, and then he says, "Well now. That *is* bad news."

"Oh?"

"More paperwork, I'm afraid."

She loses her smile. She wants to close her account. Why should that generate any more dreaded paperwork than a deposit or a withdrawal? What possible difference can it make if she withdraws her funds because she wishes to move to another town, or because she wants to put the money in a tin can behind her cupboard? She is about to say as much when he catches her off guard with a playful grin.

"And besides, we've only just met."

She closes her mouth and settles into her chair. "That *is* a pity. But it can't be helped."

"You're the schoolteacher. You live in the rooming house on . . ." he checks his file. "Redden Road. Every Tuesday about this time, right before we close for the day, you make a small withdrawal."

She nods, hoping he doesn't also know that she has been dismissed from her position over the altercation on the school grounds. She has been in Canada for nearly seven years, and what has she accomplished? She enjoys teaching, but she is "too progressive and makes too many decisions without asking permission." If he hasn't heard that already, he will soon enough. The longest she has remained in any one community is only three years—not much of a record.

He continues to twirl his fountain pen. When he notices her glancing at it, he stops and sets it on his desk. "Miss Rowbotham, I'm genuinely sorry, but it will be impossible to close your account tonight."

She starts to object, but he raises his hand to stop her.

"If I promise to make it my first priority tomorrow morning, can I convince you to have dinner with me tonight?" He leans back in his chair to fold his hands across his stomach. She can see by the way his shirt rests under his clasped fingers that he is solid underneath. His expression is pleasant and confident, as if she has already decided in his favour and has accepted his offer, but he adds, "I hope it's an invitation you'll accept."

Following his example, she uses his surname, and stresses it ever so slightly. "Well, Mr. *Skottowe*. I'm genuinely sorry myself, but I can't possibly have dinner with you until I know that you're a man of your word." She stands and extends her hand. "Shall we speak again in the morning?"

Her mother has warned her never to let a man lose face. "Better to swallow your own pride than damage another's," she said, meaning specifically that her daughter should be protective of male pride. And perhaps she is right, because she has had few dates in Canada, and certainly no offers of marriage, not that she was interested.

She returns to her room and examines herself in the dressing-table mirror. Has she lost weight again? There is a possibility that she looks even slighter around her shoulders. And though her waist is already tiny, wouldn't that be a better place to lose inches, if she must? As it is, she's beginning to look like one long, lean bone.

What could marriage offer that she doesn't already have? She pursues her own interests, as she always intended, and earns her own living. Or did, anyway. Now she's not so sure. The one thing marriage does have going for it is security. A home, social accept-ance, companionship. She's done fine on her own, so far, but she can't deny a certain loneliness. And she does have to eat. Her sav-ings will take her through a couple of months, but then what? She hates to admit it even to herself, but the thought of marriage to someone as handsome and able as John Skottowe doesn't offend her quite as much as it once might have.

"I was a constable before the Union Bank hired me," John says. "With the Royal North West Mounted Police." It is their third dinner out.

"You wore a uniform and rode a horse?" She tries to visualize him set in the saddle, dressed in the commanding red jacket and Mountie hat.

"It was all very low-key. First I was a clerk. Later they made me manager."

"Manager of what?"

"Of the most top secret information we had."

"Oh yes?" She knows there's a joke in here somewhere. He has that look about him.

He handles his knife and fork easily, and chews carefully before he continues. Partly this is good manners, but already she notices that timing is everything with John. He won't be rushed.

"I managed the supplies. The officers were the ones who had it good. I did favours for them, got to be a clerk in the officers' quarters. Then I shared what they had—canned lobster, potted meats, good tobacco, you name it."

"Roast ham? Good wine?" She indicates his plate. She has never known anyone to eat all his meals in a restaurant, but John appears to. They each have ham, scalloped potatoes, and a small glass of red table wine, and as he doesn't scrimp on anything, there will be sherry with dessert. Already, her hollow belly has plumped out. The restaurant doesn't serve alcohol, but John brings his own bottles and quietly slips the proprietor two dollars for serving the drinks with his meal.

"What can I say? I like the good life."

She hasn't often drunk wine, not because she dislikes it or agrees with her mother, who is in favour of temperance, but because she finds the extra cost in her budget unnecessary for the small pleasure she derives from it. All the same, at least part of her enjoyment with John comes from the warm sensation of wine slipping down her throat, pooling somewhere lower.

"The police here frighten me more than the bobbies in England ever did. What did you have to do to be hired? Look grim?"

John laughs. "As far as I can remember, they wanted to know: Was I in debt? Did I have any untoward entanglements with a female? And was I the parent of an illegitimate child? In that order. They also wanted to know if I could ride a horse."

"And were you?"

"Able to ride? Not well."

She eyes him over her glass of wine. Has he misunderstood, or is he deliberately teasing her?

He wipes his mouth neatly with his napkin. His eyes sparkle with humour. "I'm having you on. I could ride fine. Still can."

So she laughs, a bit, and won't permit herself to ask again about the debt, the women, or the children. "Did you round up many troublemakers?"

John glances over at an elderly couple, the only others in the restaurant, and then back at her, and he says, "From what I hear, I've got a troublemaker right here."

"That's not fair!"

"Would it bother you not to teach?"

So he does know she was fired. "I went into teaching because I thought it would be undemanding. I wanted time for my own interests. As it turns out, it's much more demanding than I imagined, but I'm a good teacher. I learned that I want to make the lessons interesting for the students. I want to challenge them. But when I stop, *if* I stop," she says, stressing the word *if* as though the choice is still hers to make, "I won't be sorry, either. I'm tired of all the old bastards."

She wonders if he will be shocked by that, but instead of answering, John leans close to her and says in a low voice, "I can't even say I heard all that. All I can think is how much I want to kiss you."

An hour later, in the privacy of his car, he does kiss her, skilfully and at length. She has been kissed only occasionally before, and those kisses were nothing like his. His lips press on hers with such varying degrees of intensity—and need—that almost immediately she knows what it is to feel real, aching desire for another.

"Mabel," he says. "We can pretend this isn't happening, or we can do something about it."

"What do you mean, 'do something about it'?"

"We could drive to Saskatoon, where no one knows us."

Is he serious? His hands are strong. They hold her in an embrace that pushes her breasts into his chest, and she can only push harder. A part of her wants to say *yes*, to drive off and learn what lovemaking is all about. She imagines the drive across the prairie pressed close to his side, slipping into the city, finding a hotel. She'd wait in the car, anonymous while he secured a room. And then what?

"I can't," she says. "I want to, but I just can't."

"You're torturing me." He pulls her to him and kisses her again, repentantly, and then as eagerly as before.

She has experienced orgasms alone, small, guilty, secretive ones that cause her hips to shiver and twitch, so it isn't as if this is the first time she has felt *anything*, but she has certainly never felt *this*. And with the desire comes alarm. If she doesn't stop, she will soon be shuddering like her father's new Big Bull tractor. So while what she wants more than anything is to stay exactly as they are, she allows herself another few seconds, until she feels such a softening of her senses that she knows the time is *now*, and then she uses all her will to pull back and push him away.

If he reaches for her again, she will be lost, will lift her skirts and crawl onto his lap, showing herself for the hungry four-limbed creature she has become, but he remains gentlemanly, and laughs slightly when they separate, and says, "my God," exactly as she is thinking the same thing. Then he squeezes her hand before he puts the car in gear and drives her safely home.

It is not the last time they steam up the windows of his car. She is twenty-seven years old and she has never been with a man. Before she met John she sometimes wondered if she ever would be. But her desire for him is so strong she can hardly think of anything else when she is not with him. She would like to know what other women do when they feel like ripping through seams to get at someone. Must she wait for marriage? Because what if he is not interested in settling down and she never fulfills this incredible longing? She knows some women don't wait, but this is only evidenced by their big bellies. And what if *she* got pregnant? It is unthinkable.

"This war must be a real boost for the bank, a real shot in the arm, wouldn't you say, Mr. Skottowe?"

She expects John to look a little pained at his client's question, mercenary as it is, but John smiles agreeably.

"Oh, I don't know, Mr. Whyte. The automobile business seems like the winner these days, war or no war. I hear Ford Motor Company's spitting one out every thirty seconds with that assembly line of theirs."

"Now that's a fact." Ronald Whyte is youngish to have made such a success of his auto business, and he flushes with pleasure when John turns to the subject. "I'll drink to that."

He raises his glass and John does the same. Mabel can see by the way John savours his that he is happy it is good drugstore whisky, and not the illegal stuff in a second bottle on the counter. Mr. Whyte must have claimed one illness or another and stood in line at the drugstore for this medicinal bottle to share with John. With Christmas coming, the lines will only get longer.

"So much for prohibition." Mrs. Whyte says this in an aside to Mabel, and then lifts a small glass of blackberry wine.

Mabel nods. "When I was teaching, I had to lecture thirty minutes a week on temperance—the school board required it. But what son cares about anything I say when he sees his father slugging moonshine out behind the barn?"

"Or drinking whisky and wine at the dinner table," Mrs. Whyte agrees, gesturing around the dinner table.

"Prohibition won't last." Mr. Whyte catches the gist of his wife's words as his conversation with John ends. "The laws'll be rescinded before we're into the next decade, that's my guess."

She hopes he is right. She's not a heavy drinker herself, and John will have a couple of shots, and then he will make a third last the rest of the evening in order not to embarrass himself in front of a client, but the rise in organized crime worries her. She thinks her father is right—once organized crime finds a crack, it is not easy to dislodge.

"What about the war?" John says. "Any forecast there?"

"French soldiers will stage another mutiny and President Wilson will lead the world to peace, all before the year 1920."

"It's almost 1918 now. Surely not another two years!" Mrs. Whyte looks to John for confirmation of her husband's predictions.

"Mark his words. Your husband is an extremely sharp man," John says. "He should be running for politics himself."

Mrs. Whyte simpers under the effect of John's smile.

Her husband lifts the bottle of whisky. "Give me your glass, my friend."

"Not at all," John says, covering the top of his glass with his palm. "You save that for yourself. God knows it's hard to come by."

And even that, she thinks, is calculated to make Mr. Whyte understand that John knows the sacrifice his client has made by sharing the good stuff.

He glances over at her and winks almost imperceptibly. He's

used to people falling over themselves to entertain him, but now she is included, and if, in the past, she sometimes felt that her contributions in conversation were dismissed, or that she tended to elicit more stern irritability than real interest or acceptance, all that has changed with John at her side.

His ideas are plastic, not as abrasive as hers, and readily accepted because he shapes his arguments to the listener, makes the ideas more palatable by stressing something minor or by neglecting to mention something of importance.

The Whytes, like most people, inevitably find themselves agreeing with him, and by the end of the evening, they pump his hand vigorously and treat him like their very best friend.

She knows John well enough by now that on the ride home she asks him outright, "Don't you mislead people, just a little? Aren't you a little *too* persuasive?"

"How can anyone be too persuasive? I don't browbeat anyone. They want to agree with me."

She can't argue with that. Others *do* want to please him. Yet he is so certain of his own infallibility. He feels entitled to anything he wants, certainly to anything anyone gives him, and while on one hand that appeals to her, she can't help but wonder if he isn't, well . . . just a little *slick*.

"One thing I've learned," he says, "is never to tell anyone more than he wants to hear."

"Does that apply to me, as well?"

"Especially to you," he says.

He slows to a stop on a side road and backs into the entrance to a field. He puts one arm around her and scoots her along the front bench until there is no space between them.

"Shh," he says, his face very close to hers. "How can I ask you to marry me if you're asking all the questions?"

Aside from an owl hooting somewhere, all she hears is her own breathing, which sounds far too loud in the confines of the car. Is he serious? She gives him another second and then she says, "You want to get married?"

"Of course I do. It's time I had a wife to show off, like tonight. Don't you want to marry me?"

She presses herself up against him and kisses him with all the pent-up passion of the past two months. Doesn't she? And if she didn't, what other choice would she have? When they finally separate for air, she is shaking. "Where and when?"

They began dating in mid-October. It is now early December.

"Anywhere, and as soon as you can arrange it," he says. "The sooner the better."

"He's lovely," her mother says to her, after an evening with John. She is clearing dishes from the kitchen counter, preparing to wash up.

"A self-made man," her father adds. He has followed them into the kitchen and stands in the doorway. "He's risen above his background, and he knows the value of hard work. You've done well."

She nods. She longs for her father to be right. She has been educated to take care of herself, but does she really want to be alone for the rest of her life? She used to believe that she did, but somehow everything was simpler then, and she hadn't known John, either. In his presence, life is exciting. Dullness transforms itself the second he arrives, so that she is both fascinated and fascinating, and there is no question that they are attracted to each other. He has not attended college, as she has, but he is more interesting than many who have.

"He makes me laugh," she says. She scrapes the plates and stacks them for washing.

And if she marries John, there will be no more worrying about another teaching position. Married women don't teach; that is policy. The thought comforts her—no more interviews, no trial period, no kowtowing to bigots and buffoons. She imagines all those hours, hers to fill as she will. She has never had to run a household on her own, has always lived either at home or in rooming houses, but how much time can housework take? She imagines time stretching ahead like a road unexplored.

"Leave these," her mother says, indicating the dirty dishes. "I have something I want to show you."

She leads Mabel into her bedroom, where a satin wedding gown the colour of thick cream hangs draped over the door of her mother's wardrobe. Its simple lines are accented by embroidered lace at the yoke and one thin strip of velvet trim at a high neck. Chiffon hangs in long graceful ruffles at the cuffs, and if the lace has yellowed somewhat in the years since her mother packed it away, the colour detracts nothing from the overall elegance of the gown.

"You're my only daughter," her mother says, her voice catching a little. "I've been saving it for you."

"It's beautiful." She fingers the fabric, overwhelmed, and imagines herself in it. Her own throat constricts as she silently acknowledges that in the beginning, her mother must have saved the dress for Honora. She has only recently begun to consider what it must be like to lose a child, and she can't imagine. Like losing a sister, she supposes, only worse.

They marry quietly, on New Year's Day, 1918, in the tiny Anglican church her parents occasionally attend. She wears her mother's beautiful satin wedding dress, and John wears a black suit, stiff white shirt, and well-shone black shoes. They have no bridesmaid or best man, but Mabel's father gives her away. John's father—the Reverend John Coulson Skottowe, from Pensacola, Florida—attends, as do a handful of friends, mostly friends of her mother and father, and John's friends. She invites Leo and his family, including his sisters and their husbands, and Leo is the usher. Her family isn't the sort that can afford to cross oceans to attend events, however momentous, and just as she has now missed the weddings of Paul and Albert, they miss hers.

John carries her across the threshold and struggles out of his over-shoes in the front entry, kicking snow as he does. He gives her a little toss in his arms, adjusting his hold to cradle her against him as he ascends the stairs and goes straight into their bedroom. They have chosen the house together, a white two-storey with a turret for reading, a baby's room, two extra rooms, and a wide, bright kitchen. They have electricity, indoor plumbing, and a coal furnace. John must have had someone stoke the furnace earlier in the day, because the house is warm, and hot embers still give off heat in the bedroom fireplace. That thought preoccupies her more than it might another. An open fire shouldn't be left unattended, should it?

She wears her "going away" outfit, a green suit consisting of a long jacket over a calf-length skirt. When John deposits her onto the mattress, she immediately stands and twists her buttons free. She slides the jacket off her shoulders and drapes it over the back of a slipper chair near the window.

He yanks on the knot of his tie, loosening it, and shrugs out of his own jacket, placing it alongside hers. Before she has reached behind her to unbutton her skirt, he has released his belt buckle and tugged his shirttails loose from his trousers. She has never seen a man undress before, and she sits on the edge of the bed in her slip, watching until he is down to his socks and underwear, and then she raises one long leg and points it at him. She unfastens her garters and waits for him to roll the stocking down.

He removes the first one with care, and then lets it slip from his palm so that it spills into a silky puddle on the floor. She lifts her other leg and he repeats the movement. And then, with daylight fading through the uncovered window, and firelight flickering across the hearth, he bends over her and together, they slide backward on the bed. Seen from below, his shoulders are broad rounded corners. Muscles gently ripple in his arms and chest, and soft dark hair curls out from beneath his undershirt. Through the thin fabric, his nipples are small and dark.

She catches the corner of the top sheet and strips it back so they can crawl under together, and she folds it over them both, pulling him down on her. He puts his lips on hers, and then rolls sideways so they lie side by side. With his face still close, he runs his hand up under her slip until he cups her hip and stretches his fingers around one buttock. She kisses his forehead and slides her hand past the waistband of his undershorts until she hears his breath catch.

John's father, the Reverend Coulson Skottowe, is sixty-eight. He has been married twice, once to John's mother, who died in childbirth, and again to Emily, John's stepmother. Emily died of influenza just three years ago. Unlike Mabel's father, who wears thinning hair short and combed close to his head, Coulson's thick white hair hangs loose, all one length to his shoulders, and he habitually pushes it back off his forehead in a gesture so natural she imagines him performing it since boyhood.

Earlier this morning, her mother told her that Coulson is a Spiritualist minister. She spoke of the news as if it were a secret, whispered and with a slight giggle of embarrassment. Now that Mabel knows, she wonders why she didn't immediately guess.

She waits for an opportunity and catches him alone, sitting quietly by her parents' fireplace contemplating the flames. His face has lived a dozen lives. It is that of a sage, old and wise in the eyes, and crisscrossed with the sort of deep lines that speak of amiability, thought, and sadness, and a life of genuine concern for others, as wrinkled as an elephant's hide.

"John never told me that you're a *Spiritualist* minister—"

"He tends to keep that one to himself."

"But why? I've been fascinated by Spiritualism for years, but I'm not certain there's a movement in Canada. I never hear of anyone, and I've asked."

"Who have you asked?"

"I wrote to the Theosophical Society in Illinois."

"It could be as simple as that there is no centre yet. That may change as people find one another." He turns toward her, away from the heat. "On the other hand, I met a doctor from Winnipeg not so long ago. He was in Pensacola on vacation. Dr. Glendenning Hamilton. A Spiritualist. Said he's been having seances in his home, and he wants to photograph the sessions. He said he'd send me the evidence if anything came of it."

She has been watching him closely. "I can't believe John never said anything."

"I suspect he'd rather I was less interested in the occult side of things."

She accepts this information reluctantly. She has had plenty of opportunity to speak of her visions, but always she's held back, thinking there was plenty of time to tell John later. And what a sad irony if, by not mentioning something so important to her, she has found someone actively opposed to it. Nervously, she sets the thought aside and focuses on his father.

"Why's that?" she asks. "What do you do, exactly? Hold seances?"

"Sometimes seances, privately, if someone requests it. But Sunday at my church is about the same as anywhere else. Sermon and song." He smiles. "Sometimes interrupted by someone who has passed, wanting to make contact—which would make it sermon, song, and spirit, I suppose."

"How do you know you've been contacted?" She hears the desperate edge in her voice. Here's someone who knows what she wants to know. And who actually helps others. Guiltily, she suppresses this thought. Who could she help? She's seen a few muddled images, nothing more.

"I know things. It's difficult to explain. Sometimes I see an image. Sometimes I hear a name. It's a way of knowing that's different from anything else."

She understands completely. "Have you ever seen something and had it happen later?"

"That's clairvoyance. I'm more of a medium."

He looks at her strangely, and for a moment she thinks he knows. There is relief in that. She'd like to talk to him about it.

Instead, he says, "I've been picking up on someone around you. A woman, I think. Maybe a beekeeper. I get a sense of a humming noise, like bees. And I've been seeing honeycombs."

The hair on her arms stands up and a chill runs down her spine. "Honey?" Just saying the word leaves her overcome with emotion. She presses her lips together to keep them still.

"She's nodding. Does that mean something to you? Did she sell honey?"

"Honora. She died when I was seven. We called her Honey sometimes."

He looks directly at her then, and his eyes reflect all the sadness she once felt. "I'm so sorry, Mabel. You must have missed her terribly."

She doesn't trust herself to speak, and only nods.

"I know how this will sound, but is it possible that you're . . . Have you . . . ?" Coulson runs one hand through his hair. "I'm sorry, Mabel. Are you with child?"

"With child!" A burst of startled laughter escapes her, a release of the emotion he has elicited, and then she blushes. "I assure you, I'm not pregnant!"

He rests a warm hand on her arm. "Forgive me. I was rude. I see symbols. Things. Gestures. I don't always know what they mean.

It would never have occurred to me otherwise, but she's rocking a baby in her arms, and I thought . . ."

She waits for him to finish, and then she tries to help. "Maybe she's saying I will be soon? John and I thought we'd wait."

He shakes his head. "I'm certain it's one you already know about. Is there some other child that would have been important to you both?"

"My brother died not long after Honora."

"An infant?"

"No, he was four. And my brothers have had children."

"Sometimes it's difficult to know. She's smiling and waggling a finger, almost as if it is a joke between you, or a source of great pleasure. Now she's showing me a picture. Do you draw? Or have an interest in photography?"

She watches his face intently and feels herself on the verge of tears. She has imagined herself doing exactly what he is doing now, communicating what others can't see or know. And he is confirming what she has always known—that Honora *is* with her. She has not been deluding herself. There is such relief in that, and she envies him.

He looks up when he asks questions, as if in thought, and his eyes move the way they would if he were remembering something, but aside from an extra bit of shine in his pupils, he might be any man in thought.

"I do draw," she says.

"She's pointing at herself. She may want you to draw her." He glances at Mabel. "Or perhaps she means only to encourage you."

"Thank you," she says, softly. She hasn't drawn Honora for some time. Could her sister really be trying to convey that the drawings mean something to her? Or is this a message meant to show her she can trust Coulson? Someone—her parents, John—could have told him that she sketches, but she has never admitted to drawing Honora, not to anyone. And no one would have mentioned Honora's nickname, either. No, even supposing Coulson wanted to fool her—and why he would she cannot imagine—he couldn't have had that information.

"You have no idea what this means to me." She is about to tell him about seeing Honora, about the visions, but just then her mother pokes her head around the door frame.

"Tea?" Mrs. Rowbotham says.

That night, she wakes while it is still dark. *Trea.* She smiles at the knowledge. The baby in Honora's arms was Trea. That's why Coulson perceived it as a joke, as something Honora might laugh about, or take pleasure in. *She* got the doll they both wanted, but only because Honora died. She always felt a certain amount of guilt about that, but Honora was happy for her. She goes back to sleep with the smile still on her face.

"I like your father a lot. Why is there such tension between you?"

They have followed Coulson home and are honeymooning in Pensacola, but John has been edgy since they arrived. He is fine when they are off somewhere, downtown or at the beach, but whenever he enters Coulson's tiny, comfortable home, he seems too large for the rooms. It is not only his size, but his energy—he is like a grown man in a playhouse.

They have been walking the streets of central Pensacola, streets with Spanish names like Tarragona, Alcaniz, Zarragossa, admiring the big old Victorian houses together. She has her arm through his, and she looks up at him expectantly, waiting for an answer.

"You're reading too much into it." John runs his hand through his hair in exactly the same way his father does. "Or if you're not, it's only because I'm embarrassed to have you listen to him. He used to be an intelligent man."

"He's a fascinating man. Is this all because he's a Spiritualist?"

"Good God, Mabel, he believes he can communicate with the dead!" John's mouth curls disdainfully.

She releases her hold on his arm and feels an icy chip form deep in her stomach. Until now, they have had one tentative conversation about Theosophy, nothing more.

"Where do you hide your glossary of terms?" he said then, when she tried to explain the principles of the movement. "Masters of Wisdom. The Great White Lodge. Adepts. Chelas. Who can remember it all?"

She only laughed. "So it's unfamiliar. You're a smart man. And what about the Christian concept of divine spirits? Angels? Heaven and hell? The Father, Son, and the Holy Spirit."

"It's all enough to make me an atheist. Leave me be. I'm a satisfied agnostic."

"And Chela is only another word for disciple."

"Really, Mabel," he says now. "You're an intelligent woman. Don't let my father convince you that it all makes sense."

"On the contrary. None of it makes sense. But what if it's not meant to? Not everything is logical. And what if he *can* communicate? Why would he pretend? And why does it bother you so much?" She feels almost queasy now. What would he say if he knew? About her?

"It's rubbish, that's why. Let me know when he makes contact with the past owner of a lost mine, or when some spirit leads him to buried treasure. Then I'll suspend my skepticism."

"But what if it's a gift that can't be used like that? Merely for personal gain, I mean. What if its only purpose is to comfort or protect others?" And is this where she has gone wrong? Has her silent obsession gone nowhere because she has selfishly focused only on herself? Silently, she begs him to open up and understand, to relent just a little.

"Then I'll continue to think of it as rubbish," he says. "Idle rubbish."

For the next month she makes the house her focus; she has purchased basic furniture for the living room and has added a few accent pieces. John already owned several interesting paintings, so the walls are not as bare as they were. Now she stands in the doorway to the dining room and surveys the front room.

So far, he has been lavish in his praise of what she has done in the house, and of her appearance, as well. She has always attended to her hygiene and was by no means slovenly, but she never fussed over fashion. But John compliments her when she makes the effort, and she likes to please him.

Gone are the navy schoolmarm's skirts and cardigans. In their place she wears soft dresses that accentuate her waist and, as hems rise, her shapely legs, as well. She has never dressed for anyone but herself, but now she dresses for John, and she undresses for him too, often slowly, deliberately, one item at a time. She marvels at how his touch causes her senses to explode. Tiny, solitary orgasms of the past have been replaced by mutual, mind-crashing events, sometimes so strong her limbs are useless for minutes after, and if anyone were to suggest that sex is a duty, she would find their ignorance astounding. For Mabel, duty never once enters into it.

A knock just then causes her to start. Through the glass at the front door, she sees three women standing there, neat and ordinarily dressed. From this distance she recognizes them only as two blondes and a redhead. The woman with the red hair raps on the outside windowpane just as Mabel opens the interior door. Her smile is broad when she sees Mabel coming.

"Hello," Mabel says, opening the door. She is not expecting anyone but she is happy to see them. She is determined to make friends of her own in her new, married role.

One of the blonde women carries a plate with a tea towel covering it. She peels it back now to show Mabel an assortment of small sandwiches and sweets. "We came for tea," she says. "I'm Phyllis. This is Rose, and Anne."

Rose is the woman with the broad smile and the surprising red hair, much redder than Mabel's.

"What a surprise," she says. "Please come in." She recognizes Phyllis and Anne as parents of children she has taught.

"We can't stay too long," Anne says. "The kids will be home from school soon."

"Yours is Jimmy, am I right?" She has settled them in the front room, with the plate of sandwiches and sweets on the coffee table, and she needs to make tea.

Anne looks puzzled. "How do you know that?"

"I taught him last year. He's a smart, sweet boy."

"Mabel Rowbotham?" Anne looks dumbfounded. "I'm sorry, I never made the connection. You look different." She turns to Phyllis. "Did *you* know?"

"Not for a minute!" Phyllis says. "What have you done to yourself? You look positively elegant."

She has her hair twisted up and she is wearing a smart dress. She wishes she could say, *Marriage. It's heavenly in bed.* Instead she sidesteps the compliment to address Phyllis. "I remember your girls, too. They used to walk with me on the school grounds. Catherine and Alda."

"Well, isn't that something. Who would've thought?"

They look at her with interest, and as they do, she senses something. There is nothing specific she can pinpoint. No fleeting image, or voice, or sound of any sort. Nothing except a small chill in her spine and a vague uneasiness that tells her all is not as it seems. She pushes the thought aside.

"You left just after school began last year," Phyllis says. "To get married?"

She considers for a moment. Should she follow John's example and tell them only what they want to hear? It would be easy enough to agree that she stopped teaching to marry John. But isn't she hiding enough already? She trusts no one with her inner psychic life, but if these women will disapprove of her for the outward choices, as well, shouldn't she find out now, rather than later?

"I was fired," she says. "They told me I couldn't control the students."

"Why that's just silly. My daughters loved you," Phyllis says. "I remember now—it was one of those ones from the settlement that started something, wasn't it? With the Connor boy? Why anyone thought a settlement child should join our children is beyond me. And to let you go because of his unruliness. It hardly seems right."

"I invited him to join our class." She says so matter-of-factly. She hopes she sounds confident, not defensive. "He was a very good student. I felt he had as much right as anyone."

All three women gape at her honesty. For a long second she expects them to stand, take their plate, and leave, but then Rose speaks.

"I agree with you. I've argued the same thing myself. Segregation only pits *them* against *us*. There's enough of that already."

When Anne nods, they all turn to Phyllis.

She has gone a little pink. She leans forward to pick up a sandwich, and then she meets Mabel's eyes. "Maybe you're right," she says. "After all, you knew him. I didn't."

"You're very gracious," says Mabel. But how to recover the light mood she has spoiled? "Please excuse me. I'll get tea now."

In the kitchen she runs her hands under cold water, dries them, and then presses her hands against her cheeks to cool them. She prepares tea, and puts cups, saucers, sugar, and milk on a tray. When she returns to the living room, the three women are chatting again, the crisis seemingly forgotten. They all look up and smile when she enters.

"We need a fourth for bridge," Rose says. "Do you play?"

"I played with my parents."

"Every Wednesday, if you're willing. I've been without a part-ner since last summer, when Ida moved away. They lived here before you. But we're itching to start up again."

"It's settled then," she says. "Wednesdays. Do you alternate houses?"

CHAPTER 8

"You're a bully." She is crying. "I'm not to talk to your father about the occult. I'm not to talk to you about Theosophy. You get angry if I read a book about it, even. I'm especially *not* to waste money on fortune tellers. I can't cook hamburger because only poor people eat hamburger." Her voice has risen so much she's almost shrieking, and yet she continues. "And now I'm not even allowed to talk about the possibility of psychic abilities without you ridiculing me? *What is the matter with you?*"

"What the hell is the matter with *you?* Where did all this rage come from? If you want to talk rubbish with idiots and ruin my credibility, do as you like. But you'd better also decide how I'll make a living when I'm a bloody laughingstock."

"Right!" She stands and whirls on him. "Let's talk about you, yet again." And then she catches sight of herself in the mirror. She immediately slumps down on the vanity bench and covers her face with her hands. She brushes her tears away and composes her features. "Fine. You're right. Your career is more important. I'm sorry."

"Come here." He holds his arms out, and his expression loses its doggish look. "Why is it so damn important to you?"

Rather than openly defy her husband by seeking out others interested in the occult, she looks inward. She rushes through household chores so that she will have time to lie on the sofa in silence. She takes deep breaths, holds them, and then exhales slowly. She counts backward from twenty, imagining as she does that she descends a ladder. When she steps off the final rung, if she is sufficiently relaxed, she feels warm and floaty, as if she has ingested a powerful dose of laudanum, and in this state, she focuses on nothing at all.

Her goal is to place her mind in a realm above consciousness, a supraconscious state in contact with all time and all thought. If her ears feel full and hum a little, the sensation only adds to the feeling of being suspended in time and space. She doesn't sleep, but hovers near sleep. Sometimes she is able to sustain the sense of weightlessness for many minutes—up to two hours at a time. Sometimes she becomes conscious of odd images or symbols—a swan standing on a precipice while a small black dog leaps nearby for attention; a woman with bare breasts flying so close to the ground that the tips of her breasts must brush over objects in her path; an oriental fan that opens suddenly into a large parachute, from which a tiny doll hangs suspended.

The hypnotic state ends when she consciously brings herself out of it by ascending the ladder and opening her eyes, or more often, when her body's startle reflex brings her back to a state of alertness. Occasionally, she enters the hypnotic state with a particular question in mind, and today she asks about her purpose. Is she meant to ignore her visions, or do something with them?

She has been in the relaxed state for only a few minutes when she hears an unmistakable voice. *Look in the basement. The answer is in the basement.* The voice speaks with such certainty and clarity that her eyes snap open. Illogically, she glances around the room. She is alone, of course. She rises and walks to the door that leads to the basement.

Normally, she avoids this part of the house. The basement has a dirt floor and is cold and damp. John built shelves in one corner where she keeps preserves and wine. Several steamer trunks contain old clothes and papers. She descends the stairs and sits on a tread halfway down. Light streams in through small ground-level windows, and creates a pattern of thin rectangles on the floor. Nothing has changed. It is a damp, unappealing cave.

When she presses John's shirts, the scent of him wafts up from the fabric with every slide of the hot iron. The scent alone causes her to ache for his return home at the end of the day. She imagines his hand running along her thigh, over her belly, up under her arm. With the iron, she loves the fabric the way she will love his skin with the flat of her palm. If only he comes home before she is asleep, she thinks, recalling how frequently he has not over the past month. Should she worry? Surely not, but even so, she misses him.

Ironing is the least tedious of the work she does now. At the rooming house where she lived previously, the price included laundry and meals, and the arrangement suited her. She joined five other boarders in the dining room at seven in the morning for breakfast and again at six in the evening for dinner. She sat at a long oak table with benches on both sides, and Mrs. Jenkins brought food out from the kitchen. Mabel ate it gratefully, because it was hot, flavourful, and always ready.

Now—unless one of John's clients invites them to dinner—she prepares, cooks, serves, and cleans up after each meal herself. She often feels that she has just finished with one mealtime when she has to start on the next. And in between there is all the rest: laundry to wash, hang, iron, and fold. Baking, dusting, sweeping, mending. Floors to wash and polish. Meat and produce to buy. Together, these tasks take much more time than teaching ever did.

She always helped her mother or her grandmother with household work, but she was never solely responsible for every task, day after day. Before the marriage, both she and John earned a living, and they both paid for food, lodging, and comforts. Now, they both work still, but only he gets a wage. It occurs to her that she performs the same tasks he used to hire out, bartering her labour for a shared bed and basic comforts. He has the better deal.

Were it not for what goes on in that bed, she could see no advantage to marrying at all. Is it any wonder spinsterhood is so readily vilified? If it were not, how many women would choose marriage?

The answer is in the basement. For weeks she has been mulling over the phrase. She has gone through everything in the basement, just to be sure, but nothing stands out as important, so she assumes the message is a metaphor for something, but what? She doesn't doubt for a moment that the phrase is meaningful. The voice was authoritative, but otherwise indescribable. She calls it "the voice of God."

A basement is beneath the house. It is dark. It could be said to be secret. The answer is in her secrets? In her unconscious? This strikes a chord, and once again, she feels she is skirting the edges of something she should be equipped to understand.

A basement is cave-like. A cave is shelter. A cave symbolizes dark and light. And then there is Plato's allegory of the cave. Is she seeing shadows on the wall instead of the real items? *In the basement.* Under the house. Unconscious.

She has peeled about half the potatoes for dinner when her chest constricts and she sees an image of her friend Rose. Rose's back is unclothed, but she knows it is her friend by the bright red hair. She has never noticed colour in her visions before this—they have always been grainy images in black and white—but clearly it is Rose straddling Phyllis, because Phyllis's face looks up from a pillow. Those are Phyllis's pale shoulders under Rose's hands. The pillowcase has a row of embroidered flowers, stitched with violet and yellow thread.

And then rough male hands reach for Rose, wrench her violently backward and throw her to the floor. Mabel feels the floorboards as if it were her hip hitting, her elbows scraping. From that vantage point, she sees Phyllis attempt to cover herself on the bed, sees dark green trousers, and heavy brown boots with dusty laces. And then there is nothing but the kitchen sink to which she clings, and the potato peels in a mound there.

For a moment she can do nothing but stand, immobilized. Then she slaps the counter and lifts her head to wail at the ceiling. "This is not funny, Honora. What am I to make of this? *What?*" She knows Honora is with her. She feels her sister's presence in the prickle of her skin.

She opens a cupboard above the kitchen counter and slams the door just to release her frustration. What is she supposed to do with information like this? Admit to her friends that she saw them naked together? What if she is wrong?

She rests her elbows on the sink and lowers her head to her hands. Impossible as it is, she feels a warm hand on the back of her neck and then smells crushed grass, and sun on skin, and has a sense of the sea, of the faint *hush, hush* of waves washing gently against shore.

"Honora." She lifts her head and touches the back of her neck, and as she does, a ripple of goose flesh rises along her spine and on her arms. She closes her eyes, and her sister's image is as clear as it has ever been, in colour, at peace, as if she reflects the calm Mabel now inexplicably feels. Mabel hears a voice. *It's all right. Everything is all right.*

She walks to the washroom and splashes cool water on her face. What will she do about the image of Rose and Phyllis? Or are the images some sort of extension of her own thoughts, and not clair-voyant at all?

Lately, John has not been interested in making love. Could the frustration she feels at his indifference have caused her to desire her friends? She has read about Lady Eleanor Butler and Sarah Ponsonby, who eloped to Wales and became known as the Ladies of Llangollen, entertaining all sorts of literati in their comfortable cottage—Lord Byron, William Wordsworth, Sir Walter Scott. Do her inclinations have anything in common with theirs? The idea of two women together does not shock her, but the idea of Rose and Phyllis together, both married, Phyllis with children, does.

Yet haven't her visions borne themselves out literally in the past? Her mother's burn? The image of her book splayed open on the school grounds? Leo's grandfather? Without question, it was Rose and Phyllis she saw together—not one of them with her. She feels certain she should warn her friends, and yet, really, what is she to say?

"Oh, this is terrible, just terrible," she says. "Why do you do this to me?"

The next Wednesday, she is hardly present at their bridge game, and she plays her hands all wrong. She forgets to finesse a king and loses an extra trick. Rose stoically sits out her turn as dummy, say-ing nothing, though she raises her eyebrows when Mabel misses the trick.

Afterward, Rose follows her into the kitchen, where they will be alone. "What's going on?" Rose asks. "That was a mess."

She has spent three torturous days deciding, and still she hesitates. But when the silence grows too long, she juts her chin forward and gathers her courage. "Rose, look, I need to talk to you. After the others leave. Will you stay?"

"Are you all right?"

"Don't worry. I'll tell you when the others are gone."

And so Rose lingers when Phyllis and Anne button their coats. "You go on," she says. "I'll help Mabel clean up."

Phyllis, in particular, looks askance at this change in normal routine. She looks anxious, almost jealous, Mabel thinks. Or is she reading too much into her friend's puzzlement? She can hardly be blamed if she is.

"So tell me," Rose says, when the door has closed. Her concern could be written in words on her face—*puzzlement* around the eyes, *worry* between her brows, even *impatience* at the corners of her mouth.

Mabel doesn't immediately answer, so Rose moves back into the front room and sits on the edge of a chair. She leans forward and tips the teapot over her empty cup. "Do you want a dribble then? There's a little left."

Mabel shakes her head. She sits across from Rose and moves Anne's and Phyllis's cups onto a tray. She wipes the coffee table with a napkin. They have become quite close, she and Rose, and she values the friendship. She throws the napkin on the tea tray and folds her hands in her lap, a gesture she is certain must look as forced as it feels.

Rose waits expectantly.

It is difficult enough to admit to the visions themselves, never mind their content. "I'm afraid for you," she says, finally. "What

I'm going to say will sound very odd, but I worry that if I don't tell you, you'll be badly hurt. You and Phyllis—"

"Phyllis? What are you talking about?"

"I saw something—"

"What?" Now she is intent on Mabel.

"You and Phyllis—"

Rose is in a posture of waiting. She is so still she might not be breathing. "What do you mean you saw something? Where were you?" Her expression has gone from concern to alarm, tinged with anger. The freckles across her nose suddenly stand out against her pallor.

"I was here, in my kitchen. What I mean is that I sometimes . . . well . . . I see things that will happen, or that have happened. Sometimes I can't tell the difference. Most of the time, I can't make sense of any of it—"

"Mabel, *you're* not making sense." Rose sets her cup on the coffee table, missing the pewter coaster altogether. She crosses her arms over her chest.

"But this time I saw you and Phyllis. Phyllis was looking up from a pillow. You were leaning over her." Maybe if she leaves out the part about them being naked, this will be only half as bad as she fears it will be. "And then some man grabbed you and threw you on the floor and it hurt so badly you might have cracked something. I didn't see the man, but he meant to hurt you. He had green trousers and dusty brown boots." She stops. "Does this make any sense to you at all?"

"None," Rose says. She smoothes her skirt over her legs, and then she stands abruptly. She looks at Mabel with eyes wide, the contrived innocence of someone caught out. "You're sounding a little crazy."

She is angry, Mabel sees, but does she believe her? Is it possible she will now take precautions, because isn't that all that matters? And if she does, will the scene be prevented, or will it happen anyway? As Rose walks away from her, she remembers something else. "The pillowcase had little violet and yellow flowers embroidered on it."

Rose freezes, and then she turns back to her. "You've been snooping in my bedroom." Her voice is icy cold. "Unless you're trying to tell me that you can read my mind, in which case you know how angry I am right now."

Mabel makes a gesture of impatience. "I can't read your mind. And I haven't been snooping anywhere. I care about you. I know how difficult this is to believe, but sometimes I see things."

"You're making me uncomfortable. I'm leaving now."

Mabel shrugs in frustration. "I saw my Mother burn herself once, badly, before it actually happened. I've always regretted that I didn't warn her. I don't want you or Phyllis to get hurt, that's all."

Rose presses her lips into a false smile. "I understand. I'm sure Phyllis will appreciate the news as much as I do. Now goodbye. It was lovely seeing you, and I hope you've got all this off your chest."

Off your chest. What an oddly accurate expression. Given how her chest constricts before each clairvoyant experience, is she not doing just that? Getting the information *off her chest?*

Sometimes, now, John barely looks at her, regardless of the coquetries she devises. She might set her foot on a chair and roll her stocking down, or lift a blouse over her head so that her round, pale breasts rise. None of it has any effect.

"Let's come home early," she says tonight. "I'd like to go to bed before we're too tired."

They are dressing for a Halloween party at the home of the Hogans, a young couple new to Lancer. Mabel is dressed in a period costume she bought two weeks ago from a travelling salesman. The salesman said he got them from the now-defunct Hugh Grange theatre company in Winnipeg. His timing could not have been better. Her dress is boned and laced at the front to cinch in her waist and create cleavage she wouldn't normally expose. John is dressed as Henry VIII. A couple of years ago, her invitation to return early would have resulted in equally insistent passion on his part. He might have said, "Why go at all?"

She runs her hand up his chest, but he brushes it aside.

"I saw Rose's husband today, poor guy."

He's talking about Rose and Phyllis, who packed their belongings, took Catherine and Alda, and disappeared one day, an hour after their husbands left for work, exactly three weeks after she had spoken to Rose. *Don't look for us,* they each wrote in identical notes. *We won't be found.*

When Rose's husband knocked on their door later that night, to enquire as to whether she knew anything, she glanced at his boots. Brown, lace-up boots. Common as dandelions, but nevertheless. She told him honestly that Rose had said nothing to her.

"She'd better hope I don't find her. If I do, by the time I'm done with her, *nobody* will want her."

"Isn't that just lovely," she said to John, when she had closed the door after Rose's husband and he was out of earshot. "Now that puts a few things into perspective."

"From what I've heard, he's got reason."

"Nothing justifies that sort of talk."

"We'll have to agree to disagree."

"I suppose we will," she said. And then they avoided the subject of Rose and Phyllis, which suited her just fine.

It was difficult to know if she had done the right thing by telling Rose about her vision, but she hoped she had. Rose had been so angry, she thought at first she must have been wrong in her interpretation of what she saw. She tried to imagine what else the images could mean, but then, when the two women left so soon after, she felt vindicated.

She stares at him coldly now, her enthusiasm for the evening gone. "Poor man, indeed."

"Now don't get petulant." He places his fur-trimmed hat at an angle and adjusts his tunic before he looks at her. "I don't want you ruining everyone else's evening with a mood. Half my clients are more enamoured with you than with their own wives, and we want to keep it that way."

She wonders whose wife *he* is enamoured with, if not his own. "Yes, I forgot. Image is everything to you, isn't it."

"Of course," he says. "You can fake good values, but you can't fake good taste."

CHAPTER 9

"I like that. It's quite good." John moves into her line of sight and stands back, appraising her work.

It is nine o'clock Wednesday evening, and he has just returned from drinks with some client, she suspects, given the strong odour of Scotch that enters with him. He is admiring a sketch of a dandelion gone to seed, an intricate portrayal of light and shadow. She saw one outside earlier in the day. With the sun shining through the delicate globe it seemed illuminated from within, dozens of feathery parachutes waiting for flight. She drew it in the foreground, added a pale, grassy knoll in purple, and a farmhouse similar to her parents' home, indistinct in the background.

At his words, and in response to the whisky on his breath, she leans heavily on her charcoal and draws a thick, dark line. She would also prefer that John did not qualify his judgement with the word *quite* as he does, that he would merely say, "It's good," if that is what he means, leaving no question as to his intent. *Quite* good suggests only moderately good, only *somewhat* good. He used the exact words the last time he looked at her work, but when she asked him if he meant only *somewhat* good, he said, "Don't be ridiculous. I complimented you and now you're ruining the praise." But if that is so, why does he phrase his compliment in the same ambiguous manner a second time? Does he resent her ability? Does he think she should sit idly, wondering where he is, ready to drop everything the second he walks through the door? Annoyed, she turns away from him and continues what she is doing with no comment at all.

When she played bridge, she arranged her schedule to leave the afternoon free of domestic obligations, so when the Wednesday games ceased with the departure of Rose and Phyllis, she kept that time free to read or draw. She doesn't understand why the restlessness within makes each activity necessary, but together, they help to subdue a feeling that she is never quite settled, never as content as she wishes she were. It's not even that she can say exactly what is missing. Some deep sense of purpose? She doesn't know. Whatever it is, she can't pinpoint it, except to acknowledge that she needs relief from what *is*, however nebulous.

Reading takes her out of her own life completely and sets her down somewhere where curiosity is the only prerequisite. Fictional characters take her hostage, drag her down streets she has never seen, through houses and front rooms, into bedrooms and minds so much more stimulating and interesting than her own—until reluctantly she turns the last page, having seen all there is to see and imagine, and is once more catapulted into that vast arena of life and eternal dissatisfaction.

She especially enjoys reading Dorothy Parker and Edith Wharton, because although they write about New York from very different perspectives—one as a working woman, the other with characters immersed in society—they both do so with acerbic wit and great insight. She reads male authors as well: E.M. Forster, Mark Twain, F. Scott Fitzgerald. And nineteenth-century literature: the Brontë sisters, George Eliot, Henry James—and Thomas Hardy, who is another favourite. More often than not, the Wednesday reading spills over into the rest of the week, as well, and she always has a book handy to pick up at quiet moments during the day and lay aside last thing at night. If more people read and lived vicariously outside their own set of experiences, wouldn't there be less stupidity and more empathy in the world?

Drawing or painting, even when the result is not as she desires, speeds time up, allows her to pass through it in a pleasant, concentrated stupor. Images of Honora continue to haunt her, so she reproduces them as if her sister were sitting for her. She absently speaks to Honora, and examines each drawing or painting after to see if there is some clue to her appearances that Mabel has previously missed.

Occasionally now, she also draws landscapes, though seldom realistically. She prefers to draw from imagination only, and in colour, so that she more often draws rolling orange hills with slashes of green, purple ponds, and yellow trees. Today dark gashes of red and black open on the page, wound-like, and representative of what? She cannot say, and yet she won't stop, either.

John notices her portfolio sitting off to one side and opens it without asking permission. "Are these ones self-portraits?" He holds up a drawing of Honora. "You have so many, at different ages."

"They're portraits of my sister." She can't help feeling pleased that he thinks they are of her. She likes to believe she and her sister would have had much in common, had Honora lived. But she anticipates a derisive response to her honesty. So be it. She's in just the mood to tangle.

"Honora? Who died when she was ten?"

"Yes. *That* Honora exactly."

"So you've imagined her at different ages?"

"Not really. I see her sometimes. It's quite comforting." And sometimes it is not, she silently amends.

"Are you telling me you *see* her, the way my father imagines he sees people?"

"I couldn't say for certain that it's the same. I'd need to speak to him about it. In fact, I will, the next time he visits."

"Oh, for Pete's sake, Mabel. You know how I feel about all that."

"I do. But do you know how *I* feel?" She is deliberately distant, cold even, though her heart aches for kinder words between them.

When John drives home in a pale blue Packard runabout as impressive as the clear blue Saskatchewan sky, she dashes outside in her apron, if only to run her hand over the glossy fender. She has never seen a smaller, prettier car.

"Did you buy it?" She hopes he has, but she is unsure how they can afford such an extravagance.

"It's a gift," he assures her, no different than the dinners they accept or the bottles of fine wine they drink with increasing frequency. When they were first together, she drank only a glass or two, preferring to let him drink the rest. Now she makes certain she gets her share. If there is any difference at all between that and *this*, he says, it is only that the car comes from a wealthier client.

The year is 1924. And if they have not had children, they have prospered financially, at least. Though the post-war depression has deepened on the prairies, bringing lower profits for banks in general, times are good for John and the branch he manages.

"But they must expect something when they give you such an extravagant gift."

"All they want is the same as everybody else—the best rate I can give them, and priority approval on their loans. Nothing I can't accommodate. They scratch my back, I scratch theirs. It's only good business."

At some level she knows this is more than good business, but the thought of returning the pretty blue Packard is abhorrent, so she tamps down any uneasiness she feels and accepts John's explanation, preferring to tell herself that he understands business in a way she never will.

But how unfortunate that none of the dress shops wants to scratch his back. Why is that? Wouldn't it be wonderful if the dress shops and the shoe store wanted to impress John the way all these others—the farmers and auto dealer and machine-shop owner—want to impress him? And what of the jeweller? Why is it that the jeweller doesn't send home a string of pearls or that marquise-cut ruby ring she has admired in the window?

"What's wrong?" she asks.

He has come home mid-afternoon, pale and perspiring. Now he sits at the kitchen table and doesn't answer. When he lights a cigarette, he takes such long, deep pulls that the lit end glows for at least half an inch.

She brings him a cup of tea and settles in across from him. She may be lonely, she may have begun to resent his behaviour, but she has always loved him.

"Talk to me," she says.

By the look of him, he won't keep the problem to himself for long, but she can't stand to see him like this. She has not yet poured them a second cup when they both see a police car pull up outside.

"I might have to go away for a while," he says. "I did something that wasn't exactly normal banking procedure. You don't need to know, and anyway, there's not time to tell you."

She doesn't need to know? She wraps her hands around her cup of tea and thinks of all the times she has never asked. "It's the car, isn't it? I knew it was the car."

"It's not the car. Somebody's out to get me."

That's a lie, and the way he says it, with such self-pity, she wants to slug him. She knows no one is out to get him. He's still the most charming man she knows. But he's done something, and how dare he jeopardize everything they have, which is plenty? She also wants to pull him into her arms and reassure him, but there is no time for that. She loves him. She hates him.

Two officers knock on the door. When she opens it, they enter. Her ears hum strangely, and she feels she is acting some part she should have rehearsed more. She even offers the men tea, as if they might all sit and sip silently by the window. This is her husband they want. This is her *life*.

One of the officers says, "Excuse me, ma'am," as he gently moves her aside, and then they stand before John and ask him to rise. She watches as they handcuff her husband and escort him through the door and out into the street. This can't be happening.

She follows them outside, still not understanding why they have come, what he has done. Whatever it is, she wants to protect him.

And then John says, "You'll have to let our lawyer know I need him."

Curtains flutter up and down the street. She sees Anne staring from behind a bit of lace. She wants to wheel around and run back into the house, but she stands with her hand raised, her fingers spread, and waits for John to give her some sign that everything will somehow be all right. She stares at the side of her husband's unmoving face until the car pulls away and there is no longer any chance that he might turn and look at her, and then she holds her head high and concentrates on not stumbling as she makes her way back into the house.

For the rest of the day and night she can hardly think straight. Her thoughts are kaleidoscopic, tumbling over one another in a confused jumble. Jagged bits of anger get pushed aside by doubt and hope, then hopelessness when the next day John is charged with seventeen counts of fraud.

"I'll get out of this," he tells her. "And the fewer people who know, the better. I haven't done anything that isn't done all the time."

This is not a response that reassures her, and as if he senses that, he tries on an attitude of contrition. "All the same, I should never have done it. I don't know what I was thinking."

She understands that he has always attempted to inspire confidence in others by allaying their fears about themselves, but she is not moved when he adds, "You couldn't have saved me, so don't blame yourself."

He believes people will forgive almost anything if they think his overriding motivation is honourable, especially if they are first forgiven and rendered blameless themselves.

But is she blameless? She married a dishonest man, and she can't pretend she didn't have evidence from the beginning. What does that say about her? She opens her wedding albums and pores over the photographs, as if by looking she will discover what else she missed. John is middle-aged now, not so young and inexperienced that he can't couple his actions with the consequences, and she believed, or at least she hoped, that he would respect the line between self-serving behaviour and unlawfulness. She trusted him to know the difference.

She should have seen this coming, and likely she did, if only she had admitted the dishonesty to herself. She should have asked more questions, demanded more answers. So if she has not become the sort of person who believes in her own comfort above all else, she *has* let material comfort shape her values to a degree. But perhaps everyone does this, she consoles herself. Don't they?

John is not sorry he took the money, whatever he says. He only regrets that he went about the deception all wrong. She knows this because instead of focusing on his own deceit, he is concerned with learning who betrayed him. All the other prairie branches of the

Union Bank are floundering, so in the course of new, more vigilant audits, he tells her, his shady dealings might have been uncovered. But it is equally possible that someone turned him in, and this is the possibility that burns in him as the whole town learns how he made the loans.

He did not do anything complicated or difficult. He issued one amount and promised borrowers they need repay only a portion of that, as long as he also kept a percentage himself. Anyone could have done what he did. He made slight adjustments in large deposits to cover the shortfall, and no one should have noticed.

He didn't mean for it to become a regular practice. At first he only made loans for his friends, and then for a few of his most generous customers. That was his real mistake. He got greedy and wrote too many, he tells her. In hindsight, he should not have bothered with the loans at all. He should have skimmed the deposits and involved no one else. That would have been more difficult to pin on him. He could have blamed one of the clerks, and who would have known the difference? It would have been their word against his.

Mabel feels sick after he admits all this. Would she have stopped him, even if she had known? She would have worried, and berated herself for cowardice and immorality, but she can't deny she has enjoyed the benefits of her husband's career. Would she have turned him in and willingly accepted this humiliation? And if she is honest, the luxuries gave her a sense of advancement. Without them, she would have felt stuck in a world of revolving tedium, each week filled with the same chores as the one previous, nothing ever changing or improving. If others feel this way, how do they survive?

～

"The house is mortgaged for more than it's worth." She states this matter-of-factly at her next visit. She has already exhausted her capacity for accusatory anger without him. Now she speaks to him across a table in a small grey room, while a guard waits inside the door.

"I had gambling debts. I didn't know what else to do." He says this equally matter-of-factly, though he does shift in his seat and have trouble meeting her gaze.

She is shocked into silence. He has also been gambling? She never suspected, not once, and she can hardly believe this new offence will now be added to all the rest. Her hands shake uncontrollably.

"I'm trying to decide if we have any future at all, and now you tell me that on top of everything else, you've been gambling?" Oblivious of the guard, she raises her voice until it is a shrill yell. "How *could* you?"

"Mabel. Lower your voice." John places his hands flat on the table, his expression uneasy.

She lowers her volume, but her tone remains harsh. "We're in a *marriage*. That implies a union. A partnership. And at the moment I'm wondering if it's a partnership I value. The bank is selling the house, I have nowhere to go, and I have no income. What do you suggest I do?"

"You'll have to stay with your parents until I'm out of here. Then we'll make it work." He puts on a deeply sad expression. "I was afraid you'd leave if I told you, but I can see now that everything has to be out in the open. Don't give up on me. On *us*. I'll get everything back. I promise you."

She feels as if she is in one of those dreams where she strains toward something but can never quite reach it. She wants to turn around and walk away from him forever, and she also wants to believe he can make everything all right. The result is that she feels immobilized, incapable of doing anything. She feels hollow, as if all this straining might cause her to cave in on herself. She has overlooked so much. She has chosen not to see. Is she really capable of something more now? She wants to put her head on the table and sleep.

"I can't live with my parents. John, I *can't.*"

"Only for a few months. It's not easy in here, either, believe me. Sometimes I wonder if I'll survive." He stretches across the table to touch her hand. "But you've got to believe me. When I get out, I'll make it up to you."

CHAPTER 10

1926

When she steps off the train in Seattle, the platform lies in copper shadow, lit by dim lamps below which travellers scuttle, their free hands clutching collars for warmth. She looks around automatically for John, and then grasps her bag from a porter and hurries to a waiting trolley car. She misses those early days of their marriage, when John always owned a car and drove her anywhere she needed to go. Now they can barely afford their tiny, rundown apartment, and even the streetcar is a luxury. But at least he is earning an honest living. She tells herself that repeatedly. And even if he wanted to meet her, he doesn't expect her for six more days.

She hoists herself onto the packed trolley, sets her bag at her feet, and hangs on as the car lurches forward. She meant to visit her parents for two weeks, not one, but her presence disrupted their routine in a way she hadn't observed before. Her mother kept sitting and rising, conversations started and stalled, and her father cleared his throat over and over and often retreated to his study. In the end she couldn't bear their discomfort.

Last year she spent eight months with them while John served time in prison. They allowed her to stay and didn't ask a word about when she would leave. When John finally came for her, and said he'd take her to Seattle, where they would start over, her parents said nothing about that, either. Everyone deserved a second chance, didn't they? She had heard that sentiment spoken so often she believed it, as if second chances were an inalienable right, some law decreed, which of course they were not. But anyone could see that he had truly suffered.

"This is your last chance with me," she said.

"I won't need another," he promised.

And hadn't everything worked out just fine?

She stares out the window into the dark and sees her own reflection peering back, her head bobbing with the motion of the trolley. A man in a smart grey duffle coat catches her eye and stands to offer his seat. She flashes him a grateful smile and sinks into the spot he vacates, suddenly very tired.

It is true that John has settled into his new job at the Seattle steamship company with fewer complaints than she expected, but she can't help question whether he really works all the hours he claims to. If he does, where is the money? And if he doesn't, where is *he*? She can't pinpoint any one time that has given her proof, but she often has a vague feeling that something is not quite right in what he tells her. Is it possible he still gambles? Or could he be doing something even worse?

Her days are as dull and uneventful as he says his are, and new worries fill them. She cleans their small apartment in two hours. Laundry and ironing eat up several hours a week, grocery shopping another few. Meal preparation is her only domestic challenge. John earns less than five dollars a day now, not even half what he earned as a bank manager, minus gifts from clients besides, so she cooks meatless soups, vegetable stews, and plenty of potatoes. She thinks she could serve potatoes twenty-five different ways. Potato pancakes, green potato, boiled potato, baked potato, potato hash, potato soup, potato casserole.

Gone are the bottles of wine and champagne, the dinners paid for by others, all the perquisites of a banker pulling favour in a small town, and she can't deny that John has changed because of it. He can still make conversation with almost anyone, but he's harder edged, sharp where he was once witty, and if before others competed for his favour, now he competes with the rest for negligible opportunities.

When he returns home, never before dark and often much later, it is mostly to roll into bed and sleep. He smiles less spontaneously, less disarmingly, and others aren't drawn to him as easily as they once were.

"We deserve more than this," he sometimes says. "I'm earning a pittance."

"But at least you have a job, when so many others don't." She strokes his brow, or rolls up against his back to comfort him as best she can.

"At this rate, we'll never get anything we want."

There are more things than ever to want, she agrees, but would they really be any happier for having them?

When she gets home tonight, she will do something kind for him—massage his shoulders or rub his feet. It isn't fair to doubt him without proof. She will show him how she has missed him over the past week. They will celebrate their anniversary in less than a month—their ninth, on New Year's Day, 1927—and she'd like to do something special for him then, as well. They haven't seen his father in more than two years, so maybe Coulson will agree to visit over Christmas and stay on until the New Year.

She will prepare a special meal. Lamb, perhaps. John used to order lamb often when they dined out, and she has been putting aside a few cents each week. Yes, she'll purchase a fine leg of lamb.

Revived somewhat by her plans, and intent on the details, she hops off the trolley and walks the last two blocks in the dark. She peers up at their apartment from the street, trying to discern by the upper windows whether John is home or not. They rent a furnished one-bedroom in an old walk-up, and she has never become accustomed to the shoddiness of the house. The roof sags, painted boards have faded, but at night these flaws aren't so readily visible.

Some couples fall apart at the first bit of trouble, but at least she and John are still together. That counts for something. And if John isn't the cocky, successful man she married, he isn't shattered, either. He will rebound. They have survived something terrible together, and that is how love transforms itself from tenuous beginnings into something that will sustain a couple for forty or fifty years.

She has learned a thing or two about marriage through it all, and something about passion, as well. For her, desire is a result of trust, misplaced or not. With trust damaged, her desire is damaged, too. When she feels passion now, it is less spontaneous, and her responses will never be what they once were. Nevertheless, if he is not too tired, maybe they can see what happens tonight. Her clothes may not be flashy, but she can still undress with style, and it is possible that John's body, hot against hers, will calm the jumpiness that has followed her home.

"I'm back," she calls. The door is slightly ajar, but that is not unusual. The latch does not always hold, and it may have popped open when a door closed somewhere down the hall. She sets her bag inside the apartment and locks the bolt behind her. There is no sign of John, but the place is a mess. A wooden chair has been overturned; cushions are pulled off the small sofa. For heaven's sake. Is this how he lives the minute she leaves? The apartment reeks of stale smoke, even with the window wide open, letting all the heat out.

She kicks off her shoes and moves quietly and quickly, straightening up. They arrived in Seattle with only a suitcase each and a few crates of bedding and dishes, everything else sold or taken by the bank. In the months since, they have acquired few material comforts. Can't he at least take care of what they have?

She is startled by a noise in the bedroom, more of a moan than any sort of greeting, but he must be home after all. With the window now closed, she unbuttons her coat and hangs it on a hook by the door, and then she follows the sound into the other room.

A small black overnight case on the floor catches her attention. Her own bag still sits by the door, and this one certainly does not belong to John. A bit of lace pokes out from between the lid and the bottom, and something black and shiny, like a woman's slip, slouches against the wall behind it. Yet she sees no one but John in the room, which is barely large enough for the bed and one night-stand. John grimaces at the sight of her, and a groan comes from the back of his throat. He lies naked except for dingy white under-shorts, and the sheet is tangled at the bottom of the bed. His legs jut out at odd angles, and two inches of Scotch sits within reach on the bedside table.

"What's going on here?" A sense of dread makes her clammy, and her legs weaken so that she is forced to sit abruptly on the edge of the bed.

"Aaaahh," John screams.

She jumps up and he screams again. Sweat breaks out on his forehead and he grabs the whisky and takes a large swig. She looks more closely at his legs. What is it about them that bothers her? She sees his wallet on the floor, as if it has been thrown there, bits of paper beside it. She picks it up and looks inside. Empty, and only two days into a new month.

"Have we been robbed?"

Suddenly the discordant images make sense. The overturned cushions, the empty wallet. "They're broken! Good God, your legs are broken." And then, without emotion, "You've been gam-bling again." It is a statement, not a question.

He turns his head away from her, so she moves to the case on the floor and lifts the lid. She feels floaty, as if the force of gravity has suddenly lessened. Female things. Cosmetics, a lacy blouse. She picks the blouse up as if it is diseased and lets it fall again.

"Don't tell me. She's gone for a doctor." She does not immedi-ately think to ask who the woman is or how long John has been seeing her. She lowers herself to the floor and turns to stare at him. She is emptied. "Why?"

She means the woman, and the gambling, but his Adam's apple merely bobs in his neck, as if he might be trying to think what he can possibly say that will not make everything worse than it already is.

"Can you talk?"

His skin is ashen, his brows pulled together, eyes dark and narrow in their sockets, glittering with pain. The way she feels, her pallor must match his.

"I can't move," he says, the words coming out raspy. "It's terrible if I move."

She sits in silence, staring at him. She thinks she could be sick any minute, and her muscles seem to have lost their ability to hold her upright.

"But why?" she asks again. She brushes one hand against her cheek, annoyed to find that she can still cry. "Why did you do this to us?"

A drop of perspiration starts at his hairline and runs down his cheek, so he looks as if he, too, is crying, though she knows he is not. He never cries.

"This woman," she says. It finally occurs to her to ask. "Who is she, anyway? And what were you thinking—that I wouldn't notice?"

As soon as she asks, she realizes that she didn't notice, until now at any rate. Or if she did—all those unexplained late nights—she didn't confront him. Yet again. "How long—?"

"It doesn't matter. It's over."

"What do you mean, it's over? What's over? You and she?" He's fooling himself if he thinks that will change anything.

"Us."

"You and *me*? *We're* over?" Well, of course they are. She had promised they would be, and where, after all, could they go from here? But this isn't right. Can't he at least pretend he cares? Did he want this all along?

"Oh God." She buries her face in her hands. Where can she possibly go tonight? She can't very well stay, either, not with the other woman returning, as if it were she, and not Mabel, who belongs. But where?

John says, "I'd only drag you down with me."

"You already have." You lying...*bastard*. She wants to get up and hit him, but the effort is too much for her. Her arms won't move.

He looks devastated, she will give him that. She sees in his eyes that he really does not know any better than she does how to make this right, and that he is not indifferent to her. Nor is his concern practised. This time it is genuine.

"What will you do?"

He shrugs, almost imperceptibly. "I've got to get out of here. Start over."

"*This* was your new start." The accusation in her voice is back, and hearing it, she accepts what he would already know: even if she wanted to, she could never forgive him again. And why should she? Wanting something to work won't make it so.

She wipes her palms on her skirt and stands. "Well then." Her voice is very quiet. She kicks feebly at the foreign bag. "At least now we've stopped the bullshit."

He doesn't answer, so she walks out into the main room, where she plunks herself into one of the chairs. She needs to do something, but she can't think what. After a minute she rises and opens a cupboard. She removes three jars of canned tomatoes and frees the shelf paper. Stuck below it is a ten-dollar bill. She peels it away, and then without bothering to put anything back, she slams that door and opens another. She takes an oversized china teapot from the top shelf, a wedding gift from one of her parents' friends in Saskatchewan. She shakes the contents onto the counter—the emergency fund she has started. Less than seven dollars.

Now she has exactly twenty-eight dollars, no other savings, nothing of any value left to sell, and she can't bear the thought of facing her parents again, so soon after she has reassured them that everything is fine, just *fine*. She is thirty-six years old and most of her belongings are already packed in a single suitcase. As she gives the apartment a quick once-over, she remembers her portfolio of drawings. She tucks that and her pencils into her suitcase, and then spots a lone apple that has rolled into a corner. It is bruised and slightly wrinkled, but she picks it up and slips it into her coat pocket—a meal when she needs it.

It is after eight o'clock in the evening when she bumps her suitcase back down the stairs of the apartment building and out into the unlit streets of Seattle. Anger and disappointment fuel her for several blocks. She half expects to pass John's woman, with or without a doctor, and Mabel imagines she'll know her immediately if their paths cross, but no one at all appears. How well does John know her? What if the woman never comes back but leaves him there by himself? How will he get help?

"Why do I care?" Mabel asks the question aloud and then looks around to make sure the street is still empty. What does *she* provide that a wife doesn't? Is it as simple as that she was there when he wanted her? That she was different? Someone with whom he could still be believably charming? Mabel will never know.

But when she thinks of the other woman with her husband, she is glad of John's broken legs. Except then she remembers the way he screamed when she sat on the bed and she is almost sorry for him again. She walks on that way, one minute wishing him ill, the next wishing she could turn back time so that everything would be as it was in the beginning.

She is such a fool. A laughingstock, really, naive and ridiculous. She will never trust a man again. And how could she be so stupid as not to see the signs?

So immersed in regrets, she fails to notice how many blocks she has covered until it occurs to her that she no longer stamps along in the dark. She has marched out of her district and into another, slightly more affluent area, still rundown but closer to the city centre.

When at last her arm feels the strain of her suitcase full of belongings, she approaches the first house with a Room for Rent sign. The three-storey Victorian mansion must have been beautiful fifty or sixty years back, when the cracked glass in its turrets gleamed, when bow windows looked out on gardens and not trash. Now a drooping front veranda advertises its current state of neglect.

She doesn't care. In all likelihood, neither does the woman who opens the door. She is thin and pulls a thick sweater around herself. She is as droopy as the veranda, and inside, the house is almost as chilly as outside.

"Ten dollars a week. Three more for meals, if you want 'em. And no men in the room. This is a respectable place."

Mabel doesn't answer. She hardly glances around her, but when she is taken to a room and sees the bed, sagging between two iron bed-ends, that is enough. "I'll take it." She relinquishes ten dollars, more than a third of the money she has.

"So you won't want meals then? There's no cooking in the room."

"No," she says. "Thank you. I only want to be left alone."

She doesn't wash, or even unpack her nightgown. She undresses down to her slip and crawls between grey flannel sheets, which she pulls up over her chin. The musty old quilt above that feels satisfyingly heavy. Then she lies there wondering what she could have done differently.

That bastard.

Normally she doesn't swear. Once, when she was younger, on her parents' farm, she dropped a large rock on her foot and screamed in pain. "Fuck," she said, copying language her brothers in England had used in her parents' absence. "Fuck, fuck."

She didn't know that her father stood nearby, and she screamed when both his hands gripped her shoulders from behind. He spun her around. The expression on his face was almost enough to silence her forever, and his words had lasting effect.

"Any clown can curse," he said. "But you've been privileged with a fine education. You have a better than average vocabulary. I expect you to make use of it."

She took his words to heart, and she has made an effort to communicate her feelings precisely ever since, but when it comes to John, her vocabulary fails her. The prevaricating scoundrel. The two-timing crook. The manipulative, dishonest rogue. None of them has the satisfying ring of *that bastard.*

The next morning she examines her face in the bathroom mirror down the hall. Her skin is dry and lifeless, papery, even after she washes with a cloth, sunken unattractively at the cheeks. Her hair, now the colour of an old penny, is dull and tangled, and not even a good brushing brings the shine back. Her eyes have also sunk in their sockets, so they look small and simian, and she thinks she has aged ten years in a single day. But what is that they say? Wisdom is the result of experience? Better a bad husband than never to have loved at all? Horseshit. It's better to have loved well.

She will go to a public call box and telephone her parents because she has no one else to tell. *My marriage is over. Don't worry, I'll be fine.* She'll need to practise saying it without breaking down. And everyone on the party line will know by nightfall. Her parents will be shocked, and disappointed in her, possibly embarrassed at her failure. They might even believe she should stay with John, though they are not the sort to say "you made your bed, now lie in it." Either way, she longs to hear anything they might have to say.

Less sure of herself after John's jail term, she has kept to herself in Seattle, so there are no friends to turn to. At any rate, she has never been one of those women who accumulate friends with ease, the way some people accumulate hobbies, constantly fitting new ones into their schedules without ever neglecting the others entirely. Of late, the effort needed to sustain even one friendship hardly seemed worth the trouble—to have a friend one must be a friend, of course. But if she is forced to defend her position with her parents, she prefers the defence to no talk at all.

PART II

LOVE
1926–1928

CHAPTER 11

"I might have predicted this," her father says. Immediately after her call, he sent a prepaid ticket home. A boy had delivered it to the door of the rooming house, and her landlady had grudgingly passed it on.

Now her father's dark oak desk sits bare and glossy, every piece of office paraphernalia tucked out of sight. Only when he works at his desk is there so much as a pen and paper to clutter its surface. Even the spines of his books are precisely aligned. He has always been tidy, but this rigid organization suddenly strikes her as sad and restrained, and she wonders if her mother remains in the kitchen to avoid disturbing her father's sense of order.

The lines around his eyes and mouth appear deeper than they

were even the previous week, and his nod, when he takes a seat and motions her into the one opposite, is unnecessarily curt. He readjusts his spectacles to peer over them.

"I think now that I should have voiced my doubts about John, but you were almost twenty-eight when you married, Mabel. A full-grown woman with a mind of your own. You were such a bright young girl, and we provided you with every advantage. You might have done so well by yourself . . ."

She knows he does not intend his words to hurt as much as they do, and she lowers her eyes to protect him from the pain she feels. He is only thinking aloud. Once she might have asked him what he would have had her do differently, but none of that matters now. What matters is how she will correct her path. She has failed as a teacher, failed to bear a child in eight years, and failed in marriage. She needs to find the place where she will succeed, but what she has in mind will not impress her father.

In her parents' world, women—even those educated for survival—marry sensibly and produce children. Her parents don't read *Vanity Fair* or *The New Yorker*. They don't expect her to write for *Vogue* magazine, as Dorothy Parker does, or produce a best-selling book of etiquette like Emily Post.

Helen Keller graduated from Radcliffe College and now works for the American Foundation for the Blind. In the past ten years, women far younger than Mabel have won the right to vote—in all three countries she has called home. In fact, every time she picks up a newspaper or opens a magazine she learns of another woman of accomplishment.

And although her parents have never been so cruel as to say so, she has given them more cause for concern than all her brothers put together. *They* are happily married with children, all four of them. Two of her brothers still operate the warehouse in London, one is in politics, and the other has started a successful side business brokering coal to foreign purchasers. Yet all her parents expect from her is that she will live a productive life and find some way of her own choosing in which to contribute to society.

She was awakened the other night by a word entering her consciousness with singular clarity: *Pensacola.* She can't explain how she knows she's meant to go there. She heard only the one word, nothing to explain it, but Pensacola is where John's father lives, and she believes the word was directive. If only she had been able to fall back to sleep, maybe she would have learned something else. Is Coulson ill? Does he need her? Instead, she was left with this feeling of certainty, and yet puzzled, as well, as if she grasped for something she saw but couldn't quite reach.

She can't justify any of this to her father, can't even explain it to herself, as she has never considered going to Pensacola an option before now. Why would she? Coulson is John's father, not hers, but now that she has thought of it, why should that stop her? It makes perfect sense—he's a Spiritualist. He knows other Spiritualists. And besides, what are her choices here? During the war, she could have worked in a munitions plant, but who will hire her now? With teaching no longer an option, will she hide out with her parents as she did last year? Or be forced into domestic work? At her age?

Nevertheless, sitting in her father's study, her plan shrinks. To her father, moving south to stay with Coulson won't sound any better than running north to come home. Will sound much worse, in fact. So when she lifts her head, she speaks more tentatively than she likes about a plan that with its crucial omissions now seems more of a non-plan than a decisive step forward.

"You chose Canada," she says. "John chose Lancer and Seattle. Now I'm choosing Pensacola. I'll stay with John's father until I find a place of my own."

"But the Reverend lives alone, doesn't he?" Her father looks affronted. "Shouldn't you stay somewhere more appropriate? I don't doubt that he'd welcome you," he says, though he looks as if he doubts her welcome entirely. "But it would be odd, wouldn't it—a young woman and her father-in-law alone in a house?"

"I imagine he has a housekeeper, Father." She's certain that he does, if only for a few hours a week. "And besides, he doesn't know about John. I want to tell him in person."

"I can't imagine why. Surely the news won't come as any surprise."

"I think it will," she says, fighting suddenly to keep her voice from breaking. "John's father cares a great deal about him, as I did."

"As we do about you, Mabel. But I worry about you. You've changed this past year. Have you considered returning to England? One of your brothers—"

"What would my brothers want with me? They'd be horrified to have me turn up under the circumstances. Their wives would be more horrified yet."

Her father nods, and then he relaxes for a moment and they share a small laugh. She hasn't seen her brothers in ten years, since before her marriage. She'd be like a stranger on their doorstep.

Her father steeples his fingers and taps his fingertips together. He looks at her as if he has much more to say, but in the end he slides open his desk drawer and produces a bank draft, already written up and signed, for one thousand dollars, an amount only slightly less than John could expect to earn in an entire year. Her eyes open wide at the sight of it.

"I'll pay your train fare, as well, now that I know where you want to go."

"Father! Are you sure? This is too generous." Her voice falters. For all her gratitude, a deep ache forms in her chest. She looks past her father and doesn't quite meet his eyes. "When do you want me to leave?"

"Stay with us over Christmas, but Mabel . . ." He waits until he has her full attention. His expression reflects the hurt she feels. "It's not that we want you to leave. It's only that we'd like to help you get where you're going."

CHAPTER 12

1927

The Reverend Coulson Skottowe rarely has an unkind word to say about anyone. In Mabel's experience, he accepts others exactly as they are, but despite this, when she hires a taxi to take her from the station to his address, she has the driver stop four houses away. Does John ever feel as baffled and hurt as she does, unable to recall when or how they ended up on opposite sides of what must be the same deep and unending desire for love? And if he does, does he ever miss her, irrationally, as she misses him now? They should be visiting his father together. Walking hand in hand along the boardwalk as they did when they were first married. Instead, she's here, in this awkward position.

She remembers that she meant to bring a few supplies, so she asks to go to a store and has the driver wait while she buys a small jar of thick cream, coffee beans, eggs, butter, and bread. Several minutes after that, she finally opens Coulson's gate and knocks at his front door.

She has not written ahead to tell him she is coming, and when he first sees her, his expression moves from expectant curiosity to bemusement.

"It's Mabel."

"Mabel! Of course." And then his face changes completely, so that it is crisscrossed with welcoming lines. "What a wonderful surprise." He takes the small sack of groceries and her suitcase and sets them aside. Then he clasps her hands and pulls her into a warm embrace.

She hugs him just a little too long and fervently, so that he gently unwinds her arms from around his neck and takes a step back.

"Did John not come with you?"

"No, he didn't."

When she fails to elaborate, Coulson doesn't press her. "Let's get you settled."

She follows him inside his house, a cottage, really. It is a thinking man's place, like an overgrown study, with books and papers in piles on almost every horizontal surface. And yet it is clean and bright, inviting, if untidy. And it is small, only a living room, a kitchen, Coulson's bedroom, and one small room off the kitchen. He leads her there.

"Unpack. Make yourself at home," he says. "I'll fix us some tea whenever you're ready."

The room is small and rectangular, and contains only the bed she once slept on with John, a tiny wardrobe, and a chest of drawers.

Almost certainly it was once a maid's room, but she is happy to have it. When she has finished unpacking, she sits on the edge of the bed as if she is a new maid herself. Should she ease into her news, or get right to the point? It occurs to her that she might have done better to tell him about John before she unpacked. Coulson was so good when John went to prison—sent her money occasionally, and words of encouragement in long, compassionate letters—but what if he feels differently when he learns she has left his son?

But Coulson is not that sort of man. She hears him in the kitchen, the rattle of spoon against cup, the squeak of his chair as he sits or rises. He will have heard her movements, as well, as she walked between her suitcase and the dresser, opened drawers, closed them, arranged her toiletries on top. Perhaps he heard her slide the bag under the bed, or the twang of the bedsprings as she sat. Does he wonder now at her silence?

She should not have clung to him as she did when she first hugged him. He is an attractive man, still, and she is a younger woman. What if her presence disturbs him or causes the members of his congregation to object?

Both Coulson's first wife and his second died before she knew him, and if her father-in-law needs the physical satisfaction of a woman, he has kept his need concealed from John and her. She has seen the portrait of his last wife, Emily, which hangs inside the doorway of his bedroom. Emily was plump and had the same intelligent and accepting gaze that she admires in Coulson. The photographer captured her looking secretly amused, as if she were about to break into peals of laughter, and because of that, Mabel wishes she could have known her. She wishes Emily were here right now to help Coulson handle the news she brings.

John once said that his stepmother was always kind to him, and that Emily and his father had been very happy together. When Mabel and John visited, sometimes late at night they heard Coulson speaking to Emily's image as if she were still in his room, so perhaps another woman would only complicate this ongoing relationship. He believes in the sanctity of marriage, and she thinks she knows what he will say about hers. Nevertheless, when she can no longer postpone the inevitable, she joins her father-in-law in the kitchen.

John is Coulson's only child, and she wants to prepare him somehow, work up to the subject to soften its effect, but she can think of no way to do any of that. When he asks about John again, she does not put him off any longer.

They sit at his kitchen table, each nursing a cup of tea, and after a few false starts, she takes a deep breath and blurts it all out—how she found John, about the woman, the gambling, all of it.

"I went back the next day. I thought he might still be there, in pain, but he was gone. She must have got him after all."

Coulson was eating a biscuit when she began. He set it down partway through her speech, and he did not pick it back up. He watches her face while she speaks, and when she stops, he sits with his head bowed, looking at his hands folded on the table. She stares at finger markings in his hair, striations half an inch deep, and she waits as long as she can for him to respond. When he says nothing she plows forward.

"I wanted to tell you myself, but that's not the only reason I came. I'd like to stay in Pensacola for a while, maybe settle here. I've got a bit of money, so I can find a room and a place to work."

Coulson lifts his head then. He takes her hand and holds it, and then he pats it in a fatherly way. "You'll stay here as long as you like."

When her eyes brim over, he continues to hold her hand and allows her to cry without saying anything at all. His silence feels like the kindest thing anyone has ever done for her.

When finally she pulls her hand free and uses her handkerchief, he seems to struggle with his thoughts, opening his mouth several times before he finds the words to speak again. "A man shouldn't have to say this about his own son. It's difficult for me to tell you this, but you've done right. You're better without him. Your own father must have said something similar, and if he didn't, he should have."

"It wasn't always like this—"

"But it was inevitable." He breaks the remains of his biscuit into two, and then instead of eating any of it, he leaves both pieces on the plate and pushes it away.

"'*Wickedness is always easier than virtue; for it takes a short cut to everything.*' That's Johnson. I thought of him because my son likes shortcuts. He won't accept that they prevent him from appreciating what he has once he's got it. You had to stand aside, Mabel. No sensible person stays in the path of trouble."

"I thought you'd disapprove." She's not so sure she wouldn't like a shortcut herself. Or at least an answer of some sort. Possibly to a question she's incapable of articulating. All she knows is that she often feels that if only she could find the missing key, everything else would fall into place. Sometimes she thinks money would solve all her problems. Other times, particularly when she lived with John, she believed she needed more power. And isn't she here now because she thinks Coulson can provide some piece of information that will finally allow her to make sense of her visions?

His eyebrows lift slightly as he shakes his head, and when he speaks, his expression is gentle. "Who am I to approve or disapprove of anyone? We all make decisions, right or wrong. The sooner we reverse the wrong ones, the happier we are."

He's right. She knows he is, but is life really that simple? Nothing more than a series of decisions, right or wrong? Even now she feels that his words are weighted with meaning, that deep inside them is some kernel of concentrated truth, if only she were capable of seeing past the glossy, comforting surface. She commits them to memory, because she knows she can use these simple words in the future, in just such a way. She can imagine herself in any number of difficult situations, saying, *Who am I to approve or disapprove?* How much more peaceful her world would be if she could master that one small phrase and really mean it.

He pats her hand again. "I'm pleased you came here, Mabel. You did well."

In the evening, while he reads, she makes them both eggs and toast. When they meet again at the table, she waits until he dips his toast into an orange yolk, and then she says, "I came here with an ulterior motive."

And so she tells him about waking to the word *Pensacola*, and about her visions. How they may have started when she was a young child. About Honora's death, and how her sister's image survived, and then changed again, and how it appears now with visions. How she used to see only in black and white, and how that changed so that she now sees in colour, as well. About Rose and her husband, and about the chest pain.

They speak for two hours.

"And you've never discussed this with anyone?" he asks. "Not even John?"

"I've said a few things, but I've never spoken to anyone who understood. I never had a vision when John was home, and I promised him I wouldn't attend meetings or search anyone out. I did practise going into a hypnotic state, though. I didn't see how that could hurt, in the privacy of my own home." She shakes her head. "He doesn't believe in any sort of afterlife. I don't know why exactly." But of course she does. At one level, the answer sits before her. John was always mortified by his father's ability to channel messages.

"He had to resist," Coulson says. "It began as a rebellion against me, perhaps, but ultimately, he wants to believe his actions have no consequences, now or later."

"Do you believe in karma?" She wants to turn the subject away from John. She's still too angry with him to speak kindly, and she's afraid she'll say something that will hurt Coulson. She has always been attracted to the idea of good and bad karma, if only because it encourages mindfulness and kindliness.

"I believe in energy," Coulson says. "That like attracts like. That which we focus on or exhibit, we attract."

"What about after death? What about reincarnation?"

"If matter is energy, as I think it must be, it will always take another form. How that happens, I can't say."

They have pushed their plates into the middle of the table, and now she runs her finger over the rim of one. "So when you see someone in spirit, do you see them as you see any person, or do they appear in some other form?"

He considers this question. "It's not easy to describe what I see, just as it's not easy to describe a dream to another person. What is so clear fades even as you try to talk about it." He drains his coffee cup. "Help yourself to more," he says, gesturing toward the pot on the stove.

She retrieves the coffee and pours for him until he lifts his hand to indicate enough, and then she adds only an inch to her own mug. Any more will keep her awake.

"It's a different kind of seeing," Coulson says. "You think you're seeing, but really you're *knowing*. Just as you know differently in a dream. You know someone is your neighbour, even if she looks like someone else entirely. You know she looks like someone else entirely even if you can't remember her features half a second after you believed you saw them."

"Yes, exactly." She feels a keen sense of anticipation. "But it's all so much more vivid than a dream. And there's a certainty I never feel any other time."

"You've got straight to the heart of it. It's the certainty that distinguishes psychic communication from everything else. There's never any doubt involved. You can't explain that kind of certainty, and no one can talk you out of it. It has to be experienced. And judging from the number of skeptics you'll encounter, perhaps it can't be believed until it *is* experienced."

She might have drunk ten cups of coffee, not just one, for the adrenalin is coursing though her system, as if every nerve in her body is alert. "And the images overlay whatever else is there. If I saw something now, this plate would still be here, but I wouldn't see it. The image would block it out, and then when the image faded, the plate would reappear."

Coulson smiles affectionately at her. "You see, it's good to have me confirm what you know, but you knew it anyway."

"No! You don't realize what it means to me to talk like this. Any time I've broached the subject in the past, I've got strange looks. It puts people off."

"You've been talking to the wrong people."

"That's probably true enough."

"That's the thing about fitting in," Coulson says. "Once you find your people, or attract them, it doesn't matter what the rest think."

She understands that he's holding back, allowing her time to say whatever she needs to, but she already knows what goes on inside her head. It is *his* thoughts she's interested in.

"So what am I meant to do with them? I keep feeling I'm supposed to do *something*. I'd like them to be less random and sporadic."

"You want to control them, you mean?"

"I do. I don't want to be taken by surprise, and I want to see when I'm asked to."

"That's unlikely." He is silent a moment. "That's like saying you want your dreams to be less random. You might correlate your dreams to your thoughts with enough practice—tenuously, that is—but you'll never really control them. I don't think it's possible."

"You must, to see something when people ask." Or don't ask. She recalls often the message he brought from Honora, and she is eager to see how he responds to others in his congregation.

"I don't always, and it's a very passive process. I don't do anything to channel information, except relax as best I can. I consciously slow my breathing. That's all."

"So what's your advice for me then? What should I do?"

"No one can tell you that. It's something you have to figure out on your own. But I suspect you already know. Have you had any thoughts?"

She's had thirty-six years' worth of thoughts, and if there is one person she'd like to emulate, it is Edgar Cayce. Ever since the librarian at North London Collegiate showed her the first newspaper clipping she ever read about him, over twenty years ago now, she has been building her own private and parallel persona, if only in her imagination. When she was a young teacher, she grew angry at his responses to her letters and for a few years pushed him out of her thoughts, but always he creeps back.

"I'd like to help people, like you. Like Edgar Cayce." She is trying this out on him. It's possible he will think she is arrogant beyond belief, but this is what she wants. It's not fame she wants, but purpose. How many times has she imagined how Cayce must feel after he helps someone? Often he gives them their lives back. "I just don't know how to start."

"You've started already," he says. "All you really need is patience. You'll find guidance when you least expect it."

"That's it? You really think all I need to do is wait longer?"

His smile is beautiful. "I do."

It is just after nine-thirty in the evening when there is a knock at the front door. She has tidied up and is about to prepare for bed, but when she hears a man's voice, anguished and pleading, curiosity brings her out of her bedroom.

"Do you need me to leave?" she asks Coulson.

"No, stay. You can bring him a blanket. And a cup of hot tea."

The man is dressed warmly, in a wool jacket and thick trousers, but shaking uncontrollably. As soon as he speaks, she understands why.

"Ruthie," he says. "My little girl. She's been missing for two days, and we're afraid we've lost her. She's only four. You've got to help us."

Coulson's face is a map of sympathy and concern. "Of course I'll help if I can. What's your name?"

"Jackson. Abe Jackson. We don't know where else to look. Our friends the Bartons told me about you, so I came as fast as I could. I don't know what you do exactly, but anything's better than nothing. We've already combed the woods—"

"You're from Pensacola?" Coulson takes the thick grey blanket Mabel brings and wraps it gently around the man's shoulders. In response to his visitor's agitation, he has become very calm.

"Milton. We're from Milton. My wife's damned near hysterical. She's thinking alligators."

"There's a woman. Has your mother passed?"

"Three years, only."

She watches Coulson. His eyes are open, directed at Abe, and he seems completely normal, only calmer.

"Her name starts with an *S*? Sylvie? Sylvia?"

"Sophia. Can she see her?" Abe seems a bit surprised and possibly skeptical. But he glances up at the ceiling and back at Coulson. "Mama, if you're here, tell me she's safe."

"Your mother's with us. I'm seeing water. Could your daughter have reached a body of water—the ocean? A lagoon, maybe?"

She gets goose flesh as she recalls the lagoon out near the highway, and she prays his wife's not right about the alligators. Her hands shake as she drops a few leaves of tea into a cup. She takes the kettle from the stove and pours water over them.

"She's drowned—?" The man's voice breaks.

Coulson pulls his chair closer and puts his hands on the man's knees. After a long moment of silence, when he appears to be listening to something, he looks into Jackson's eyes. "Abe, listen to me. Your daughter is still alive."

"You know that? Did my mother tell you?"

Mabel has a thought, and a sudden urge to interrupt. "A well," she says, hoping Coulson won't be annoyed. "Could she have fallen in a well?"

Abe lifts his head and stares at her. Coulson does, too.

"By golly, a well would make sense." Abe's voice has a note of hope, and she can see how her idea takes hold in him.

He turns back to Coulson. "What does my mother say?"

"That Ruthie's safe. She's looking out for her."

Not well enough, Mabel can't help but think.

"But I'm also getting the sense of a tree. A very large tree."

The tea will be ready now. She stirs it and leaves it on the counter. It wasn't a vision. She never heard a voice. Was it only a lucky guess? Presuming the child is, in fact, trapped in a well and not somewhere else entirely.

"Oh my Lord. Near the bayou. Let's hope she never made it to the bayou." Jackson stands and dumps the blanket in his chair. "It's worth a check. There's an old well at the Claytons' farm near there. How she would have got over there, I don't know, but I'd better get back and find out."

"Your mother's showing me a baby, wearing a crown."

"She really *is* here!" He looks puzzled. "I never knew what to make of it when the Bartons sent me here, but you couldn't of known that. He's our youngest. Just turned one. We put a paper crown on him to celebrate." He shakes his head. "Wait'll the wife hears that! Maybe we could come back sometime—"

"Anytime," Coulson says.

"What do I owe you, Reverend? My little girl needs me." He retrieves a thin, worn wallet.

"No. Put that away." He waves the wallet aside and escorts Abe to the door. "Finding Ruthie's all that's important, so send word that you did."

Abe Jackson pumps Coulson's hand, nods at Mabel, and is gone. When the door closes after him, Mabel puts her fingers to her neck. Her pulse is racing. "Does this happen often?"

"Too often for the poor souls who seek me out."

"But you helped him." She wasn't sure, at first, that she would be so generous at bedtime, but now she sees how impossible it would have been, how cruel, to turn him away. She would have done just as Coulson did.

"*You* helped him, Mabel. Whatever made you think of a well?"

"I honestly don't know. It just popped into my head in an ordinary way."

Coulson shakes his head. "You may have saved that child's life."

"I only hope that's where she is." She's still worried that she has it all wrong. "And they have to get her out safely. Do you think they will?"

"You tell me." Coulson notices the cup of tea cooling on the counter and picks it up.

She closes her eyes a moment, and then she nods. "Yes. I think yes."

"Can't you be certain?"

The responsibility frightens her. But Coulson is sipping his tea, waiting. "Fine. Yes. They'll get her out safely."

"There now. You think you don't know how to start, but I'd say you're well on your way."

The very next day she accompanies Coulson to the Church of the Healed Soul. Unlike most church services, scheduled for morning or evening, Coulson's service begins at one-thirty on Sunday, and continues through the slumbering hours of early afternoon. There was a time when the church was his alone, but four years ago, coinciding with the election of Republican President Harding, a divide occurred in his congregation. Half wanted him gone altogether, while the rest fought for his right to share his gifts. In the end, church elders agreed to bring in a new pastor to run regular services if Coulson confined his service to once a week. As a consequence, and despite the heat, his congregation is large, double the size of the earlier service, and by the time Coulson appears in his flowing white robe, all of the pews are full.

Mabel is at first certain that, as in most gatherings, the front row will be the last to fill, but someone sits on the other end of the wooden pew not long after she seats herself, and as others arrive and slide toward her, she sets her handbag alongside her hip, hoping to reserve a small bit of breathing space. But when the last two spaces fill, a woman slides next to her elbow, smiles and glances at the bag, so Mabel is forced to move it obligingly onto her lap.

The woman is about Mabel's age, in her mid-thirties. She wears a simple cream-coloured shift with shoes and a hat that exactly match her pale green eyes. Her handbag, in an unusual contrast, is watery orange. Mabel would never have thought to mix the colours, might have worn everything matching, but she envies the effect. The woman's hair, below the hat, is dark and cut in a perfect, straight bob. She doesn't appear to wear makeup aside from lipstick, and yet her skin is so even she looks as if she has stepped out from the pages of a fashion magazine. She turns to Mabel as soon she settles and extends her hand.

"I'm Nellie Painter. And this is Roger."

A man of considerable bulk and height rises politely to shake her hand, and then he sits again so suddenly and heavily that she feels the pew shudder. He is bearded and morose-looking, exactly the sort of man she prefers to avoid. She expended a great deal of energy, during her marriage, drawing men like that out in order to please John, more often than not receiving only dull monologues in return. She assumes that Roger is Nellie's husband, but before she can clarify, or provide more than her own name in response, Coulson lifts his white-robed arms and signals that he will begin. The congregation stills, as expectant as if a show were about to start, which in a way it is.

"Friends and guests," Coulson opens. "Welcome."

He has the sort of voice she could listen to for hours, regardless of what he says, if only for the pure pleasure of the rising and falling tones. Like music, or running water.

He stands alongside, not behind, the pulpit, and as he pushes his hair back over his forehead, he tilts his head as if he hears something the rest of them cannot.

"The spirit is coming through me," he says. "And I'm seeing the letter *M*. Is anyone here connected to someone with the initial *M*? Morris? Marvin?"

An elderly man in her line of sight ventures another name. "Margaret?"

For a second she wonders if the message might be meant for her, and her heart beats quicker. Her name begins with an *M*. Is it Mabel? Her hope rises. But then she thinks that would be awfully convenient. It would make her doubt Coulson a little. The message would have to be something he could never know.

"No," he says. "Not Margaret. It's a man's name. I definitely get the sense that it's a man. Melvin? Has anyone lost a Melvin?"

A small gasp comes from somewhere in the back of the congregation, and Mabel turns, not caring that it is impolite to stare. The sound was muffled and restrained in the way of someone afraid the message is for her, but even more afraid that it is not. And Mabel is not alone in looking. Almost everyone cranes toward the sound, and many appear disappointed that, once again, they are passed over.

"Who is it? Where are you?"

In the second last row of pews, a heavy-set woman heaves herself to her feet. Coulson has already explained that while occasionally the sharp intake of breath will come from a man, twice as often the message resonates with a woman. Perhaps women are less resistant to the unknown in general, he said, but he has also read that they adapt to change more easily, and are twice as likely as men to try new products that come on the market.

This particular woman is as wide as a door and completely blocks out at least two people behind her when she stands. Coulson singles her out as if they are alone in the room, and Mabel, like most of the others, swivels between his voice and hers.

He moves closer to her. "What's your name?"

"Isabel."

"Isabel, why do I get the feeling this person is a father, or an uncle?"

"My father's name was Melville."

"Did he make a habit of wearing a carnation in his lapel? No, hold on, I was wrong. It's not in his lapel. I'm seeing him in work clothes, but he's holding a carnation against his chest, possibly a daisy. I know they're very different, but that's what I'm seeing, sometimes one, sometimes the other."

"Oh Lordy."

"Does that mean something to you?"

"Yes."

Mabel watches Isabel fold her arms on her middle and nod without elaboration, then the woman laughs, her plentiful chins wobbling agreeably. Anyone can see she will be sobbing any second.

"My father took my mother a carnation when he proposed to her. He gave her one every year on their anniversary until she admitted she preferred daisies, then he brought those instead. He did that every year until he died."

"There's something else."

Mabel turns back to Coulson and watches him closely. His eyes are open. He's not in any sort of trance. He speaks clearly. He only looks relaxed, as he told her he tries to be.

"I don't know what this means, but he's brushing at his nose. He seems to be having fun." Reverend Skottowe stares up and to his left, watching something only he can see.

For an instant Mabel wonders if the pose is pure theatrics, and then she chides herself. She knows it is not. Nothing with Coulson is anything but genuine. It is only his son who acted for effect.

"He's laughing, as if it's a big joke. Maybe it's a baseball signal?"

"Ha!" Wheezy laughter bursts from Isabel and, while the flowers on her dress bob as if in a breeze, she coughs until Mabel thinks she will choke.

"I know why he's doing that. He died when I was eight. I used to play this game with him when I thought he was sleeping. I'd sneak up to him and tickle his nose until he batted my hand away. When I got older, I realized that he pretended sleep so I could have my fun."

The Reverend Skottowe speaks gently. "Your father's telling you he's with you in spirit. He wants you to know that."

"Amen," says someone.

"Amen," echo several others.

Next to her, Nellie catches her eye. Mabel smiles back.

"He's a remarkable man," Nellie whispers.

Mabel already likes this warm, sophisticated woman. "He's vegetarian," she says, unsure why that pops out when she could remark on so many other details of Coulson's personality and life—his kindness and warmth, the way he meditates morning and evening, how people seek him out, as Abe Jackson did last night.

Nellie observes her with a quizzical expression.

"I'm cooking for him," she explains. "His son was a meat eater, so it's going to be a challenge to switch to vegetarian, but I'm searching for interesting recipes." She takes a breath and rushes on. "I was married to his son, John, but now I'm staying with Coulson, trying to make myself useful. At least until I find a room of my own."

"You're staying with Coulson? In his tiny little house?"

She nods, feeling foolish. Why has she offered so much information so soon? And mid-service, at that. She clamps her tongue between her teeth and stops. "Let's talk later," she whispers.

Afterward, people rush up to Coulson, so that he seems at the centre of a large humming nest of wasps. He speaks to everyone who comes forward, and while Mabel waits for him to finish, she talks to Nellie.

"Have you and your husband lived in Pensacola long?"

"Oh, Roger's not my husband! He's my brother. Marriage doesn't interest me."

"Really?" Mabel is instantly intrigued. She has long felt certain that women should not necessarily want marriage above all else, but this is the first time she has encountered someone who won't even bother to pretend interest.

"Men will reduce twenty-four hours to ten if you let them."

She laughs at that. It is true—she always accomplished so much less when John was home. "So you never married?"

"Never did and never will."

"You must have hopeful suitors in constant pursuit. I imagine they're awfully disappointed." She is possibly the most beautiful woman Mabel has ever seen.

"They've mostly got the message by now. I have too many interests of my own." She smiles engagingly as she waves the men's disappointment away. "My father left me an inheritance, so I need no deliverance from my plight, thank you very much. I'm a free woman. I live with Roger out of family tenderness, not of necessity."

Mabel is delighted, and laughs outright. "You could be a suffragette!" She says so admiringly, with none of the contempt that often accompanies the word.

"I *am* a suffragist. Now that we have the vote, people think we should be satisfied, but there's a lot to accomplish yet, especially in the arena of marriage. Intelligent society needs to accept that marriage isn't good for all women."

"You're right. There ought to be plenty of options open to every woman, not just the Lady Astors or Margaret Sangers." She name-drops purposefully. She has recently read quotations by both women—Lady Astor on politics, and Margaret Sanger on sexual liberation for women—and she wants Nellie to know she is at least aware of the possibilities. "I'm struggling with that very thing right now. I'm not sure how to put myself to good use."

"You'll think of something," said Nellie. "The most interesting women always do."

The more she thinks about it, the more she wants her old name back. Or a new one entirely. She plans to ask Nellie for her opinion. They have fallen into a pattern of meeting when Coulson's service concludes on Sundays. If the afternoon grows late, Nellie invites her and Coulson back to Roger's mansion for lavish dinners. Where others, if they are fortunate, may have a housekeeper and a cook, Roger and Nellie have an entire staff.

The mansion, one of only a few dozen in the small city, resembles no home she has ever visited. It is as large and busy as a small hotel, opening into spacious rooms with a staff of gardeners, drivers, butlers, chefs, and assorted housekeepers. A typical Sunday dinner at the Painters' begins with oysters, is followed by consommé, poached fish, filet of beef, roast chicken or duck, boiled potatoes, and carrots. Even dessert arrives in courses: crepes Suzette, ice cream, and then fruit, accompanied by coffee, tea, and liqueur. She eats only a small portion of everything put before her, and still she is overfed.

After dinner, the four adults often separate into pairs. While Roger and Coulson make their way to the library to smoke and drink cognac, Nellie and she stroll out into the garden or beyond, into an impressive orchid conservatory.

Tonight they choose to wander amongst the roses, where the air is cool and scented. They stop to admire a new tea rose hybrid Nellie purchased the year before, the Mrs. Anthony Modern.

"This one has just bloomed for the first time." Nellie points at a luscious display of petals the golden yellow of a harvest moon. The moon above is paler, almost bright enough to read by.

When they move on, Mabel says, "I'm thinking of changing back to my maiden name, or to a new name altogether."

"You're starting fresh," Nellie says. "You can become anyone you like."

"Ahh. Madame Bovary, perhaps," Mabel says, teasing.

"Or Madame Blavatsky," says Nellie. "She's more reflective of who you are than that whining Bovary woman."

"You're familiar with Madame Blavatsky?"

"I should be. Roger and I are both Theosophists."

Mabel can't hide her surprise. "I'd begun to think I was one of a very small minority."

"You've been talking to the wrong people. The entire movement has gained popularity since the war. There are some fifty thousand in the society now. And who knows how many don't bother with membership. Are you one?"

"I'm not, but I've read Madame Blavatsky—both *Isis Unveiled* and *The Secret Doctrine.*" She still browses her copies, sometimes finding pure genius, other times only irksome redundancies. "I've read Katherine Tingley, too. '*The greed of the world is the death of the world,*'" she quotes. "I'd like to see her colony at Point Loma, outside San Diego—Lomaland. I saw a postcard. Both the temple and the yoga centre have impressive dome roofs, and there's an amphitheatre for conferences and entertainment. It might have been transported from ancient Greece, it's so beautiful."

"I read about it in our newsletters," Nellie says. "Have you heard of Krotona, as well?"

Mabel nods. "The colony in Hollywood? I know of its existence, but that's all." They have circled the garden now, but when Nellie moves to go around again, she is happy to continue the discussion. "What got you interested in Theosophy?"

"One religion for all appeals to me." Nellie pulls free a tendril of hair that has got caught in her mouth. "I'd like to believe that we'll eventually evolve into a unified position that will end religious wars. Religious conflict in general. We have enough of it right here. With all the similarities between the teachings of Jesus, Buddha, Mohammad, et cetera, how could anyone believe we're not already part of a Universal Brotherhood, whether we call it that or not?"

"I was raised Christian—believe in Jesus and go to heaven, but believe in Buddha and go to hell."

Nellie laughs, a sound as lovely as silver tapping crystal. "Well, that certainly simplifies it."

"Doesn't it? If you take religion on faith, and of course you have to, why be exclusionary? Isn't that a key condition—to treat others as you would have them treat you? The idea that any one group should be 'God's people' doesn't sit well. It's more intelligible that all the great sages have become enlightened Masters. I can't believe that Jesus was right and all the rest were wrong."

Nellie loops her arm through Mabel's companionably. "I agree; also, Theosophy is a woman's movement as much as a man's. When did Christianity ever give us two female leaders?"

"Three. Helena Blavatsky, Annie Besant, and Katherine Tingley. Can you imagine the papal conclave that would put forth a female Pope?"

They fall silent for a few seconds, then Nellie points out another white rose so illuminated by the moon as to seem almost incandescent. Mabel is amazed that only a few short weeks ago she still felt awed and self-conscious in her friend's company. Now there is only easiness.

"I'm drawn to the occult side of it," Mabel says. "Theosophists accept the notion that energy has always been wielded, both magically and psychically."

"Then you'd like *The Three Truths,* by Edward Arthur Wilson. Do you know him? He's also known as the Brother, XII."

Mabel has never heard of him. "Does the twelve have significance?"

"The twelfth Master communicates through him, and instructed him to take the name. He's heading a colony called the Aquarian Foundation, a utopian community in British Columbia."

"Like Point Loma?"

"Similar. It's meant to be the physical counterpart to the Great White Lodge—a manifestation of work the Masters have been doing on the spiritual plane."

"Does the twelfth Master communicate with him in visions?" Her hopes go up. Is this the sort of guidance Coulson alluded to?

"Automatic writing. All of *The Three Truths* was received that way."

Mabel had attempted automatic writing before her marriage, when she lived in the boarding house, but even though she tried an hour a day for several weeks, sitting with her hand poised over a blank page, she never produced anything legible that was not a result of consciously writing. Maybe Wilson could show her what she is doing wrong. "Is he American?"

"English, and he's attracted a very educated group of disciples. Well-to-do, too. Sir Arthur Conan Doyle, for one. Sir Kenneth Mackenzie, an English occultist. A famous British astrologer. A millionaire from Chicago. Will Levington Comfort, from the *Saturday Evening Post.*"

It occurs to Mabel that Nellie might accept her visions as easily as Coulson did, and she almost admits to them now, but as much as she likes Nellie, perhaps *because* she likes her so much, she can't, yet.

"I'll lend you everything I have about the Aquarian Foundation," Nellie says. "I know you'd like him. Initiates train at the colony to reach new spiritual levels, to become a force on the ground, he said, the epicentre of the new race. I want to see for myself. But enough of that. You need a new name. Madame B."

"Madame B or Madame Zee?" Mabel rhymes playfully, but

then she makes a surprised face at Nellie. "I like that. Madame Zee. Though I'm not exactly French."

Nellie shrugs. "Pronounce it the way we do here, with the accent on the first syllable instead of the last. Would *ma*dame care for a seat? It's heads over *Mrs.*"

"*Ma*dame Zee?"

"Or Madame Zura. I know someone with that name, though Zee is more exotic. And I believe Roger already finds you exotic and mysterious."

"No!"

"Yes. But don't take him too seriously. He's already married five times."

"He's well practised then. He should be getting better at it by now." She glances at Nellie and away again. Nellie must know she has no interest in another marriage. But then, her friend is not likely to advocate marriage for anyone.

Roger is pleasant, not nearly as sombre as she imagined he would be, and while she finds him much more interesting now than she did initially, even the thought of him courting her causes her panic.

What if she were alone with him, both of them pushing food around on their plates, each trying to entertain the other without Nellie? There would be awkward questions and answers. Evasions, small embarrassments, misunderstandings, and doubt. The idea makes her shudder. She would spill food or drink on her chest, or go on and on about something irrelevant, as she did when she first met Nellie. At some point he might lean in to kiss her, all bearded and strong lipped. Is there any chance that might be good? Just thinking of sex arouses a surge of longing.

She misses that part of her marriage. But perhaps Nellie is only teasing her?

Aloud, she says, "I like Roger, but—"

"Don't explain. I would have been alarmed if you had jumped at the idea. I'm still thinking about the letter Z. Does it have any special meaning?"

Gratefully, she accepts the change of topic. "It's the twenty-sixth letter of the alphabet. That's a sacred number for Cabalists, and it's the complex variable in algebra. It provides resolution. X plus Y equals Z."

"Algebra never made sense to me," Nellie says. "If Z is the third unknown quantity, what is Y?" She reaches down to nip a spent bloom from its stem, crumples the dried petals in her palm and scatters them in the soil, and then she smells her fingers. "I didn't understand a single equation put to me."

"Oh, I loved algebra. I could teach you in a minute." Not since Honora died can she remember feeling such a strong sense of kinship with another female.

"Maybe not. But you can do something else for me." Nellie stops at a curve in the path and turns to face Mabel.

"Anything."

"Roger and I have discussed this. We want you to stay with us. I know how much you care for Coulson, but we have more empty rooms than we can count. I'd enjoy your company."

"Oh, me, too." Put to her that way, how can she refuse? She would love to have a constant companion again, especially someone with so many of the same interests. And if both Roger and Nellie are interested in Theosophy, and the occult, what else will she have in common with them? And the obvious comforts of their home cannot be denied. She doubts that there is a room as small and spare as the one off Coulson's kitchen anywhere in the Painter household. She embraces Nellie gratefully. "That's so kind of you. Tell Roger you've invited Madame Zee."

CHAPTER 13

She sits at a desk in the tennis house, twirling an expensive pen. Who could have known that changing her name—her identity, really—could feel so good? Born Edith Mabel Rowbotham, she made a formal application to change her first name to Zura and adopt her old surname. She kept the name Mabel out of respect for her parents' choice, and yesterday she received documentation in the mail. No longer Edith Mabel Skottowe, she is now Zura Mabel Rowbotham, a.k.a. Madame Zee. Simpler yet: Zee. Already she feels freer, as if she has abandoned some part of the past forever, though one problem still remains: what will she do with her freedom?

To feel useful, she is addressing mailing labels for Nellie and affixing them to pamphlets the Brother XII wants distributed.

Outside, Roger is examining something on the ground. Since Nellie commented on Roger's interest in her, she has noticed that he has no trouble inventing reasons to find her, though he encounters her at practically every meal.

The tennis house is not, as she assumed when they offered it, a small structure used to house tennis equipment, but a seven-room cottage with its own tennis court, located just beyond the orchid conservatory and opening onto Nellie Painter's fragrant rose gardens. The pen she holds is a cool, gold-tipped fountain model by Waterman, very different from the metal-tipped dip pen she used as a schoolteacher in Saskatchewan.

Now that she actually lives in Roger's house, she notices in detail how unrestrainedly opulent it is—pillars two storeys high, shiny Italian tiles, and enormous arched windows that fill entire walls, each hung with heavy draperies to protect an eclectic collection of paintings.

She has seen similar paintings in the main house, and the ones she knows to be Impressionist art fascinate her most. She admires each piece often, for several minutes at a time, and from various angles. Reviews of the Impressionists and their work have been mixed, some blatantly unfavourable, some glowing in their praise, but imagining the well-discussed canvases, however aptly described, is nothing like actually experiencing an original Monet or Renoir.

Plain, meagre lines suggest the movement of people, tiny specks hint at flowers or human heads, and primary colours laid side by side cause her eye to see blended colours where really only distinct ones exist, and yet it is as if the artist's soul is enshrined in paint. Layer upon layer of pigment allows the canvas to appear textured and of such depth that she can almost reach inside the images or feel the warmth of sunlight reflecting back at her. The fact that Roger owns these paintings at all stirs her curiosity about him—not in any romantic way, she tells herself, but because he is someone who appreciates beauty.

"There you are." He materializes behind her as if straight out of her thoughts, and indicates with a jutted chin the mailing list and labels. "What does my sister have you doing now? We didn't bring you here to work all day."

He is tall, long-bearded, and, unlike John, his smiles are hard-earned, but she appreciates how he doesn't need to charm everyone in a room. When he smiles, the effect warms her.

Roger leans over the desk as if considering the list of names she copies, and then he reaches into a nearby plant urn and extracts a mailing label. He pronounces the name on it. "Paris Singer!"

His voice leaves no doubt about his feelings for Mr. Singer. "He owns the Everglades Club in Palm Beach. He used to keep Isadora Duncan in style. You've heard of her? The dancer?"

Zee has heard of her, and in addition, her name is so similar to Honora's (isaDora, oNora) that she pays keen attention, wondering if her sister will suddenly appear while she speaks to Roger. Sometimes a similarity or even a stray thought is enough to summon her.

"She even had his child," Roger says, "but now he calls her *Is-a-bore-a Drunken.*" He winks at her. "Ungentlemanly, that."

He reaches into the urn for a second time and pulls another label from behind the plant. "Martin Post. He's legitimate. They're just back from the Philippines. He's an interesting man, but he lives under his mother's thumb. He's not easy to get alone."

"I just wrote that. How did you get it?"

"Are you impressed?"

"I should be able to catch you out, so tell me."

He smiles. "If I told you, I'd ruin the magic."

"That's exactly what my father always said. Give me your hand."

"Pardon me?"

"Let me see the back of your hand. My father used to entertain me with tricks when I was a girl, and I learned a few myself. You have tape on the back of your hand."

Roger laughs and lets her examine both hands. No tape.

"I came out here for a reason," he says, when she is satisfied that he hides nothing. "We've been invited to a gala in Miami. Nellie's reluctant, but she'll come if you do. If you agree, we'll stay the weekend. I'll book a suite for the two of you, and one for myself."

"She didn't mention it." Nellie has already admitted that she dislikes parties, but never having been to one in Florida, Zee doesn't share Nellie's lack of enthusiasm. "I'd be delighted. Thank you. And now will you show me how you're snatching those labels?"

She watches him closely, but Roger produces a third label from up his sleeve and turns it over to her. "Bernard Noble. Now there's a man with a healthy respect for business. A builder. And more interesting than that sounds. Money's never too new for him."

She glances down and reads, *Bernard Noble.* She wants to address Roger's sardonic tone, and to learn more about where he fits into this hierarchy he alludes to, but she can't let his parlour tricks pass. How did she miss his sleight-of-hand?

"That's very impressive. I've practised, and you fooled me."

"I was a magician for a few years, and a hypnotist." He shrugs and flashes a self-deprecating smile. "On the stage, before I discovered the great American passion for chickens."

Really? He was a hypnotist? Philosophers and physicists undertook the first serious studies of paranormal events in part because of the phenomenon of hypnotism. For now, she will be his audience of one, if that is her purpose, but there may be much she can learn from him.

"I've always been interested in magic. And the occult in general, of course." He pulls on his beard and strokes it in a ponderous way that makes him look less confident in himself than he had seemed earlier.

She hesitates, and then says, "I'm especially interested in telepathy and clairvoyance." There. How good it feels to say that so openly. "Do you know the Society for Psychical Research in London?"

"Of course. I've read Sidgwick and Meyers and others."

"I have, too! '*The limits of our spectrum do not inhere in the sun that shines, but in the eye that marks his shining.*'"

"Meyers?"

She nods, pleased—with herself, that she can still recall a quotation after all this time, and with him that he recognized it.

"A memory like that trumps my little trick, but I'll make it up to you. I'll introduce you to Houdini when he returns. He's the best of his kind. I saw him extract himself from a straitjacket in Boston a few years back while he dangled on a rope five storeys up. His body swelled and contracted like waves on the ocean, imperceptibly at first, then more noticeably. Next thing we knew, he was out of it—belts, buckles, straps—not one of them cut or damaged. The crowd loved him."

"I've always wanted to see him." She touches a scar on the palm of Roger's hand. "What's this?"

Roger catches her hand, and then releases it slowly, as if with reluctance. "From childhood. I don't remember where I got it." He leans against the wall and studies her. "You're an interesting woman. Is it true I'm to call you Madame Zee?"

"Well, it does have a certain esoteric appeal, don't you agree?" Almost unconsciously she responds to his flirtatious tone in kind. Then, annoyed with herself that she has blushed like a child, she tries to catch him off guard. "And if *my* sources are correct, you're a notorious philanderer—married five times already, I heard. That's got to be a record, even in Florida."

He laughs, as she intends. "That's too boring to substantiate. I understand that Canadians pronounce the letter *zed. Madame Zed* doesn't have quite the same ring to it."

"In that case, perhaps I'd best not return to Canada."

He takes her pen and squeezes it through a hole in his closed fist until it disappears and a cigarette emerges out the other side. He taps it on her desk. "That will most certainly be our gain."

CHAPTER 14

For her first big gala event, she wants to make the right impression. While this is not exactly a date with Roger, she senses it is a beginning of some sort, and she wants to play her role in it successfully. She wears a beaded cloche to hold her hair close to her head, and an evening gown Nellie has helped her choose, a slinky satin-backed silk crepe that reveals much more than it hides. The dress falls above her knees, not below them as she is accustomed to, but its length, or rather lack of it, showcases her greatest physical asset—long, shapely legs.

The fabric drapes in such a way that the heavy silk catches low on her breasts and exposes a great deal of cleavage, and then drops straight to the hips, where beaded ribbons weight the fabric so that it pulls taut from shoulder to hip. The overall effect is one of loose, straight lines, but she has never felt more curvaceous in her life.

The dinner itself is lavish and takes hours, and afterward, they are drawn along with others to the main ballroom of the hotel, an enormous marble hall easily able to accommodate a thousand or more, but already she wishes she were anywhere else. She expected something different entirely—friendly people, more than anything. Instead, she is shoulder to shoulder with people who won't return her smiles but have a way of looking past her as if she is invisible, or worse, someone they have already summed up and dismissed.

Most of the younger women, including Nellie, are dressed as she is, in the "flapper" style, and they wear either straight bobs or waves similar to the ones beneath her own cloche. They have silk stockings and strappy silk shoes, and plenty of bare skin. Their gowns are no more beautiful than hers, their cosmetics of no better quality than the ones she applied to her face, and yet somehow they all have achieved the lithe presence of *Vogue* models, while she feels like someone who has mistakenly arrived in costume.

The women of the white-haired set speak to one another through smiles that strike Zee as imitations of smiles, not genuine at all, but a careful setting of teeth on teeth. Even while smoking they smile for photographers who circle the room in a manner not so different from the seagulls outside on the beach. The women turn their heads slowly, and their scalpeled chins remain perfectly level except when they lift them occasionally to receive a kiss on a powdered cheek. Others have forgone powder for a becoming shine.

"They look like they've been basted in honey," she complains to Nellie.

Her friend nods and stifles a laugh behind a gloved hand. "Don't get me started. That long trip for an evening of this—I'll never understand Roger."

Mabel nods agreeably and then speaks primly, tongue in cheek. "Who knows what depths of private pain lie behind the perfect facades? In matters of the heart, isn't everyone equal?"

Now Nellie laughs aloud. "You'll have to save that for someone who doesn't already know you!"

So they talk about an upcoming orchid show that Nellie plans to attend, and when they have exhausted the topic, Nellie stands gracefully. "And now you'll have to excuse me."

"You're not leaving?"

"I may be back."

But she knows better. Nellie often excuses herself with no explanation and never returns. "You won't. You're off to the suite and you'll be lounging in bed before I've lured Roger back."

Nellie laughs again and touches a hand lightly to Mabel's shoulder as she glides away. "You'll be fine. He'll be along in a minute."

Roger has left them to join a small group of men talking only to one another. They are so obviously in control of their environment. They have no need to prove anything to anyone, and unlike her, they are fully capable of enjoying themselves with or without company. In fact, except for the numerous waiters, one for every two or three people, she thinks she is the only one not entirely confident and pleased with the evening in general.

After Nellie leaves, Mabel wonders if she should walk away, too. She could thread her way past the closed groups clustered around the edges of the ballroom and return to the suite with her. Instead, she is at first immobilized by awkwardness, and then noticeably fidgety. She folds her hands in her lap, and then stands and allows them to hang loose at her sides, where they feel clumsy and out of proportion to the rest of her body. Finally she snatches a champagne flute from a silver tray—even with Prohibition, there is no shortage of good champagne—and moves toward Roger. He sees her coming and nods goodbye to the men in his cluster.

"Would you like to dance?"

When she shakes her head, he guides her through several archways and into a smaller salon. The Atlantic scent of fish and salt blows in through open windows, and heavy oak writing tables line walls lit with lamps. The atmosphere in this room is muted and mellow, in part because of dimmer lighting, and because the gilded horde populates it less densely. Roger indicates a row of pipes and thin, rolled cigarettes.

"You need to relax. You can always find something in one of these side rooms to loosen you up. Look."

He draws her closer, so that they form a unit one would hesitate to approach, and then he chooses one of the carved wooden and ivory pipes that lie fanned out along the table in a delicate curve.

"Opium, mixed with a little marijuana or tobacco. It'll leave you languid and content."

"Alcohol. Drugs. Are there no laws in Miami?"

"Not too many they enforce. Al Capone owns this hotel."

"Al Capone?" She has read the papers. "Don't tell me you know him?"

"Never met the guy." He passes her a pipe.

She sniffed cocaine once, with John, and she enjoyed the immediate lift and sense of confidence she experienced, but she has only heard about opium. "Is it safe?"

"That depends on who you ask. It's big business for your countrymen. The Brits sell it to half the world, but it's banned in England. Same thing in Europe and over here. None of us wants to poison our own race, but it works wonders if you give it to the servants when they're tired. They'll do double the work. And pity the poor Chinese sailor who smokes a bit after a hard day's labour. He gets arrested here for doing what he's encouraged to do at home."

"And yet *you* use it."

"Not often. Would you like to *give it a go,* as your British friends would say?"

She doesn't immediately take the pipe, so he lights it himself, draws on it, and holds the smoke in. When he offers it to her for the second time, she takes it and follows his example. Someone moves between her and the window and cuts off the flow of fresh air. The room is hotter immediately, more so when she inhales and bursts into a bout of coughing.

"Pull on it a bit less. Like this." Roger expertly lifts the pipe and directs the thin blue flame of his lighter over the pipe bowl. He draws in slowly and then blows out a small pocket of smoke. When he finishes exhaling, he flicks his lighter again. "Opium burns hotter than tobacco, so you need to hold the flame while you inhale."

This time he holds the smoke in longer and only exhales a little through his nose. When he passes the pipe to Zee again, she takes it. She inhales and looks into his eyes as the sweetish, pungent odour rises around them. His pupils are huge. He rests his hands on her shoulders. They are warm and heavy and exciting.

She cups the pipe bowl in her palm. Its warmth runs up her arm in a pleasing way, and she finds herself smiling, tentatively at first, and then continuously, like the others. Across the room she notes several groups lifting pipes to their mouths and others sipping drinks. Some huddle together intimately, heads tilted as if to guard their words, while others tip their faces back and laugh openly, abandoning the tight personal control prevalent in the main ballroom.

She leans against Roger. Every nerve in her body demands attention, and when he cradles the back of her neck and slides his fingers across her throat and down between her breasts, she isn't offended at all. More than that, she wishes he would keep going. He is about to kiss her when someone else brushes up against her, a life-sized yellow butterfly with startling red lips and a tinkling voice. The butterfly flits around them. The sheer silk of her dress floats and settles. She kisses first Roger's cheek, and then Zee's, before she lights on them, stretches a cool arm over Zee's bare shoulders, and follows Roger's path down Zee's chest with light fluttery fingers of her own.

"You're being naughty in public."

Roger reaches up and runs a curved finger down the woman's cheek in a gesture every bit as natural as his recent intimacy with her.

"Meet Ruby."

His voice sounds deep and close, yet also very far away, and she laughs, they all do, maybe at the sound of Ruby's name, which matches her lips and puckers Roger's as he pronounces it, or at the way she kisses him again, lingering and on the mouth.

"Don't be jealous." She moves her sweet-smelling face in so close that Zee can see damp clinging to her upper lip, and she speaks in breathy bursts. "Roger is a doll, a great giant lug of a doll, and you're a doll, too."

The words elongate as she mouths them, and they reach Zee's ears distorted but still comprehensible. Ruby's face is pretty hovering over hers, and when her soft lips land on Zee's, the sensation is light and warm, her tongue just a tickle, very unlike Roger's as he also leans in and lays his lips on hers, his tongue thick and heavy, demanding, and distinctly male. She kisses him back, fervently. And then they all laugh more, and Ruby compliments her on her dress, on the way it hangs off her breasts.

"Off your nipples, really."

She has only said what anyone else might think, because the silky fabric accentuates how they have gone stiff and are impossible to ignore, jutting out like eager buds seeking light. Ruby touches her own breasts lightly as she comments on this, but she looks at Roger, not Zee, though Zee's breasts strain even more, toward each of them, toward anyone, if only someone would grab her and squeeze and satisfy the delicious ache that suddenly defines her. Then Ruby's laugh tinkles again and she moves on as quickly as she arrived.

Roger places a firm, guiding hand on her waist and walks her down a corridor and up a long, sweeping set of marble stairs until they reach an even quieter level. He steers her toward a closed door where she hopes they will be alone, and for a moment she believes they have arrived at his suite. That, too, is somehow perfectly acceptable, but the room they enter holds dozens of people. Smoke fills it, and the occupants are in varying states of undress, many of them completely naked, sprawled languorously or chewing at each other openly, and while this fact would certainly shock her normally, she only notes it now filtered through an eerie, but not uncomfortable, distance.

Roger's arm still encircles her, and rather than letting his hand rest at her waist, he cups her breast tentatively. With her dress hardly covering her to start with, she is immediately exposed. She feels a vague need to object and cover herself—sometime, if not immediately—but really, their behaviour is hardly out of place amongst so many others doing the same or more, so the need to protest passes almost as quickly as it occurs to her, and aching need prevails.

A waiter approaches them. He balances a tray of drinks with one hand, and when she makes a half-hearted attempt at modesty, Roger pushes her fingers back and wraps them around a flute of champagne instead. He takes another flute for himself and sips from it.

"Hold this, will you." He hands the glass back to the waiter, who grasps it while Roger leans down and clamps his lips on her bare breast.

Her eyes flicker to the expressionless face of the waiter, who gazes straight ahead and not at her, and then she closes her eyes and gives in to the sensation of pleasure. After what could have been one second or many, she opens her eyes and watches, curiously removed, as Roger's tongue moves in circles. Gradually a feeling of awareness replaces the fog of desire, and she pulls away and covers herself.

The waiter continues to look off at some distant point on the wall until Roger straightens, and then he once again offers the champagne. Roger brushes it aside.

"Take it away," he said. "I don't need it." Then to her, "Are you happy?"

"Me?" Where a moment ago she felt pleasantly spongy, she now feels vaguely but consciously uncomfortable—with their treatment of the waiter, with the level of intimacy, with her own lack of dignity. And with Nellie's brother of all people! She wants to reconcile her conflicting emotions, but her thoughts continue to hover just outside their normal cognitive boundaries. One thing is certain: to agree she is happy will create a shift from acquiescence to approval, and she can't have that.

Rather than answer, she raises her glass and drinks. Off to the side, Ruby winds her way toward them. This time she carries several pipes on a tray.

"I like her," Zee says, turning when she senses that Roger has noticed Ruby, as well. "She's honest. Do you know her well?"

Roger laughs. "She's a hotel whore. Half the women in here are hotel whores."

Chapter 15

She wakes the next morning at seven. Still groggy with sleep, and still thinking like a wife after nearly three months of separation, she reaches over to pull John to her, and as soon as her mind registers the fact of his absence, and further, how it is the morning after the night before, she covers her head with a pillow. What on earth came over her last night? If only the opium had also affected her memory, maybe she could get through the next few days, but how will she ever face Roger when she remembers everything she allowed him to do?

Reluctantly, she gets up and opens the draperies a modest width for fresh air. How can the day move forward so ordinarily after a night like that? Her entire knowledge of herself has changed, and who is she that her inhibitions can be overridden so easily? And who besides Roger witnessed her behaviour? Even if no one else noticed anything, what will she possibly say to him on the train back to Pensacola? And what will he tell Nellie?

The beautiful dress lies draped over a chair, and she looks at it with distaste. If only she'd worn something else, maybe none of this would have happened. She rolls it in a loose ball and stuffs it into her suitcase, and then she chooses her day dress carefully, a pale yellow cotton that suggests decorousness and restraint.

She wants to emulate Nellie, who looked summery and elegant the previous afternoon, in shades of cream and buttery yellow. If only she can look calm and unruffled, maybe she can also project the same impression of nonchalance that Nellie manages.

Zee is most concerned that Roger will try to use this new information to his advantage. He might think he can take liberties she doesn't want and won't allow.

He had his mouth on her breast, for heaven's sake. And she wanted him to! Well, she won't give him the satisfaction of seeing how the experience has rattled her. She'll say nothing about last night to anyone, and if he dares to bring any of it up, she'll ignore him and walk away. She'll leave their house if she has to.

She brushes her hair forcefully and takes pleasure in the sting of bristles pushed hard into her scalp. *She* is no hotel whore, and if Roger thinks she is, he'll soon learn otherwise.

"Over here." Nellie pokes her head out from behind a tall white *phalaenopsis* and waves a trowel in her direction.

Zee smiles cautiously and waves back. The trip home from Miami was not as bad as she had expected. Roger made himself scarce and spent very little time in their day car, and all week he has been absent from the house. Nellie told her yesterday that he was rising early and arriving home late—something to do with an expansion at his chicken-processing plant. Nevertheless, she feels transparent. She approaches her friend with a vague sense of foreboding, and with the knowledge that she will have to talk about what happened with Roger if she wants the discomfort to go away.

"I knew I'd find you with your orchids. I'm surprised you don't sleep out here."

"Sometimes I do—not sleep, but I wait for the nocturnal flowers to open. Some of them are only fragrant at night." Nellie motions around. "Aren't they perfection? What faultless, short lives they live."

"They might be a little less faultless if they weren't trapped in their pots. It's not as though they have any free will to exercise."

Nellie approaches her with a puzzled smile.

"I mean, even a plant must feel the difference between the earth and a pot."

"You may be right. It's possible their roots ache when it rains— all that water, and they only get the little bit I dole out."

"Hmph."

"I'd like to create a twenty-four-hour garden that would tell me the time all night." Nellie's placating words are nevertheless tinged with impatience, as if warning her not to get mired in her sulky mood. "Like Linnaeus's diurnal garden clock, only with flowers that open through the night, as well."

"Dandelions open at nine a.m.," she says, "And close at five. I've retained that much botany."

"Did they open an hour later in 1918 and 1919, when we had daylight saving time?"

"Ha, ha." She can't help herself, she smiles a little.

Nellie points at a cluster of flowers. "Look at them. We'd be a better nation if people said so little and smiled so much." Once again, she encompasses the garden with a sweeping gesture. "Wasn't it Emerson who said, '*Earth laughs in flowers . . .* '? They're like hundreds of painted mouths."

"This one looks miserable." She points at a white rose as large as her hand. "It's as down in the mouth as anything I've seen."

Nellie laughs, beautifully, spontaneously. "You're in a real mood, aren't you."

Zee removes her finger from her mouth. She has been sucking where a thorn stuck it. "For all that, they're still on the attack." She holds her finger for Nellie to see the drop of blood.

Nellie hardly glances at it. "Don't be silly. They attack nothing. They only defend themselves."

For a while after that, they move around the conservatory in companionable silence. Though there are small sections of varied plants—ferns, roses, epiphytes of a type other than orchids—the majority of the space is given over to orchids, hundreds of them, some rare and valuable, others commonplace.

She has always been intrigued by the reproductive columns of orchids, how they combine both male stamens and female pistils. She finds the enlarged labellum, or outer "lip," almost embarrassing in its overt sexuality, yet it is captivating for that same boldness. When they stop to admire a *Cymbidium,* she estimates its two long flower spikes at twenty-four inches or more. Between them, the spikes bear at least twenty flowers measuring two or three inches across.

"They're spectacular."

"They are," Nellie agrees. "And yet some serious collectors hardly notice them any more. They're so eager to find something new, they can't enjoy the ones we've catalogued."

She moves several steps ahead of Zee and slowly makes her way between raised beds. "Look at this one." She points to a *Cattleytonia*, a single flower in the bright clear colours of watermelon and lemon. "It's the purest simplicity." She tickles its middle with a small brush and then moves on to touch the brush to the centre of another flower.

Zee has to comment. "They're a bit erotic, don't you think?"

"Disarmingly so. I suppose you could say I just satisfied both the male and the female."

Zee shoots her a look. "If only we were all so easily satisfied!"

"Only under my skilful touch."

Her skin is a perfect match with the almost translucent petals of a pale pink *Lailia,* and Zee notices the enticing fragrance of damp earth combined with subtle flowery undertones. She wonders if she has caught the scent of Nellie or the plants she tends. Either way, she registers an impulse to find the source and bury her nose in it.

She draws nearer for a closer look at Nellie manipulating the centre of each flower, and when they are both huddled over the same plant, she inhales deeply, trying to reclaim that wafting scent. As she inhales, her chest swells outward so that her bosom presses lightly into Nellie's. For an instant neither woman breathes, and then the colour intensifies on Nellie's cheeks. They stay close, pushing against each other ever so slightly. She doesn't want to move and break contact, but Nellie turns away suddenly and reaches for another pot. She holds it between them to show Zee a new bud.

She has a dozen questions she wants to ask Nellie. Has she *never* wanted to marry? Has she ever loved anyone? Or felt desire for another? Nellie has already told her that she cared for her mother when she was ill, and that she has lived with Roger for the past five years. Is this arrangement all she wants?

She pretends to listen as Nellie points out the singular peculiarities of yet another beguiling hybrid, but she hardly hears a word. Only last weekend she got all itchy with desire around Roger, and now her physical response to Nellie is equally strong. Did her marriage awaken such a strong need that she can't even discern between the sexes? For a moment she allows herself to wonder what she would feel if she kissed Nellie, but then Nellie startles her by placing a hand on her arm.

"You might want to be careful with Roger."

"Pardon me?" She feels blood surge into her face. What has he told his sister?

"I don't know what happened in Miami, but you haven't been yourself since. Roger has that effect on people sometimes. He's unpredictable. He doesn't know when to stop."

"Oh." She feels a wave of relief that she won't have to explain anything after all. "I'm fine. Really. A little more prepared for next time, that's all."

"I don't want you to get hurt. Maybe you won't have to see it, but he has a foul temper."

She shrugs. "Thanks, but I'm not proud of my own temper, if it comes to that."

Nellie turns toward a row of flowering orchids, and with a quick snap of the shears she decapitates a *Dendrobium.* Zee isn't sure what to make of the violent action, but Nellie turns and tucks the flower into her hair.

"Roger tends not to consider others as much as he should, that's all I'm saying. He's always been like that. And desire is a poor judge of character." She levels a meaningful look at her. "That's why I've never given in to my own."

Later in the afternoon, they play a game of tennis. She has decided that her best course of action is to keep her regrets to herself and act as if nothing has happened. She's in a different world, after all, with different rules than those in rural Saskatchewan.

She has only rudimentary tennis skills, but Nellie coaches her and seems not to mind chasing all over the court for Zee's wild returns. When she loses two sets—six to two, and six to one—Nellie takes pity on her.

"Match. That's enough for one day. I'm ready for lemonade."

So they lounge in the shade with sweating glasses of cold lemonade and watch ruby-throated hummingbirds hover over the Christmas berry shrub.

Her heart rate has hardly slowed before she feels a hard ache in the centre of her chest, and almost before she can take a breath, the tightness increases until she thinks the life is being pressed out of her. To make matters worse, Nellie doesn't know about her visions, and even if she could get the words out, what would she say? *Oh, by the way, I'm clairvoyant.*

She sees a flash of Roger, and then she has trouble breathing, is completely unable to speak, and it is too late to warn Nellie or explain what will happen next. She pushes hard on her breastbone with both hands. If the moment of knowing is unpredictable, the discomfort is not, and sometimes when she feels it, she believes that *this* time the pain really has to be caused by heart failure. Surely nothing else could hurt so much. But just when she thinks she must die from the crushing weight, an invisible screen drops down between her and the rest of the world, and she watches the grainy images as if she were there. She loses consciousness of Nellie altogether and sees instead Roger hunched over, clinging to his middle as if in great pain. His face has the strained, grey complexion of someone injured or weak.

"What's happening?"

She hears Nellie's voice from a great distance and then her friend blurs into focus. Nellie grips the table and leans toward Zee. Her face has gone very pale. Zee's lemonade has spilled, and her glass lies shattered on the stones. Zee registers these details, as if she has just awakened from a faint, which in a manner of speaking she has. She still sits upright, but she trembles uncontrollably.

"Are you all right? Is it *petit mal?* What do you need?"

She knows from past experience that her consciousness has been altered for only a few seconds, but even so, everything has changed. The air is too warm and close. Shapes are distorted. Nellie's expression is one of fear as well as concern.

Her tongue makes gluey sucking sounds when she moves it. "Did I say anything?"

"You sounded like you were in terrible pain, and you may have called out Roger's name, but it wasn't clear."

She takes this news in. There is nothing there to help her understand the purpose of what she saw. She has the sense, by way of a cottony smothering of sound, that she has entered a vacuum. She hears her own voice and Nellie's clearly enough, but all the other ordinary sounds of the garden—music from inside, birds, water splashing in the fountain—are filtered, so that she feels at once both able and unable to hear.

"I saw Roger looking ill."

"What do you mean, you 'saw' him?"

In all the years she has had visions, she has spoken openly about them so rarely. To her mother, Rose, and Coulson. But it is a relief to talk to Nellie. "My sister made them seem normal when I was young. She called them daydreams. When she died, they stopped until I was fifteen. Then they came back with this terrible chest pain."

Nellie is the only person she knows who never interrupts when someone else talks, and when she listens, she does so intently, not as if she is merely waiting for an opportunity to jump in. "I saw an old man break through the ice and fall headfirst into freezing water. I could see, and hear, and feel him go under. I'd never seen deep snow, and the old man was no one I knew, so I didn't understand why I saw him or what the vision meant. I tried to tell my mother, but she looked so frightened I couldn't talk to her. And then later, she and my father lived on a farm next to this family in Canada—the Parsonses. I used to go for walks in the snow with their son, Leo. He told me his grandfather had fallen through the ice right there, on their farm, and he described it just as I had seen it when I was still in England."

"Good heavens," Nellie says. "Did the old man live?"

"He did. I even spoke to him, but I learned nothing, except what I already knew—that the vision made no sense at all. Mostly they're like that—meaningless, or after the fact. I've only had one where I might have actually helped someone. If I'm clairvoyant, shouldn't I understand what I see?"

She still occasionally worries that the visions are a sign of mental illness, and she hopes Nellie won't conclude the same.

"You don't know they're meaningless." Nellie has regained her composure completely. Even after playing tennis, and this shock, she looks cool and unruffled. "The Brother XII says we're all portals to the spirit world. Or we have the potential, at any rate. And that we're all utilized in different ways. So maybe he's right. Maybe this has nothing to do with clairvoyance."

"You mean I could be providing passage of some sort? As Coulson does?"

"But for some other purpose. We could read what he says for clarification, because he's very articulate on the subject. And accessible."

She uses the word as a compliment, not as his critics might, slyly, as if they actually mean to say he is *too* accessible, as if everything of value must first be confusing.

Nellie reaches across and gives her arm a gentle squeeze. "Whatever the cause, I think your visions are a fantastic gift."

"Honestly?"

"Of course I do. You may be helping people in ways you'll never understand. What if something happens in the moment of the vision that allows good to come of it? Maybe having that vision when you were young somehow saved that old man. And if it did, what does it matter if you don't understand?"

Zee blinks back tears. It is just like Nellie to accept her reality as something positive and good. The effect on her is that she wants to crawl close to Nellie and hold on like a child. That impulse triggers a memory, and as suddenly as that, like remembering a dream she has long forgotten, she recalls lying in Honora's arms when she was very young.

"Oh!" she says. Memories of her sister present themselves, a flash at a time. Honora running with her in a field. Honora in a nightgown brushing her hair. Honora whispering in her ear. The memories of her sister tumble over one another, and she remembers how inseparable they were. Before now, she saw mostly static images of Honora. Zee waited for her to present herself, she looked on her sister when she appeared, but she never really *recalled* Honora as a living, breathing person. This time, she is flooded with love and contentment.

Nellie reaches out. "Is it happening again?"

"No. I'm fine. I don't think I've felt this happy since I was a small child. You're very much like my sister in that you make everything so acceptable."

Nellie rings a small brass bell. "Let's get you another glass. You should drink something."

A maid appears almost immediately. As soon as she leaves, Nellie turns back to Zee. "How did she die?"

I killed her. And then aloud, "There was a fire . . ."

"I'm so sorry."

Zee nods, and then changes the subject. "We were talking about the Brother."

"Of course. He says we're entering a new age—of Aquarius. We're meant to be more intuitive as a race. You already are."

"Good luck getting the entire human race to accept intuition!"

"You'll have to read him and decide for yourself. Or maybe you'll go to Canada with me and take a look at his Utopia. At least he's beginning with values I can believe in."

"Why do you suppose he chose Canada?"

"It was chosen for him. The Masters designated the spot. At Cedar-by-the-Sea, partway up Vancouver Island. He says it is verdant and mystical—practically an imaginary realm."

She has never been farther west in Canada than the Alberta border, but she remembers everything west of Ontario as flat green or golden planes, iced over with white in the winter, beautiful in their own spare way. "I suppose the coastline could be similar to Seattle's. It isn't much farther north. Though it's nothing like Florida, I can vouch for that."

They both accept a fresh glass of lemonade when the maid returns, and Nellie raises her glass and touches it to Zee's. "We'll have to see for ourselves."

"You're serious, aren't you?"

"I'm going. I've already decided."

She puts her elbows on the table, locks her hands under her chin, and stares until Zee begins to feel that same pull of discovery. What if there really is something to this Aquarian Foundation? Whatever he has written—this man, Wilson, the Brother, XII—he does have Nellie fired up. She's acting as if he's the new Messiah, so there must be something to him.

"When will you go?" If only she could sell a few drawings, it would not be impossible to think she could travel with Nellie.

"I haven't decided. Summer?"

"But you said 'Utopia,' earlier. Do you really think the Utopian ideal is possible?"

"I hear what you're saying—the great, wonderful nowhere we all dream of."

"Yes. Like the end of a rainbow. Oscar Wilde said, *'Progress is the realization of Utopias,'* but I don't know that they're ever realized. Even when one looks attainable, it's not."

"But didn't he mean only that in trying to attain one thing we often learn what we want in another?"

True enough. And what else has she got to do, after all? She has become a bit idle, living this comfortable lifestyle at no personal cost. In coming to Florida, she meant to find a way to put her abilities to good use, and what has she done with them—except perhaps to stop hiding them?

CHAPTER 16

Well before dawn, she wakes from the most vivid dream. She sits up in bed and runs over it again, wide awake now, certain the dream is prophetic. It had that feel—everything so clear and certain, as if burned into memory, and impossible to forget.

She was on a train with a man—the Brother. She has been reading his book *The Three Truths,* and also his collection titled *Foundation Letters and Teachings.* Nellie lent them to her, and the latter work in particular has kept her up at night thinking. And though she can't say what he looked like, she knows it was him on the train. They sat in adjacent seats, leaned toward each other, and he asked her a question, but however hard she tried, she could not form the answer. He waited and waited, until she worried that he would walk away. Finally, the melodious chimes of the dinner bell saved her from having to reply. She can hear them still.

"If I may?" He rose and offered his arm. "I understand they handed up fresh mountain trout in Montana. There's no dinner course better than that. Unless, of course, it's the Wenatchee apple pie for dessert."

Then they ate dinner in the dining car. Everything from the pale striped chair covers to the crisp white table linens looked freshly laundered and starched. She even distinctly remembers the place setting: three spoons, two knives, and two forks, all silver. Silver condiment bowls and a glass water pitcher with a silver handle. Surrounding them, gleaming mahogany panels and arched windows with the shades partly pulled. Above, white globe lights, all in a row.

But he kept calling her Myrtle instead of Mabel, and she wanted to correct him, except she couldn't get the words out, because she didn't want him to call her Mabel, either. He should call her Madame Zee. And then she felt his leg press warmly against hers and he clasped her hands in his, which were very small, with neat, buffed nails. In keeping with his insistence that he is nothing but the messenger of the Masters, she still did not see his face, but she heard him distinctly.

"You have the fathomless eyes and the flawless complexion of a goddess." He reached out and ran a curved finger down her cheek. "You take your beauty for granted, but you are a goddess. You are Isis, and I am Osiris."

The words rang so clear—*You are Isis, and I am Osiris.* Isis: the great Egyptian mother of all, loving, clever, loyal, and brave, mistress of powerful words, goddess of nature; she embodies both magic and nature. Osiris: beloved pharaoh of Egypt, god of agriculture, husband of Isis.

In the dream, she is certain that he means them to govern together, but surely not? And yet she was with him, and they were intimate. What else could it mean? She knows there is no chance of sleeping any more. She must write the dream down and date it, and show it to him when she goes to the colony.

She has already sold more than a dozen of her drawings. Coulson suggested she sell them to members of his congregation. He even bought one himself, a starry sky scene in navy and pink, and he invited others to his house for a private showing, her first. Already she has earned enough money to pay all her travel expenses and more.

Symbolically, would it be such a stretch to imagine herself as Isis, mistress of magic? She contemplates this for a moment and then cringes inwardly. It's absurd. She is clairvoyant, yes, but no "Mistress of Magic." And what about the Brother as Osiris, god of agriculture? He has already created the colony, has overseen the building and clearing and planting. He is already revered by a multitude of followers. Feeling sheepish at her interpretation, and yet excited, as well, she reaches for her notebook.

If she had not met and married John, she would not have known Coulson. If not for Coulson, she would not have met Nellie and Roger. If not for Nellie, she would not be meeting the Brother XII. Absurd or not, the only way to learn what comes next is to remain open to whatever happens, however ridiculous it may seem now.

At breakfast, Roger says, "I'm going out to the poultry plant this morning. Would you like to see what we do out there?"

He is speaking to Zee, but Nellie makes a face and shakes her head at her. "It's horrible. You'll hate it."

In the weeks since the gala, Roger has said nothing of what occurred between them there, and he hasn't, as she feared, interpreted her behaviour that night as open permission to treat her with further impropriety. On the contrary, he has been considerate in every way. He rises when she enters the room, seats her at the table, and has several times complimented her dress. When she speaks, she has his full attention, and more than once she has caught him watching her. As his guest, it would be rude to refuse his offer.

So she smiles brightly at Nellie and says, "My mother always said, 'Any experience is an education,' so why not?"

They arrive around noon, when the heat is at its most unbearable. Three buildings sit long and low, centred in a square of parched land surrounded by wire fence, and everywhere she looks she sees chickens. She has never heard such a clatter, as thousands of them squawk at once.

Roger shows her the hatchery first, where his employees can set twenty thousand eggs a week. "Several hundred baby chicks will be sold right here," he says. "To local farmers."

Some families buy only three or four newborn chicks, while others want up to a hundred at a time, he says, but these sales make up only a small part of his business. The majority of the chicks are kept and grown in the second building to an average weight of four or five pounds. These are broilers, for sale at auction, and it is the broilers that have brought him more wealth than he could have imagined.

"But that's only the beginning. Processing is the future."

Fresh packaged chickens, he tells her, have much more potential for profit than live ones, and this new plant has begun as a small experiment for the city wholesale market, which pays highest of all.

"People in the city don't want to choose a chicken and wait to have it dressed. They want to be in and out of the market as fast as possible. That's the future, and almost no one knows it yet."

Inside the last building, the air is fetid and almost as hot as outside. All the workers look bored and unhappy and like they wish they were not standing on a concrete pad in a sweltering processing plant. But when Roger hands her a cotton overcoat and rubber boots, and dons a set himself, she does the same. Then she balls a handkerchief under her nose and follows his lead, noting that as they approach each station, his employees grow busier at their tasks.

They walk to the far end of the building where live chickens enter, still flapping and protesting, their feet bound together and clipped to a heavy cable strung the length of the factory. The clips move easily along the cable so that workers can slide birds backward or forward as necessary.

"You have more people working here than I expected." She wonders if he notices how strained and tired they look.

She has imagined the factory differently—quieter, cleaner, with only a few employees, and each of those busy over one bird at a time. In fact, the birds move swiftly from person to person along the overhead cable.

"We call this the disassembly line. It's tripled our output," Roger says. He looks pleased with himself. "And we still can't keep up to the orders."

Everywhere she looks she sees a mess of feathers, blood, and other, glutinous-looking bits in piles she carefully avoids.

"See here." Roger nods to an employee working over a trough where the water runs bright red. The fellow acknowledges Roger and tosses her a curious look, but he keeps on with his job, and as she watches, he takes a chicken by the beak with one hand and stretches its neck. His other hand wields a large knife, and he decapitates the unfortunate creature with one quick slice, deftly tosses the severed head into a barrel behind him, and unhooks the chicken from the cable. It continues to flap even as he dunks the neck in the trough of water. The chicken's bowels released when he cut off its head, so when the flapping lessens, he scrapes that evacuation into the water, as well.

Roger raises his voice over the racket. "Come closer." He motions her over where she can see into the trough. "I've devised a system where water fills and drains continuously so the level remains constant but fresh. If you kill chickens at home, a bucket of water will do, but we're processing so many here, he'd soon have more blood than water."

She winces at that. The thought of a tub full of warm blood, combined with the very real odour around her, causes her to press more firmly at the handkerchief she holds to her nose.

When the chicken stops flapping altogether, the man reattaches it to the cable and pushes it along, even as he reaches for another live one. They move on then, to watch as a different employee grabs a drained chicken and dunks it in water.

"That's hot water," Roger explains. "He holds the chicken under for a few seconds to loosen the feathers for plucking. They'll go in that barrel." He points. "We sell them for pillows and feather beds."

She watches as the older man pulls feathers at a remarkable speed and tosses them aside.

"The world record for plucking is ten seconds." Roger gestures toward the line. "He's been with us since the beginning, so he's almost as fast. A beginner like you might need fifteen minutes. Would you like to try?"

Why not? she thinks. How difficult can it be?

Roger motions the man aside, and he smiles encouragement as Zee tentatively pulls a few feathers. They come out more easily than she had expected, but when she finishes a patch, the skin isn't as bare as she'd hoped. She tries picking at a few of the smaller feathers and hairs that remain, but that only tears the skin, so she stops.

"They singe those," Roger says. He takes her elbow and guides her farther down the line, where the chickens move faster from person to person. One man cuts the legs and feet off. Another slits up the back and removes the windpipe and the neck. A third removes an oil gland and cuts around the anus.

She hasn't realized that a chicken passes through so many hands before it touches her plate, and she is about to say so when they reach the eviscerating station. The stench here is strongest of all.

"Wait." Roger motions an employee to stop just as she moves to put her hand inside a chicken, and he nods toward Zee. "She'd like to do it."

"No. I don't think so." She is content to watch, or to move past without watching at all. She has had enough of the chickens, their noise and odour. She doesn't know how anyone can work in such disagreeable conditions day after day, and she doesn't want to consider the sorts of lives that force these people to. For her own part, she has begun to feel so dirtied she doubts she will ever feel fresh again. She could be reduced to this if she's not careful.

"No, Roger, that's fine." She places a hand on his arm to stop him. "Let's not interrupt her work."

"She doesn't mind. She'll catch up. It's the last step before we rinse and package them."

The woman on the line waits. Another chicken joins the first, so now she is two behind. Put on the spot, Zee reluctantly pushes her sleeves up past her elbows, grips the chicken with one hand, and plunges the other inside it, up to her wrist. She doesn't know what she expected, but suddenly she understands, as she hasn't until that very second, that she has reached into the cavity of a creature that, until only a few moments before, lived. Her horror couldn't be more real if she had forced her hand down someone's throat and into his chest cavity.

She makes herself clutch a handful of warm, slippery entrails, wincing as cords and soft lumps squish between her fingers. When she withdraws her hand, the entrails plop out like placenta after a birth, and slime and blood cover her fingers up to the wrist. She clenches her jaw and swallows urgently, willing the contents of her stomach to stay put. She's certain nothing has masked her revulsion, and yet Roger urges her on.

"That's the way. Scrape with your fingers until you get it all." He focuses intently on the activity of her hands.

Once again she violates the chicken. She thinks she is indeed doing something immoral, as if she performs some sick sideshow, and the intensity of Roger's observation causes her to wonder how frequently he stands at this particular table. Just as quickly as she has the thought, she tries unsuccessfully to blot the resulting image from her mind.

"Feel around in there. Get it all."

She hears an extra note in his voice that wasn't there earlier—not excitement, perhaps, but some inappropriate cousin to excitement that she can't quite name. Once again, Roger has pushed her beyond what she knows of herself, into a dark arena of discomfort. She looks down on the chicken, and on her hand fumbling and twisting inside it. Already, high on her narrow wrist, thin red strands have begun to dry.

"That's it." She drops the chicken on the worktable and sinks her arm in a bucket of clear water she has spotted next to the station. "I'm finished." She snatches the stained towel Roger offers and turns away from him.

CHAPTER 17

Nellie slides into the garden chair next to where Zee is sketching, and she smiles at her friend. "You're good," she says, observing Zee's confident strokes, the quick smudges of colour.

"I'd like to draw you, if you'll allow me."

Nellie isn't a vain woman, and yet she looks pleased. "I'd like that."

"But not posed and stiff." She wants to draw Nellie in a way that causes her to admire herself. "I'll draw you at work in the conservatory, when you're at ease."

"How was your tour?"

She adds a couple of quick lines to her drawing before she sets it aside and grimaces. "Horrible, just as you said. If I never see another chicken again, it'll be too soon."

In the clear, bright light, away from the stench, she can almost believe that she overreacted to Roger. Almost, but not quite. She gives Nellie the highlights, including how contrite he was in the car on the way back, and then she changes the subject altogether.

"Roger told me about your father's cigar factory in Tampa." John used to buy hand-rolled cigars, fat, fragrant rolls that contributed to his overall look of success when he played the part of successful banker. It's a safe topic.

"This state is a natural humidor. Our house was always full of people and cigar smoke. I remember talking to buyers from Europe when I was ten years old, during the Spanish-American War. We were at war with Spain, and thousands of young men were stationed in Tampa. My father used to invite them home just to toy with them. He'd pit people against one another, all in fun. He'd have one opinion one day and a completely different one the next, just to stir things up amongst people who couldn't possibly agree on anything anyway."

Zee thinks how different he must have been from her own father, who would never argue with a guest. "Roger says it's a dying business."

"Oh, he always says that. My father was no different with him than with everyone else. He used to try to get a rise out of him. They argued about the future of the cigar industry all the time. And especially about Ybor City. Do you know it?"

"No. Only where it is."

"It has an interesting history. Don Vicente Martinez Ybor was in exile from Cuba. He and Ignacio Haya moved their cigar factories from Key West to Tampa because land was cheap, and he thought he could build an industry there. They attracted thousands of immigrants, not only Cubans, but Spaniards, Italians, Jews, and Germans, and a socialist community grew almost overnight. They built their own hospital, restaurants, clubs, aid organizations, everything. Growing up near there helped to shape how Roger and I view socialism, and it's one of the reasons why I'm so interested in the Brother's colony. I believe people can do more by working together. My father always said the social programs would ruin the business, but now there are over a hundred factories producing more than two hundred million cigars a year. It's the cigar capital of the world. And the Ybor factory is the largest anywhere."

She takes up her sketchbook as Nellie speaks, trying to capture some sense of the animation in Nellie's features. She wonders what Nellie would say if she mentioned her conviction that she is meant to work side by side with the Brother. Would Nellie see it as aggrandizement or opportunism, or would she understand the certainty of her dream?

"Roger sold the factory when my father died. Despite the Ybors, he's convinced the industry won't survive the next economic downturn, while poultry will only continue to grow. It seems to me that both are still thriving."

"How did your father die?"

"Heart failure."

"And your mother?" asks Zee.

"Tuberculosis. You would have liked her. She was lively, and kind, and unlike me, very active socially."

Zee lifts her eyes to catch the depth of Nellie's expression, which has saddened. She adds a few more strokes to her sketch. "Aside from that, you're very like her then."

"I miss her." She cranes her neck toward Zee. "Can I see what you've done?"

Zee covers her work protectively. Nellie should be an easy subject because she looks good from every angle, but there is something unique in the beauty, an element of serene composure that she hasn't caught yet. "Soon. When I'm happy with one."

Later they meet up in the conservatory. She carries her sketchbook and pencils.

Nellie is transplanting a miniature *Cattleya* from a window bed to one in the centre of the room.

"It needs a little more heat at night," she explains. Then she adds, "I received a letter back from the Brother XII this afternoon. He said we can visit anytime we like, but he'd prefer if we waited until summer. They're having their rainy season now. I think he wants our first impression to be good."

"Not two months!" She can't hide her disappointment. "I don't care about a little rain!"

When she reads his literature, she feels as if he is writing directly to her. Just this morning, a couple of lines jumped out at her: "*There is a Purpose, which underlies the surfaces of life; a Power which moulds all outward circumstance to ends invisible.*" She's been feeling that power of late. In the circumstances that brought her here. In the dream that placed her alongside him. She is meant to be there. She must be. He says himself that his message will resonate with some and not others. It has resonated with her, and now she is impatient to be there.

She says as much to Nellie, who reacts with habitual calm.

"He also says to look for truth inside yourself, not in books, nor with priests, but in your own heart."

"It's only that I feel I should be there already," she says. "Have you ever felt like you were being guided by a force outside you? That's how I feel now."

Nellie listens attentively, but she says nothing in response, just carries on attending her plants. This, too, reminds Zee of what the Brother wrote in *The Three Truths*. *Knowledge is born of silence,* she paraphrases silently. *It's not found in argument or insistence, in affirmation or denial.* And there is truth in the statement, for although nothing in Nellie's look or posture is judgmental, her silence causes Zee to notice her own illogic. If she truly is guided, then isn't it possible this delay is also part of the plan?

"The time will go quickly," Nellie reassures her. "It always does."

She hides her irritation. It's not the same for Nellie. She never feels a sense of urgency, about anything. "Did he say if there are accommodations for us?"

"He said not to worry, they'll make us comfortable."

"And how long can we stay?"

"As long as we like. He said everyone contributes as they're best suited. If they have a greenhouse, I'll send a selection of orchids out and tend them. Roses, too. If not, I'll get one built. And he mentioned plans for a school. Will you teach?"

"I learned quite a lot about medicinal herbs when I studied botany. I could do both." Nellie's beauty distracts her; her expression is as content and acquiescent as a Bodhisattva's, and it begs to be sketched.

As if to belie this impression, Nellie says suddenly, "What if the colony really is as Utopian as it sounds? I can't imagine ever feeling completely satisfied, can you? What would we do if there were no more painful choosing between one thing and another?"

As Nellie did earlier, Zee opts for silence, sensing that she is not meant to ask what painful choosing Nellie alludes to. But she wonders, what has Nellie, who seems to have everything, ever given up? She supposes Nellie will tell her, in time. For her part, Zee's always had to choose between the acceptance of others and the exploration of her clairvoyance. And until a few weeks ago, Coulson was the only one she knew who took the occult seriously. Now she has only to attend his services to be surrounded by Spiritualists. She has Nellie, and though she is not entirely comfortable around him, Roger as well, and soon she will meet the Brother and his entire colony and see for herself what place she has there.

"I hope you don't mind," Nellie says, interrupting her thoughts, "but I mentioned your visions to the Brother. He very much wants to meet you."

"Did he say anything else, about why I might be having them?"

"You can read the letter. I believe he said, 'Clearly, she is one of us. Few are chosen. Fewer yet answer the call.'"

Clearly she is one of us. She opens her pencils and brings out her pad of drawing paper. To be considered not odd, but chosen. Even at her age, she still longs to belong. She finds a seat several feet away from Nellie and chooses a pencil.

"Is the Brother married?"

"Good question," Nellie says. "I'm not sure I've ever heard."

She waits for Nellie at breakfast, and after thirty minutes, she checks the gardens. Finally she knocks on the door of Nellie's room, where she finds her friend still lying in her large four-poster bed, propped up on pillows. The sun shines through a crack between the edges of her draperies, and her bureaus and chests are faintly outlined with a gilded glow.

"What? Aren't you lazy today? I wandered all through the gardens and the conservatory looking for you, and here you are still in your nightclothes. I've hardly slept thinking about the colony. I'm all jittery and impatient."

"I'm a bit ill, I think." Nellie pulls the covers over her shoulders and runs one hand through her hair.

"What is it? Do you have a fever?" She cannot see Nellie clearly enough to judge her colour, so she walks to the window. "Shall I open these?"

Before Nellie can answer, Zee pulls the draperies wide to let the light stream in. A palm frond stands out as a dark curve against the pale sky. Birds chirp, and already heat radiates in visible waves off the flagstones.

"Let me take a look at you."

"It's my stomach. I have problems sometimes, and nothing helps. I need to sleep it off, I think."

"You're very pale. Should we send for the doctor?"

"No, please, it's nothing. I'll be fine if I lie here a while. Really."

"Can I get you anything?"

"Nothing. Just don't fuss."

Nellie rarely speaks so sharply, so she hesitates, and then asks anyway, "Are you certain you wouldn't like me to stay with you? I could keep you company."

Nellie shakes her head and closes her eyes against the bright sunlight.

She touches her hand to her friend's forehead. It's clammy but not hot. "I'll let you rest, but I'll check on you later. If you think of anything I can do . . ."

Nellie opens her eyes and pleads silently. Zee sees the question. Why is she hovering when Nellie has already asserted her need for privacy? She closes her mouth.

Nellie rewards her with a weak smile, and her eyes flicker appreciatively when Zee returns to the window and adjusts the draperies until the bed is again in shadow. Then Zee leaves, closing the door softly behind her.

She takes her pad of paper and case of pencils and crosses an expanse of lawn, and then a small footbridge. She knows where she is going, and at last arrives at a remote corner of the grounds, where she sits on a bench in a secluded arbour, out of the morning sun. A small table is situated off to one side, and she pulls it closer.

As so often, too many thoughts tumble through her mind, each jostling another aside so that none holds steady, all of them as insistent as children. *It's my turn! No, mine!* When she tries to focus on one over another, she finds that the thought stutters under attention, and is after all incapable of articulating its pressing need. She counts on her drawing paper to silence them all.

She now has many preliminary and impromptu sketches of Nellie, and she flips through them before she begins afresh. Here is Nellie bent over a flower. There Nellie speaks earnestly, eyes wide. Nellie with head on hand, eyes soft, staring off at something unknown. Each drawing has its own focus. In the latter it is the hand that is important, the curve of the fingers, the oval of each fingernail, all shaped carefully, if quickly. In another it is the intensity in the eyes, the angle of the brow.

Already she has an image of Nellie forming in her mind, can see the expression on her face, and from these disparate poses caught on paper she hopes to form a composite whole that will come alive so that it is no longer only a drawing, but the imagination made recognizably tangible.

She lays a preliminary outline in quick, bold strokes, makes decisions between marks faster than she can blink—the angle of the head, looking left, right, or straight on, eyes wide or partly closed, lips smiling or not, muscles firm or relaxed. She sees each bit as a piece in itself and then wonders that it blends in at all, when the image in her mind disappears and reappears at whim. She adds a curve that's all wrong, that damages the mood all on its own, then quickly removes it with a ball of eraser gum and tries again, more successfully.

After a while, she's no longer conscious of the heat, or the birdsong, or the shadows, or even her own breathing. All that exists is the page and the marks she adds and subtracts. Even her own doubt retracts so that she no longer worries that she can't do Nellie justice, but simply draws her as she imagines her, pausing now and then to flip backward through the pages to consult a previous sketch.

By the time she adds the last bit of shading, the heat is less stifling and the light has changed. It no longer sears into everything, and colours washed out in an earlier glare now reflect vividly. She has missed lunch altogether, and has instead fallen in love with every line and curve that makes up the whole of Nellie's face. She might well have been following her fingers into the hollows below Nellie's eyes, into the cavities of nostrils and ears. She has felt the heavy silkiness of smooth, straight hair, the softness of a cheek, the plump firmness of each lip, now slightly parted in an expression both antic-ipatory and seductive. She knows this face, and she adores it. When she holds her drawing up to view it from another angle, Nellie's eyes follow her. Light reflects off her forehead, the tip of her nose and her chin. Her neck is long, slim, vaguely sinewy, and perfect.

Finally, she has something to show her friend that won't insult her, may even please her in its wholly natural elegance. If she is still unwell, the gift may cheer her, or perhaps she has recovered and is ready for a bit of company, is waiting for her already.

She wanders back across the lawns, and as soon as she opens the door, knows something is wrong. Most of the house staff loiter uncertainly in the hall, and a few of the women sniffle and wipe their eyes with balled handkerchiefs. Everyone looks stricken.

"For goodness' sake, what's happened?"

"It's Miss Nellie." The butler speaks when no one else does. "Mr. Roger is waiting for you in the library."

"What about Miss Nellie?" Everything slows down, and her centre of gravity changes, so she reaches out for the wall to steady herself. Just like after a vision, sound in the room becomes strange and muffled. Clocks stop ticking, feet no longer scuff the floor, and while some of the women still push handkerchiefs into their noses, their sniffles have been silenced. Some sensory registry shuts off all peripheral sound, and yet she still waits for an answer, knowing from experience how it will come—odd and distant through the fog of silence. She clutches her drawing pad to her chest and still no one gives her the answer she already knows. They look at each other blankly, and then at her, until one of them wails pitifully. She turns her back on them and walks down the hall toward the library until Roger calls to her.

As she approaches, he hunches over, clinging to his middle as if he is in great pain. She feels tears on her face and she swipes at them. When Roger stands erect, she sees in his face that the news is terrible.

"My God, *what*? What has happened to Nellie?"

"She died."

He opens his arms and she walks into them unthinkingly, but when he crushes her to his chest and holds on, she pushes him away.

"That's impossible. I saw her a few hours ago." Roger only closes his eyes and shakes his head, so she finds a chair and sinks into it. "She told me she didn't need a doctor."

"Her appendix ruptured. Fatal peritonitis. Her maid heard her scream and called the doctor immediately, but it was too late. He said he should have been called hours ago. She died before he could move her."

"Hours ago?" *She* could have called hours ago. Instead she sat oblivious in the garden.

She pushes out of the library and walks up the wide staircase and down the hall to Nellie's rooms. A lamp dimly illuminates the bed, though it is still afternoon. The draperies remain pulled closed, and the air is sour. Nellie's bed linens and feather bed have already been removed, and the mattress below lies empty. Zee sits on it and covers her face with her hands.

After a moment she feels Roger's hot, heavy hand on her spine. He rubs small circles into her back. His voice, when he speaks again, is dull and toneless.

"I can't believe it. She was fine last night."

"I finally got her drawing right, and she'll never see it. Why does everyone I love die?"

Of course they don't. She admits the inaccuracy as soon as she says it, and yet together Honora and Nellie—the only two people with whom she's ever felt entirely herself—seem like *everyone*.

Roger sits on the bed beside her and pulls her into his arms.

"I had a sister, once," she says. But she only shakes her head when he asks what happened. Instead, she tries to explain her childish disbelief, the great wash of grief, and the ultimately luxurious self-pity—tears enough to fill a bath, and months of rubbing her own thumbnail the way she used to rub Honora's. She hadn't understood at the time how Honora could go to heaven, but she understood well enough that she had been the cause of her going.

She tells him how she lay on Honora's side of the bed and refused to talk to anyone, even her grandmother, who tried so hard to bring her around: Didn't she want to help with the biscuits? Would she like to scrape the cake batter from the pan? Always the cajoling tone, the gentle hand. And, finally, she felt the cold blade of anger—as if someone had openly stolen something of hers and refused to return it. Worse, that someone came back and took William, too.

She can't help but think she could have prevented Nellie's death if only she had warned Roger. And then she remembers something else. That day with Nellie in the garden, the way she envisioned Roger doubled over, just as he appeared in the library moments ago. This thought fills her with such rage that she pounds the bed with a closed fist. What is the point of seeing anything at all if the images only make sense after the fact?

PART III

LIFE

1929

CHAPTER 18

There is a mix-up over which ferry they are to take from Vancouver, and so she and Roger arrive at Nanaimo two hours later than they wish, in late morning.

They have gone only a few miles in their hired car when Zee calls out to the driver. "Pull over here, please." She steps out of the car and lifts her nose to the salty breeze flowing in from the bay below, and then she points. "Look, an arbutus tree." She walks to it and runs her palm over the flesh of the exposed trunk, green-gold and new, where a thin, delicate layer of brittle coppery bark has curled away. "It feels like skin." She smiles at Roger out of politeness, not expecting him to care, and moves to another, thrilled by the sight. Crisp strips of exuviated bark snap underfoot. "They grew along the coast in Seattle, but I've never seen them anywhere else."

"They're quite something," Roger agrees. He surprises her by admiring the broadleaf evergreen, by touching it himself. "The entire terrain is quite something."

He stares off toward the bay, and she stands near him. When has moss ever grown so green? Thick luxurious towels of it wrapped around everything in sight. It covers the boulders at the top of the embankment and clings to mammoth fir trees surrounded by yet more moss, a pea-green foreground for a panorama that slopes steeply down to even more green, the tops of trees poking through wisps of fog parted like tossed veils over emerald waters. Stunned into silence, they move together. He puts his arm around her, and she leans into him, their earlier arguments forgotten. It is not possible, she thinks, for any place to be more magical.

It takes another twenty minutes to arrive at Cedar-by-the-Sea, and when the car finally bumps gently down the grassy lane, she rolls down her window. It is spring, and all around, everything looks new—pale mauve crocuses in bloom, bright green tips on the cedars, and tight russet cones dripping from fir trees. The air is fragrant with cedar and fresh earth, and she inhales deeply. She is in the back seat, straining forward, one hand on the seat in front, eager to see everything.

There are two colonies now, here at Cedar-by-the-Sea and over on Valdes Island, together making up the core beginnings of a universal Brotherhood. She wonders how many of the more famous members have ever visited. Will Levington Comfort has come and gone, she knows, and too bad—as a novelist and correspondent for the *Saturday Evening Post,* she imagines he has an excess of interesting stories, and she would have liked to meet him. James Lippincott, of the Philadelphia publishing family, remains, and Alfred Barley, a well-known English astrologer. She is eager to meet them all, but it is the Brother she can't wait to set eyes on.

Though she has dreamed of him and they have corresponded so openly she sometimes feels that she knows him already, she has come across only one description of him, found in one of Roger's Theosophical newsletters. The author said he is a "small man, wiry, intense, compassionate, and indefatigable in the service of others," but the description left her with no mental image beyond the small brown hands that held hers in her dream. What does she expect? Jesus? Buddha? Coulson? An eye in the middle of his forehead? Now that it is time to find out, her insides are jittery with the possibilities.

He stands facing them at the turnaround when the driver pulls up, and when she sees him, she looks at Roger for his reaction. Excited or not, he gives no evidence of either, but only dips his head and looks out the window curiously. She, on the other hand, feels momentarily deflated. For all his presence and eloquence on the page, there is nothing overtly commanding about the Brother, XII, at first glance. She despises herself for it, but she is again disappointed. He has a trim, neat appearance and a proportionate build—though he certainly is small. She knew he was not a large man, but when she exits the car and approaches him, he barely reaches her shoulder, and she can look down on the top of his head. His hair is flinty grey and parted to one side, and a neatly cropped stiletto beard only accentuates the sharpness of his features.

He wears a tie and a grey suit, well cut and fashionable, as if he intends to look good for them—a point in his favour. She has also dressed carefully for the meeting, in a simple camel-coloured skirt and jacket that shows off her auburn hair. She wears stylish low-heeled shoes and a creamy satin blouse with only a single strand of gold for jewellery. It's all out of place here. Amongst the others, who have gathered in their work clothes, the three of them stand out like celebrities.

"At last." The Brother grasps both Roger's hands and holds them as he welcomes him, and then he repeats the gesture with her, excluding all others while he turns his gaze to her.

His hands exude such energy and warmth that her initial disappointment falls away. She hangs on longer than she needs to, reluctant to release him, and then makes an effort to calm down. "I hope we didn't keep you waiting."

They rose early that day at the boarding house in Vancouver where Bo suggested they spend the night. That is how she thinks of him now—as Bo, her affectionate shortening of *the Brother*. He had assured them that he and his wife, Elma, frequently lodged there, but when Zee and Roger arrived, she wondered if Bo had recommended the place to prepare them for the asceticism of life at the colony. The rooms were all small, dark, and unnecessarily Spartan. Their hosts went beyond frugality and instead gave the impression of outright penury. Narrow mattresses sagged hammock-style toward the middle, the blankets so thin they might suffice as sheets. Rough towels had holes worn through.

After a fretful night, they accepted only tea and dark, disagreeable toast for breakfast, made somewhat more palatable with too-sweet preserves, after which they spent the entire morning on a ferry.

"I've been waiting almost a year," he says now.

His smile is so genuine, his eyes so blue, that when he looks away she instantly feels the loss, as if he has taken back something she just now learned she needs.

"And now you are here." He takes her arm and once again his hand feels warm, dry, and charged with energy. "Come. They're all eager to meet you."

The strength of her physical reaction to him shocks her into uncharacteristic silence. His hand on her arm produces a prolonged sensation of pleasure all along her spinal cord, and when he releases her arm and presses lightly on the small of her back, the result is that she almost stumbles. Do others have this same response?

She has hardly entered the building before a woman approaches and skilfully separates her from Roger and Bo. She will learn later that the Brother separates all couples as soon as possible, no exceptions. The woman is about her age, of similar height and build, with a strong handshake. She is practical-looking, someone who might be capable of any task. Certainly she seems determined to take charge of Zee.

"I'm Gerda." She has the manner of someone who wishes she were somewhere else, but when she positions Zee off to one side of the room, amongst a mixed group, she offers a damp face cloth. "I've brought this for your hands."

Zee uses it immediately, touched to find that it is even warm. She smiles her thanks. "You must travel, to know how grubby I feel."

"I travelled here."

"And what do you think of *here?* It's even more beautiful than I expected."

"I suppose one way or another we all find more than we expect in the end, don't we?" She looks past Zee's shoulder and excuses herself then, abruptly, leaving Zee to consider her cryptic remark.

But others sidle up to introduce themselves. The names and faces slip by—Georgia, Margaret, Alfred. Bruce Crawford, the brawny, brusque one who immediately grabbed their bags. That good-looking boy, Leon, with his two sisters and their annoying mother, Irena. Annie Barley and Sarah Puckett. The latter two women are older and ordinary in appearance, but their names make an impression because Zee hears them one after the other so that they link together in a singsong chant that she repeats silently as she smiles her gratitude. Annie Barley and Sarah Puckett, Sarah Puckett and Annie Barley. Annie Barley and Sarah Puckett.

She glances over to where Roger still accompanies Bo and notices that an older woman has joined them. She is gaunt and slightly bent, her body suggesting appetites suppressed and with-held. She carries wine, so Zee mistakes her for a servant, not remembering that there are no servants here, or that all members do the work of many servants. Another woman follows with stemmed glasses, and together the two pour and distribute small portions of wine.

Something about the way the others hold their wineglasses is ritualistic and odd, and it takes a moment before she can discern what it is that bothers her. Each person cups the bowl with both hands as if the glass has no stem. But for what purpose? Not want-ing to be the odd one out, she holds her glass in the same manner, which elicits eye contact and a brief nod of approval from Gerda. She waits to ascertain why.

They are all so conscious of the Brother, XII, that the moment he lifts his head and surveys the room as if preparing to speak, everyone falls silent and defers to him.

He motions the group—perhaps thirty in all—to gather around him, and then he cups his wineglass as they do. "Peace be to all beings." He raises the glass to his lips and drinks from it, as from a bowl, and then takes it by the stem in normal fashion and turns to Roger.

This appears to be the cue for everyone to parrot him: "*Peace be to all beings,*" they say in unison, and then they each sip as he did. Both she and Roger join them.

"You all know by now how impossible it is to convey a spiritual reality by written or spoken words. All we can do is set the right chord vibrating in the consciousness, and intuition will accomplish the rest. Your intuition has brought you here, partly because we have already met on other planes and sub-planes of consciousness. And remember, the whole process of evolution is the gradual extension of, and unfolding of, consciousness.

"All the planes are within ourselves—potentially. This is what Christ meant when He said, '*The kingdom of God is within you.*'"

He stops to take another sip of wine, and then he gestures toward Roger. "We've met countless times on the spiritual plane, but I never dreamt we'd be reunited on earth."

She looks around to see if anyone else expresses surprise at this revelation. She has read his thoughts on reincarnation, and he is very clear that all consciousness is one, that no single atom is self-subsisting, and that stone, plant, animal, and human are all from one origin. The boundaries separating each from the other only mark steps to increased perfection, Bo says, and wider fields of consciousness and will.

Humankind is imperfect, and so holds a midway place, rising through experience. He likens it to steam rising from a vessel's vent, in an ever-widening column, as consciousness ascends to wider views and reaches formless levels—as unconfined as space itself. Consciousness is life, he says, and nothing that lives can ever cease to live.

She tentatively accepts this. Most Eastern religions take reincarnation for granted, and even if they are wrong, won't the electrical energy in her body—the impulses that allow her to think and feel—won't they take some new form, as well, just as liquid becomes gas, or gas liquid? But this is reasoning, not faith.

She shifts her weight to her other hip and watches the Brother closely. He is a spiritual initiate—someone so advanced spiritually and psychically that he can already communicate with the Masters—but she can't help a small surge of doubt when he says he has met with Roger. Are these "spiritual meetings" in any way like her visions? And if so, what will he say about them? Did *she* meet Roger on another plane when she saw him doubled over before Nellie's death?

But Bo isn't finished. "I knew you," he says, "as the great John de la Valette when you defended Malta against the Turks." He raises one hand, palm out. "You have a scar across your left palm. You may not have known why until today, but I saw you save one of your men from death by catching the blow of a sword with your gloved hand. I've had the privilege of seeing this re-enacted many times."

Roger takes a step forward, and when he raises his large left hand for everyone to see, a pale white gash, clearly visible against the pink of his palm, runs diagonally from his index finger to his wrist.

His expression registers genuine surprise. "You've just made sense of a recurring dream I've had for years," he says. "In it, I march up the side of a long hill in terrible heat. I never knew where until you said, but Malta makes perfect sense."

Bo allows a moment for the inevitable murmurs to subside, and then he lifts his glass and concludes his speech. "For leading the Knights of Malta in a brave defence, and for being the man you are today, each of us honours you. The Masters have instructed: you will be known as the Brother IX."

"To the Brother IX." Their voices echo Bo's as they toast Roger, and then silence follows as everyone sips.

It irks Zee to see some of the members approach Roger with new reverence. But not everyone is interested in contact, and others only direct furtive glances in his direction. She asked Roger about that scar herself, once, but if he provided an explanation, she has no memory of it. And of late, they haven't spoken much at all. Some people laugh more easily the longer they are together, but Roger and she laugh less.

Nellie's death changed everything between them. She was determined to follow through with the plans she and Nellie had made, but in the first weeks after her friend's death, she felt overcome with such lethargy she hardly cared to get out of bed. When she recovered somewhat and explained to Roger that she would leave for the colony, he surprised her by breaking down.

"No," he said, his voice ragged. "You were her closest friend. *We're* friends." He crossed the room to her and opened his arms.

In her embrace, he clung to her and his shoulders shuddered under the flats of her hands.

"Please don't," he said. "It's too soon." He pulled back to look at her, and she couldn't refuse him. "If you'll stay until I get my business in order, I'll come with you."

At some level, she thinks she wanted to be persuaded. Roger was familiar, and though she was certain she belonged at the colony, she didn't want the Brother's first impression of her to be that of a sad, middle-aged frump lacking spirit. She would do her grieving with Roger. She owed him that much. He had lost a sister, and she, better than anyone, knew the pain of that.

But without Nellie between them, silence took on a new, clumsy quality that sent them in search of sound. They resorted to outsiders to put them at ease. Attempting normalcy, they invited guests in and attended parties without pleasure. One night, having both drunk a little too much, the inevitable finally happened.

They didn't fool themselves; they had no illusions, she felt, but sought solace in each other, and while their couplings provided an intimacy of sorts, they had sex purposefully, sometimes fast and cruelly with little or no foreplay, like animals in heat, rolling away after to lie separately, only to come together again with the same intensity. With unbridled libidos they staunched their emotions, and sex became a momentary escape from loss.

Then, in the latter half of 1928, scandal descended on the Brother. On a train between Seattle and Chicago, papers reported, Bo seduced Myrtle Baumgartner, a married woman. The "Isis and Osiris" scandal.

She couldn't believe what she read. He was married, after all. And Myrtle. That was the name in her dream about Isis and Osiris. Immediately, she felt foolish. Had she misunderstood her dream and placed herself alongside the Brother on that train, when in fact the woman was Myrtle all along? Had she dreamed another woman's experience? She must have. And why not? She had experienced her mother's burn, so was it not also possible that she would experience Myrtle's seduction? Usually she would receive information like that in a vision, not a dream, but perhaps that only meant that Honora was right all those years ago, when she said that daydreams were as night dreams, only easier to remember.

At the time Zee had the dream, the meaning had been clear and simple. As Isis and Osiris had governed together, so would Bo and she. But she had it wrong. Bo had meant to place Myrtle at his side. She was willing to bet they even had Wenatchee apple pie for dessert.

For several hours she puzzled over these questions. As straightforward as it all seemed, something still did not sit right. She could not shake the feeling that somehow she played a role herself. Osiris was taken from power by his brother. Likewise, in a court battle that went on for months, some of the founding members stripped the Aquarian Foundation of its society status, based on claims that Bo had misappropriated funds. James Lippincott had brought a second case against the Brother, for wages he claimed had been promised, and his disgruntled secretary had taken him to trial after that. Wasn't it possible that just as Isis did her best to restore Osiris and bring him back to life and power, she is also destined to help the Brother rebuild? That Isis wasn't successful, she refused to consider just yet. Clearly, she was meant to make the attempt.

And poor Mrs. Baumgartner! Zee had pains in her chest when she read the account of the affair in the *Vancouver Province,* one of the papers Roger had had mailed to him as soon as he heard the news. To have become pregnant and miscarried. To have had her husband refuse her when she tried to return to him. The scandal. The disappointment. Zee braced herself for a vision, meditated in an attempt to bring one on, but none came, only further news that many members of the foundation had defected on moral grounds. So then she railed against the defectors. He had only proven himself human, and when had he ever claimed to be anything else?

And were these dissenters responding to the affair or to the article he had recently published, espousing his views on the different types of marriage? In the Brother's view, the most common marriage is one of short-lived sexual attraction, often a sad mismatching of personalities joined in a lifetime contract presided over by the Church and State, dissolved only with shame. That marriages of this sort should be "perpetrated and erected into a national institution is nothing less than a tragedy," he wrote. Thinking beyond her own failed marriage to others she had seen bound unhappily together by law, she felt inclined to agree.

The second type of marriage is one of deep friendship, based on a true knowledge of and affinity for another. A marriage of this type could be highly satisfying, especially if it were not "jeopardized by the imposition of a galling *legal* yoke," he said. The third and highest marriage is between two initiates, such as him and Myrtle. This type of marriage is dissolved at will, and the sexual pleasure of the participants is irrelevant. The marriage is consummated for the purpose of conception, with no consideration of sexual enjoyment, to assist passage of an important and expected incoming soul.

This last idea in particular is admittedly radical, perhaps even far-fetched, and certainly the Brother might have done better to promote these views *before* his ill-timed relationship with Myrtle, but regardless of the timing, he was ahead of his time in one respect. How could anyone, in good conscience, uphold an institution whereby grizzled old men regularly bought girls as young as eleven from their fathers and, as their husbands, raped them with impunity in the marriage bed?

She went to Roger. "He needs us. We can't wait any longer."

Now she sees how pleased Roger is to have arrived, and she is happy for him, despite the chasm that has opened between them. Of late, she has been distant with him, and Roger has responded to her coolness by taking perverse pleasure in annoying her, until sometimes she can hardly stand to be near him. The reasons themselves are often silly. He has grown his facial hair to chest length, and he strokes his beard the way another man might idly stroke his penis, over and over until, irrationally, she longs to snip it off.

He never told her how or why his marriages dissolved, but she suspects he purposefully drove his wives out with a sequence of planned irritations. In company he remains courteous, but in private he picks his teeth and runs his tongue behind his lips to make squishing, sucking sounds that cause her to clench her jaw until it locks. He has frequent moments of flatulence. He burps long and loudly. He taps idly with his fingers, a pen, a glass—anything his searching hands find that can be lifted and struck upon a surface fifty or a hundred times in succession.

She practised merely observing his actions, believing that if she could watch him dispassionately, as a stranger might, she would have no strong reaction, but her attempts failed. Sometimes he merely offends her. Other times he repulses her.

Even now his lips swell loosely, almost obscenely, from between a furry muff of stained beard and moustache, and she moves to turn away, sickened by her own distaste, feeling in her failure less of a friend to Nellie. Now, even more than she needs Nellie's presence, she needs her forgiveness.

But then Bo approaches Roger, and she watches them together. Perhaps, in fact, everything is working out exactly as it is meant to. They share a fervent embrace, and then Bo raises his hand, asking for silence.

"I'd like to welcome a second member to our fold, for she, too, has worked tirelessly as secretary for the foundation. For the past year I have corresponded with her frequently, and I've learned the value of her insight. Please welcome Madame Zee. Henceforth, she will also be known as the Brother III."

This gives her a start. He has conferred the title of "Brother" on only one other woman: Mary Connelly. But Lady Mary, as she is sometimes known, has contributed almost as much to the financial health of the colony as Roger has—some thirty-five thousand dollars, according to figures that came out in Bo's last court battle. Roger has sent frequent donations of five and ten thousand dollars at a time, and he has brought an astounding ninety thousand with him in cash.

She has read the back of her program at the theatre, and she accepts the concept that some will be "Friends" of an organization, while others will be "Donors" or "Patrons," according to the size of their supporting donation. She supposed the same would be true here, that only inaugural members and those who made large donations would ever become honorary Brothers.

So why her? Her only material assets are her meagre savings and the small trust her father set up for her when he sold his farm last year. He and her mother came to Florida to present the money to her privately, before they boarded a ship back to England. Not even Roger knows of the fund, but it is her father's gift of independence. She won't live lavishly on it, should she decide not to stay at the colony, but she will certainly subsist. But Bo must know she is not the one with money.

His pronouncement causes more than a few frowns. It can only be seen as gratuitous, and the others will resent it. At the very least, she will have to work twice as hard to gain acceptance. Nevertheless, she hides her dismay and pulls her lips into an appreciative smile. He could only have done this to please her, so she approaches him with shoulders purposefully squared. Their eyes meet and hold, and then she smiles—the instant where she might have objected gone.

"Thank you. I'm honoured."

Bo receives her and embraces her with the same fervour with which he embraced Roger a moment previous, perhaps even more fervour, for the clinch lasts several seconds. When he releases her, she sees that the woman she mistook for a servant is already glaring with open hostility, and it dawns on her that the dour-looking woman must be Elma, Bo's wife. She has sparse grey hair, worn pulled back in a severe, unstylish roll, and if her body once had curves, no evidence of them remains; her dress hangs like an old man's shirt. The entire membership knows of Bo's affair with Mrs. Baumgartner, and Elma's expression says she perceives Zee as a new threat.

One woman to another, Zee offers her a reassuring smile. In return, Elma's eyes bore into her with an unnatural intensity, so that within a few seconds of Elma's hostile response, she dismisses the older woman as the cause of her own troubles.

Then, as she becomes once again the object of Bo's fixed absorption, she momentarily forgets the others and focuses only on how he has focused on her.

He speaks quietly and takes her arm. "I've been waiting like a small boy to meet you."

She feels vaguely light-headed under his attention, reckless even, ridiculously so.

"Your letters of support have been such an inspiration. The Masters instructed me to send for Roger, but our correspondence compelled me to send for you."

His proximity and the faint pressure of his fingers on her arm distract her, so she doesn't notice that he feels he has sent for them, when in fact they have come on their own as quickly as possible. He stands a little closer than others normally stand, and though she feels she should, she cannot pull away. If anything, she is compelled to move in closer, though she does not, and suffers the sort of instant attraction one learns by experience to distrust. She makes an awkward attempt to change the mood.

"Your wife already has me singled out as someone to watch." She is aware that others have glanced in their direction, as well. "We're speaking longer than courtesy demands."

"Elma?" The Brother shoots a look over his shoulder toward where Elma stands her ground, still glowering. "We never married. But don't take it personally. She's been odd lately."

She can't resist. "Since Mrs. Baumgartner?"

Bo's eyes flick away, and then return to hold hers. "I know you read what I wrote about incoming souls needing an enlightened vehicle."

"Of course I did. You only wanted to impregnate Myrtle for the benefit of the world." She tells herself she is sparring with him in self-defence.

"And if circumstances had been different?"

She can construe his question in any number of ways: if Myrtle had not miscarried, if the members had not defected, if Elma did not exist. If it had been she on the train . . .

She backs away in an attempt to break his spell. "Not too many incoming souls would find me a suitable vehicle, Brother. Regrettably, I've discovered that I'm barren. These days, I only have sex for pleasure."

CHAPTER 19

Alfred Barley approaches and touches Roger on the sleeve. "If you're ready, I'll show you where you'll stay."

Zee moves to follow, but Alfred shakes his head. "I'll call someone else for you." He beckons to Gerda and waits until she lifts her hand to indicate she has seen him.

So she won't be staying with Roger. She assumed they would be housed together, had even worried about how she would disentangle from him now that they had arrived at the colony. But this is good. It will ease them into the separation she desires.

They haven't spoken about it. She hasn't come right out and said, *Our time is up,* but she feels that is the case, and she has little doubt he feels the same.

And so Gerda leads her away from the main lodge. A path takes them through towering, fragrant cedars, past a series of small homes and temporary structures, many of them canvas tents the colour of Zee's suit. Gerda walks alongside her, seemingly uninterested in conversation, and intent on her own thoughts until Zee interrupts them.

"Have you been here long?"

"Over a year."

She tries again. "Have you learned much since you arrived? Is there a schedule of events? Courses? Private instruction, that sort of thing?"

Gerda laughs. "I've learned a lot about work. You'll be on the roster yourself, tomorrow."

"But I assumed I'd teach."

Gerda glances at her as she leads her toward a fork in the path. She gives a little snort. "Half the women here are former teachers. But there is no school yet, and no classes to teach. Everyone starts the same way—on the duty roster. There's a lot to do. And believe me, the work never ends." They walk a short distance farther, and then she stops and gestures toward a tent. "Here we are. You'll want to get settled."

Zee has never in her life slept in a tent, not even while her parents built their house at the farm. "Are there wash facilities? A toilet?"

"There's a bowl for water inside, and the well is over there." Gerda points down the path. "We passed the path to the outhouses on the way here. You'll see it when you walk back. Keeping them clean is one of the jobs on the roster."

"Wonderful." The light is much dimmer here in the trees, and that raises another question. "Is there a torch? A flashlight? Otherwise, how will I find my way back in the dark?"

"There's a lantern." Then Gerda grins, as if she has taken measure of Zee and recognizes her as more vulnerable than she first thought. "You'll be fine. It's a lot to take in at first, but it's not so bad. In some ways, it's everything it's meant to be."

"Only in some ways?" She might be more interested in how it is not.

Gerda shrugs, but when she turns to leave, Zee attempts to detain her. "What do you like to do here?"

"I write poems, when I have the time. The work goes quicker if I imagine them during the day and write them down at night." She shifts her weight on her feet and brushes her hair back from her face, losing some of her distance, softening in her expression.

"What do you write about?"

"They're meant to be philosophical, sometimes metaphysical. I just finished one I called 'Consciousness.'"

Zee is surprised, though she's not sure why she should be. To cover, she says, "I'd like to read them."

But Gerda curls back into herself like a dry leaf, hunching her shoulders and crossing her arms. "I don't show them off much." She gestures toward the tent. "I'll leave you now."

For the second time that day, she walks off abruptly, and Zee is left to face her new home. Tiny spots of mildew freckle the canvas flap at the entry, which she pushes aside to enter. A covered straw pallet takes up more than half of the floor space, and someone has stacked her luggage in one corner. Folded sheets, a blanket, and a pillow sit ready on the bed. So there will be laundry duty, she can count on that. And yet she feels invigorated, on an adventure. She is camping out in the most beautiful spot she has ever encountered.

An overturned apple crate holds a galvanized bucket and provides a makeshift stand for the washbasin. Inside the basin: a towel, a face cloth, and a bar of plain soap. On the floor, a roll of toilet tissue—Waldorf—and the lantern. She laughs aloud. What else can she possibly need?

There is relief, at least, in the privacy of her own space. However simple, it is a place away from everyone else, where she can rest, think, and read in privacy. Were Roger with her, they would have to take turns sitting on the bed to accomplish anything.

So she concentrates on practical and immediate needs. If she waits until after dinner to heft her bucket and walk to the well for water, she will have to search in the dark for something she might not readily locate even in daylight. But instead of moving to leave, she folds her legs and sits on the straw pallet. It is peaceful here, alone, with only the birds chirping outside and the occasional buzz of bees and flies. Besides, she always travels with a full hot-water bottle in her luggage.

She believes this idiosyncrasy could prove useful in any number of emergencies, and though she has never once had an emergency, she has often used her own small supply of water to freshen up between stops. They only crossed the strait today, but she filled the bottle in their Vancouver lodgings out of habit. If she uses the water already in the bottle, she can nap now and find the well tomorrow.

So she washes her face and neck and arms, and finally her underarms. She soaps her hands and scrubs under her nails, which have accumulated a thin line of dirt from the day's travel. Then she wrings her washcloth into the basin and shakes the folded linens out over her pallet. They are nothing like the silky smooth sheets she has grown accustomed to at Roger's, but they will provide a layer between the coarse mattress cover and her skin. She removes her shoes, suit jacket, and skirt, attire which now, in such primitive surroundings, seems almost ludicrous, and she slips between the sheets and falls into a strange uneasy sleep.

She dreams she is deep in the bottom of a ship, where orphan children sleep in steerage, twenty and thirty to each makeshift room, tripping over one another like animals confined to inadequate pens. Adult passengers, those lacking the financial resources that would take them anywhere near a porthole, share the remaining space with equipment and cargo. Don't go *down there*, she hears her mother warn her, for even those without portholes themselves believe that *down there* is the bottom, both of the ship and of humanity.

What she sees and what she knows without seeing get muddled so that in her dream world she knows the ship is nearing its destination even as she sits with another woman on a wooden box in steerage, watching the orphans play. Their mouths open in shared laughter, are still hanging open when coal off-gases explode in the fore hold. Her friend is blown into the air, and a small, stunned child stands frozen in that millisecond when the nervous system strives for a correct response and fails. The little girl is splattered with blood.

Zee's dream self grabs the terrified child and bolts up the stairs. At the top, she pushes the girl from her and then grabs her again, only to drag her along as in her panic she dashes frantically from one spot to another.

She hears a resounding *boom*, like that of a cannon, and feels a second explosion shudder through the thick planks beneath their feet. A moment of woolly, unnatural silence occurs, and then immediately she hears the wailing and shrieks of passengers from below deck as they emerge from every companionway, many of them cut, bruised, their skin blackened and bleeding.

And then, although she was a woman below deck, she becomes also a young girl with her mother. Her mother turns to her and says incongruously, unkindly, *Even a bad experience is an education, darling.* She can't fathom why her mother would say such a thing just then, but as smoke billows out from below in dark volumes, she can't stop to think about it. She runs to her mother's arms.

They watch the captain jump from the bridge, gesticulating and yelling orders to crew members, who sling hoses over their shoulders and carry their burdens down into the smoke, flooding as they go. Some who might have perished get pushed or carried onto the open deck while the captain hurries his passengers toward the ship's rails.

Husbands and wives call for each other and mothers scream for their children. Everywhere people scurry and shout in confusion. Her mother's fingers bite into Zee's waist as she pulls her close and cranes her neck to peer over and around the crowds swarming the deck. Soon some three hundred bewildered people block her view, and still Zee's father has not appeared.

"Open the sluices," the captain yells. "Open the sluices now!"

Then another ship pulls alongside theirs, its horn bellowing, reassuringly large and afloat as their ship settles noticeably lower in the bay. They all press forward in a move toward safety, but

Zee is left behind, and then the boat tilts. The bow rises and the stern sinks so that she slides slowly downward, feet first, while her hands claw at the deck and catch nothing. Something pushes into her chest painfully. She tries and tries to scream, but only the smallest sound rasps from her throat, until, gratefully, she wakes in the tent, sweating, her throat sore and aching. And, oh, her chest. Oh God—her chest.

She focuses on the washbasin. There is no doubt, she has stopped dreaming. And yet an image of Gerda replaces the basin. The other woman lies atop a patchwork quilt, unsmiling, staring at the ceiling, in a simple blue dress that stands out brightly against the darker colours of the quilt. Her skirt is lifted above her waist and her hips and legs are naked below. Roger's fingers are inside her. She doesn't see Roger, doesn't notice anything distinguishing about the hand that fondles Gerda, but she knows it is Roger the way she always knows these things. And then the image fades, and her nightmare is over.

She has thirty minutes before dinner, and an urgent need to find him. She had thought they might drift apart with no need to speak of the change at all, but now she feels a vague, irrational ache at the thought of Roger with Gerda, or anyone else. It's not that she wants to stop him. Ultimately, what she saw is exactly as it should be if she is to be free herself, but he should know freedom is what she wants.

She dresses in khaki slacks and a simple blouse, and chooses low, suitable shoes. As she hurries back along the path toward the main house, she rehearses what she will say to Roger when she locates him. She will tell him that she had a dream, one of those especially vivid ones that inevitably come true one way or another.

"Was it a vision or a dream?" he will ask.

She will say nothing about her vision and will tell him only about the feeling of foreboding she is left with. From there, it will not be such a big leap to suggest that they clarify their expectations.

She has no idea where to find Roger, but she starts back along the path. A forest of fir and cedar, hundreds of years old, towers above her. Some trees are so large in circumference that five or six people with arms outstretched and hands joined might still have trouble circling the trunk. Along the edges of the path, lady ferns grow as high as the little girls she once taught, their arching fronds like ruffled skirts, and behind them, dense patches of shining salal. Above her, and in the woods beside her, birds fill both the canopy and the underbrush with their calls and song. As she walks, she identifies those she can—black-capped chickadees, a ruffed grouse, a Steller's jay. A ruby-throated hummingbird hovers near her head, its tiny propeller sounds accompanying her for several feet before it veers off and disappears into the mottled green backdrop.

She has just decided to abandon her search, to wait for Roger at the Centre, when she hears his voice, deep and immediately recognizable behind one of the larger houses. A pile of rocks, heavy grey fists set one atop another, mark the entrance to a narrow stone pathway that runs in the general direction of the sound, so she walks forward until she spots him leaning against a porch railing. Gerda is with him, her loose dress yellow, not blue as in the vision.

Regardless, Gerda has her head cocked in a coy, flirtatious manner, and Roger has the smug, self-satisfied look of someone pleased with his own performance. He wore the same expression when he first met her, and she half expects to see him pull a flower or a coin from the collar of Gerda's dress.

When she sees them together, her breathing becomes shallow, and she can't immediately move, even when Gerda and Roger instinctively turn. They both notice her at the same time.

"Zee! What are you doing here?"

"You're staying *here?*" Her astonishment is more than a necessary cover-up. Compared to her tent, the house is luxurious, a charming cottage with a gabled roof and eight-paned casement windows. "I'm in a bloody tent."

Gerda glances at Roger. "I'd better go. I'll see you both at dinner."

The way he watches her walk away suggests a future Zee has already predicted. And then he turns and motions with his head, inviting her inside.

The front half of the cottage is essentially one large room, with a stone fireplace dominating one wall. Her small tent wouldn't crowd the area around the hearth. A couple of easy chairs and a sofa face the fireplace, but aside from that and a table and four chairs beside a window, there are no other furnishings. Only plenty of warm, dry space.

"There's not much to it, is there." He points to an interior door. "The bath is through there."

"You have a *bath?*" She forgets why she has come. The disparity in their lodgings is too great.

"Don't you?"

"In a tent?"

"Right." He has the decency to look chagrined.

"Where's your bedroom?" She wants to see if the covers match the patchwork quilt in her vision.

Roger takes her down a short hall. "Three small bedrooms, right here."

She peeks into the smallest one and then the second. Each contains a single bed and not much else, and then she stops at the doorway to the master bedroom. "This looks comfortable. Nice bed." A plain brown coverlet hides whatever blankets lie beneath.

"Yes. I took a nap. It's as restful as it looks."

She walks over and sits on the bed. "If you had a nap, who straightened the covers?"

"I'm not completely inept."

She raises her eyebrows and fingers the coverlet, wanting to flip the edge up to expose the blanket below. Instead she smoothes her hand over the rough cotton.

"Gerda made it up for me. That's why she was here, to see if I needed anything."

"Oh, just forget it." She jumps up and pushes past him. "I wanted to talk to you, but it can wait."

At the main path, she turns in the opposite direction from the Centre, where she is expected for dinner. It is unthinkable to isolate herself so early, to make herself both unpopular and easy prey by not coming to dinner on her very first night. Nevertheless, she can't face the others until she cools off.

"Offer my apologies," she says, and without waiting for Roger's response, she takes the trail to the beach.

Her pace is furious, and she reaches the water quickly. A cool breeze causes her to wrap her arms around her middle.

What difference does it make if he wants Gerda or not? She's not about to have it out with him in some horrible exchange of accusations. Why didn't she say what she had come to say and leave with dignity?

She picks up a flat stone and tries to skip it in the waves. It sinks as soon as it touches water. Because he's so damn self-satisfied, that's why.

CHAPTER 20

Work in the kitchen, as everywhere else, begins with an affirmation: *Today and every day, I align myself with the source of all that is good and true and powerful. I leave my personality aside, to work in harmony with others for the good of all.*

It is not so much a prayer, the Brother says, as a reminder that each of them is here as part of an elite group—in effect the gentry of mind and spirit—charged with carrying out the wishes of the Brotherhood.

There are many rules, never set out in a list, but demonstrated and enforced. In the kitchen, hair is coiled under a white scarf at all times, and white, starched aprons worn. All cloths, sheets, napkins, and towels are folded in a particular manner: in half lengthwise, in half again, and then in three equal parts. Pans are oiled before they are put away, and arranged according to size. Food is stored so that always the freshest is at the back, the least fresh at the front, and all labels face forward. Ingredients for a recipe are laid out first, and then added as necessary to a dish, never found and tossed in as needed. Water glasses are filled three-quarters full. A stack of bread may be eight slices high, no more. One dozen toothpicks should be placed in each pewter holder. Potatoes and vegetables are cubed to one inch. Floors are swept and washed after each meal. Meat must begin circulation from the north end of the table, dairy from the south, and all food is rotated counter-clockwise.

At first, she finds these rituals time-consuming and illogical, but constant exposure causes her to recognize them for what they are: rites of practised conformity, and then she watches with interest, and concern. When she is no longer the newest member and can observe others who come after, she notices how these small movements toward compliance change people, and she sees that when there are so many rules, only some of them practical, one stops requiring explanations and simply does as one is asked. And because not all of the practices are unreasonable, it is possible to believe that the less comprehensible acts might actually be justifiable, too, if only someone had time to explain. As time passes, whether a task is reasonable or not becomes less important than that it is performed according to expectation, because when it is performed correctly, every once in a while someone offers a bit of praise, so that praise becomes a replacement for rational thought.

With a growing sense of alarm, she catalogues the changes in herself. She holds her wineglass as the others hold theirs. She sits in her prescribed place at dinner, never thinking to sit anywhere else. She counts out toothpicks, rises at dawn, chants when others chant. *Watch it,* she warns herself.

It is a Monday, so there are six of them on household duty this morning—Sarah, Annie, Margaret, Irena, Mary, and herself. She is responsible for the day's bread and pastries. Sarah and Annie are peeling and chopping vegetables, Mary sews in a chair by the window, Margaret irons, and Irena flits in and out noisily as she cleans the other rooms. Earlier, Zee ground grain with Irena, and in the first ten minutes of work she disclosed that she was once a stage actress and starred in *A Parlour Match, Papa's Wife,* and the silent film *Madame la Presidente.* She has an ability for the opera, as well, she said, and that was proven when her son came looking for her. As soon as she saw him she burst into song and then suddenly stopped to quiz him.

"Leon! What am I singing? Quick, quick!"

"Puccini, Mama." He pronounced *Mama* in the Spanish way, with the accent on the last syllable. "It's *La Bohème.*"

"Good boy. You make your mother proud."

Zee has noticed that others watch Irena with a slight, wary smile on their faces, as if she is a strange specimen that may be poisonous, and about which they haven't quite made up their minds. She might have been merely vivacious once, but at her age, such exuberance and hysterically urgent tones are exhausting, meant only to draw attention back to her when it moves elsewhere. It is simply not possible that everything from a light spatter of rain to the colour of the surrounding moss can be a matter of such extreme agitation for her.

"Oh, look!" she shrieked yesterday. "Children, look at the cater-pillars! There are caterpillars all over the walls!" She was still shriek-ing when Annie grabbed a broom and swept them off, small brown streaks commemorating the fate of those that didn't survive.

Now she rushes into the room and bends near Zee to retrieve a cloth from a drawer. Zee hears something fall and roll along the floor, but by the time she sees what it is, Irena has already gone again. She retrieves it, a pretty little pocket sewing kit etched in a floral pattern. But holding it, she feels suddenly very sad, to the point of tears. The kit belonged to Irena's mother, and she sees her suddenly. Her name is Prudence, and she is very beautiful, with fine bones and dark hair piled in coils atop her head. She died young, Zee thinks, and then she sees horses and feels such terror that she immediately drops the kit into her pocket, wanting only to be rid of it.

"Are you all right?" Sarah asks.

Zee glances at her, and out of habit hides her anxiety. "I'm fine. Why?" She wonders if her face is as flushed as it feels. Part of her wants to reach into her pocket again. Another part recoils from the object there.

"You've been standing in a stupor. I'd like to use the table when you finish."

Her tone says *if you ever finish,* and Zee feels a twinge of irrita-tion. She folds the bread dough over on itself and nods. "I won't be long."

She glances at Sarah again, but the older woman has gone back to chopping potatoes into small cubes. She is the eldest of the women, in her seventies, Zee guesses, with silver hair and a frail body. Like Zee, she was a schoolteacher once, and she was lonely before she came here, Zee guesses. She must have imagined life at the colony as a sort of family, to replace the one she had missed out on.

And what has Zee missed out on? Children, like Sarah, and what else? A happy marriage. Good friends. As she turns the dough, she tries to recall exactly what the Brother wrote in *The Three Truths*:

What is it that everyone seeks so madly? What drives them headlong through the days and years, without rest, without ceasing, lacking pity? Only one thing, under many guises. One person might want love, in the form of family, or a great beauty to hold or possess. Another seeks fame or power. Some desire wealth and strive for it, forgoing the gift of leisure, companionship of friends, of books, of nature. Others cling to faith, narrow and fanatical with unenterprising minds, warped by tradition, their vision of truth distorted, hating knowledge lest it spoil "belief."

However anyone defines need, they're all after happiness, in the end. But attaining the heart's desire won't quell need; it is merely reshaped, re-formed. That's the paradox.

But all truth is paradox, he says, and he urges readers to strive for that which is already within themselves. They must become that which *is* themselves.

Whatever that means. Whenever she reflects on this, on becoming that which *is herself*, she understands clearly what he means for about a fifth of a second before the meaning curls away from her again, like a ribbon twirling on a gust of air. She attempts to hang on to that brief understanding, or lack of it, in this way: if there is her real self—which *is* her—and her self-image—a figurative, constructed, and constantly changing template that should, but doesn't, fit exactly over the real self—she believes he means that the more the two align, the truer her life will feel. If that is the case, contemplating and striving for that alignment, rather than for a myriad of other imagined needs, will render "happiness" irrelevant.

As she forms the dough into ten separate loaves and puts each loaf into a heat-blackened pan, she thinks that these moments—the visions, the glimpse of Prudence she just experienced—bring her closer to becoming that which is herself, because it is in these moments that she feels most excited and alive.

She touches the item in her pocket and the sadness she experienced earlier returns, and with it, the thrill of discovery. She remembers that in her father's pawnshop she occasionally felt that when she held an item, she knew something about the person who owned it. But these feelings about Irena and her mother are stronger, and much clearer, as if they have been boosted and amplified. By age or experience? Because she is here at the colony? Or possibly because her practice is finally paying off.

She lines the bread pans up on the table and inhales the yeasty scent of their contents. The loaves are lovely and elastic, already plumper than when she formed them. She sets them in a warm, sunny spot on the counter, covers them with a damp towel, and checks the roster for her next task. Windows. But not for a minute or two.

She catches Sarah's eye. "I'm finished. It's all yours."

﷼

"You dropped this." She holds the pretty sewing kit up for Irena to see. She has found her upstairs, sweeping the bedrooms.

"Did I lose that again?" She speaks at twice the volume Zee does, and then laughs as if it is a big joke. "I swear that thing jumps out of my pocket."

Zee steps back as Irena takes the kit from her. Irena has the annoying habit of standing too close to people, so Zee must either step back or collide with a heavy shelf of partially clad bodice. "Have you had it long?"

"Forever," Irena yells. "I always have it with me."

"It was your mother's."

That slows Irena down. "Why do you say that?"

"My mother had one something like it." And immediately she regrets the response. She's *here.* She shouldn't have to hide who she is.

"She died when I was young, and it's one thing I can keep close to me."

Zee takes a breath. "That's why I felt such sadness around it."

"What do you mean?"

"Just that. When I picked it up, I almost wept. And then I saw a beautiful woman. Prudence, I think. And a horse." Irena stands silent for the first time since Zee met her. "I got the sense she died on a horse."

"It's true."

"Were you her only child?"

"Why do you ask?"

"Her last thoughts were of you. I'm certain of it."

279

For all Irena's usual theatrics, she makes no sound now. She holds one hand to her heart; the other clutches the sewing kit. Then she recovers. "How do you know all this?"

"She had her hair in coils, and she wore a green riding skirt with a brown jacket. Sometimes I see things."

"My God." Irena sounds shrill, more like herself. "You really did see her! We kept those clothes in a trunk for years." Now she clasps both hands to her chest and moves closer to Zee. "You said her last thoughts were of me. What were they?" She holds out the sewing kit. "Do you need this?"

Zee moves back and shakes her head. "I don't know exactly. There was the word *Izzy*. And the sensation of great love and sorrow. I wish I could tell you more, but that's all I have."

Except now there is something else, just the briefest image in her mind, not about Prudence, but about Irena's husband, Fernando. She sees him with his hand cupped over the breast of Irena's oldest daughter, Verona, and she feels Verona's fear and confusion, mixed with a surge of arousal.

"My mother called me Izzy sometimes."

"Well." Zee turns aside, almost angrily, at a loss for words. Why does such troubling knowledge have to find her? Why not someone else? Someone who might know how to respond to knowledge of this sort? She can easily imagine how Irena will fly apart, fly at her, if she dares to put this new image into words. But for Verona's sake, she can't keep quiet either, can she? She lifts her hands and gestures unhappily.

"That's it then." She struggles for something more. "But I get the sense she's proud of you. She sees you."

"Thank you!" Irena throws her arms around Zee and squeezes her tightly.

Tentatively at first, and then with more feeling, she returns the hug until she finds herself holding as tightly as she is held, and when they step back, she smoothes her hair back from her face, wipes her hands on her apron. She opens her mouth, hoping the right words will come out of it. But as so often happens, Irena beats her to it.

"Imagine, you telling me all that," she says. The cackle is back in her voice, and she waves Zee off as she returns to work.

Somehow the sound irritates Zee less than it might have an hour earlier.

At dinner that evening, the Brother, XII, chews thoughtfully on a slice of bread. Between two bites, he waves it at the group. "Who made this?"

Zee fakes indifference, even as she awaits his criticism. "I did. It's a little on the heavy side, I admit."

This morning when she returned to put the loaves in the oven, she found the window open alongside where they rose. The kitchen was not hot, and there was no reason to open a window, but she was too late. Someone—Mary? Sarah?—had either inadvertently or purposefully allowed the cool breeze to make the dough somnolent, and as a result, the loaves did not rise properly. The bread is heavy and dense.

"It's perfect," he says. And then he holds her eyes a little longer than usual. "Like my mother used to make—more substance, less air."

Later, she notices Fernando checking something under the hood of his Model T Ford, recently signed over to the Brother. She walks close, and waits until he lifts his head to throw her a questioning glance. When she says nothing, he straightens up and smiles flirtatiously. He's a good-looking man, as fit as a teenager, and she can understand why Irena was drawn to him.

She knows nothing of their marriage now, except that they both have a knack for turning the most ordinary statement into sexual innuendo, and that they're eager to hug almost everyone except each other. They both look hungry and predatory, as if whatever they need they have not found together.

So when Fernando lifts a greasy hand and seems about to put it around her waist, she says what she has come to say with no prelude, and no apology. She doesn't always interpret what she sees correctly, so she is well aware that she could be wrong—but in her heart, she is certain she is not.

She holds up her palm to keep him at a distance, and she looks directly into his eyes. "If you touch Verona again, I'll cut your penis off in your sleep."

The look that flashes across his face tells her all she needs to know, and one more thing: he believes her.

CHAPTER 21

She stands under a Douglas fir and waits for the shower to pass, a short respite from the back-breaking work of rock picking. Since dawn she has been at it. She stoops over, loads as many stones as she can carry into a bucket, straightens, stretches, and carries the bucket to the edge of the field, where she distributes the stones in a drainage ditch. Then back into the field for more.

Her fingernails are jagged and broken, the dirt under them impossible to remove completely, even with scrubbing. If her mother could see her now, she would weep, and there have been days when she has wondered if she is mad to be here. Some of the Brother's ideas already irk her, and the work required is unreasonable by any standards, but she is withholding judgment for the moment because when she pushes past this external discontent, she has to admit that the hard labour soothes something restless within her.

She hears his voice now when she works, the voice of the meetings, of his Letters to the Members. *If you want to find Spirit, find it in the rock you pluck from the field.* And if she's not exactly *plucking* rocks, which implies an eagerness she doesn't feel, she has been hauling them away with a certain amount of pride. There is urgency in doing, and an afterglow of satisfaction that accompanies physical exhaustion.

What they are meant to learn through their labour, she thinks, is that the job most likely to lead to inner peace is the job at hand. Any work is right work, if one approaches it with self-awareness.

As if thinking of him has caused him to appear, he walks purposefully toward her now, in the rain, and all thoughts of inner peace are replaced by skittering sparks of awareness. Although she avoids looking at him directly, she follows his progress peripherally. It has been like this since the first day. She dreams of him. She senses him before he arrives. Thoughts of him sometimes overlay every other thought, so that she feels irrational and obsessed. What is it about him? The strength of her infatuation embarrasses her. It is unwarranted, and wrong. Foolish. Adolescent. And necessary. Just this morning she woke from a dream of him with a solid pulse between her legs. She even touched her cheek, where she still felt the goodbye kiss of her dream, warm and light, and checked the flap of her tent for movement.

Now, unlike the rest of them, he is clean, and he carries an umbrella, a smart black one, as if he is a country gentleman just stepping out for a stroll.

"Good work," he says as he comes up to her. "Wherever I place you, in the kitchen or the field, you work without complaint."

She masks a surge of pride, mindful of his reminder that the personality is nothing—the work of the Masters, everything. She swipes her face with the back of her hand, hoping she's not just adding streaks of dirt where she means to remove them. "Thank you," she says. "There's a lot to do, and I'm happy to do it." If that's not completely true, it does feel like the appropriate response, and she offers it decisively.

She has been at the colony two months, and in that time she has chopped firewood, cleaned outhouses, painted, cooked, done housework and laundry, picked rocks, dragged stumps, and weeded a garden—one of six.

She hasn't complained—she has seen Bo's impatience when anyone complains—but she hasn't stopped thinking, either. She may be developing an appreciation for hard work, but she doesn't plan to do it forever.

"I've been considering your interest in plants," he says now. He broaches the subject as if he's thought of it on his own and is unaware that she's been trying to steer him in that direction for days. "And I've decided that we're wasting your talents out here in the fields. I want you to plan an apothecary. To gather whatever you need. Dry the plants. Bottle them. We'll keep them in the small room off my office."

Yes, finally! On several occasions she has mentioned her former interest in botany, and last Thursday as he walked with her to her tent, she pointed to an odd sponge-like mushroom. "That's a black morel. They're edible, and highly prized as a delicacy. We should be eating them. Or selling them." Earlier in the week she had offered him a handful of dried kelp. "It will lower your blood pressure."

So now he has made the decision she hoped he would—that while back-breaking work in the fields will occupy her as rightly as any other, her skills may be put to better use. She rewards him with a warm smile and a light touch on the sleeve. A room off his office is perfect.

"When do I start?"

"Now," he says. And then he turns his umbrella over to her, despite the fact that he is dry and she is already wet. "You'll find me upstairs after you've cleaned up."

She isn't blind to the resentment in the eyes of the others as she walks past. But she has not done anything any one of them could not also have done, and she wishes they, too, would take the initiative. After all, if everyone were really working according to his or her greatest talent, wouldn't there be far less resentment?

She is partway up the stairs when the pain in her chest starts. Not knowing how long the vision will last, Zee sinks down onto one of the treads. She sees a woman—a beautiful woman with straight, dark hair—clutching a large fir cone to her chest. Someone has painted its edges gold and silver, so that it catches light and reflects it like mother-of-pearl. The woman, who has a childlike demeanor, holds her treasure out to someone in the uniform of a hotel chambermaid.

"I found it on the stairs," she says, "but you might as well have it. They'll take it from me if they know I like it. They take everything I like." Her voice, too, is very childlike.

The chambermaid, plump and rosy, twentyish, examines the pretty cone. She looks into the woman's eyes, and then she produces paper and string, and together they wrap the cone and mark it.

"You see, now it says right on it: *For Myrtle.*" The girl places the package under the Christmas tree. "No one who's got a heart at all will take away a gift put under the tree."

The woman—Myrtle—runs outside then, into the woods in slippers and dress. Zee sees as if through her eyes, and everywhere she turns things are gnarled and twiggy, covered with trailing wisps of Spanish moss and bark mould. Branches tangle and arch, and above her, curled dead leaves, cracked and stained as old cups, fill with snow. Even the evergreens loom wet and black, as if she views everything in grey tones and has forgotten how to get caught up in colour.

She picks her way, haphazardly, through the darkening forest, stopping to chastise squirrels that retreat up trees to scold her.

"Shush," she says, putting her finger to her lips.

And then Zee feels her clothing as Myrtle must have, as a sudden constriction that means to bind or even strangle her. She sees Myrtle tear at her collar and her buttons, open her dress to the wet flakes so that they melt as they land, and run in tiny rivulets between her breasts. She feels the wet trickles. She feels how Myrtle wants to cleanse herself, and watches as she removes each article of clothing, first her dress, then her underslip and brassiere, slippers and stockings. As each item comes off, she folds it neatly and piles it atop the last at the base of a tree.

When she is naked and the cold nips at her, she stands confused, her arms wrapped around her chest, less for warmth than to cancel out breasts too firm and abundant, a useless luxury if she cannot use them to mother. Tears pour down her face as she tries to remember what it was she wanted to do next.

Still badly shaken, Zee doesn't immediately tell Bo that she has envisioned Myrtle. The woman was too sad, and Zee felt her pain too acutely, to have it all explained away as neat as can be, which is what she believes Bo will do.

She has learned from the other women at the colony that after Myrtle miscarried, Mary Connelly took her to a hunting lodge for the wealthy and famous, located on Sooke Harbour, off the Strait of Juan de Fuca. They arrived just before Christmas and waited there while Mary made arrangements for a nurse to accompany Myrtle to Toronto. It is likely that the forest she just envisioned Myrtle in is the land surrounding the Belvedere Hotel, but she'd like to know more before she brings the subject up.

"I just had an odd feeling," she says, to cover and provide an explanation for her shaken appearance. "Like I do before a vision, but it passed."

"When you have visions, do you see the past, or the future?"

"A little of both. Sometimes I think everything we do and think is as available to others as a conversation on a party line, should they pick up the receiver, and who knows who's listening? It's a bit disconcerting. "

"We're all potential channels," he says. "Both in and out, though most people aren't aware that they are. There was a time when divine knowledge flowed through us at all times. Now we're provided with brief glimpses, but the glimpses originate in the divine, and we yearn for more."

He moves a stack of papers off a red armchair and motions to it. "Most people misunderstand the scriptural allegory of Adam and Eve and take it literally. But the garden was the astral world, and we were excluded from it when we fell into matter. Before that, all knowledge came to us as you sometimes experience it, as a faculty of general awareness. We *knew,* but there was no need to question why."

Perhaps, she thinks, feeling a prick of impatience with his explanation, but what caused this alleged fall?

Certainly his suggestion of a more generalized awareness is appealing, but how is a fall from the astral world any different, really, than a fall from the Garden of Eden? Either way, he's saying humanity made one monumental error that changed everything, and while that's not impossible, wouldn't it be more likely that intellectual change happened over time? She opens her mouth to ask, and then closes it when he lays a hand on her arm.

CHAPTER 22

Meetings in the assembly hall are rarely held unless there is a problem, and tonight's problem is larger than usual. Some of the members have hoarded bits of their monthly allowance in an attempt to accumulate savings that will allow them to leave. An hour ago, she overheard Bo tell Bruce Crawford, "I want everyone here. Spare no doors."

The disciples are slow to arrive, but eventually they sit before him, most of them still unwashed from the day's work. A few look as if they're about to drop. All in all, they're an unkempt lot, and all look wary and concerned.

He begins without preamble, only a long look of great disappointment. "Personal wealth is of no use to you. Search through your hearts, think your own thoughts. Keep an open mind. Do not be swayed by others. This is how you find Truth. Truth never resides in money or things, books or priests, but only in your own heart.

"Buddha knew the value of non-attachment, and Jesus, and all the other great prophets, as well, and I am telling you now: *you,* too, must know it before you can advance to the next plane."

Whenever she sees him with the others, she marvels at how well he times each word for maximum effect. It is dizzying sometimes to watch him hold the others captive. Every eye is on him, and no one looks away. There is a magnetism about him that she can't explain, an energy she feels every time she is near him, and especially when he touches her, but it is more than that. Perhaps he offers each of them an opportunity to realize a vision of themselves they could never imagine without him. And yet, sometimes she believes the others fear him. Other times she thinks it's more that they want his approval so badly they yearn for it. Certainly when he turns his smile on her and says, "well done," she experiences a sense of accomplishment she does not with anyone else, and that's partly because his approval is so difficult to get. When praise doesn't come easily, it becomes a reward in itself.

Wisely, now, he chooses not to rail at them, but speaks to their consciences.

"For your own good, you mustn't hoard a single penny. Hoarding jeopardizes not only your own spiritual well-being and future but those of everyone around you. You must strive to forgo the personality, the individual, and you forget that. If you're saving to leave the colony, as I know some of you are, if you're certain you are not one of us, then come to me directly. I'll give you money, as I've given you everything you need, according to the Master's wishes."

He makes eye contact here and there. Many look ashamed. Despising herself for it, Zee longs for even a quick glance.

He walks to the table at the front of the hall and reaches for the Bible lying there. It is weathered and well thumbed, and he lifts it over his head. For an entire minute he holds it still, and then, just when tension is at its highest, he lowers his arm, finds a marked page, and opens to it.

"Joshua 7. You will remember Achan, who was a soldier in the Bible. Achan went off to war with instructions to bring the spoils back for God. Instead, he kept some for himself. He kept two hundred pieces of silver, a bar of gold, and a valuable robe from Babylonia. He hid them under his tent because someday he would need them. But when things started to go bad in Israel, God spoke to Joshua about the cheating. Achan was found out, stoned to death, and burned. His family was killed, his cattle and his land destroyed. Those few items he kept cost all their lives. And what was he trying to say? That he knew better than *God* who should own what?

"Is that the message you wish to give the Spirit you've been sent to assist? Like Achan, you have insulted the Spirit of Grace, and the Masters are not pleased. Achan's mistake has been preserved so that we might learn from his error, and I'm warning you now. Come forward and declare everything you've held back, or be like Achan, and you *will* be struck down."

He slaps the Bible shut and stands at the front with crossed arms. Zee is amazed that within seconds, they begin to approach.

He motions to her, and asks her to make a written record. First the Jeffersons come forward, and then the Barleys, until one by one they hand over whatever cash they have—some even promising to go home for the rest. Some disappear right then and return quickly with banknotes or coins dangling in a sock or rattling in a tin.

When they have all left, she stays behind and hoists herself up so she sits atop the table, where only moments before she recorded the amounts each disciple turned over. All of their cash amounts to less than one donation cheque she saw on his desk this morning. She is troubled, too, by the way he frightened them. He began with sympathy and ended by terrorizing them.

"Would you really give them money if they came to you and said they wanted to leave?"

"Of course. What would be the point in keeping them?"

"How much would you give them?"

"Enough to get them off the island. A little more, perhaps. They're resourceful. They'd manage."

"But they've turned over their life savings!" She is stunned by his lack of generosity.

"You're forgetting why they turned it over. This is renaissance work. Not child's play, but crucial to the survival of the species. It is the most important work occurring in the world right now. Discipleship is a choice and a decision that no one should make lightly, and a donation is a commitment to expenditure, not a deposit in a savings account.

"I told them when they joined that they could have no other allegiance, to any other group or teacher. Who wouldn't be confused if their teacher said one thing and I said another? And the desires of the outside world might as well be another teacher, for it pulls them in a direction that is not of us."

From what Zee has seen, the colonists are mostly intelligent adults. Their doubt and questions would only confirm that. But she supposes he has a point. How would the Catholic Church respond if on Monday, the parishioners asked that their Sunday offerings be returned? A compassionate priest might do exactly as Bo has suggested and give some small amount. A less compassionate one might turn them away with nothing.

And it makes no difference to argue that their gifts are larger than a Sunday offering, because what of a wealthy man's donation to a hospital or a library? If he changed his mind once the new wing was built, the new stacks filled, or even before, who would return one dime?

"I'm feeling a sense of responsibility, that's all." She had been hanging a wet sheet, and was hidden from view when she overheard Annie tell Sarah Puckett how difficult it is to save anything from their allowance.

"We'll never be able to leave at this rate," Annie said.

Sarah agreed. They were all having the same trouble.

Zee hadn't meant to betray them. She asked Bo only why they wanted to leave, and then he called the meeting.

"Your guilt is misplaced," he says now. "You did what you should have—you alerted me to the problem."

But she followed him into his office, and she saw him sifting through ledgers, noting who had exchanged their allowance for goods and who had not. "But you led them to believe the Masters reported their hoarding to you."

"To protect you. Would you rather they knew I heard it from you?"

She crosses her legs and says nothing. She has to admit, she's grateful he didn't pin it on her. "It's only that they all seem so frightened. Why are they afraid of you?"

"Not me." He reaches out and runs a finger down her arm. "They believe I've been possessed by a black adept."

She rubs her arm where he stroked her, annoyed that a mass of goose flesh has risen there. Her body should not betray her by responding with a ripple of interest even when she doubts him. "Why would they think that?"

"It's as if they look at this table and see nothing but the surface of the table, while I am looking at the table and see it from somewhere up amongst the stars. I see the Earth, and the continent, and then I see this tiny piece of land, the houses on it, and the Centre, and finally I see the same table they do, from a much different perspective. They see it looming large, as all there is, while to me it is a mere speck amongst all the other specks."

The self-aggrandizement in this statement takes her aback. She says nothing, waiting. She won't argue that perspective is unimportant, but what has that to do with black adepts?

His tone is impatient. "Whatever they don't understand they attribute to black adepts. They'd rather believe I am possessed than accept that their perspective is so limited. So naturally they're frightened. No one wants to tangle with the force of a black adept. I've witnessed men standing alone, writhing in pain as the life is squeezed out of them. They're everywhere around us, but most people can't see them. They're in constant battle with the white adepts for control, so it's a difficult matter, knowing when we're being guided by adepts and when we're being misled by black adepts."

She withdraws from him slightly. He sounds demented talking about black and white adepts like this, and she has no response. She has never known what to make of accounts of black magic of any sort. But others would be just as uncertain about her visions. She has experienced firsthand the same sort of discomfited look she is likely bestowing on him right now. As he says, it's all a matter of perspective. And experience. So she gives him the benefit of the doubt and treats his remarks seriously.

"Have *they* witnessed anything like that?"

"Not to my knowledge. But they got an eyeful of what I could do during the Lippincott trial. That fool sued me for wages when everyone knows we don't pay members. When our own Mr. Turnbull got on the stand, I focused all my energy on him, until he crashed to the floor in the witness box. Then his counsel became so tongue-tied he couldn't manage closing remarks. And when Judge Barker tried to speak, he couldn't either." He laughs. "When he could croak something out, he adjourned the session. Next day he threw the whole case out of court."

"What do you mean you focused your energy on them? What did you do?"

"I stared at him and concentrated until I saw him crumbling to the floor, silent as a stone. I imagined it and made it happen. I could kill a man by hacking him to pieces in my mind. The others will tell you if you doubt me."

She narrows her eyes. "I don't doubt you. I only wondered how you did it. And so now they think you're a black adept?" To a certain extent, she sees their point.

"The Masters exercised the control. I merely channelled the energy."

"To frighten them?" She sounds unsure. And didn't he just say they "got an eyeful of" what *he* could do, that *he* "imagined it and made it happen"? She's certain he did.

"Not to frighten them, but to show them that all is not as they, in their limited way, believe it is. They were silenced, in the best interest of the colony."

He stands so close she can feel the warmth of his breath as he speaks.

Then he says, "You *do* doubt me."

She swings her legs sideways and jumps off the table. "I don't at all. I only wondered how it feels, to wield such a power."

He grins. "You feel invincible." A minute too late, he adds, "Even when you know you're only the instrument."

When Bo walks her back to her tent a few minutes later, they stroll side by side in the fading light. Over the past week she has been wandering the forested acres unearthing bark, mushrooms, roots, and berries. He has joined her for an hour or two every day, and always there is the same underlying sexual tension she felt after the meeting. Even with all his inconsistencies, and a dark side she can't ignore, she still desires him. He must know, just as she knows he wants her, and yet he never presses her, has said nothing overt.

When they arrive, he holds the tent flap aside for her and ducks in after. He moves the washbowl onto her pile of luggage in a proprietary gesture that allows him to sit ungallantly on the upturned apple crate while she is left standing. Her eyes drop to the bed, the only other place to sit.

"This won't be comfortable," she says. He is a powerful man, but she has learned a thing or two about men. A woman's influence is at its greatest when a man wants what he hasn't yet had.

"Let's go outside," she says, "on that patch of moss between the trees."

Though it is not quite dark, she takes the lantern with them and lights it. Odd how after all these years, lighting a lantern still causes her anxiety. She hangs it on a branch, and then she sits opposite him.

In the weeks and months since they arrived at Cedar, she has not had time to talk to Roger as she meant to. Even at dinner, he is seated near one end of the table while she is at the other. She knows he spends time with Gerda because she overheard Annie complain to Margaret that Gerda hasn't done much work since the "anointed giant" arrived. But Zee no longer feels jealous. Roger and she had exhausted the passion and potential between them before they ever arrived, and now she experiences a new and satisfying lack of interest in his whereabouts.

"I want to talk about your visions," Bo says. "You're being used as a medium in this first phase of the restoration. You've been what we call an *unconscious medium,* meaning you haven't understood the significance of your visions."

"Lately some of my dreams have had that same quality of certainty I've always associated with the visions. And I've had a few episodes of psychometry."

"Of what?"

"Psychometry."

"What's that?"

She hides her surprise. The term was coined by an American physiologist in the mid-1800s. Can he really not know it? "Sometimes when I hold an object I get a sense of its history."

"Ahh, yes. You experience the soul of the thing."

Is he covering for a lack of knowledge, or has she merely refreshed his memory? She has no way of knowing.

"Your receptiveness is expanding. It may be that you'll experience your clairvoyance in other ways, as well. The visions, the dreams—however else you will receive information in the future—they're all platforms for messages from helpful spirits. To date, you haven't received any information relevant to the colony, but it's clear to me you're being prepared."

She still has not told him that she saw Myrtle in both a dream and a vision. She has the feeling that to do so would be a betrayal—and hasn't Myrtle been betrayed enough already? Whether rational or not, she feels protective of the woman.

"I often meditate," she says. "And I've been practising automatic writing again, but nothing much comes of it."

Their lantern hangs from a low branch, and it has turned dark, so now shadows tremble all around them. She sits with her back to one tree while Bo has his back to the other. The trees are old, three or four feet across at the base of the trunk, and she can feel the rough bark through her sweater. She spots an ant crawling on her arm and she flicks it away as she waits for his response. Moths flutter around the lamp, the silver flicker of their wings an irregular tic caught in the corner of her eye as she listens.

"When the Masters first contacted me, I went into a trance every morning, and during the winter of 1925, I received the first pages from the Masters of Wisdom."

"When you wrote *The Three Truths.*"

"I wrote every page of it in a trance."

"But you'd already had some success with automatic writing?"

"You need only to practise more."

She wonders if that is true. Wouldn't she be better to practise, as he did, the technique with which she has already had some success? When she meditated on Myrtle, she didn't learn anything immediately, but her vision of the woman in the forest came only a few days later.

"However it happens," he adds, "you're being prepared. Remember, I knew nothing of what I'd written until I came out of the trance and read what I'd scribbled. The same will happen to you. Everything I wrote I did under the power of the Brotherhood. Without their message, I am a very ordinary man."

"No," she says. "Whatever else you are, you are not ordinary."

"That's where you're wrong. I'm not a person filled with power. I'm a Power using a personality. And you're no less capable."

The intensity behind the statement transforms it into a magnanimous compliment, and when he leans forward to grasp her hands, she allows him to hold them for several seconds before she pulls away.

He reaches into his trousers pocket and extracts a handkerchief and a small porcelain snuff bottle. He opens the bottle and holds the tiny spoon to first one nostril and then the other, snorting sharply each time.

She flicks another ant off her skirt. It lands on Bo's arm and begins crawling up his white sleeve. She reaches forward and flicks it off him, as well.

He lifts the spoon and snorts from it again. Then he wipes his nose with his handkerchief and moves to return both items to his pocket.

Zee stops him. "Let me see that. What's in there?"

He lifts his hand dismissively. "Just something I take for pain."

"Can I see the bottle? It looks unique." She extends her hand and he turns it over to her, a whimsical piece of Chinese antiquity, a tiny porcelain bottle glazed with laughing, brightly coloured deities, some of them clapping or playing instruments.

"It's magical," she says. "Where did you find it?"

"In China, when I was at sea. I have several, but I use this one the most. Each of the deities represents something—good fortune, good health, prosperity." He points them out. "They're all there. Happiness, longevity, desire."

The silver scrollwork stopper is equally unusual. Embedded in the top is a tiny piece of red coral. She unstops the bottle, removes the miniature spoon, and holds it to her nose.

"Careful there," Bo immediately objects. "Give it back."

"Why?" She takes a tentative sniff and then gawks up at him.

"What? Give me that."

"You have cocaine in here."

"They gave me morphine when I was in the hospital, but it's not so easy to come by these days. What do you know about cocaine?"

She shrugs and takes a quick snort herself. It is his turn to look astounded, but she merely sniffs and brushes at her nose, then returns the bottle. "You see everything in Florida. Are your other bottles as interesting as this one?"

He shuffles his bottom forward across the soft, spongy moss so that he sits very close to her. "You'll have to see them and decide for yourself."

Already she forgets her earlier skepticism. He's incredibly handsome to her now. And his eyes are mesmeric. Once she gazes into them, it is difficult to look away again. And the closer they are, the bigger they seem. She almost believes she could dive into them and end up somewhere else.

Soft rustling sounds hint at nocturnal life outside the soft pool of light in which they sit, and nothing but salt air hangs between them. A surge of energy and goodwill overtakes her.

"Kiss me," she says.

CHAPTER 23

She can't sleep.

They kissed for several minutes, and while they did, there was nothing in the world more important than exploring that soft wet place, but then, when they pulled back for air, she felt differently and jumped up. "I'm sorry," she said.

"Don't be. I'm not."

Maybe he wasn't, but that didn't change her response. "Please go. I need time to think."

And then, though it was already late, she gathered her things and walked to the bathhouse, enumerating the reasons why she needed to avoid intimate contact with the Brother. One: He was married, and she didn't sleep with other women's husbands.

Two: He is not always as humble as she thought he would be, as she believes an enlightened being should be. Three: Sometimes he seems a bit deluded—perhaps because of the cocaine he uses so frequently? And deluded people are irrational people.

She shouldn't even *think* about it. Not for a second.

Four: If it was cocaine making him odd, that could be a problem. He could become violent, and she had already heard him screaming at Elma. Would she want that? But she didn't want to *live* with him, did she? She only wondered what it would be like to sleep with him. Once.

She heated water and filled the tub. She undressed and lowered herself into the water. But even as the warmth soothed her aching muscles, her mind remained on him. Her body had responded exactly as she had thought it would, and she felt the effects of him still.

She half hoped he would see the light of the lantern and would knock on the door. Her mind flitted over the tantalizing possibilities of that, and then she looked down at herself. She would remain sprawled in the bath, her meagre breasts uncovered, hard chocolatey nipples jutting above the water, her entire long body visible beneath it.

When he entered, she would point to the remaining hot water in a pitcher beside her. "Don't burn me," she'd say. She would spread her legs like two silvery scissor blades and press them against the sides of the tub so he could pour the water between them. He might try to look only where he poured, or he might not, but either way, he couldn't avoid a glimpse.

"You can join me if you want," she would say. "There's room for two."

But that is as far as her imagination would allow her to go, and then the water cooled, and her little game struck her as silliness.

So now she is in bed reading D.H. Lawrence's *Fantasia of the Unconscious* by lamplight. The book is not at all what she had thought it would be. She bought it because of the word *Fantasia* in the title, because of two chapters titled "Cosmology" and "Sleep and Dreams," and on the basis of a few lines read at random in a bookseller's shop. Lawrence's witticisms amuse her, and his well-spun sentences weave a spell of their own. Nevertheless, for a writer so censured for his sexual themes, she finds his ideas in this book as old-fashioned and moralistic as the Old Testament. His concern with male masturbation, in particular, is as obvious as a sausage on a bare plate, and she pities the boys whose fathers will read the book and heed the author's advice to frighten their sons off ever touching their poor pending members. They'll be frightened into lying, at least, for what boy can help but try to quiet himself when he hardens with excitement? She can't believe Lawrence still takes the business so seriously, and if he feels strongly enough to write at such length, she wonders how he manages to relieve himself, or if he squats to piss like a girl to keep his hand from loving what rests in it.

These are the roving thoughts Roger interrupts when, without calling out or asking permission to enter, he pushes her tent flap aside and stumbles in.

"Well, hello," she says. "Where did you come from all of a sudden?"

He wastes no time on preliminaries. "I saw you kissing."

"Is that a fact?" She won't deny it. Instead, she places a marker in D.H. Lawrence and draws the bed covers around her as she sets the book aside. "Have you taken to peeping in the dark?"

"I provided for you. Your life was easy from the day we met."

"And is not much worse now." She pulls the covers tighter.

"You're a user, Mabel." He resorts to her given name when he wants to show his displeasure with her, like a disappointed parent. "I might have agreed to a bit of play, under certain circumstances, but to deceive me—I won't tolerate that."

A tic starts in his cheek, a familiar tocsin of imminent rage. She's only seen him furious twice, once with her, and once with his manager, but both times the tic came first. When he was angry with her, over nothing, over some small remark she made at the wrong time, he slapped her so forcefully she fell to the floor. Then he threw a glass of Scotch into the fireplace, and kicked a chair and tripped over it. By the time he had finally spent himself and come seeking forgiveness, she had locked herself in her bedroom.

"From what I hear, you're well occupied with Gerda."

"You ungrateful whore." He unfastens his belt.

She takes her book up for protection and wishes too late that she had heeded the signs. He looks as if he truly wants to tear her to pieces, and this time he has a weapon.

He tears the covers off her with one hand. She wears a long flannel nightgown that catches as she tries to slide into a sitting position. He wraps the leather end of the belt around his knuckles and swings the buckle.

She screams and lifts the book to protect her face, but it flies off to the side as Roger bloodies her lip and nose.

Metal glints as he swings again. "You unfaithful bitch."

She catches the end of his belt and gives a sharp pull as she tries to gain control. Instead, she pulls him heavily on top of her.

His bulk momentarily stuns her, and he uses that to his advantage, pinning her body to the bed with his weight. He catches one of her wrists, but her other hand remains free and she pulls at his hair and claws his face. He releases her wrist and grasps her head with his two hands, holding it still while he presses his lips against her mouth, smearing them over hers, groaning audibly when he tastes the blood he has drawn.

His tongue slathers her face until there is nothing more to lap up, and when he lifts his head, she screams.

"Shut up," he says, and he draws his fist back and pummels her. Bone connects with bone.

Her awful screams. His grunts. Their blood intermingling.

"You unfaithful whore. You *fucking* unfaithful whore."

She registers the sounds now as if they come from somewhere apart. Was that foreign, anguished voice really his?

There is blood on the pillow, so much of it, and crimson. Again and again he pulls his arm back, until suddenly his fist stops in mid-air as his body arches and his hips jerk. And then there are more screams, not her own, and shouting.

"It's over." It is a man's voice, a mixture of disbelief and disgust. "Christ, get him off her."

Chapter 24

For two days she is sedated, her eyes swollen shut, but on the third day, she implores Bo from between horizontal slits framed by spongy, discoloured flesh. "I didn' see this coming. Nod'd all." Her words come out slurred and heavy, as if her tongue is glued to her lower teeth, but she wants him to understand. Her visions are random and unpredictable; not a single one has ever been useful, and when she needed advance warning most, she saw nothing.

"Shh. He's gone. I sent him back to Florida. He told me to tell you he's profoundly sorry."

"Hmph." She moves her mouth to say something more, but the pain is too great. Later she will tell Bo: she will not be bullied again.

She saw herself in the mirror when Margaret helped her shuffle to the washroom earlier. Her lips are split and swollen, her nose is broken, and the rest of her face is puffed to twice its normal size. The ends of sutures stand up like stick pins in a badly bruised fruit, and her normally light skin is now an unattractive purplish blue ranging to brownish yellow. She moves her tongue over her teeth, which, remarkably, remain intact.

Bo has installed her in an upper bedroom in the Centre, next to his study and at the opposite end of the hall from his and Elma's own bedroom, and she overhears him warn anyone who wants to enter, "Prepare yourself, it's bad." She also hears him arguing with Elma so loudly that she catches a few words. *Shrew. Bastard. Pointless.*

Elma has been in twice. Once she filled the empty water pitcher, clunking it down with such force that Zee started awake and called out, momentarily disoriented and panic-stricken. The second time she entered quietly, eerily, to lay an extra blanket over the back of a chair. Both trips were unnecessary, except to give Elma an opportunity to study her, but when Zee turned to look, the older woman averted her eyes. She doesn't know how to read Elma, but she recognizes controlled anger in the set of her jaw and in her movements. Any minute now she half expects her to finish off what Roger started, and her muscles tense with the possibility. And yet shame keeps her silent. Where Elma is concerned, she is the guilty one. Never mind that Bo would have tried to kiss her anyway, had already scooted over to do just that.

She dozes fitfully, and takes pills when Bo or Margaret offers them, and late in the afternoon when the light has already dimmed, she wakes to find Elma sitting at her bedside, staring so intently, in her unblinking way, that Zee instinctively sits up and shifts away.

She glances toward the doorway, expecting the door to stand open, which would provide at least the possibility of being overheard if she has to call out, but Elma has closed them in.

"For ten years I've stood by him." Her voice is harsh, the words brittle with anger. "I don't suppose he mentioned that? Or that he was nearly dead of hepatitis when he met me?"

Zee has no response. Judging from Elma's face, which has the look of a rumpled rag, there is a lot more she intends to say. Looking at her, it is easy to believe that in those ten years as his wife, the moments of happiness were rare, and if she has endured ten years of festering anger, her emotions are ready for a cleanse.

As soon as Zee meets her eyes, Elma resumes speaking. "I met him when he was very ill. In the South Seas. Did he tell you that?"

Zee shakes her head and feels the wall at her back. She must not show her fear. And then remembers: she looks frightening herself. Oddly, she finds strength in that.

"He wouldn't have survived the month if I hadn't nursed him back to health. When he was well enough, we went to France, and then England, and here, all on my pension. Because I believed in him, and I still do. He's the only man I've ever loved. But do you think *he* believes he owes me anything? He's like an angry ferret over every little thing."

She doesn't doubt that. Even in the short time she's been at the colony, she can see that they are like flint and tinder, sometimes Elma the flint and Bo the tinder igniting, while other times he sets Elma off with equally slight provocation. She has seen the same behaviour in other couples, has felt the beginnings of it herself, with Roger, as if some people can live together only so long before their abrasiveness resides at the surface, no longer protected by patience or even common courtesy, but laid bare by years of struggle, so that any contact at all naturally results in sparks.

"I held a pillow above his head while he slept last night. I could have easily pinned him under it."

Zee goes absolutely still, and then grips the sides of the bed under the covers. If Elma comes at her, Zee will need to pull her down and hold her tight. She hopes she has the strength, and that there is someone in the Centre to hear if she screams. Her eyes dart to the night table—she might make a grab for the water pitcher, if she needs to.

"You're not so exceptional. He's had most of the women here. He's decreed it. Any woman he wants—married or single—has to couple with him up to nine times. Not that anyone has ever objected."

Has to, she says, as if against their will. But isn't that only compatible with his views on marriage? And yet none of the women has complained. That surprises her more. Then again, why should it? She wouldn't refuse him either. He exudes such an intense energy—who wouldn't want to claim that for herself? More likely she would be disappointed when the nine times had passed.

"So why did you stay with him all this time?"

"Why do you want him now?"

Fair enough, but she doesn't answer. She has been asking herself the same question, because she *does* want him, though not at all in the same way she once wanted John, possibly even Roger. She wants him quietly and certainly. She wants to *know* him, and be known, as neither John nor Roger ever knew her. He conveys an aura of power, and she wants to radiate that power, too.

"When does he ever lift anything heavier than a fork?" Elma spits the words out now. "His back, he says, or his heart. And all the while he has me out picking rocks to build a wall. At my age. But you'll see."

"Why are you telling me this?"

Elma ignores her. "Do you know that he used to work in Victoria? He claims he's never been here before, that the Masters pointed him here, but he worked for a shipping company and delivered up and down these channels. He told me all about it."

Why does this news not surprise her? And yet, even so, she finds herself on the defensive. "You're saying he's a fraud? And that you participated in the deception?"

"I'm saying nothing of the sort. I'm saying that he deceives himself. If you can't recognize that, you're more of a fool than I thought."

Zee checks her anger so as not to incite any further rage in Elma, but the woman is volatile, and she is toying with her. She wishes she understood what Elma wants from her, and she watches her warily, uncertain what to expect. After they have sat for a minute or two in silence, she thinks it might be within her power to provide some reassurance, and she reaches out tentatively.

"I didn't intend—"

"I don't care what you intended." Elma waves off her hand. "But if he wants you, I'm not going to stand by and watch. I've already booked my passage to New Zealand. And it was *my* decision, not his, though I'm sure he'll pretend otherwise."

Zee nods to indicate she has heard. She breathes a little easier. All Elma wants is to leave with a shred of dignity. The purpose of her visit is not to make Zee pay, but to prevent her gloating. As if she would. In a moment of empathy, she says nothing at all.

Deprived of any further fuel for anger, Elma looks sadder, and shrunken. Still, her parting words are bitter. "He's got a wife in

New Zealand, and three children. Ask him about *that.*"

Elma leaves within the week, quietly, with no formal farewell gathering, though Sarah, Margaret, Annie, and Mary all wave goodbye from outside the Centre as the Brother drives Elma down the lane. She wears a hat with a brim, and she looks very small beneath it.

Zee watches from the upstairs window. She feels quite well and has the energy to leave her bed and walk outside, but she remains in her room because her face still horrifies her. Her mouth and nose remain swollen and her colour ranges from yellowish blue to black. She hasn't slept through the night since she first woke after Roger hurt her, and at least once a night she relives the brutal beating, awaking in a panic as she fends off an imaginary intruder.

Alone in the bathroom down the hall from her bedroom, she has plenty to think about. Elma is gone. Roger is gone. The secretary-treasurer disappeared last fall before Zee arrived. On some levels the colony is idyllic. It resembles a large summer camp on the ocean, with everyone pitching in and the smell of fresh cedar always in the air. The children race down paths and hide in the bushes. Young enough not to mind the cold water, they swim in the ocean and warm themselves around campfires. They laugh freely and are brown and healthy looking. But on another level, something—plenty—is drastically wrong.

It's worse than you think. The voice comes out of nowhere, and it is not hers. Then again, the sound didn't originate outside her, either. She raises her face and looks in the mirror. *Hello?* That was her interior voice, completely different from the previous one.

She opens the door and peers out, but there is no one there. She can't help but wonder if she has pushed herself more than she should have today. Once, when she was younger, a fever made her delirious. She feels a bit delirious now, but she reminds herself that she hasn't had a fever through any of this, and when she touches her hand to her forehead out of habit, she is perfectly cool. She turns back to the mirror and almost chokes on her swift intake of breath. Then she immediately begins to hyperventilate.

She cups her hands over her mouth and forces herself to breathe slowly. Honora's face has supplanted her own in the wall mirror, but she is only visible for a few seconds, and then the image changes. There is smoke, a lot of it, billowing up around her, and she is looking for someone—for Bo, she thinks. She smells diesel fuel and feels an intense heat. Red, orange, yellow flames burn on the surface of the water, and when she whirls away from them, chaos surrounds her, like the aftermath of an earthquake. Things everywhere—broken glass, something sticky, smashed window-panes, an axe stuck in the wall. And then the flames again, a mast snapping as a boat rolls on its side. Now the horror of it hits her physically. Terror. Panic. She begins hyperventilating again.

When the images fade, her eyes are huge in the mirror. She vomits into the sink. Something terrible has happened, or is going to happen. She couldn't articulate her thoughts now if she had to, except to say that she has never been more frightened in her life.

CHAPTER 25

The response of the colonists is immediate. While they don't actually mutter their discontent, their rustling and startled glances can't be ignored.

"I repeat," Bo says, in response. "I have appointed Madame Zee my aide and second-in-command. Some of you may think you could serve me better. Some of you resent her and already refuse her when she asks you to carry out my wishes. But I've called you here to tell you: neither the Brotherhood nor I grant authority lightly. Of all the Brothers, Madame Zee knows my wishes best. More than Herbert, or Roger Painter, who has disappointed us. More even than Alfred Barley, for whom I have so much respect."

He glances at Alfred, who listens with his arms folded across his chest. He rocks slightly on his heels and glares off to one side of the room rather than look at the Brother. His wife, Annie, doesn't sit with the other women but stands by his side, an anguished expression on her face.

Bo has told her a little about the couple. Part of the first small group of followers to leave England and come with him to Canada, they have been here longer than anyone. Alfred is a famous astrologer, as well-known for his work with the magazine *Modern Astrology* as for his scholarly works. Annie was a teacher for thirty years, and after, secretary of the London Astrological Society.

The Brother looks around at his other disciples, and then his gaze returns to Alfred and Annie. He stops speaking and stares hard at Annie until she looks up. She turns her head from side to side and even glances behind her. When she understands that she is the focus of his attention, blood rushes to her face and she looks down at the floor.

"If I'm to carry on my work," the Brother says, "I can't continue to manage the minutiae of every day. Think of our Brother Blavatsky. Her work failed in part because people around her couldn't conceptualize the Masters' plan."

Zee wonders if this is true. She'd argue that Bo and others continue to carry out Blavatsky's work, at an intellectual level at any rate. The real downfall for Blavatsky came when the Society for Psychical Research investigated her and determined that so many acts of "magic" were actually fraudulent—"astral" letters written in her own disguised hand, these same letters fluttering from cracks in the ceiling, hidden doors between the "occult room" and her bedroom. Zee has had the same concern about Bo, that he sometimes resorts to deception for effect, when in fact the truth should be good enough.

"This must not happen to us, and I'm striving to understand correctly everything they ask. But imagine what this entails. As the personal Chela of the Twelfth Master, I'm constantly surrounded by that intense energy. I live within the powerful vibrations of his immediate aura, and this puts an immense strain upon a lower vehicle like me. The result is that I'm left hypersensitive. Ideally, I'd be in complete seclusion because that's necessary for the work, but I'm trying to remain available to you at some level. I can only do that with your help. My body is too weak."

She contemplates this. Is he really surrounded by the energy of the Master? Is this why he exudes such intensity? She wants to believe in an afterlife, wants even more to believe it is possible to communicate with those who have passed, but somehow faith and certainty continue to elude her. From experience, she knows that some people genuinely do have access to seemingly private information—Coulson does, possibly Bo does, certainly she does—but where does this knowledge originate? Is it really coming from those who have passed, or is it information somehow collected psychically from those of this world, either present or not? Or is *this* world and *the other* world really all one?

What if, despite all our talk of *passing,* and *moving on,* whether to reincarnate or settle in heaven, there *is* nothing else, but neverthe-less, all that ever *has* been, in terms of thought or energy, remains, so that only matter is lost or changes form? Isn't it possible that a huge and ever-growing compilation of information—both important and mundane—lies available to anyone who can somehow perceive it, either accidentally, as she sometimes does, or through practised effort? Wouldn't that make as much sense as Masters and Gods and Spirits? Wouldn't that *be* the God within, the all-knowing power of the universe, to which everyone has access?

And if Darwin's theory of evolution is correct, wouldn't the body of knowledge and thought also evolve, making new information available to all? But Bo doesn't believe in evolution. He'd say that *nothing* can ever truly be new, because everything known, or waiting to be known, already awaits manifestation, and *will* be manifested through him, or any of them, when the Masters deem the time is right to pass this knowledge along. Somehow, this doesn't sit right with her.

Bo has taken a few steps toward Annie, whom Zee knows to be hesitant at the best of times, and easily agitated. At first, Annie ignores him, as if she hopes he will pass her by, but as he continues his intense staring, she lifts her head and meets his gaze directly.

"By appointing Madame Zee in my place, I'll find respite. Not enough, certainly, but any amount will improve my current state. If you—any of you—resist Madame Zee's authority, you'll risk not only my wrath, but the wrath of the Brotherhood, and of the many powerful spirits that surround us." He lowers his voice and speaks earnestly. "I've seen disbelievers struck down as they walked. I've seen them pinned to their beds, writhing in agony before they fell unconscious, never to awaken again. I wish that fate on none of you, and I hope to prevent it. But if you bring this wrath upon yourselves, I'm helpless to intervene. I cannot."

She shakes her head in dismay. Poor Sarah clutches the front of her dress. Others have grabbed on to each other. She asked him to request their support, because they respect him and because she thought a request would stop them from resisting her every step of the way, but she had hoped he wouldn't bully them.

Both Annie and Alfred have the discomfited look of those who, finding themselves in the spotlight, wish only to escape it. The Brother ignores Alfred and focuses on Annie, so that as he draws closer, she loses colour in her cheeks. Behind him, a burst of white flame shoots into the air and subsides in a puff of smoke.

To Zee, the flash of fire behind him looks suspiciously like the flames caused by the white phosphorus she once used to impress her parents and her brothers with magic tricks. Perhaps they all want to believe in burning bushes and oceans parting, but Bo's moments of glory are rare these days, and when they occur, she can't help but suspect they have been planned well in advance.

But the others look as if at any minute a spirit could appear before them and cast them down. The room is so silent that as a group they might well be holding their breath. Annie stares back at Bo with a blank, dazed expression, and then, just as he reaches her, she collapses in a faint.

Zee turns away in disgust. These theatrics are unnecessary, and they're exactly the sort of thing that brought Blavatsky down, for the same reason. She meant to impress others even when her own powers failed her, and what she couldn't count on naturally, she orchestrated herself. He's no different, except that he means not so much to impress as to frighten the colonists into acquiescence. As often as he says that his own personality is irrelevant, that he is at the Master's bidding alone, he disproves that today. He wields power, but not spiritual power, and whether the others can recognize it or not, focusing on Annie is a cheap trick. Don't they know how easily she succumbs to pressure, and if they do, why can't they see this for the gimmick it is?

"Don't hurt her." Alfred catches his wife's body as she crumples and turns away to protect her, but the Brother places a hand on Alfred's shoulder and then scoops Annie into his own arms.

"There's nothing to be frightened of," Bo reassures him. "She's been touched by a spirit with a message. Why they chose her, I can't say, but I knew, and I wanted to be near her to balance the energy around her. When she wakes, perhaps she can enlighten us."

He is not a strong man, but he carries Annie to the table and lays her out on its surface. He places one hand on her forehead and one below her breastbone. Alfred is at his side.

"You will wake feeling refreshed and in good spirits. You will be composed and certain in your beliefs, ready to pass on the message with which you have been entrusted." The Brother says this quietly, calmly, as if he is bringing someone out of a hypnotic trance, and as he does, Annie opens her eyes.

She smiles uncertainly and reaches out for Alfred. When he helps her into a sitting position, she swings her legs off the table and moves to step down, but the Brother stops her.

"You've been given a message from the spirits," he says.

"I have?"

"Close your eyes and recall your last thought as you saw me walking toward you. It's important that you remember. You may have seen an image. Anything you thought or saw just before you fainted."

She has none of the anxious look she had before she collapsed. "I did hear a voice, very clearly. It said, *There is nothing to fear, and everything to be gained.*"

Zee stifles a sigh of frustration. Unwittingly, Annie has played Bo's hand out perfectly, and while she should be relieved—he has likely frightened most of them into accepting her new position—she's not. If the Masters really did work through him, he wouldn't have needed this pretence. And now she wonders: what if there are no Masters? The thought feels blasphemous, akin to saying, What if there is no God? But at the very least, what if there are no Masters speaking through him?

"Thank you," Bo says, taking Annie's hands in a heartfelt manner. "I'm sure we all needed to hear that. Sometimes, just as we feel we can't go on, there is a message like this. If we're open to it, we're revived, and reminded of *everything to be gained.* There is *nothing to fear,* and *everything to be gained.* Let us all remember that."

As Alfred helps Annie down, a supportive group forms around her, and now Zee, too, feels a strong compulsion to attend to her. She joins the group, garnering the other woman's attention by laying a hand on her shoulder.

Annie looks up immediately, her face puzzled. "You're so warm," she says. She lays her own hand atop Zee's and then removes it almost as fast.

"Warm oil will clear your ear," Zee says, and then she lifts her hand and takes a step backward and away. Now that she has made the comment, the urgency that pulled her forward is gone.

The muscles in Annie's face confront the question of what to make of this. "Yes," she says, when finally she decides. "I should have thought of that. Thank you."

Zee turns away, and a thrill runs through her. Where did *that* come from? Is it a sign, and if so, of what?

"That's all," Bo says, waving a hand to dismiss them. "Go, and let us work together as we are meant to."

Later that night, she and the Brother share a glass of wine in Bo's log cabin on Valdes Island. He has named this portion of the colony the Mandieh Settlement. It is only the second of three planned settlements, and soon the colony will expand farther, to DeCourcy Island, situated between Valdes Island and Cedar-by-the-Sea. Mary has already purchased the island, and Bo has begun building a smaller home on the point where he and Zee will live until he finishes the mansion he calls Greystone, intended as a place of refuge for Brothers from around the world. Mary may live there, and others who wish to replenish themselves when necessary contact with the outer world wears them down.

For now, he spends most of his time on Valdes, protected from all but a few of the original members. And so she relaxes with him in his study, a cozy room filled with leather-bound books and a variety of carved masks and personal effects he collected during his travels.

"You and I will have a separate wing for our quarters," he says of Greystone, "and another on the other side will house the servants."

It is the first time she has heard him speak of servants, but she doesn't doubt that he believes some of the members are just that, servants meant to do his bidding. She wonders if he is aware of this verbal slip, and it serves to remind her of how he misrepresented himself earlier. Just how often does he perform his tricks? And how many people has he taken in because of it? Myrtle certainly— and is *she* intended to be another?

Now that Zee has had time to reflect, she is embarrassed that she interpreted her dream about the two of them to mean that she was destined to be Isis to his Osiris. That was no more than naïveté and wishful thinking. In retrospect, the dream was more likely a warning—away from the same aching desire she feels right now, though however much she distrusts these feelings, she can't resist them, and doesn't want to.

She knows intuitively that if she were smart, she'd walk away now, before they progress any further, but she deliberately ignores the warning. She can handle this. Just once, and then she'll decide.

As if to counteract her doubt, he is speaking of their future together. They may be able to move to the smaller house by fall, he says, and the new residence will allow them almost complete privacy.

Yesterday she visited the spot with him on his tugboat, the *Khuenaten,* and he's right, the building site is very private, situated on the southernmost point of the island, at the head of three jade-green bays—with plenty of sun, a good sandstone beach, and lush evergreens. Summer or winter, the view will never change.

For now, though, they have brought her personal items over to Valdes. She swirls the wine in her glass and takes a sip.

He approaches with the wine bottle and refills her glass, which she immediately sets aside, and then he sits on the sofa near her. The bottle is empty, so he places it on the floor, carelessly, and so it clatters on its side and rolls against the wall. He ignores it and takes one of her wrists and very gently draws her closer, looping her arm over his shoulder.

They kiss, tentatively at first, and then fervently, until he pulls her to her feet and leads her out of the study and down the hall. The window in the large bedroom is open and the breeze has made the room fresh. There is nothing left that would suggest Elma—it is almost as if she were never here, though in noticing the lack of her things, Zee gives her a presence—and the bed is already turned down, and made with crisp white linens, fold marks still visible on the sheets and pillowcases.

He kisses her temples, and embraces her, and then they undress each other. For such a small man, he is well-endowed, and she reaches down to hold him and then winds her arms around his back to press him against her. He pushes her hair aside and nuzzles between her ear and shoulder until the soft skin there shivers and tightens. He runs the tip of his tongue over the scar on her chin, now as much a part of her as the crease on her neck, and he says, "Dr. Schmidt is coming from Switzerland next month. He'll look at these for you."

Right now, she doesn't care. All she wants is for him not to stop.

And then he moves her onto the bed. His movements are slow but sure and precise. He applies pressure with his fingers and his tongue, with a knuckle, with the heel of his hand. They move together like expert dancers, comfortable and smooth. Her pleasure is immediate and prolonged; she is buoyant with sensuality and goodwill. She loves him. She adores him. She is happy, ridiculously happy. She loves his little brown hands, his small body and twiggy toes, the way he slides over her and into her.

She wallows in excess. They are greedy but unhurried, and not particularly noisy, giving way more often to stifled moans and sharp intakes of breath than to violent sound. And when, finally, they lie side by side, fingers and legs entwined, whole bodies equally spent, she can't say how many hours have passed. She has only one thought: *Once is not enough.*

PART IV

DEATH

1932

CHAPTER 26

Zee stands by, watching Bo as he bends over a series of drawings he has spread on the table in the Centre. Her main purpose now, she thinks, is to protect the others from him. Over the past two years she has come to respect many of these people, the women in particular, and incredibly, they still believe all is well. Not entirely, of course, but they have always known him to be a little eccentric, a little volatile. They roll their eyes on occasion, or mutter amongst themselves, but they accept his outbursts as the result of too much strain or of fending off black adepts.

She has considered revealing the extent of his madness, as only she really knows it, but for what purpose? The men would strip her of authority in a matter of minutes, and which of them could manage the affairs of the colony any better? She has grown to like it here. There are picnics, and children's pageants, swimming, and long strolls through the surrounding woods.

There is an ever-changing group of like-minded people sitting around the firepit when it is warm, or inside the Centre when it is not. Once she wondered how others survived the day-to-day tedium of their lives. Now she sees that the experience of tedium is only blindness to the needs of others, and to the inexhaustible beauty found everywhere. Here there are lively discussions, and communal meals, and while she never would have believed it in her first months at the colony, often such a sense of camaraderie, after shared work, that at times she believes they really have created, if not a Utopian world, at least a co-operative, communal one—as long as the extent of Bo's illness remains a secret.

In addition to her responsibilities overseeing all day-to-day operations and special projects, she has become a naturopath of sorts. The women have accepted her now, and she has helped many of them with herbal remedies. More than that, she has developed a way of sensing what ails them even when they don't seek help on their own. Margaret had gallbladder trouble, Annie had an allergy to moulds, and even Lady Mary, skeptical at first, thanked her sincerely when chickweed juice and milkweed sap cured a crop of warts she had mentioned to no one else.

She is good with children, and while the colony still does not have a formal school, she has created informal outdoor programs designed to teach the children about their surroundings, and she doubts there is a child present who can't identify at least ninety percent of the native habitat—plant, animal, and mineral.

All in all, this situation has worked very well for everyone over the past couple of years. Because Bo told the members to accept her as his eyes and ears, most ideas—both Bo's and the colonists'—must pass through her first. Where Bo had begun to veto almost every idea that wasn't his own, she approves everything they can afford, and then arranges situations that allow Bo to believe he initiated the changes. Likewise, if his ideas are sound, she has them carried out promptly, and if they are not, she is sometimes able to subvert them or even quash them without notice. Occasionally, however, he conceives of something of which no amount of cajoling, persuasion, or outright manipulation will dissuade him.

This is one of those times, and all she can do is stand by and observe quietly, so that she will be aware of exactly what the colonists have seen and heard. In this case, the drawings he has spread before them illustrate six forts he has designed and wants constructed along the shores of DeCourcy Island, where he and Zee now reside. Little more than ditches with a roof, the forts will have earthen walls and floors, cedar fronts with holes for rifles, and cedar roofs with openings for crawling in. He explains all of this to Leon, Bruce, Alfred, and Roger, who has been allowed to return to the colony against her better judgment. Bo discussed the reasons why he wanted him back—primarily Roger's business sense and the size of his donations, which anyone could see the community needs—and then he said they would have him return to manage the colony while he took Zee to England, where he hoped to buy a sailboat. As she would see her family at last, she reluctantly agreed.

Roger returned with his new wife, Leona, a woman twenty years his junior. Bo and she returned with a sleek sailboat, a sixty-two-foot Brixham trawler christened the *Lady Royal.*

"I want these forts to be invisible from the water," Bo says. "Surprise is the best weapon we have."

"Against who?" Leon is still young and trusting; confusion is evident in his expression.

"Against intruders. Let them go to Cedar or Valdes. This is my refuge, and no one comes here unless they're invited."

He has a crate of .303 Lee-Metfords, ordered from an army surplus store in Edmonton, though what he wants to protect, she can't say. Either his cocaine or his gold, she guesses, though the gold, at any rate, is already sealed in Mason jars and well hidden. In her view, neither one is worth killing over.

She was with him when he sealed the gold in jars—two leather pouches full of U.S. twenty-dollar double eagles. Each one featured a robust and full-length portrait of Liberty in high relief, her torch in her right hand and an olive branch in her left. Behind her the sun's rays rose from the horizon to illuminate her dress. On the reverse—a magnificent eagle in flight. The coins were works of art, and with so many of them at her fingertips, she couldn't help but think of pirates and stolen loot—except that the gold was not stolen, but freely given by new arrivals. And all of it on top of the smaller bills and donations that arrive each month, routinely enough to cover the operating costs of the colony.

They processed the gold as ordinarily as if they were canning apricot halves or yellow beans. Bo filled two quart-sized Mason jars with the gold, and she melted squares of paraffin in a saucepan on the wood stove. At his instruction, she poured liquid wax around the coins the same way she might pour sugar water over fruit, filling each jar until not so much as an air bubble of space remained. When the wax hardened, the contents were barely discernible. To an unknowing eye, they could be dull disks of meat or vegetable, set in lard. He fit each jar snugly in its own cedar box, specially made by Bruce Crawford, and secured the lids to the boxes with brass screws. As far as she knows, the two boxes are still hidden in a milk bucket in the cistern.

Now Bo is attempting to incite their enthusiasm. "You're the Metford Defence. You'll build the forts and man them from dusk to dawn. It's an important position. You're my first line of protection."

It is insane, this compulsion to arm them, and she can imagine their silent groans at the thought of all those tedious hours in the ground. Not only that, but the first time anyone fires one of those guns, they'll have more unwanted attention on this island than he can imagine. And what if they actually hit someone? What then? But she has already argued this point with Bo. She has learned from experience that the quickest way to get him to abandon any project is to let him play it out until he forgets about it and goes on to something more benign.

Now he swipes at his nose with his index finger, a gesture that has become habitual. He has a bad sinus drip, and though his nasal membranes are sensitive and bleed easily, he uses his snuff bottle more frequently than ever.

She stands by without a word as the others shoot one another glances. *They* know the idea is mad.

So the forts are built, each one hardly larger than a packing crate, and the watches begin. Bo gives each of his Metford Defence a rifle and sets them on guard in alternating shifts. The men, including

Leon, take their turn scanning the Ruxton Passage for boats. The Brother has instructed them to fire at the first sign of a hostile vessel, but she overhears them later, asking one another what constitutes hostility. "Zee," someone says, and they have a laugh at her expense.

The joke is not entirely unwarranted. If the women of the colony have warmed to her, the men still fight her at every turn. Just the other day, Alfred so frustrated her with his patronizing tone and deliberate taunting that she succumbed to a fit of temper. She swore at him, called him a jackass, and whacked at his heavy boots with her riding crop. He couldn't have felt the blows, but by dinner, everyone in the colony knew she had "taken her whip to Alfred." Even Bo asked her to explain what she thought could be accomplished by "horse-whipping" a colonist.

Despite what she would overall call a contented life, she has never suffered such fits of temper as she does now. All the great tyrants of the world rolled into one have nothing on her. It's odd how a change like that creeps up on you. You go through life believing you're a certain kind of person, not noticing baby steps in a new direction, and then one day someone tells you you're not who you think you are, and you realize they're right. Thinking back, she believes the change began after Roger so violently beat her. She doesn't know if it is her age that altered her, the circumstances here, or something that happened as a result of the beating. She doesn't believe in violence, and didn't even cuss much in the past, so these angry outbursts startle her, and hurt her confidence. In an attempt to curb the problem, she regularly drinks chamomile tea, and she has searched the open woods for hypericum, a weed that might lessen her anxiety, but so far she has found none.

She waits until Leon is settled in his fort and the Brother has gone off to check on someone else, and then she walks to Leon's post with a lunch—two tuna sandwiches, a couple of chocolate cookies, and an orange. So intent is he on his watch, he doesn't hear her approach. She looks in through one of the chinks between boards and watches him heft the rifle and wedge it against his shoulder. He holds it steady and sights down the long barrel. "Bang," he says. "Gotcha, you rotten maggot."

"Everything all right?" Zee bangs on the wall and opens the hatch from above. "You know how to use that thing?"

"We practised," Leon says. "I got pretty good at it."

"You know how to unload it?"

"Sure."

"I want you to take the bullets out and put them in your pocket. Can you do that?"

"The Brother wouldn't want me to."

"The Brother isn't going to know. And if he does, you tell him I made you do it. How's that?" She passes him his lunch and sees that his face is red and damp. "It gets hot in there, does it."

Leon rips the paper off his sandwich. He takes a bite and then answers with his mouth full. "It's hot as an oven in here."

"How about you unload your rifle and go find your friends? Take a swim or something."

Now she has something to offer. "Really?" he asks.

"Sure. Just leave the gun here. And let me have those bullets." She confiscates the ammunition and sets him free. She'll rescue him every day if she has to.

Yesterday Bo ranted about a knife left in the sink, a potential weapon for anyone who wanted it, he said, and then he went to an open closet and fiddled with his cache of rifles and ammunition. Out in the shed, she knows, he also has dynamite. They need it for blasting the site for the new Brothers' Centre, he says, but she wonders.

The two tablets she took for her headache half an hour ago have done nothing to relieve the pain behind her eyes. She wishes she could go to bed for a week, but instead, the sun has just risen and Bo has sent her to Mary and Sarah's house at Cedar-by-the-Sea. Once again, he has demanded that she oversee Bruce Crawford and his "wrecking gang" as he moves people about like chess pieces on a board. When Bo is ill, and bed bound, she can neglect to follow through on orders like this, but with all the recent excitement over his new forts, he is more alert, and she can think of no way to postpone.

Once, when she refused to uproot a couple, he circumvented her wishes by allowing Bruce and his men to handle the move alone. The results were so disastrous that the tormented couple fled the colony as soon as they could flag down a boat. A few days later the *Vancouver Province* ran their story under the headline *Disciples Used as Slaves at Vancouver Island Work Camp.*

This is exactly the kind of publicity she hopes to avoid. She has seen too much delusion and deception from Bo to believe any longer in his ability to commune with the Masters, but he is not a complete charlatan. He has not created the colony for his pleasure alone. He genuinely believes he is saving the world. He has, through erudition, experience, personal charisma, and great vision, inspired others to follow him—as he once inspired her—and he has created something good here, if only he can be prevented from also unwittingly destroying everything he has built up.

Bruce and his burly crew, however, are ready to carry out their orders with a perfunctory coldness that frightens her in its lack of compassion. They are accustomed to moving certain members of the colony frequently, with little or no notice, and depending on the direction of the move, the change is either reward or punishment. A move toward DeCourcy, where the Brother barricades himself, is a reward, a step up in the hierarchy, while a move toward Cedar-by-the-Sea, where he established the first settlement, is punishment. The more sudden the move, the more severe the punishment.

But where he once made decisions with purpose, now he is sometimes like a small child who does not yet understand the game, but nevertheless likes to rearrange the pieces according to colour or size, or merely to move them. When she cannot subvert his wishes, she must go along with them to protect the colonists as best she can, though they seldom read her behaviour in the same way. More often than not, they act as if the moves are her idea.

"Let's do it." She motions to one of the men, the one who stands glowering, sucking defiantly on a cigarette. "Just pick something and go." And then to Annie and Mary. "You two need to get your overcoats and follow them. The tugboat is waiting." Angry that she is the one who has to enact this ridiculous ritual, her voice is harsher than she intends.

Mary was writing a letter when they arrived, and now she moves to gather her papers together into her desk. *They're to stop what they're doing and go with no questions,* Bo said. *Make them* leave whatever they're doing. If they're in their nightclothes, they go in their nightclothes.

"Don't cling to your things now," she says. "Stop fussing and go, go, *go!*"

"Can't I at least gather my papers?" Mary looks stunned at the injustice of such unnecessary treatment.

"Quick then." She feels a bit stunned herself. But why *should* she make them drop everything the second she arrives? In this, at least, she can soften the blow. *It's a test,* he tells them when they ask, *to see if you're ready for the next level of responsibility,* but everything is a test these days, and there *is* no next level of responsibility.

It is not only Mary and Sarah that the crew must uproot. He has told Zee to move the Barleys with them, and also Leona Painter, the young wife Roger has brought. She is twenty-five, Bo said, although she looks even younger. She stands taller than the morning's other victims, her flesh firm, plump, and flawless. The others are like chalk figures in comparison—Sarah the eldest, but all of them past sixty, their hair ranging from silver to white, and the backs of their hands spotted and corrugated by protruding veins and bones.

When their things have been loaded helter-skelter onto the tug-boat, all their clothes and furniture mixed with the belongings of the others, they cross the chilly waters to Valdes Island, and not one of them looks pleased to be moving in the right direction.

The moment Bruce pulls up alongside the dock, the wrecking gang hops out and begins transferring everything ashore, not up the steep embankment and a half-mile beyond, where the cabins stand out of sight, but just clear of the water's edge, unprotected from the persistent drizzle.

"Careful, there." Zee cringes each time she hears wood crack or the tinkle of glass breaking, but there is little she can do to prevent it, as nothing has been properly packed or protected.

A spreading mound forms—of bed-frame parts, mattresses, linens, tables, lamps, cabinets, boxes, clothes, trunks, books, kitchen utensils, food, and miscellany. When it is all unloaded, Bruce revs the engine and waits for Zee to step aboard. But she finds she can't leave. The small, abandoned group stands in a confused huddle. Rain has plastered the women's kerchiefs to the shape of their heads, and they all hunch their shoulders against the cold, staring forlornly at the heap of goods before them. After several seconds of silence, Alfred turns to Annie.

"Not even up the slope," he says, shaking his head. "You'd think they could do that, four big men. Look at us." Each one looks at the rest with blank, unbelieving eyes. Mary and Sarah. Leona Painter, and the Barleys.

Zee turns to Bruce. "Get your men to move this stuff up the bank and nearer to their cabins."

"They can manage it. We've got to get back." The boat is ready to go.

"For God's sake, man. Open your eyes. Take a look at these people. Whatever you're supposed to be doing, it can wait."

While the men grudgingly move the load farther up the island, Zee inspects the cabins. There are two. Alfred and Annie's isn't too bad—rustic, but solid. The other one is a shambles.

"Oh *my.*" Sarah's voice breaks when she sees where they're meant to live. "This is hardly better than no shelter at all."

She isn't far wrong. The cabin, in fact little more than a dilapidated shed, is uninhabitable as it stands. The unpainted boards have grown silver and hairy with age. The door has to be lifted on rusty hinges before it will close, and even then light shines through wide cracks. Beneath a large hole in the roof, wood has rotted away on the floor, and various clans of small creatures scurry and scuttle out of sight with each step. Leaves and fir needles have accumulated in piles against the side walls and in corners. Cobwebs stretch like intricately paned windows from one wall to another.

She wonders how these women can keep going. They will be hours cleaning and making repairs. They could stuff cracks until dark and hardly be further ahead. And for what purpose?

Just then, Sarah confronts her. "You've really got it in for us, haven't you."

There are tears of frustration in her eyes, and more than anything, she resembles a hurt child. Though Zee is wounded by her words, she has an impulse to pull her into a comforting hug, but Sarah is too angry.

"You must really want to try our spirit to put us here. Do we really deserve *this?*"

Zee presses her lips together to hide her anger with Bo. "Who am I to try anyone?" She says the words sincerely, drawing them from a time when she felt vulnerable and Coulson comforted her by saying, *Who am I to approve or disapprove of anyone?*

But while she means well, the words have no similar comforting effect on Sarah. These women have been tested over and over again, and still they would rather blame her than Bo. He is their leader, real or imagined. If he fails, what recourse do they have? He is the icon they admire and follow. As much as she would like to say to all of them, *He is ill. Follow me,* they would never transfer their loyalties so easily. He stands for everything they have given up and hope to gain. When he fails, they fail.

Weak with pent-up rage and a pounding headache, she turns her back on them. But before she can walk away, she feels the telltale pain in her chest. She moves to the doorway for support and clutches the cracked casing. She sees an older man in a bed. He is thin and pale, with round wire spectacles and an unusually large mole on his earlobe. Sarah is at his bedside, humming. Zee hears the tune. "Amazing Grace." And then he speaks. "Bring me the Bible. I need to study for my final term." And that is all. The image fades.

"I said, *excuse* me."

Sarah and Mary stand stony-faced, arms full of leaves and debris they have scooped from the floor of the shed. They want past her, but she blocks the doorway.

She doesn't know which one of them spoke, and she stares at them dazedly until Mary says, "May we move past?"

She stumbles forward, out of their way, holds her hand to her chest, and then stands straighter and turns to Sarah. "I'm going to say something to you, and I'd like you to tell me if it means anything to you."

Sarah puts her hands on her hips. "What now?"

Softly she repeats what she heard: "Bring me my Bible. I'm studying for my last term."

Sarah's face lights up and she laughs spontaneously, and then just as quickly, her eyes fill with tears and she glares at Zee. She clutches Mary's hand and practically spits the words at Zee. "That's what Wesley said before he died. Who told you he said that?"

Wesley is the man Sarah would have married had he not become fatally ill. "I heard him just now."

"Get away from me." Sarah pushes past her as if Zee doesn't exist. "You are a vile and vindictive woman."

"Oh for God's sake." She reaches into her pocket and extracts the sharpened pencil she always carries, and then she looks around until she spots a cardboard box. Tearing the flap from one side, she sits on a rock and sketches quickly. The round, bald head. The equally round spectacles on a longish nose. The ear with the large mole, and the thin frame under the bedcovers. Her strokes are fast and confident. By the bedside, she sketches Sarah with her mouth open, singing. Altogether, the sketch has taken five minutes at most.

She finds Sarah inside and shoves the drawing at her. "Here. You were singing "Amazing Grace." He said, 'Bring me the Bible. I'm studying for my final term.' I get the feeling this is a message of some sort, meant to comfort you. Now, if you'll excuse *me*."

And with that, she turns and stalks back down to the shore.

The men have moved all of the group's belongings, and Bruce is revving the engine impatiently. "Let's go," he says. "Get aboard."

She jumps on board and grabs her whip from where she left it anchored under a pile of rope. "Move it," she says. It is all she can do to resist the urge to whack something.

Chapter 27

It is three months before Zee can move Sarah and Mary and the others back to their homes. Bo has been weak and depressed all month, so the colony environment has been stable and restful, with all going about their business without undue anxiety. Zee has disbanded the Metford Defence, though the forts still stand, some with rifles and ammunition stored on a ledge within.

Sarah, having "failed" in Bo's eyes at every unreasonable task put before her—rock picking, field plowing, stump dragging—has finally had a month of rest. At no small cost to her pride, Zee thinks, Sarah apologizes to her, and then pulls a list of questions from her apron pocket.

What was Wesley wearing when she envisioned him? Did he look happy? How did she know he meant to comfort her? Did she say anything else? Does Zee think there was a message in the song she sang—"Amazing Grace"? Was there anything else she might have forgotten? Could she see him again?

So Zee tries her best. She holds the gold watch Sarah has brought with her, Wesley's watch, but what she envisions is someone else entirely, a woman, plump and cheerful, rosy cheeked and white haired—Mrs. Claus in an ordinary housedress—yeasty smelling, with a collie at her feet. She sketches the image and gives it to Sarah. "She was a contented woman. She was happy. Others were happy to be near her."

But Sarah doesn't recognize her. "It may be his wife. She died first, a few years before I met him."

And then others come. Mary wants to see her son. She was at his bedside and watched helplessly as his lungs filled with fluid. Until then, rarely a day had passed that he did not stop by to visit his mother. She said she felt his loss as a quiet melting down that left her with a searing and constant pain in her heart. She feels the ache still, but each morning when she wakes, she welcomes it because if it ever lessens, she worries her memories of him will fade with it.

Zee sketches her son with Mary's daughter-in-law and two pretty granddaughters, who remind Zee of her own nieces, Elisabeth and Eloise, and she advises Mary to let the pain go if it will.

"Your memories will survive," she says.

And then Mary, who manages always to be poised and composed, breaks down and admits that those are the last words her son ever said to her. She has been superstitious about them, has repeated them to no one.

Somehow, a woman from Nanaimo learns of Zee's sketches and asks to visit the colony. Zee meets her at Cedar-by-the-Sea, where she draws the woman's father—large, stern, dark-complexioned, and holding a chicken. Feeling uneasy, Zee tells the woman what she needs to hear—that she was the single greatest source of her father's joy. The woman, as Zee knew she would, breaks down and weeps. They had sharp words, she says, and when her father became ill unexpectedly, he died before she could return home and tell him that she loved him.

"He knows," Zee says, almost swooning with a sense of the man's anger. "He was a stubborn man, but he always knew, and he forgave you everything."

That is an outright lie. He was not a man who understood that the uniqueness of the individual is essential to freedom. And while Zee's mind is anything but a safe and predictable place, she cannot look on this sad woman and reveal that her father's anger went with him into death. For what purpose? Who would be helped? So she lies, and hopes the distortion is not harmful in a way she cannot fathom.

"He has always been proud of you, and never more than now." And then with a sense of immense relief, she adds what she knows to be true. "He says that your daughter, May, is just like you once were, the sweetest child on earth."

"How did you know her name?"

"I can't say for certain." She has thought about this often. Does she really communicate with the deceased party, or does she receive information, unwittingly, from the survivors? Or from somewhere else entirely? She has decided that there is no way to discern that, and what's more, it doesn't matter. She extends the finished sketch to the woman. "Names just come to mind. I never know if they're right or wrong, I just pass them along."

The woman thrusts two dollars into Zee's hand, enough to buy a pig. At first she refuses, but when the woman insists, she accepts on behalf of the colony. "I'll only take it as a donation," she says. "Thank you."

After that, more people come, two or three a month, all of them happy to make a donation—some in cash, others with a hen or a bag of peas—and then that many strangers a week begin to visit, until finally she puts a sign at the entrance to the Cedar-by-the-Sea settlement that says she will sketch on Fridays from ten until two.

At first the colonists are excited by her ability. Many of them come to her for their own sketches, but after a few weeks, they begin to grumble. From various sources, she learns that she is *uppity,* that she is *trying to take over,* that *strangers have overrun the place.* Yet never in her life has she felt as complete as when she is able to sketch for these people who seek her out.

Bo has not rebounded from his last bout of illness, and he remains thin and pale. He is out of bed and sits at the front window in discussion with Zee. His depression has lessened, but the nature of his thoughts has gone over the edge into real insanity.

"We can only ask her," he says. "It will be her decision."

"You want Sarah to drown herself so she can communicate with us from the dead?"

"I won't force her. It will be her decision."

"You honestly believe that Sarah is willing to drown herself for the good of the colony?" She is incredulous. "And how will she accomplish this?"

"Leon can take her out in the rowboat. You can go with her to make sure she does it."

"It's not going to happen. I won't be a part of it."

"It's why she's here. It's why she's never succeeded at anything else. This is her purpose. Will you deny her that?"

He stares hard at Zee, but she says nothing. The idea is preposterous, but how will she shake him free of it?

"If she's successful, we'll converse on the astral plane. She'll be the first to describe in detail what happens when we cross from this world to the next. She'll dictate, and I will write her experience for everyone to know."

Rubbish, Zee argues. Coulson is alive and well, and he communicates information just fine. So does she.

"I'll get Bruce to go in your place."

"You'll have to."

She has just opened her mouth to say more when they hear a gunshot. And then a second. They jump out of their chairs to peer out the window. Zee sees a movement at one of the forts, and hears someone screaming. When she sees a thick mat of curly hair appear, she leaves the house on the run.

"What happened?" She reaches Leon before Bo does. He has clambered out of the fort and now stands white and shaking in front of her. "Are you hurt?" She looks him over even as she asks—his hands, his chest, his feet. She sees no blood anywhere.

He feels his shoulder. "That gun kicks pretty bad."

"What did you shoot at?" She struggles to get her breathing under control. She has an urge to shake him.

Bo reaches them just as Leon points into the bay. "Someone was coming, so I shot at them like the Brother wanted."

She glares at Bo, who is bent over trying to recover his breath. *You see what you've done,* she wants to say. "Did you hit them?" She prays he didn't.

"I don't know. One of them dropped down."

"In the boat? As if he was hit?"

"I don't know."

"Where's the boat now?"

"I don't know. It took off."

She stares out at the water. Whoever the boaters were, they're gone now, and not even a disappearing wake shows which direction they went.

"Let him be," Bo says. He is perspiring and has a strange, excited look on his face. "He probably scared the pants off them, and that's what we want."

Leon glances from him to her.

"You did fine," Bo reassures him.

No, he didn't, she screams silently, but she will wait until she is calmer to speak to Leon. "Did you see a Coast Guard flag?" That's all they need, to have gunned down a Coast Guard.

"I didn't notice."

Bo rumples his hair. "You'll be sporting quite a bruise on that shoulder tomorrow. But you did well. You're Captain of the Metford Defence now. What do you think of that?"

When he lays an arm across the boy's back and turns him away from the fort, she doesn't follow.

She stays behind and studies the ocean instead. To a bystander, she might look as calm as the bay, a woman alone, enjoying the view, but inside, her thoughts churn as the sea might on another day. She thought she had managed this charade well, but now she is not so sure. To stay, or leave: it is not a simple choice. She has always wanted to use her visions to help others, and now, after all this time, she has found the means accidentally. But Bo has become dangerous. This incident with Leon. His talk of Sarah. Will Zee wait for an actual death before she takes action? And yet what is she meant to do?

Brotherhoods, disciples, initiates, adepts? This whole hierarchical structure—what does it have to do with ideals of unity and collectivity?

Bo doesn't communicate with any force higher than his own thoughts. And he is *not* enlightened. Money speaks louder than character to him. A barrage of foul language regularly escapes him. He is paranoid. He has heaped verbal and written abuse upon her and others, both at the colony and beyond, through letters. And while there may remain in him some vestiges of that mysterious, redeeming *something* that initially attracted her and the others, it is clear to her now: he is not the man any of them thought he was.

CHAPTER 28

Sarah Puckett has made her decision. Though Zee would never have believed it could happen, the elderly woman prepares to drown herself by falling backward out of a wooden rowboat into the deep, dark waters of the Pylades Channel. She sits in the stern of the simple craft, her seventy-eight-year-old frame arranged in a prayerful pose, silver head tilted back, hands clasped tightly to her chest, her only movement caused by the metallic slap of waves below her. And though Zee also swore she would never be party to any of it, she faces her in the bow, and Leon rows between them. His hands rest lightly on the oars as he allows them to drag momentarily.

Zee miscalculates the time and believes it must be several hours since she donned a headscarf for protection and stepped into the boat, but in fact, they have been out for little more than an hour. She prays that Sarah will come to her senses. She wishes she knew what sort of thoughts allow the woman to be here at all.

She stares at Leon's back. The fibres of his sweater stretch with each new pull on the oars, and she wonders, too, what the boy makes of Sarah's decision. Bo has convinced her that this is her final chance to prove herself, that as the oldest, childless member of the colony, Sarah will enter the afterlife through the cold watery funnel of the sea and will find a way to communicate with the colony from the other side.

Without Zee's participation, Bo would have asked Bruce to take Sarah out. Maybe he would even have asked Bruce to bump Sarah overboard, as he suggested Zee might do, and she has no doubt Bruce would have complied. Incredible as it seems, Sarah has already stated that she will fling herself backward off the edge of the rowboat as soon as she hears that tiny interior voice she believes will rightly summon her from this world to the next. This idea that God summons people, takes them when he wants them, causes Zee to seethe silently. Bad things happen. End of story. We die because we're old or sick or stupid or accident-prone. Or because of someone else's stupidity or carelessness. *Not* because God calls us.

Or perhaps Sarah fancies herself like Abraham, ordered by God to sacrifice his son Isaac as a burnt offering. She may be willing to follow through, confident that before any harm comes to her she will be saved and exalted for having faith. Or maybe she's just fucking crazy.

Zee's speculation is interrupted when she hears a muffled huffing sound. She sees nothing, but the sound is there, not precisely a snuffle, nor even a snort, but unique to itself.

"Whales!" Leon says. "To port."

She cocks her head, and soon they are all rewarded with a sound like the sharp exhaling of breath.

"They're too far out. We won't see them." Leon sounds disappointed.

"That's exactly where we want them," she says. "I already feel the difference in the water."

It is true; the waves lap slightly higher from the activity. The boat rocks more noticeably, and they fall silent again, listening.

She stares down over the side of the rowboat at the cold metal sheen of icy ocean. Moonlight shivers on its surface, and she shivers with it. Sarah leans against the side and dangles her fingers in the water. She has not held her hand in for five seconds before she pulls it out and buries her fingers in her armpit.

There is another mighty slap on the water, and she peers out, looking for the large, looming arc that will signal the presence of an orca.

They listen, but they hear nothing else for several seconds. This indicates one of two possibilities to Zee. Either they have caught the tail end of a resident pod, which has already swum out of earshot, or this is a transient pod. Unlike resident orcas, which travel in large groups—sometimes as many as thirty together—a transient pod usually consists of only three whales, an adult female and two of her offspring.

The silence, so soon after hearing the initial spoutings, suggests to Zee the latter group. Most likely a transient pod is silently stalking a porpoise or a sea lion. They are the mammal eaters, whereas resident whales prey on fish or squid, noisily communicating to other pod members as they hunt. Neither type is known to eat human flesh, so it's not that which worries her. But they weigh in at two to nine tons. With that sort of water displacement, she wants them at a distance.

Leon stops rowing and pulls the oars in just as a large, numbing splash drenches the entire right side of Zee's body.

"Look!" Sarah screams, attempting to stand.

"Sit down," Zee says.

The whale is a glistening black wall of magnificent mammal rising and huffing in the moonlight, and so near Zee could reach out and touch it, if she dared. So close, its intelligent eye gleams, the proud body torpedo shaped, the white markings in stark contrast to the predominant black. And then a second splash drenches them all, and even dripping wet, Zee is speechless, oblivious of the cold for the moment and awash with awe at the sight of perfection so near. Three other whales surface around them, glossy black fins erupting out of the ocean, and in their midst, only two oar lengths from the boat, is a black-and-white calf the size of a large man.

Sarah, possibly startled, has again attempted to stand.

"Down," Zee shouts, too late.

Just as Sarah bends her knees, the boat rocks violently. When her hand stretches for the side of the boat, she misses and grabs at nothing but air. In a motion strangely familiar to Zee, she tumbles headfirst into the water.

"Damn her." With only the slightest hesitation, knowing there is no way Sarah will ever get back into the boat without a push from below, Zee dives in after her.

Nothing in her experience has ever been so cold, and the pain in her ears is as intense as anything she has ever felt. Her shoes cause her legs to sink, and each laboured kick increases her sense of panic until she somehow scrapes free of them. *Kick,* she tells herself. She knows she has to reach the surface, but still she sinks, with no way to take a breath. Finally, just as she no longer cares, when the numbness has taken over, when she believes she has sunk a mile deep, she resurfaces, naturally buoyed up by the salt water, and gasps for breath. But there is so little air, so much ocean.

And then there is Leon's head bobbing over the side, just before a swell forces her under again. But this time her arm hits something solid, and when she tries to grab it, she brushes fabric. Sarah—limp and unflailing. Operating more by instinct than thought, Zee dives under Sarah's body and then thrusts her head up from below with all the force she can muster.

She is rewarded when Sarah's weight lifts off her, and somehow Leon drags Sarah into the boat. She attempts to throw her own arm over the gunnel, but her cold limbs are now almost useless. She slides back into the water.

There is the sensation of twirling, of a slow spiral downward. Because she cannot move or swim, she wonders how long it will be before she arrives at the bottom, if there is a bottom, and what will happen to her then. But the sinking never ends, and there is only the weightless, fathomless fall. And then the water seems suddenly infused with the scent of apples and strawberries, and fresh-cut roses. In all her forty-two years, she has never encountered anything so sensually sublime, and what she feels now is the most wondrous inner peace. She suspects that such serenity is only possible in death, or near death's edges.

But, cruelly, she is yanked back. Not sinking, but merely bobbing in the water. She coughs and sputters, turns her head and vomits salt water until her throat burns. When she can look up, Leon is still there, his sheer bulk and strength hovering over her.

She dreams of Honora. They lie in a field, and her sister's body is warm beside her. Honora smells faintly of seaweed, and she murmurs comforting words. And then something wakes Zee. Thunder, perhaps, or something heavy dropping. She listens, and hears only silence. There are no sounds in the house.

Sliding her legs out from beneath the covers, she pushes free and rises from her bed to spread her arms wide. Her limbs are stiff, but stretching them provides a pleasurable sensation. She is alive! And judging from the light at the window, she has slept well into the morning.

A sheet of paper has fallen to the floor. Perhaps a note from Bo? But when she retrieves the paper and turns it over, the handwriting is not his. She walks into the light and reads the first few lines absently. *To the Brother, XII. I'm sorry it has come to this, but too much has happened that cannot be undone. We have for many months now experienced significant concern and a growing and inexorable sense that you are no longer capable . . .*

She scans the rest. *Sarah's near death . . . impossible to believe . . . must ask that you not continue this charade . . .* The remaining colonists have all signed it. Bo must have brought it in for her to read when he received it.

Zee lifts her head. They want him to leave. And her, too. But who can blame them? She crosses to the bedroom window and raises her hand to brush the curtains aside for more light, and then she leans forward with her hands on the sill and gasps at the destruction below. The *Lady Royal* has rolled onto her side and is surrounded by flames, huge black clouds of smoke billowing from between gutted ribs. *What has happened?*

She trembles so badly she cannot consider dressing. Fumbling as she slips into her shoes, she snatches her robe and then rushes down stairs that now seem oddly spaced; twice she almost trips and only her grip on the handrail saves her. At the bottom, she swings around the newel post—and stops, aghast. All is destroyed. Furniture and paintings are slashed, bookshelves overturned. She steps over and around the mess and picks her way to the door. Her chest hurts, as before a vision, but no vision comes. Could the colonists, in anger over Sarah, have hurt Bo?

She crosses the grass in long leaps until she reaches the dock and steps onto it, and then intense heat and roiling black smoke stop her. Her legs shake uncontrollably as she surveys the damage, and then it is all too much, and everything changes, as if something inside has been shaken loose to change her perception. She sinks down onto the rough planks of the dock, dizzy. Distinct images peel away from the whole. A tin mug floats just below the surface of the water. Scattered papers make wet skins, and a partly submerged cushion still burns. Splintered wood litters everything, and the far end of the dock is burning. The graceful *Lady Royal* lies crippled, embers glowing red in places, volumes of smoke rising from others. There is no thought of saving her.

The smell of burning oil hangs in the air, and it is perhaps this, more than anything, that has immobilized her, that causes her to remember. How the lamp oil caught fire and spread, quicker than her young mind could ever have imagined. The initial pain of her own burns, before numbness set in. Her sharp screams in contrast to Honora's weak mewling. The way Honora's hand reached out, and then fell to the bed, her eyes confused as flames leapt to life around her. And then the rest of the family suddenly in the doorway. Her father pushing everyone aside.

"Go get your blankets," he boomed, grabbing Honora. "Now!"

How he stripped the burning covers from the bed, stomped on them, then scooped Mabel into a blanket and tossed her to Gram. His grunts as he moved. Her brothers stumbling into the room under bundles, their bodies hazy and ghostlike through the smoke. Curses. Her mother's panicked shrieks.

And still she sees Honora's face, flushed pink, eyes glazed and confused, hands falling limply . . .

When she becomes aware again of her current surroundings, she lies prone on the dock, a raised nail pushing into the back of her head, bits of debris and ash floating through the air above her. She knows she dropped the lantern and started the fire. Because of her, Honora died. And yet these remembered details are all new, and still they won't stop. She remembers how her mother and grandmother fussed over her on the main floor of the house—Honora *and* her, one at each end of the living room sofa. And then the doctor, checking her burns, applying salve to her arms. And Honora, still shivering and whimpering as her mother pressed a cloth to her face and arms.

Whatever Honora died of, she did not die in the fire.

How could Zee not have known this? And how much of a fire could it have been, that she was back in her old bedroom as soon as she returned home from the Stantons'? She recalls the odour of smoke mixed with paint—the room yellow now, clean and bright, and empty of Honora.

All these years, believing Honora died because of her childish mistake. But why had no one corrected her?

She sits up on the dock and rubs the back of her head. Had she voiced this belief, likely someone would have set her straight, but when did anyone in her family ever speak of such things? She has vague memories of her grandmother shushing her, telling her Honora was happy in heaven. Of sudden silences on happy occasions, when it seemed to her that the others must be remembering her sister and brother, but no one ever mentioned their names or admitted to wishing they still lived, as if doing so might unleash something caged and unmanageable. It was no different when Gram died. The family gathered around her bedside while she took her last breaths. They held a small service, and then she lived only in their memories. Zee cannot think of a single spoken reference to her deceased grandmother after she and her parents departed for Canada a few weeks later. And she must have had a grandfather. He doesn't even figure into memory.

But when Honora has shown her so much, if indeed she has, why could she not show her the fire as she just now remembered it? Has she been wrong in assuming the messages had something to do with her sister? Or has she finally remembered what Honora intended her to all along? She will have to think more about all of this, but already she feels lighter, as if the stone in her chest has cracked open and can never again weigh her down quite so heavily. And while Honora's image does not present itself now, she has the sense that she has pleased her sister, that if the two of them could sit on the dock together, they would do so in companionable silence, nothing of importance separating them.

Then something else explodes—a fuel barrel?—and she pushes herself to her feet at once. She's still a little dizzy, but she needs to find Bo. He's not on the boat, she would know if he was, but he could be hiding somewhere. Earlier, on her way past the storehouse, she noticed bullet holes in its walls, and she moves in that direction.

She doesn't have to search. When she reaches the doorway and steps in, he is in full view, not hiding at all. He sits calmly on an upturned bucket, his hand wrapped around the barrel of a .303 Lee-Metford.

She lifts her arm and gestures around her. "Did you do all this?"

He turns to her with a vacant look. "It's worse than you think."

CHAPTER 29

Summer afternoons in Querétaro are long and hot. Anyone who is able stays inside, or outside on a terrace under an umbrella with an iced drink in a tall glass that sweats as if it, too, were only human. Even dogs slink under tables and into the shade, their incessant barking silenced by tongues lolled out, dusty-pale and parched.

Expectations are tamped down, set aside or forgotten until evening once again allows for the necessary vigour of activity. Mid afternoon is the quietest of the daylight hours, and her preferred time of day.

Inside, she has Mozart piano concertos playing softly in the background. She plays them often as she sketches. They make a soothing accompaniment to volatile thoughts, to the various burdens of knowing, and when they play, her whole body moves differently.

She has no windows on to the street. There were two when she bought the house, but they let in noise and dust so she had them bricked up and plastered over, preferring to get her light from behind the house and above. Eighteen-inch walls keep the inside temperature comfortably cool, but her house is no dark cellar, no ruins in the making. The ceiling above her table opens into a cupola so that the front rooms are light and bright. The back sitting room, her favourite of all, opens into a garden, an opulent tropical microcosm she has tended for more than three decades. It is its own world of soothing, muted sounds. Silvery fronds swish in an occasional breeze. Leaves the size of plates fall audibly onto patio tiles or clack gently against each other. A slow drip feeds a shallow clay bowl she has set out to attract birds. And always the subtle scent of something blooming—frangipani, jacaranda, cosmos, and more than a dozen varieties of delicate-scented salvia. It is from a shaded corner of this refuge that she has so recently been summoned by the young woman who sits before her.

She pulls the top card from a worn tarot deck the woman has given her, and flips the Six of Coins face-up on her kitchen table. The woman has so many regrets, all visible in the sad lines of her face. And then Zee sets the deck aside and with quick strokes begins sketching what she sees. A middle-aged man in his bed, this young woman beside it. He died recently, after a long bout of illness, and the young woman here misses him, as Zee misses her own loved ones—Honora and William, her grandmother, her parents, both of whom have long passed on. Occasionally she paints all four of them as she imagines them, and sells her paintings in a gallery alongside the locals'. And rarely, one of her family will speak to her in a vision.

The man she draws now is small and slight, with angular features and a pointed beard that remind her of the Brother, XII, as he was when she delivered him to Dr. Schmidt in Switzerland. She heard Bo died there. Mary wrote and told her, years after the fact.

If you ever need anything . . . Dr. Schmidt had said, when they met at the colony. He had visited and stayed for two weeks just after she and Bo moved to Valdes, and then returned later for an entire year. He had looked at her scars as they healed and had given her a special oil meant to fade them, so she remembered him when Bo collapsed. *If you ever need anything,* he said, *I run a hospital in Neuchâtel.*

So she took the two jars of gold coins from the cistern and hired a nurse to accompany them, first to England and then to Switzerland. She had a vision there, of a city in Mexico. Of a small house, with a garden where she sketched. And a name came to her: *Querétaro.* She knew nothing of Mexico then, but it is home now.

"Your husband adored you," she says to the woman. She feels certain that he did, and she no longer cares one whit how or why she knows. As with love, which can be measured only by the certainty with which it is known, so it is with psychic ability. "You carry his silver cigarette case with you."

Had the man not smoked, he would have lived much longer, but that was his business and not hers. She is tired, and she wants a nap. The fat and the elderly should always be forgiven a nap.

She pushes the drawing across the table. "The deceased need no sacrifices," she says. "It's not the dead we need to make peace with, but the living."

Author's Afterword

Madame Zee: Psychic, Fiend, or Femme Fatale?

The real Madame Zee has been described as both *mistress of the devil... without a saving grace... a complete sadist[1]* and as *very feminine, and very clever at handling men ... an adventuress.[2]* As mistress to Canada's most infamous cult leader, the Brother, XII, Zee lived with him from 1929 to 1934. *He* founded the Aquarian Foundation, a utopian colony in British Columbia with Theosophical roots. *She* carried a whip everywhere and flayed anyone who got in her way. Or so the story goes.

Here was a woman, strong by all accounts, loathsomely

1. From MacIsaac, Clark, and Lillard's book, *The Devil of DeCourcy Island: The Brother XII.* (46)
2. From John Olipant's biography, *Brother Twelve: The Incredible Story of Canada's False Prophet and His Doomed Cult of Gold, Sex, and Black Magic.* (242)

unattractive or seductive, depending on which account one believes, and about whom no more than a few anecdotes are known and repeatedly presented. She is often mentioned in relation to the Brother, XII, every account vilifying her for cruel and sadistic behaviour, and yet she remains an enigma.

According to biographer John Oliphant, she was born Mabel Edith Rowbotham, in Lancashire, England, in 1890. As a young adult, Mabel immigrated with her parents to Lemsford, Saskatchewan, where she taught school in a series of small prairie towns until she married John Skottowe, then manager of the Union Bank of Canada and a former North West Mounted Police officer. When the bank uncovered Skottowe's fraudulent loan practices, the couple moved to Seattle, where their marriage dissolved. A visit to her father-in-law, a mystic minister in Pensacola, Florida, resulted in her meeting Roger Painter, a wealthy entrepreneur and former stage-hypnotist, nicknamed the Poultry King of Florida. In 1929, after Mabel changed her name to Madame Zee, the couple joined the Brother, XII, at his utopian colony at Cedar-by-the-Sea, just south of Nanaimo on Vancouver Island.

I first learned of Madame Zee from a History Channel documentary about the Brother, XII.[3] Questions about Zee plagued me. Was she really as cruel as accounts would have us believe? And if she was, how did she get that way? What caused her to become so angry? Was it frustration at the way the other colonists treated her? A desire for power? The fluctuating hormones of mid-life? Childhood trauma, or post-traumatic stress disorder? Any one of these seemed a possibility, and because no one had yet explored

3. History Television. "Edward Arthur Wilson—Brother 12." The Canadians: Biographies of a Nation series.

her life, I was free to invent one for her; the resulting book is *story*, and by no means a factual account, though I've based many events on historical ones.

I have chosen to make Zee a good-hearted character at her core, as I believe she likely was, if only because we're all sympathetic at some level, even if monstrous at others. Common sense and intuition tells me that she must have been a product of her environment, subject to the same hurts and stressors as anyone else, and I've tried to provide these triggers over the course of the story. I gave her psychic abilities because historically so many of those around her were preoccupied with Spiritualism and the occult. It makes sense to me that her own hidden psychic talent might have drawn her to the Brother, XII, who professed to communicate directly with the "other world."

With the exception of the Brother, XII, all my characters are inventions. Some, like Madame Zee, retain the name and possibly a few of the characteristics of historical people. In the case of the Brother, XII, I have imagined many of his actions, but wherever possible I have ascribed to him his own words, sometimes paraphrased, but quoted primarily from his first book, *The Three Truths* (The Camelot Press, 1927). I do not mean to pass his words off as my own, so while I have italicized them wherever possible, readers should assume that any philosophical thoughts originating with the Brother are his, and not mine. Nellie Painter and all of Mabel's siblings are complete fabrications.

And while I have written from a contemporary perspective, in contemporary language, I have made every attempt to present an historically accurate picture of the period, something that required extensive research. At times, I could hardly write a sentence without having to stop and investigate a detail. In the first few pages alone, I needed to research dozens of particulars: Which plants grow in an English meadow? What sort of dolls were available in the late 1890s, and what were they made of? What clothing did children wear? What diseases commonly killed them? What books did people read? Would they use string or twine? What were the most common given names? How large was the average family? What would a typical meal consist of? Did people use coins or paper money? As the book progressed, the list became endless—research on geographical locations in the United States, England, and Canada; schools for girls; salaries and living expenses; women of the times; the availability of drugs; historical background on the North West Mounted Police; Ukrainian emigration; reincarnation; suffrage; the Tarot and even the letter Z.

Larger concepts required weeks and months of research: I began by reading everything I could find on the Brother, XII, searching for information on Madame Zee. I spent fabulous, absorbing days reading newspaper articles and archival materials. In the Nanaimo Community Archives in British Columbia, I leafed through yellowed poems and booklets written by former colonists, and held a worn cloth copy of *The Three Truths.* I couldn't help but wonder if Zee had once held it also. I went on to research the Theosophical Society and its founder, Madame Blavatsky; cults and cult behaviour; mind control; Spiritualism and psychic phenomena—clairvoyance, telepathy, psychometry. I read "around" these subjects as well, often only to create a paragraph or two, or to include the most telling detail.

At times, I thought I would never finish this book: it took almost five years from start to finish. A 1989 story in the *Nanaimo*

Times claims that anyone who writes about the Brother, XII, will be jinxed—cursed with one problem after another. At one point, having suffered ongoing family and personal illness, and then the death of three members of my immediate and extended family, financial difficulties, missing files, and frequent computer glitches, I began to wonder if there might be something to this amusing superstition. A good friend joked that the book might have progressed more quickly and easily had I called it Madame A, instead of *Madame Zee*. But the gestation period is finally over. She is birthed now, or perhaps reincarnated, as a gifted psychic—neither fiend nor femme fatale.

Acknowledgments

I could not have written this book without the help of many individuals and organizations. For my understanding of the Brother, XII, special thanks go to Ron MacIsaac—for an interesting conversation, for archival materials, and for his book *The Devil of DeCourcy Island: The Brother XII*, co-written with Don Clark and Charles Lillard. My appreciation to John Oliphant for his book *Brother Twelve: The Incredible Story of Canada's False Prophet and His Doomed Cult of Gold, Sex, and Black Magic.* To the Nanaimo Community Archives, specifically Christine Meutzner and Dawn Arnot, for their invaluable research assistance. To Nanaimo Law Courts, particularly Diana Paulson and Merle Cram, who were very helpful. To North London Collegiate

School, especially Karen Morgan, Tamara Milberg, and Rebecca Pennells. And to the Parapsychology Foundation in New York. Thanks to Brad Belchamber for architectural details concerning the historical houses at Cedar-by-the-Sea.

For various acts of kindness, I am indebted to Shirley Graham, Peter Levitt, Robin Rudgley, Richard Rudgley, Patricia Fibiger, Li Read, Grover and Jill Wickersham, Lyn Goertzen, Allan Markin, and especially my agent, Denise Bukowski. Many thanks to my editor, Iris Tupholme, for her patience in working this story out of me bit by bit. Thanks also to Noelle Zitzer and Allyson Latta. And for the gift of her own evocative words, blessings for Crystal Andrushko.

I gratefully acknowledge the generous support of the Canada Council for the Arts, the Alberta Foundation for the Arts, the British Columbia Arts Council, and the Writers' Trust of Canada's Woodcock Fund.

With love and gratitude for encouragement and character insight, I wish to thank my daughter, Amanda Ziola. And for their love and generosity of spirit, my stepchildren, Breanne and Austin Hilles. For countless reasons, I am deeply indebted to Robert Hilles, who patiently suffers the writing alongside me.

SELECTED BIBLIOGRAPHY

Berton, Pierre. *My Country*. Toronto: McClelland and Stewart, 1987.

Hodgins, Jack. *The Invention of the World*. Toronto: Macmillan of Canada, 1977.

MacIsaac, Ron, Don Clark, and Charles Lillard. *The Devil of DeCourcy Island: The Brother XII*. Victoria: Porcépic Books, 1989.

Oliphant, John. *Brother Twelve: The Incredible Story of Canada's False Prophet and His Doomed Cult of Gold, Sex, and Black Magic*. Toronto: McClelland and Stewart, 1991.

——. "The Teachings of Brother XII." California State University, Fullerton; College of Humanities and Social Sciences Page. Retrieved 02/10/2003. <http://hss.fullerton.edu/comparative/oliphant_brxii.pdf >

Santucci, James A. "The Aquarian Foundation." Theosophical History Web Site. Retrieved 02/16/2003. <http://www.theohistory.org/aquarian_foundation.pdf>

Scott, Andrew. *The Promise of Paradise: Utopian Communities in B.C.* Vancouver/Toronto: Whitecap Books, 1997.

Wilson, Colin. *Rogue Messiahs: Tales of Self-Proclaimed Saviours*. Charlottesville: Hampton Roads Publishing Company, Inc., 2000.

Wilson, Edward Arthur. *Unsigned Letters from an Elder Brother*. 1930. Reprint Montreal: Aura Press, 1979.

——. *The Three Truths*. London: The Camelot Press, 1927. Gertrude Phillips fonds.

Nanaimo Community Archives.
——. *Foundation Letters and Teachings*. Akron Ohio: Sun Publishing Co., 1927. MacIsaac Collection (unprocessed). Nanaimo Community Archives.